HIGHFALUTIN PRAISE
FOR AWARD-WINNING AUTHOR
SANDRA HILL AND HER NOVELS

RED-HOT CAJUN

"In need of a laugh? Look no further than this funny, sexy, warm-hearted tale."

—*Romantic Times BOOKclub Magazine*

✦

"Ms. Hill provides a Louisiana summer heat romance filled with passion and humor."

—*Midwest Book Review*

✦

"For people who like to laugh, people who like to cry, and people concerned with the state of the earth."

—*Booklist*

✦

"Hill's thigh-slapping humor and thoughtful look at the endangered Louisiana bayou ecosystem turn this into an engaging read."

—*Publishers Weekly*

✦

more . . .

THE CAJUN COWBOY

"Hill will tickle readers' funny bones yet again as she writes in her trademark sexy style. A real crowd-pleaser, guar-an-teed."
—*Booklist* (starred review)

✦

"An intoxicating addition to her Cajun Bad Boys series."
—*Publishers Weekly*

✦

"A pure delight. One terrific read!"
—*Romantic Times BOOKclub Magazine* (four stars)

✦

"Sandra Hill's writing is fabulous. Look forward to a book by her because it will be a great read."
—*The Literary Times*

✦

"Ms. Hill has a marvelous way of weaving a story chock full of frivolity, sensuality, and delight. . . . Her talent for comedy brings a unique quality that entertains."
—*Under the Covers*

TALL, DARK, AND CAJUN

"Flat-out funny, sexy, and touching. A treat!"
—*Romantic Times BOOKclub Magazine* (four stars)

✦

Also by Sandra Hill

The Cajun Cowboy

The Red-Hot Cajun

Tall, Dark, and Cajun

Pink Jinx

Sandra Hill

WARNER
VISION
BOOKS

NEW YORK   BOSTON

Copyright © 2006 by Sandra Hill
Excerpt from *Pearl Jinx* copyright © 2006 by Sandra Hill
All rights reserved. Except as permitted under the U.S. Copyright Act of 1976, no part of this publication may be reproduced, distributed, or transmitted in any form or by any means, or stored in a database or retrieval system, without the prior written permission of the publisher.

Warner Vision is a trademark of Time Warner Inc. or an affiliated company. Used under license by Hachette Book Group, which is not affiliated with Time Warner Inc.

Warner Vision is an imprint of Warner Books, Inc.

Cover design by Diane Luger
Cover art by Tom Hallman
Lettering by Jon Valk

Warner Vision
Hachette Book Group USA
1271 Avenue of the Americas
New York, NY 10020
Visit our Web site at www.HachetteBookGroupUSA.com.

Printed in the United States of America

First Printing: November 2006

10 9 8 7 6 5 4 3 2 1

This book is dedicated with much appreciation to all those fans who have told me over these past ten years how much you appreciate my unique—okay, warped—sense of humor. You know who you are. You are teachers, pilots, therapists, ministers, housewives, Norwegian sailors, college students, nurses, men and women from all walks of life. I have been particularly touched by those of you who say my books have helped you through some life struggles and by those readers who are nobly serving in harm's way in the military.

When I first started writing romance, I had no idea that humor could touch readers so strongly. I thought only books with serious messages helped people. The most extreme example I can offer is the precious fan of mine who died of cancer and asked to have one of my Viking books placed in her coffin so that, at the viewing, people would look and then smile. Yep, humor to the end. But I am equally touched by the working mothers who need a little humor in their lives at the end of the day.

Let's face it, in these often depressing post-9/11 times, humor can make anyone's life better.

Please visit my Web site where I have something FREE to offer you, in a show of my appreciation.

And be assured, Tante Lulu and Tee-John, those outrageous Cajuns, are along for the ride in this new treasure-hunting series.

Wishing you smiles in your reading,

Sandra Hill
www.sandrahill.net

Dear Readers:

Welcome to my new Jinx series.

First off, let me introduce you to some of my friends, the main characters in *Pink Jinx*. Lawyer Veronica "Ronnie" Jinkowsky and her four-time ex-husband, Jake Jensen, a professional poker player, have been conned by Ronnie's wacky, polka-playing grandfather into taking over Jinx, Inc., a treasure-hunting company.

There will be an ensemble cast in all the Jinx books, characters who will recur in subsequent books, but each with a different hero and heroine. We writers like to say that we create "worlds" with our series, whether they be vampires, Vikings, Cajuns, or historical families. When readers like a particular book, they tell us they want to come back to that "world." So, welcome to my new world.

Those of you who have read my previous books will be pleased to know that Tante Lulu and Tee-John from my Cajun series are still around and spreading mischief. For the many of you who asked, yes, Tee-John will have his own story someday. Before that can happen, he's got to get a few more years under his belt, literally.

It's important to note that you do not have to have read the Cajun books to start the Jinx series. Likewise, the Jinx series is loosely linked, meaning the books can be read out of order.

A wise editor once told me that in the best of books, the writer makes the reader laugh as well as cry. Well, I can guarantee that Ronnie and Jake will tickle your funny bones, but I also hope your heartstrings will be tugged as well. These two love each other so much, but they just can't get it right, as evidenced by their four divorces.

As a special thank-you to all of you who have been faithful supporters of my books, please visit my Web site, where I have a special, free surprise for you—a never-before-published novella called *Jinx Christmas*.

You can also look forward to reading about the ex-Amish, ex-Navy SEAL Caleb Peachey in the next Jinx book, *Pearl Jinx*.

Wishing you smiles in your reading and joy in your life.

Sandra Hill
www.sandrahill.net
shill733@aol.com

Chapter
1

Her chips were definitely down. . . .

The scent of salt water always made her sick.

Which was really unfortunate for Veronica Jinkowsky, because not only was she being sucked into a venture that would place her on the high seas, but also here she stood on the boardwalk in freakin' Atlantic City, the saltwater-taffy capital of the world. On a sucky scale of one to ten, her day was hitting about fifteen. And it was not yet over.

The rhythmic click of her high-heeled Christian Louboutin pumps on the boardwalk planks vibrated throughout her body and up to her head, which, not surprisingly, throbbed with a killer headache. Swinging through the back beachside door into the Taj Mahal, she blinked against the assault of cigarette smoke, raucous music, flashing lights, and the ching-ching-ching of slot machines. It was midnight, and the gamblers were out in full force. In the midst of all this "splendor," she stood out like a sore thumb in her beige silk designer suit.

Distracted, Veronica bumped into a short, elderly woman with red curly hair carrying a purse the size of Idaho. The jolt forced the woman against a slot machine, which began to make loud noises: "Wheel . . . of . . . Fortune. Wheel . . . of . . . Fortune . . ."

Yikes!

At first, Veronica was alarmed. The woman, a combination of Sophia Petrillo from *The Golden Girls* and Granny Clampett from *The Beverly Hillbillies,* had to be at least seventy years old. That's all she needed—to knock down some old lady in a casino.

But the old lady righted herself and asked in a heavy Southern accent, "You gots any idea where the Chippenduds is dancin'?" She was so short she had to crane her neck to peer up at Veronica.

Huh? Ohmigod, she must think I work here.

Then the old lady asked, "Are you a hooker?"

"I beg your pardon! Why would you ask such an absurd question?"

"You doan look like the other folks here. No offense. Some of my best friends is hookers down on Bourbon Street. Well, okay, one of them was . . . back in 1952. Marie Boudreaux, bless her heart. Anyhow, you look like yer high class, and I heard they has lotsa hookers here in Atlantic City, and I figgered you mus' be one them call gals or sumpin'. You know, high-priced ladies of the night. Ain't you ever seen that Elizabeth Taylor movie *Butterfield 8?*"

Veronica clicked her jaw shut. She hadn't realized she'd been gaping. *Me? A hooker? Is she blind as well as batty?* Veronica refused to answer such a ridiculous question. "Back to your question—your *other* question. I've never heard of Chippendudes. Do you mean Chippendales?"

The lady furrowed her already-wrinkled brow. In fact, she had so many wrinkles she could probably screw a hat on.

"No. They's definitely dudes, not dales."

Veronica had to smile, despite her foul mood. "Are you looking for male strippers?"

"Tsk-tsk-tsk! Do I look like I could do anything with a nekkid boy toy?"

Not in a million years was Veronica going to answer that question.

"Now, Richard Simmons, thass another story. Hubba-hubba, that boy is ten kinds of sexy! Betcha he's got a real nice hiney. Betcha it's an onion butt. My niece Charmaine says an onion butt is a butt that's so nice it brings tears to yer eyes."

Good grief!

"Nope. I come all the way from Looz-ee-anna to rescue my great-nephew. He jist grad-je-ated from college and got hisself a summer job flashing his bee-hind in front of a bunch of horny wimmen. Talk about!"

Oh, boy! Leave it to me to find myself a looney bird after only five minutes in a casino. Why me? "Sorry. I don't know where there are any male strip shows. You might try asking at the front desk."

"The rascal's prob'ly hidin' from me. That Tee-John allus was slicker 'n hog spit. But I'll find him, guaranteed."

"I've got to be going." Veronica backed away. But her innate sense of kindness wouldn't let her abandon the woman, who was clearly lost or, worse, stranded here. "Are you alone?" *Please, God, don't let her be. I can't solve my own problems, let alone someone else's.*

"I came with Henri Pinot. He said he'd be back

quicker 'n a gator kin blink. That means in a minute. Henri is my third cousin. A widower. But his dead wife, Margie, talks to 'im all the time. Margie was a voodoo priestess. Henri went to the restroom. Between you and me, he has a little prostate trouble."

Way more information than I need. Time to make a getaway. "Uh, nice meeting you. Good luck."

Granny Clampett had already turned around and was putting a paper voucher in a slot machine.

Veronica inched away. She felt a little guilty leaving the aged damsel in distress, but Veronica was a woman on a mission herself. And she damn well wanted to get it over with as soon as possible.

Wending her way through the casino—past a city of slot machines and roulette, craps, and blackjack tables, she finally arrived at the poker room in the front of the hotel. A banner proclaimed, "U.S. Poker Championship." A poster read, "No-Limit Texas Hold 'Em . . . $1 million Grand Prize."

ESPN camera crews were there filming, and somewhere in the background, probably coming from another part of the casino, she heard that catchy country song by the duo Big and Rich. Coincidentally, the rowdy song was the lead-in to some of ESPN's TV poker programs. Something about a guy who walks into the room, passing out hundred-dollar bills, buying the whole room a double round of Crown, and "it kills and it chills. . . ."

She shook her head in disgust, definitely chilled. Inside the room, spectators were cordoned off by velvet ropes from the finalists' table about fifteen feet away. Six players were still in the game with piles of chips in front of each of them. The tour director was calling out the action: "Sabato bets . . ." "Molene raises . . ." "Here comes the river . . ."

She didn't recognize the middle-aged guy in the cowboy hat or the young Vietnamese fellow, but she did know the others.

Grace O'Brien was a cynical ex-nun. Correction—a cynical ex-nun with a sense of humor. The first time Veronica had met her, four years ago, Grace had cracked a joke: "What do you call a one-legged nun? Hopalong Chastity." Veronica had been to Grace's Cape May cottage several times and liked her a lot.

Mark Molene was a Denver oncologist who'd given up his high-stress medical practice a couple years back. Mark was dark and a little scary, giving new meaning to the word *unsociable*.

And Angel Sabato. Veronica had to smile, seeing the guy with the long ponytail who was famous for his collection of Harleys—and Harley groupies. She recalled a harrowing trip she'd taken with him one time down the Garden State Parkway. Angel, not surprisingly, had posed for *Playgirl* last year. His photos had appeared below the suggestive headline, "His Poker Is Hot." She wouldn't admit it to just anyone, but Veronica had checked out the issue—only because she'd wanted to see if he really did have piercings in his penis, as had been rumored. He did. And, yep, it was hot.

Then there was the last player. You *could* say that she was acquainted with him. Well acquainted. He was her ex-husband, Jake Jensen.

Actually, he was her fourth ex-husband.

Okay, he was her only ex-husband. They had married and divorced four times, each of the marriages ending in a standoff and Jake ultimately leaving.

Trying to have a sense of humor about their multiple weddings—it was either laugh or cry—she and Jake had given names to their four marriages.

First was the Sappy Marriage, where they had been so much in love it practically leaked from their pores. They'd foolishly thought love conquered all. The wedding had involved a church service and a lavish reception, despite her grandmother's disapproval of Jake. The marriage had lasted a record three years.

Next had come the Cowboy Marriage. Hey, what woman could resist a guy in Aruba wearing cowboy boots, a cowboy hat, and the sexiest grin this side of the Texas panhandle? All she knew was that she'd somehow landed in the honeymoon suite of a local hotel with Jake, him wearing nothing but cowboy boots and an open snap-button shirt and her wearing nothing. *Whew!* She got shivers just thinking about that one. Too bad it had ended two years later.

Third came the Tequila Marriage. Think Mexico and a gallon of tequila. Enough said! One year for that mistake.

Fourth was the Insanity Marriage. They had actually gone into that one with their eyes wide open. No heated rush. No booze. Just a pathetic hope that they could make it work. That marriage went out with a roar in a pitiful three months.

Thus, four marriages and divorces.

It was embarrassing, really. She was a corporate lawyer, albeit a burned-out, bored one. Presumably intelligent. She was sensible to the max. And yet she didn't have the sense to stop marrying and divorcing the same guy over and over.

She continued to watch Jake as he played.

Some people thought he looked like a leaner, younger George Clooney. She thought he looked better. The years gave her cellulite; they gave Jake charisma. Her heart skipped a beat then hammered against her chest, making her breathless. That was the reaction she always had on first seeing her sinfully handsome ex. You'd think the hair-trigger attraction would have faded in the two years since she'd seen him last.

Not that any of that mattered.

Veronica shook her head to clear it of the unwelcome temptation.

He was thirty-five years old, wore a baseball cap over his short black hair, and sported day-old whiskers. He had on his lucky gray T-shirt with the logo "Up that!" She'd bought it for him sometime during the Tequila Marriage. Dark sunglasses covered his compelling, pale blue eyes.

"How much are each of those chips worth?" she asked the elderly gentleman next to her.

"This is the cadillac of poker tournaments, so . . . Let me see, the orange ones are one thousand each. Gray ones, five thousand each. Buy-in fee was ten thousand dollars."

"Holy moly!" Stacked in front of Jake was about—she did a rough mental calculation—four hundred thousand dollars. He sure had come up in the world, if gambling one's life away could be considered an achievement. There was an old Armenian saying: "What the wind brings, the wind blows away." She and Jake had been in more windstorms than she could count.

She must have spoken louder than she'd thought because Jake's head shot up and turned right to her. He lowered his sunglasses down his nose and peered over them to get a better view of her. Then a slow grin crept across his lips, just before he slid the glasses back up.

Instantly, he morphed into his zen mode, something he'd perfected over the years. Focus, focus, focus—that's what was needed to be a winning poker player in the Bible According to Jake. He gave away no "tells" once he was in that mode—not a blink, grimace, or gesture, nothing to indicate whether he held a winning or losing hand.

Everyone at the table seemed tense. She knew from living with Jake that in no-limit Texas hold 'em, fortunes could change from hand to hand. Some pros refused to enter this kind of game because of the heart-stopping swings.

The three flop cards were already on the table. As spectators looked on, the dealer flipped the turn card, which left only Jake, Mark, and the Vietnamese guy in the hand. Mark bet $400,000, enough to put Jake and the Vietnamese player all in. Jake folded some thought, but the Vietnamese called and was disgusted to see that he was "drawing dead." As the meaningless river card hit the felt, Mark scooped up his winnings, and the tournament clock hit zero, indicating the end of the level and a short break for the remaining players.

Jake immediately made his way toward her, which she'd expected. He knew she wouldn't step foot into a casino, or come searching for him after all this time, unless it was important. People kept patting him on the back and shaking his hand, but he merely nodded at them and continued on his way. Even the ESPN reporter was waved off.

When he got to her, he took her elbow and steered

her down a side corridor labeled "Employees Only." Not a word did he utter. But then she was a bit speechless herself.

He stopped and stuck one hand into his jeans pocket, something he did reflexively when he was nervous. No one but she knew that he was probably fingering the silver worry beads she'd bought him during their Sappy Marriage. Or was it the Cowboy one? Taking off his sunglasses, he leaned his left shoulder against the wall. "Hey, Ronnie," he greeted her in that low, husky voice that made her melt. Had made her melt *at one time,* she amended.

"Jake," she said back, matching his husky voice.

It was a greeting routine they had played often in the past. To her surprise, he didn't appear pleased. "What's up?" he asked with equal measures of irritation and concern.

She leaned her right shoulder against the wall, facing him. Forget old feelings of tenderness . . . or lust. She was angry once again. "My grandfather," she snapped.

He arched both eyebrows. "Frank?"

"Yeah, Frank." Veronica had called her grandfather Frank from the time she was only a few years old. *Grandpa* or *Gramps* was too soft for the man, even then.

"What's the old geezer done now? Did he find any more gold toilets?"

Her grandfather owned a treasure-hunting company, Jinx, Inc., a play on his last name, Jinkowsky. A *treasure detective,* that's what he called himself. Sort of like Clive Cussler's Dirk Pitt, she supposed. Sometimes his projects involved deep-sea expeditions, sometimes archaeological digs, and sometimes just tracking down mysterious, missing objects. While he supposedly had a great reputation among historians, scholars, and museum curators for having made some important discoveries, he was known to take on infamous cases as well. Last year, he recovered a solid-gold toilet once owned by Mussolini. Some Italian prince paid a million dollars for the stupid thing. The story made all the newspapers. Frank had been quoted as saying something about even Mussolini needing a crapper and other unsavory observations. Her Boston family was not amused.

Veronica refused to play teasing games with Jake, though. This was business. Serious business. "He signed Jinx, Inc., over to me."

Jake's mouth dropped open before he clicked it shut. "You're kidding!"

She had his attention now. "But not only the treasure-hunting company. He's given me his boat, *Sweet Jinx;* the Barnegat warehouse; his Long Beach Island house; and a bunch of his personal belongings. Without my permission, by the way."

Veronica had become increasingly dissatisfied with her job as a corporate lawyer this past year. But that didn't mean she wanted to, or would ever, become a treasure hunter, for Pete's sake. That would be like Donald Trump deciding to become a hula dancer. No, it was the field of corporate law that no longer appealed to her, not the law itself.

Jake was clearly startled by her news, but he remained silent, waiting for her to explain. Talking to Jake was like playing a game of cards—she never knew what he was thinking, unless he wanted her to.

Jake laughed. "You? Running a treasure-hunting company? Last time I talked to Frank, he said he was planning a venture that involved deep-sea wreck diving. Hell's bells, Ronnie, you get seasick in the bathtub." He was still laughing.

"It's not funny. I have a job in Boston. A *steady* job," she added for his benefit. "I have no time for this nonsense."

Jake didn't rise to her "steady job" bait. He'd heard it enough in the past. "So? Decline all the . . . gifts."

"I can't. His lawyer says the trust he's set up is iron-clad. I just came from Harley Winston's office in Asbury Park."

Jake's eyes swept over her. "So that's why you're all dolled up."

She felt herself blush, though she hadn't a clue why. Jake had said and done much more to make her blush over the years. "I went to a charity event for my grandmother in Spring Lake before I met with the lawyer."

He nodded, his face suddenly grim. Jake didn't like her grandmother any more than her grandfather did.

If he only knew how her grandmother had flipped when Veronica had told her where she was going tonight!

"Can Frank do that—give you something you don't want? Isn't it illegal or something? Oh. Forget I said that."

They both knew her grandfather was up close and personal with all the politicians in New Jersey. Criminals, too, for that matter. Sometimes they were one and the same. He could probably do just about anything without being arrested.

"If he's given it to you, then sell it. No big deal!"

"Hah! You would not believe the conditions he's set up for me to liquidate anything. I'd be spending the next few years in court. Besides that, I'm not sure what Frank's financial situation is until I look through the paperwork. I have a two-foot pile of folders in my car that Winston gave me. I might be liable for his debts as well."

"Frank always was a cagey one." He said *cagey* as if it were a compliment. Jake frowned then. "Why would Frank do this? Turn over his precious company to someone who knows diddly-squat about treasure hunting—and who has no interest in learning?"

Veronica winced at his last remark. Jake had always pushed her to get closer to her eccentric grandfather, who had often been downright cruel to her. Frank had assumed she was as judgmental as her grandmother, Lillian, who had divorced him more than fifty years ago. "I don't know why," she replied finally.

He waited for her to say more. When she didn't, he said, "I'll bite, babe. Why not just ask him?"

"I intend to. In fact, I've already spoken to my own lawyer back in Boston. He suggested I talk to Frank before I do anything." She put a hand to her forehead and sighed.

"Headache?"

She nodded, waiting for him to say something sarcastic, like, "What? Your halo on too tight?" It wouldn't be the first time.

He said nothing, though, just continued to worry the beads in his pocket while watching her.

"So, Ronnie, you came to me first before confronting Frank. Why?" Slowly, his eyes went wide with disbelief as he came to his own mistaken conclusion.

"Un-be-friggin-liev-able! Don't tell me you missed me."

That was a low blow. She would always miss him, and he knew it.

Instead of appearing pleased, Jake shifted uncomfortably from foot to foot. Judging by the movement of his fingers in the jeans pocket, he was worrying those beads like crazy.

"Why? Did *you* miss *me?*" She regretted the words the second they left her mouth. "Never mind."

But it was too late. Some words couldn't be taken back.

Whatever discomfort he'd been experiencing melted away, and sparks sizzled in the air. The sexual attraction between them had always been spectacular. It was probably why she'd given in to him when she was a freshman and he was a senior at Boston U. It was probably why they kept marrying. But then, they'd learned the hard way that good sex didn't necessarily mean good marriage. Even love didn't guarantee a good marriage, as had so sadly been drummed into them four bloody times.

He put a hand over his mouth and rubbed it back and forth, watching her intently. But he didn't say anything. He didn't have to.

"I'm not here because of . . . us." To her chagrin, her face heated. She was a corporate lawyer who had no trouble talking with high-powered clients and judges, but now she was floundering for words like a teenager.

"Obviously! The last time we were together, you told me to hit the road and stay out of your life forever."

"Of course I told you that. You were already halfway out the door. Running away. Like you always do."

"Sure I run. You provoke me into leaving every single damn time."

"You avoid arguments."

"You love arguments."

"Maybe if you had stuck around one of those times, you might have discovered how untrue that is."

"I stuck plenty." Jake's jaw tightened as he visibly suppressed his temper. Apparently their last parting still rankled him. Finally, he ran his fingers through his hair and said, "I didn't run. You pushed me out."

"Oh, Jake. That was two years ago."

"Uh-oh!" Jake stiffened at the sudden softness of her voice, and fear flashed across his face for a brief moment.

Good heavens! Does he think I want to hook up with him again? And why would that scare him? Well, okay, that would scare me, too. Like a bad B movie. Return of the Living Idiots. "Don't uh-oh me. I haven't changed my mind. I am not interested in you *that way*. I came to you because Frank's lawyer gave me some interesting information. It appears you are a major investor in Jinx, Inc." She narrowed her eyes at him. "Since you invested in Frank's company, you must know what he was up to regarding me."

"No, I didn't know Frank was handing the company over to you."

"It's a corporation, isn't it? Jinx, *Inc.* He can't make that big of a decision without consulting his shareholders."

Jake laughed. "The *Inc.* to Frank means *signed in ink.* It's not legally a corporation."

"Why did you just happen to dump that much money in his lap? Why not invest in something else, like, oh, let's say, real estate?" It was a question she shouldn't have asked. Jake was a rounder, a person who plays poker for a living. Taking risks was in his genes. She, on the other hand, was a *grinder,* a person who played safe; it was not a compliment, in her case.

Jake exhaled with exasperation at her persistent questions. "I like Frank. I had a stretch of good luck. Simple as that. And why the hell not?"

"Good luck? Good luck?" She was practically shrieking. "Give me a break! A hundred thousand dollars is not *just luck.*"

"Let's not beat that dead horse again." His jaw, under the day-old stubble, was stiff, and his eyes blazed. Her criticism of his gambling was a perpetual hot button—a dead horse, for sure.

"Couldn't you have bought a savings bond or some IBM stock? I'll bet you don't even have an IRA yet." Veronica grimaced as she realized that she had fallen into lecturing him again about being conservative with finances. Jake used to tease her about it. In fact, he had often joked that her idea of doubling her money was folding the bills and putting them back in her pocket. Still, she blathered on. "The investment-to-return ratio on blue chips has got to be better than treasure hunting and almost risk-free in comparison."

He relaxed and smiled at her. When he smiled like that, his dimples emerged, and Jake's dimples pretty much amounted to lethal weapons of the most erotic kind. "Cupcake, when did I ever play it safe?"

And that is the crux of our problem. Always has been. Always will be. "I want you to pull your money out and talk some sense into my grandfather."

"Still afraid of the old man, are you?"

"I'm not afraid . . . oh, all right, he does scare me a

little. I never win an argument with him. And he has a way of making me feel like I'm a condescending clone of my grandmother."

He gave her a quick once-over that said he agreed with that opinion.

The jerk!

"What makes you think I could do any better?" Jake asked.

"He likes you. He always has."

"He likes you, too, Ronnie. You never gave him a chance."

The unspoken message was that she had never given Jake a chance, either, which was ridiculous. She'd given him four chances. She waited for him to say that he liked her, too, which he would normally have done, but he didn't. *Something is going on here. Jake is not acting his usual self.* "Let's put the subject of my grandfather in the 'dead horse' category, too." She and Jake had never agreed about Frank and probably never would.

He glanced at his wristwatch. "Listen, I have only another half hour before they resume play. I need to go meditate for a few minutes. What do you want from me?"

Ouch! Talk about blunt! There was a time when he would have had me in the sack by now, game or no game. "I told you, Jake. Go talk with Frank."

"*You* go talk to Frank."

Blunt again. "Come with me to Long Beach Island." She slapped a palm over her mouth. She couldn't believe she'd said that.

"I can't," he said sadly. "Five minutes next to you

and I'm already all twisted up inside. You make—oh, shit!"

Veronica turned to see what had caused Jake to curse. A young woman was approaching. As if watching a slow-motion vignette, Veronica saw the woman smile at Jake, ignoring her as she came up to them, then put her hand on his arm.

In the old days, Veronica would have actually snarled at that hand on his arm. Now she just snarled inwardly.

The girl—woman—couldn't have been more than twenty-five. Definitely no cellulite here. Her wavy blonde hair was any woman's dream . . . or man's, for that matter. Her tall, perfect figure put Barbie to shame. *Is Jake her Ken?* She wore a black suit with a brass name tag. Probably a casino or hotel employee.

"I just got off work, sugar."

Sugar? I think I'm going to be sick.

"How are you doing in the tournament?"

Probably good since he was one of five finalists in a million-dollar tournament.

"I'm doing great." He didn't sound great. The bimbo—it was unfair, but that's how Veronica labeled any of Jake's women—tilted her head in confusion, first at Jake and then at Veronica.

He sighed deeply, then said, "Trish, this is my ex-wife, Veronica—Ronnie—Jinkowsky." His eyes held Veronica's for a long while, as if he was sorry for something. Then he put his arm over the bimbo's shoulders and said, "This is Trish Dangel." There was a long pause before he added, "My fiancée."

Someone said, "Congratulations." It had to be Veronica, but she couldn't be sure since she was stunned. She couldn't have hurt more if she'd been kicked in the stomach. *It's been lovely, but I think I'll go scream now.* Loud white noise roared in her head. *Do not cry in front of him. Do. Not. Cry.* She turned slowly and walked away from the couple. Jake called after her to wait, but she *couldn't* stop.

Once she had gone some distance, nausea overcame her and she rushed into the first ladies' room she saw.

The scent of industrial-strength pine cleaner and a floral deodorizer assaulted her senses. Luckily, the restroom was empty.

Apparently, Jake had moved on with his life. It was unreasonable for her to be so stricken. Their relationship had always been doomed.

Still, Veronica's heart hurt, despite the divorces, despite not having seen him for two years. She was reacting so strongly because his announcement had blindsided her, she concluded.

Satisfied with that explanation, she walked woodenly into one of the stalls, locked the door, and leaned against the wall.

I don't care!

I don't care!

I don't care!

Then she gave in to the sharp pain in her abdomen, clutched herself around her middle, crumpled to her knees, and retched violently.

Chapter
2

Desperate men do desperate things. . . .

Frank Jinkowsky lay in his big antique bed late that night with his longtime girlfriend, Flora Clark— Flossie—nestled in his arms, her face on his chest. They were both naked. And both panting.

He had no business shaking the sheets like this, being seventy-five years old, but then Flossie was a young chick—only fifty-five—and he never could resist her. She was so sexy she could turn on a cadaver.

And who was he kidding? He had every business getting it on. As long as he was able. Contrary to general opinion, there were probably a whole lot of senior citizens doing the same thing right now. Use it or lose it. Definitely.

When he'd first hooked up with Flossie, he'd been fifty and she a mere thirty. A scandal! Especially to his ex-wife, Lillian, who had a permanent pole up her ass.

Although he'd learned the hard way that matrimony wasn't for him, he would have married Flossie long ago, for her sake. But she'd balked, having suffered a bad marriage herself. Now, after all these years, the idea of a legal document seemed downright silly.

"Was that as good for you as it was for me?" he joked, giving her a squeeze.

Flossie peered up at him, without raising her head, and smiled. "Not bad for an old codger . . . especially without Viagra."

He chuckled. He didn't need those blue pills yet, but he'd use them in a heartbeat if he had to. Pride went out the window when it came to a man's favorite body part.

"My breasts are sagging," Flossie said out of the blue. "Do you think I should get a boob lift?"

Now there is a loaded question if I ever heard one. He leaned down and kissed her. He loved her, sagging breasts or not. "Don't you dare."

She giggled.

Seventy-five years old and I can still make a woman giggle. Am I good or what?

"I know why you wanted to have sex tonight," she said, pulling the sheet up over them.

Another loaded comment. But he was no dummy. He settled for a simple, "Oh?"

"Yeah. You're trying to divert my attention from that loco, asinine, stupid, impossible, harebrained scheme of yours. You've done some insane things in your day, but this time you're going too far."

He laughed. "Why don't you tell me what you really think?"

She slapped him lightly on the shoulder.

"Now, Floss, come on. You have to—"

"I mean it, Frank. Nobody is going to believe you're broke, especially not your granddaughter."

Frank wanted Ronnie to work for him, but he knew she wouldn't come unless he gave her a really good reason. So, he'd come up with the idea of pretending to be on the skids financially and needing a successful project and her help to get him out of trouble.

Time was running out on him, and he had to correct the mistakes of the past couple of decades that involved his family. That meant Ronnie, since she was the only family he had left. That's why he'd invited Jake to invest in his company last year. That's why he was turning his company over to his prissy granddaughter, whom he hoped to unpriss. That's why he had taken on the Pink Project for his old friend Rosa Menotti.

Yeah, it was a crazy idea, but he'd done crazier things in his life. "I can pull it off, honey."

"All she has to do is go in the attic and see what you've stashed there."

"She is *not* going to go into the attic," he assured her. "Hell, I can barely get her to come into the house, even for a short visit."

"And whose fault is that? You should have fought harder to see your granddaughter. Not to mention Joey, when you first got divorced." Joey was Joseph Jinkowsky, Frank's son and Ronnie's father. Long dead now.

"I know, I know. The first couple years I was just too boiling mad to do anything. After that, I admit it, I was having too much fun being a wild adventurer with no marriage ties. Then, when Ronnie's mother died so young and Ronnie and Joey moved in with Lillian, it seemed an exercise in futility. They were totally under her thumb then."

"She did paint a wicked picture of you from day one."

"I have my faults, but no one this side of Satan's parlor has *that* many sins."

Flossie sighed, and he could feel her breath against his chest hairs. "It's your ridiculous pride. That's what it is."

Maybe. But he was for damn sure swallowing his pride now.

"You could tell Ronnie that you're sorry, that you love her and want her to take over the company. Tell her that you want to retire; then the two of us can ride off into the sunset in our miniyacht."

Last Fling was a fifty-foot cabin cruiser he had hidden away in a Barnegat slip. It wasn't a yacht by any means; although it had all the luxuries of one, it was still small enough not to need a crew. Just the two of them. Flossie called it a *miniyacht* because of all the extras he'd added, like a Jacuzzi and a restaurant-quality kitchen.

"Yeah, right. And then she'll just hop onto my lap and give me a grandpa hug," he scoffed. "And don't forget I want a great-grandchild in there, too. Ronnie and Jake belong together, and I'm gonna make sure it happens. This time I plan to be around when a baby is born and growing up."

"You're setting up bad karma with that poverty nonsense."

"Karma, smarma!"

Flossie tsked. "Well, don't ask me to help. I won't tell such a ludicrous lie."

"You don't have to lie. Just don't give me away."

Her silence was answer enough. He could trust Flossie.

"I expect she'll show up here tomorrow, madder'n a hen in heat." Tossing in one last argument, he added,

"It's the only way. Ronnie will never agree to help me unless it's something really drastic."

"Drastic is getting down on your knees and begging. Drastic is getting down on your knees and praying. Drastic is not your pretending to be almost in Chapter Eleven." Flossie inhaled and exhaled with exasperation, then added softly, "I hope you won't be hurt."

He kissed the top of her head and prepared to fall asleep.

How could I hurt more than I already do?

✦

Welcome to the funny farm . . .

It looked like a creepy haunted house.

Veronica arrived at her grandfather's oceanfront home at ten the next morning, after crossing the bridge from Manahawkin where she had spent the night in a motel. The turn-of-the-last-century mansion was located in Loveladies at the northern end of Long Beach Island, New Jersey—a strip of land bracketed by the ocean on one side and Barnegat Bay on the other. Nearby was the historic Barnegat Lighthouse.

The house, which sat on more than an acre of land, would probably bring a cool five million in today's market, even though her grandfather had certainly let it go. Shutters dangled from some windows. Blinds were pulled down in others. The weathered wood shakes appeared really . . . weathered. The mansard roof probably leaked, if some of the tiles that had fallen to the ground were any indication. And the sea grass in the front yard was a shoulder-high jungle.

What happened in the past three years, since she'd been here last, to bring on such neglect? Her grandfather was a nutty old coot, but he cared about this family home—or at least he used to. She remembered something then. This was *her* family home now, if the lawyer was right. *My God! I don't have the kind of money to refurbish or keep up a place like this. The taxes alone would eat up a good portion of my annual salary.*

It was springtime, and, although it was balmy, the summer crowds had not yet flooded the town or beaches. Long Beach Island, like much of the Jersey shore, was loaded with commercial enterprises, but not so much here at the northern end. The stillness of the off-season atmosphere, combined with the crashing of waves on the beach, gave a lonely feeling to her grandfather's house.

Even though she'd taken a Pepto-Bismol tablet to settle her stomach, she held her breath to block out the scent of salt water while she knocked on the front door. No answer. She tried again. Still no answer. But Frank's vintage black Mustang convertible and a late-model red pickup truck with the Jinx, Inc., logo were parked in the driveway. He must be around. Turning the doorknob, she realized it was open and stepped inside.

"Anybody home?" she called out.

She thought she heard voices coming from the opposite side of the house, the one facing the beach. Walking down the corridor, she saw rooms covered with dust and filled with draped furniture. Paintings were missing, judging by the lighter rectangular spaces on the faded wallpaper. There were no antiques or the horrible Buddha with the foot-long penis that had given her nightmares when she was a child. In the library, she noticed that the floor-to-ceiling bookshelves were half-empty, and assumed it was the collection of first editions that was gone. Even the stuffed animal heads mounted on the paneled walls—the taxidermied nightmares bagged by some nitwit Jinkowsky on an African safari years ago—were gone. Thank God for that.

The Jinkowsky brothers—Frank's grandfather and two great uncles—had made their money making kielbasa in the early 1920s, first in a butcher shop in Jersey City and eventually in a Newark factory. The Kielbasa Kings, they'd been called. Those days were long gone. In fact, the year Frank married Lillian prior to both entering Stanford Law, the Jinkowsky company had been sold due to the grandchildrens' lack of interest in entering the business. Frank had come into a small fortune along with the Long Beach Island mansion. Instead of hotfooting it off to law school—a tradition in Lillian's family that he'd promised to follow—he'd decided to use his inheritance as seed money for a treasure-hunting company. That had been the beginning of the end for him and his wife, who'd felt betrayed by her husband's change of career. The worst abomination, according to Lillian, was that Frank had gotten her pregnant before leaving.

Dreary would be the best word to describe the house now. Or *plundered*. Had her grandfather needed to sell everything in order to raise cash? She could think of no other reason for the house's condition.

She continued down the hall to the great room, with its fireplace big enough to roast a boar. That room and the kitchen were clean, with nothing removed, as far as she remembered.

She could see her grandfather out on the deck with Flossie, his live-in girlfriend. A wide expanse of beach extended from the deck to the ocean, and seagulls squawked as they swooped down for food.

Frank and Flossie sat at a large, round patio table with an unfurled center umbrella. Polka music played loudly on a tape deck; her grandfather did love a good accordion. Flossie, who was fiftysomething, resembled an aging stripper, which she could have been, given Frank's habits. But actually, she'd been a Las Vegas showgirl. Even though Veronica had been only seven at the time, she could still remember the uproar when fifty-year-old Frank took up with thirtysomething Flossie. Lillian hated Flossie almost as much as she did Frank.

To say that Flossie was well-endowed would be a colossal understatement—another reason for thin-as-a-rail Lillian to hate her "replacement." This morning Flossie wore tight black jeans, a revealing red tank top edged with sequins, and red high-heeled slides. The woman had more than twenty years on Veronica, but Flossie had a better figure. Her blonde hair, dyed of course, sported the biggest metal rollers Veronica had ever seen, possibly empty soup cans.

Her grandfather was a big man, at least six foot three and burly, like the mountain men in old westerns. Needless to say, he had scared her a little when she was a child. He was reading the morning newspaper, a burning cigar in one hand and a glass of some amber-colored beverage in front of him. Probably bourbon. *Booze before noon? No wonder he has money problems.* He wore denim shorts, which were full of holes; a threadbare, once-yellow T-shirt; and his trademark suspenders—he had more than Larry King, he sometimes bragged.

They were Mickey Mouse ones today. The canvas shoes on his feet were so worn, they were more sole than anything else. He was usually rather vain about his appearance, but today he was unshaven, and his white hair stood out like Don King's. He'd always been a handsome man. Now he looked like Nick Nolte's mug shot.

She could have sworn they'd noticed her approach, but maybe not because Flossie was arguing with him about eating his breakfast.

"I don't want any of that frickin' egg shit," he said. Not bothering to peer up from the paper, he blew enough smoke into the air to make Flossie choke.

Waving her hand in front of her face, Flossie said, "It's not egg shit, darling. It's eggs benedict. I got the recipe from Vivian over at the Nail You manicure shop."

Veronica glanced at Flossie's hands. Yep, she still had those inch-long sculptured nails, painted bright red today and matching her shirt.

"Pfff! That doesn't look like any eggs benedict I ever saw. It's green, fer chrissake!"

"It's jalapenos in the sauce—Mexican eggs benedict." Flossie smacked him on the shoulder. "Eat the eggs, dammit."

"I can eat shredded wheat, like always. Why are you wastin' money on this other food?"

Eggs are expensive? Since when? Oh. He really does have financial problems, then.

He slammed the paper down, took a huge slug of bourbon, and shook his head. On an empty stomach, it must hit like five hundred proof.

With a frown of disapproval, Flossie began to gather up the dishes, then for the first time noticed Veronica near the open French doors. "Ronnie!" Flossie exclaimed, giving Frank a strange, warning glower. Then she set the dishes down and came over to give her a hug. Veronica and Flossie were both about five-nine, but with the high heels, Flossie towered over her. She wore so much Shalimar perfume, it wiped the scent of salt water from Veronica's nose.

Flossie rolled her eyes meaningfully at Frank and then at her. Except Veronica wasn't sure what message she was being given.

"Frank." Veronica walked over and stared down at her grandfather. *Should I hug him? No! He would probably shove me away.* Just being near him made her stomach churn and made her want to bolt, but she had important business to discuss first.

Frank frowned. "It's about time you got here, girl."

"What do you mean? You never invited me."

"What? You need a hoity-toity engraved invitation to visit your grandfather? Your grandmother turned you against me a long time ago. The bitch!"

Flossie harrumphed her opinion.

Well, this is a pleasant start to our visit. Veronica sat down opposite him and let out a whoosh of frustration at the same old direction their conversation was heading. "Listen to me, old man, you are not going to lay a guilt trip on me. You are the one who threw me overboard into the bay when I was only five years old."

"*That* again! I was tryin' to teach you how to swim, for chrissake. You were babied too much by that Boston bunch. Besides, you had a life vest on. You were never in danger of drowning."

"How was I to know that?" she cried out. "You don't teach children to swim by tossing them overboard."

"Oh, yeah? You learned to swim that day, didn't you?"

And to hate the ocean and salt water, which she'd swallowed about a gallon of.

"Then there was the time you terrorized me by taking me on that roller coaster in Asbury Park—the one that went out over the ocean." She'd smelled the salt air that time, too.

"It was fun," he protested.

"For you, maybe. Not for me. I was scared."

"Kids like to be scared on rides."

"Not this kid!"

He shook his head as if she were a freak.

"Then there was the waterskiing incident. And the deep-water fishing trip—for sharks, of all things." *No wonder I have an aversion to salt water. I don't need a shrink to diagnose my Pavlovian association.*

Flossie made a clucking sound at their juvenile squabbling, then picked up the dishes again and walked toward the kitchen, tsk-tsk-tsking the whole way.

"All that is beside the point. I'm here because of this." She slammed some legal documents on the table. "What is this all about?"

He didn't even look at the papers. Instead, he spoke around the cigar in his mouth. "I'm taking care of business."

"Why me?"

He shrugged. "You're the only family I have."

"How about Flossie?"

Flossie yelled from the kitchen, "I don't want it."

"Floss wouldn't know treasure from tulips." Her grandfather downed the last of his liquor.

"And I would?"

"She thinks pink flamingoes are fine art."

"Do not!" Flossie yelled again.

"Even if I wanted to, which I don't, I wouldn't have a clue how to run a treasure-hunting company."

"I'll teach you."

I'd rather swim with sharks. "No, thanks."

"Anyhow, your job would be more like supervising. Hiring. Budgets. That kind of crap. You're a corporate something-or-other, aren't you?"

He doesn't even know what I do for a living. "Why should I?"

"Like I said, you're the only one."

There was an insult in there somewhere. "Why now?"

"You figure it out, girlie. You got one of them phi beta thingees, dontcha?" There was a nasty tone to his voice. For a man trying to convince her to do something she didn't want to, he was doing the opposite.

She tilted her head to the side. Something was very strange here. More strange than usual. Enough with beating around the bush. "Are you in financial trouble?"

His face reddened with what she assumed was embarrassment. Men and their pride! "I'm not about to go belly-up . . . yet . . . if that's what you're asking."

She noticed the nervous tic in her grandfather's jaw and the strange expression on his face. Then she noticed Flossie standing in the doorway, wringing her hands, frowning at Frank. Meanwhile, the "Beer Barrel Polka" blasted through the speakers.

"What? How bad is it?" she demanded.

Her grandfather gulped several times and held Flossie's gaze, as if pondering whether to tell her something or not. But he was saved from having to respond because company arrived.

And what company it was!

Chapter
3

You could say she was the Godmother . . .

A woman and two men came strolling toward them from the side walkway. They'd probably knocked, as she had, and not been heard.

About sixty years old, the petite woman wore a Chanel dress, Manolo Blahnik shoes, and enough jewelry to make an Oscar nominee on the red carpet envious. Auburn hair, perfectly coiffured, framed a face that had surely had a face-lift or two and a skin tone that spoke of Enro Laszlo makeup.

Between this woman and Flossie, Veronica could easily get an inferiority complex.

Wait a minute. The woman looked familiar. Veronica tapped her closed lips thoughtfully with a forefinger, then gasped. It was Rosa Menotti, widow of Mafia boss Sam Menotti. Veronica recognized her from the photo spread in *People* magazine last year that had highlighted wives of notorious men. The two burly thugs who accompanied her—could they be Mafia hit men? The jackets they wore—could they be hiding guns? *Oh. My. God!*

"Franco!" The woman smiled and waved as she approached. *"Buon giorno!"*

Franco? Veronica's eyes shot to her grandfather, who stood to greet the trio. "Rosa! How good to see you! Come sit down here, darlin'." Then to Flossie he said, "Get us some more iced tea, would you, sweetie? And more sugar this time."

Okay, so it was iced tea and not bourbon. And his full-body shudder was due to the bitterness of the drink, not to its alcoholic potency. Those weren't the only surprises. Veronica was also taken aback by her grandfather's hospitable behavior. He must really be losing it. Either that or she was the only one who got the rude treatment.

Rosa sat down, along with her two male companions, both in their mid- to late-thirties, Veronica guessed. About five-ten, they wore expensive jackets, one black and one gray, over massive shoulders and chests, with Rolex watches on their wrists and gold chains around their thick necks. One had black hair that was slicked back, and the other's spiked upward in a sort of long military cut. Both could probably bench-press a boat. Or a getaway car.

Her grandfather had moved his glass and newspaper aside to make room for them and was about to douse his cigar when Rosa raised a hand. "Don't put that out for my benefit. I love the scent of a good cigar. My Sammy, he always . . ." She sniffled and took out a tissue, dabbing at her eyes in a way that would not smudge her mascara.

Is she sniffling over Sammy the Goon—the guy who single-handedly killed more than twenty men one night?

The two men were oddly mute. *What do I know? Maybe hit men aren't supposed to talk. Maybe it's a Mafia code.* The two men and Rosa glanced at her, then at her grandfather, before he said, "This is my granddaughter, Veronica. Ronnie for short. Her grandmother hates that I gave her that nickname and it stuck. Ha, ha, ha!"

Could he be any more obnoxious?

"Isn't she a beauty? And smart, too," Frank continued without missing a beat.

Veronica couldn't believe her ears. *My grandfather just said nice words about me. Holy cow! I'd better be careful. Either his nose is going to grow or the sky is going to fall.*

Flossie set a tray on the table and passed out frosty, mismatched jelly glasses of iced tea. What happened to the Fostoria crystal they used for everyday? Amazingly, Flossie had not only made the beverage in that short time, but she'd also taken out her metal rollers and managed to tease and spray her hair into a poufy, Dolly Parton–style do.

Her grandfather proceeded to add sugar to his iced tea. One teaspoon. Two teaspoons. Three teaspoons. Four teaspoons. Five. No one else noticed, or else they were being polite.

Veronica's mouth dropped lower and lower with each addition.

Even more amazing, he took a long swig of the drink and said, "That's better."

So, Frank still had a sweet tooth. She'd forgotten

how much he liked sweet things, especially ice cream. As a little girl, it had been a marvel to open his freezer and see a dozen different flavors of ice cream . . . right next to all the kielbasas.

Rosa put her hands on the arms of the two men on each side of her. "And these are my two sons, Anthony and Stefano. They are smart and beautiful, too, are they not?"

If one likes steroids.

Everyone nodded. Veronica could swear there was a matchmaking glint in Rosa's eyes. That was confirmed when she asked Veronica if she was married. When Veronica said no, Rosa smiled and said, "Neither are my sons. They have been waiting for the right woman." She stared directly at Veronica as she spoke.

The two olive-complexioned men sort of smiled at her. Some women might consider them attractive, in a barracuda sort of way. They gave her a lengthy, head-to-toe survey, as if she were a choice piece of meat being offered to them. A kielbasa, maybe. One of them even winked at her.

Oh, no. No, no, no, no! I am not getting involved with some Mafia guys. Jake was bad enough. But Mafia? No way! And what is my grandfather doing with these people?

Her grandfather then spoiled the effect of his earlier nice words about her by adding, "Like I told you before, Rosa, my granddaughter is going to take over Jinx, Inc., for me. She'll be heading the Pink Project diving operation, under my supervision, of course."

Veronica gaped at the old fool.

Rosa lifted her eyebrows with concern. "I know we discussed this before, Franco, but are you sure she can help us find the pink diamonds?"

The two of them talked as if she wasn't even here.

Whoa, whoa, whoa! I am not taking over Jinx, Inc. I am not supervising any diving project. Did she say "us"? Oh, Jeesh! Did the Mafia commission Frank to do some project involving pink diamonds? What pink diamonds? Are they stolen? Damn, he must have taken this on because of his money problems.

Hard to believe that her biggest concern this time last week was boredom with her job. *Can my life get any worse?*

Turned out it could.

In walked Jake, cool as a Jersey shore breeze, wearing a Hawaiian shirt, khaki shorts, and athletic shoes with no socks. He tipped his head at everyone, kissed Flossie and Rosa on the cheek, patted her grandfather on the shoulder, and shook hands with Anthony and Stefano, saying "Tony. Steve." Apparently, he knew the Mafia gang. *Why am I surprised? That's what comes from hanging around casinos.* He plopped down in the seat next to Veronica, took a sip of her iced tea, then turned his baby blues on her. "Hey, honey bun! Your nose is getting sunburned."

Veronica had been crushed by Jake's fiancée announcement last night, and she still felt like a raw open wound when she thought about Jake marrying someone else. For just a second, she considered castrating him with her iced-tea spoon.

He put a hand on her arm and whispered, "Hi!"

She slapped his hand away and sputtered for something to say, but all she could come up with was, "Where's Barbie?"

He flashed her his dimples. "Trish's at school."

She must be younger than she looked. "School?

Oh, you are such a sleaze. Fooling around with a schoolgirl."

"Premed," he said, chucking her under the chin. "She works part-time in the casino between semesters. And, for your information, she's twenty-five."

Well, that makes me feel lots better. Not!

"Jake is Ronnie's husband," her grandfather announced out of the blue.

She wasn't sure if her grandfather had forgotten the divorces or if he was just being obnoxious.

"*Scusi,* but I thought you said . . ." Rosa's forehead furrowed.

"Ex-husband," Veronica pointed out.

"Oh," Rosa said, relieved.

Rosa's relief sent little alarm bells off in Veronica's already-pounding head.

"Four times ex-husband," Jake the Snake pointed out, smiling.

She elbowed him in the arm, and he pretended to be hurt, like an immature idiot.

"Huh?" Rosa and her two sons asked.

"Ronnie and I can't live with each other, and we hot damn can't live without each other." Jake regarded her with amusement. "Isn't that right, cupcake?"

Why is he doing this? What's his game this time? "Jake is engaged to someone else," she informed everyone.

The Mafia group appeared pleased, but Frank and Flossie stared at Jake as if he'd committed some heinous crime.

"Actually, I might not be engaged anymore."

Veronica turned slowly to look at him. "*What?* That's not what you said last night."

Jake winked at her.

"What in blazes does that mean?" Frank wanted to know. "Are you engaged or not?"

"Ronnie and Jake, you were together last night?" Flossie homed in on the least relevant thing Jake had said. "How romantic!"

You wouldn't have thought it was romantic if you had been there. Nope. Definitely. Not. Romantic. "What do you mean, you *might* not be engaged anymore?" she asked Jake, even though she knew she shouldn't encourage him in any way.

"Trish seems to think I still have you under my skin." His eyes held hers for several moments.

Under his skin? Me? Veronica was not pleased . . . much. "Why would Doctor Bimbo think that?" she asked. "Until last night, we hadn't seen each other for two years."

"Maybe because she practically had to wrestle me to the floor to keep me from going after you." He shrugged. "Anyhow, Trish gave the ring back and told me not to darken her door till I get you out of my system." He smiled at her as if he'd just told her she'd won the lottery.

"And I'm supposed to be flattered by that? Like I'm going to welcome you back till *you* get tired of *me*? Like I'm the other woman or something?"

"Yep."

She snorted. "That would be a first."

"Hey, I never cheated on you. Ever. And don't arch your eyebrows at me, babe. It's the truth."

"Give me a break. Never let it be said that Jake Jensen would allow a little rust to grow on his zipper. You've had more women than . . . than Hugh Hefner."

"But not while we were married."

"Yeah, but you were bed-hopping before the ink was dry on our divorce papers. All four times."

"Doesn't count. Everyone knows testosterone is a natural IQ suppressant, but I never cheated while I was with you."

"Go right ahead, blame it on testosterone."

Frank cleared his throat a couple of times, trying to get their attention. "Do you two mind saving your lovers' squabbles for later?"

"We are not lovers," Veronica protested, but no one seemed to be listening.

She glanced around the table and suddenly realized that she and Jake were making spectacles of themselves. Jake, on the other hand, looked pleased that he'd managed to rile her. The lout! But, no, he had his hands in his pocket, rubbing the worry beads. That meant he was nervous. Hmmm.

"What brings you here?" Frank asked Jake with a cat-who-got-the-cream smirk.

"Yeah, why aren't you playing poker?" Veronica snapped.

"Tournament's over and I'm dropping out of the circuit for a while. Luckily, I'm free for the next month or so."

Lucky for whom?

"Good. Then you can help Ronnie with the new project," her grandfather suggested, a crafty gleam in his eyes.

Whaaaat? she screamed inwardly. *Am I being set up here?* "No, no, no! Not that I'm getting involved, but no, definitely not. No Jake. No treasure hunting."

"We'll see." Frank smiled at Jake, who smiled back.

Worms "R" Us!

"You know, that reminds me. Life is like a poker game," Jake began.

Veronica groaned. That was her usual reaction to his hokey poker platitudes. She'd heard that he used them as headers on each chapter of his poker how-to book.

He ignored her groan. "Life is like a poker game—you gotta ante up if you're gonna win the prize."

Everyone at the table was silent for a moment as they tried to figure how what Jake said related to the treasure-hunting project.

"Is that sorta like, your ship can't come in if you don't send out any boats?" Frank asked.

"Precisely," Jake replied.

"Yo, Jake! How'd you do in the tournament?" Anthony spoke up.

"Second place," Jake replied. "Just can't manage to win the championship."

"Hey, second place ain't bad. Half a mil, wasn't it?" This time it was Stefano speaking. The two goons had tongues after all.

Then Stefano's words sank in.

"Half a mil?" she squeaked out. "Dollars?"

Jake nodded, suddenly serious, a defensive cast to his eyes. He was reminding her of all the times she'd doubted his ability to make a living from poker. "To answer your question, Frank"—Jake tipped his chair back against the deck rail—"I'm here to show Trish and the world that I can resist Ronnie."

Veronica choked on the iced tea she'd just swallowed.

Jake clapped her on the back. Too hard. "You should be more careful, honey."

"You've got some nerve. Coming here so you can

prove I'm no longer a temptation. So you can then go marry the boardwalk bimbo?"

Jake laughed, unrepentant. "Yeah. So don't go hitting on me or anything."

Veronica sputtered with disbelief. Well, she shouldn't be surprised. Jake had once told her that laughter was good medicine, like jogging for the soul.

He waggled his eyebrows at her, ignoring her outrage. "Ronnie and I go way back," he said to no one in particular, though everyone was staring at him—at the two of them, actually. "Why, the stories I could tell you about the things we've done. Whoo-boy! Makes my toes curl just to think about it. Like the time she handcuffed me to—"

Veronica stood suddenly and pointed at Jake. "You! Come with me. Now!"

He grinned.

She growled, started to stomp toward the beach, took a deep breath, dug in her pocket for a Pepto, popped it into her mouth and proceeded to chomp vigorously, then pivoted and walked back into the house. He followed after her.

"You always did have the greatest ass," he murmured.

She stopped and turned. "What did you say?"

He just waggled his eyebrows at her again.

Veronica entered the library before him and stopped in the middle of the room. That's when she heard an ominous clicking sound.

Jake had just locked the door.

Uh-oh!

They both noticed the leather chaise lounge at the same time.

❋

The plot thickens . . .

"Honey." Flossie put a hand on Frank's shoulder, calling him back to the present. "Rosa just asked you a question."

Frank shook his head briskly to clear the cobwebs. "Sorry, Rosa. I was thinking about my granddaughter and that rascal husband of hers. I can hardly remember being that young . . . or so full of piss and vinegar."

"Tell me about it," Rosa said, rolling her eyes.

Flossie ran a caressing hand over his forearm. "You've still got plenty of piss and vinegar, old man."

She was reminding him of last night. *What a girl!*

Without speaking, Rosa's two sons stood and walked to the edge of the deck. Because of the unseasonably warm temperature for late May, a scattering of people could be seen near the shoreline. An elderly couple wearing matching sweatshirts, holding hands as they strolled along the water's foamy edge. Several children digging for sand crabs. A college-age jogger, bare-chested, wearing only nylon shorts and running shoes.

Frank loved the ocean. He couldn't imagine ever living or working away from it for long. Not all his treasure hunts were aquatic, but he always came back. That's why he couldn't understand Ronnie's aversion to it.

Anthony and Stefano surveyed the area as if they expected some mob bosses to pop up out of the dunes. Which wasn't totally out of the question, even though their father was long buried. Family vendettas had a way of sticking like glue. And the Jersey Pine Barrens were presumably loaded with the casualties of those feuds.

Flossie went into the house, probably to check on her stock portfolio. Most people didn't know she was quite the investment guru. While Frank had made his fortune in treasure hunting, Flossie had amassed an equal fortune playing the market.

Rosa pulled out a cigarette and put it into one of those silly cigarette holders that were supposed to filter out nicotine. "I don't like to smoke in front of the boys," she confessed.

Hmpfh! Those "boys" have seen lots worse than their mother smoking.

Sheepishly, she lit up, inhaled, and blew out an impressive series of rings. Then, sighing with pleasure, she turned her attention to him. "So, Frankie, give me an update on the project."

He pulled out some maps from a tube at his feet, along with spreadsheets listing costs, items yet to be purchased for the dive, and briefing notes for the six-man crew. The Pink Project would involve deep-sea diving about forty miles off the Jersey coast. It would not be a salvaging operation, because there would be little historical value in raising the wooden-hulled Italian boat, the *Sea Witch*, which had gone down in a storm about sixty years ago. Therefore, no archaeologist would be on board, nor any representative of the U.S. Park Service, which usually had jurisdiction over shipwrecks. The value was in the iron chest supposedly located in its hold and that contained, in today's market, roughly twenty million dollars in diamonds.

Rosa knew the details because her Sicilian family had sent the diamonds as a dowry for her mother in this country. In addition, Frank had done extensive historical research and made two trips to Italy, one of which included Flossie, Rosa, and a contingent of Rosa's stateside family. The map of the site had been drawn and redrawn over and over, and still was a guesstimate . . . but a sound one. In many ways, treasure hunting was like doing a puzzle. In this case, all but a few pieces were in place.

The diamonds had not been stolen, which would have been a definite no-no for Frank. But they had been smuggled across international waters, presumably to avoid customs. He'd bet his left nut there was a story there. In addition, there was no existing cargo registry anywhere, just family letters and the word of one survivor, now long dead.

While the legalities of it all were iffy, the ethics were not. Frank had friends in high places who'd approved the six-month permit to dive within a one-mile radius of the wreck site. He had friends in low places, too, but that was beside the point.

Rosa wanted the handful of pink diamonds, which she considered family heirlooms. Pink diamonds, once available only to royalty, were the most rare of all diamonds, known to fetch up to one million dollars each. Frank and his crew would get the nonpink diamonds, as much as a hundred of the buggers. Dollar-wise, the split should approximately amount to fifty-fifty.

The wreck was a virgin site. No one had made an effort to recover the diamonds in many years, and only a few people knew about the treasure—all members of Rosa's family. It wasn't until recent years that technology had enabled them to pinpoint the area where the boat had gone down. Plus, Rosa had waited till her husband died before investing a hundred thousand of his dollars in the venture. Sam had always refused to risk money for what he'd referred to as a "bag of rocks."

Despite his friendship with Rosa, Frank was cautious. There might be more to this sunken boat than Rosa let on. In addition, he did not entirely trust her two sons to hand over the remaining diamonds. Partnering with the mob was dangerous under any circumstances. And when money was involved, people of any ilk reverted to their baser selves; at least that had been Frank's experience.

He spread all the documents on the table. After a half hour of back-and-forth questions on issues they had gone over many times before, Rosa smiled at him. "This is so exciting, Franco. When do we start?"

"Two weeks, if I can get my granddaughter to agree to work with us."

She frowned and took a deep drag on her cigarette, blowing the smoke out slowly in a thin stream. "I don't know, Franco. She has no expertise." This wasn't the first time Rosa had raised these concerns.

"Ronnie is a deal breaker for me," he said adamantly. Then he softened his tone. "I have my reasons. Not to worry, sweetheart. I'll be there supervising everything."

She tapped her ridiculously long, red nails on the table; they were just like Flossie's. "Why is it so important that your granddaughter be involved?"

Rosa was the one who originated the search, and she was ponying up a hundred thousand. He had to be careful not to offend her. So, while he would like to tell her to mind her own business, what he did was shrug and reply tersely, "Family."

"Ahhhh," she said. "We Italians know better than anyone—family is everything."

Not quite the same.

They shook hands then, sealing the deal.

Frank had always liked a good chess game. Now that all the pieces were on the table, he couldn't wait to see who won. He was betting on himself.

Chapter

4

Let the games begin . . .

Jake leaned back against the locked library door and took his time studying his ex-wife. It was the first time in more than two years that he'd been alone in a room with her.

"We are not going to make love," Ronnie said, wagging her finger at him, even as she backed up till her butt hit the round table in the middle of the library.

That was the last thing Jake had been thinking. It was just that the chaise lounge had thrown him for a loop. Too many memories!

She wore a white silk shirt tucked into a short, black, pin-striped skirt. Miles of silk-encased legs were exposed down to high-heeled patent-leather shoes that would have appeared librarianish if not for peep-toe openings. *Her toes are painted pink! Does she want to give me a heart attack? Note to Jake: Ronnie doesn't dress to please you anymore. Another note to Jake: You're here to show that you're over your ex-wife, not to jump into the fire again.*

She'd let her thick, chestnut hair grow longer than when they'd last been together. It was upswept into a knot at the top of her head. Ronnie worried about getting wrinkles. All women did. But he thought she looked just as good as the first time he'd spotted her across campus thirteen years ago and fell in love on the spot. It had been the same the second time around when he'd fallen in love with her all over again. And the third. And the fourth.

While Jake was feasting his eyes on her, Ronnie's honey-brown eyes stared back at him, but not with admiration. In fact, she was as jittery as a deer caught in a hunter's crosshairs, not sure where to run, or *if* she should run.

You should run, he would tell her if he was a better man. *I should run.*

"We are not going to make love," he agreed, but took an instinctive step toward her.

"Stop right there." She put up a halting hand and moved backward till she was on the other side of the table.

"Why are you here, Jake?"

He'd seen how crushed Ronnie had been last night when he introduced his fiancée. He'd never intended to blindside her that way. They may not love each other anymore, but they had too much history to take the other's romantic relationships lightly. To tell the truth, he wasn't sure how he would have reacted if the tables had been turned—if she'd introduced him to a potential husband.

But someone needed to lighten the tension in this room. "Life is like a poker game, sweetie. You gotta have alligator blood if you're gonna play with the big boys." *Alligator blood* was poker lingo for *nerves of steel,* and, yep, they both could use a pigload of that.

She didn't acknowledge his attempt at humor, not even with a frown. *Okaaaay!* Glancing around the room, he noticed that lots of the books and furnishings were missing. *What is going on?* Then he noticed that one particular object was missing. "Oh, no! What happened to Buddha?"

"I have no idea." Ronnie blushed at the reminder of the statue.

He'd forgotten how much he enjoyed making Ronnie blush.

"Man, I hope it didn't get broken or lost. One of my favorite sexual fantasies involves me, you, and big ol' Buddha."

"You can file that in the Department of Wishful Thinking. I repeat, Jake, why are you here?"

Because I like banging my head against a brick wall? "Hell if I know. To get you out of my system, I guess . . . or to see if you're still in my system, like Trish says."

"Like an exorcism?" she scoffed.

"Uh-huh. Minus the green vomit. Or Richard Burton." He grinned at her.

She didn't grin back. "And you plan to do that, how?"

"I'm thinking about helping Frank—and you—with the Pink Project."

The horror on her face should have offended him, but he was beyond being offended. Being married and divorced four times tended to build a thick skin on a guy.

"Not gonna happen," she said.

He didn't say anything. He didn't have to. They both

knew that if they were in each other's company for any length of time—say, an hour—they would be all over each other, like honey on a hot rock.

"Cut it out, Jake. Your teasing isn't helping matters."

She inhaled and exhaled a few times. That usually meant he was annoying her. *Big whoop!*

"I need to talk with you," she said after she finished her inhale-exhale exercise.

He could see that she was genuinely distressed. Time to back off. With a loud sigh of resignation, he plopped himself down on the leather chaise and stretched out. It was the same chaise where he and Ronnie had rocked each other's worlds one time while visiting Frank. He wondered if he should remind Ronnie. Probably not. Besides, she must recall every vivid detail, same as he did.

He folded his hands under his neck and crossed his legs at the ankle. "It feels like I'm in a therapist's office or something. Not that I've ever met with a shrink. Oh, don't look at me like that's just what I need."

She fought a smile and shook her head at his antics. Well, at least she wasn't still frowning. "You promised to quit teasing."

"I did?"

She pulled up a desk chair and sat down. "Have you noticed anything odd about Frank?"

"He's always been odd."

"Odder than usual."

He furrowed his brow, thinking. "Nope. I've talked to him plenty on the phone, but I haven't seen him much in person the past year. Do you mean 'odd' because he left you all his worldly goods? Or a different kind of odd?"

"Both." She worried her bottom lip with her teeth.

She really shouldn't do that. Anything involving her lips, which he had a particular affection for, was a definite no-no.

"When I first got here, I overheard him arguing with Flossie, and he mentioned her wasting money—on eggs, for heaven's sake. He was being crude and, well, not nice."

"C'mon, Ronnie. Your grandfather has always been a bit grouchy, even with Flossie. And crude? He makes *me* blush sometimes. Remember the time he asked me if I could get it up more than five times a day? Of course, I told him yes." When she didn't smile, he decided that she was not in the mood for a stroll down memory lane.

"Something about him is different," she insisted. "And have you looked around? All the artwork and antiques are gone."

He pondered what she'd said. "Maybe he just got tired of the old things. Maybe he and Flossie want to redecorate."

Unconvinced, she tented her fingers in front of her closed lips and studied him. "Another thing I'm puzzled by. You."

Uh-oh! He mouthed the word *moi?*

She was not amused. "There is no way you would let a woman decide whether you are engaged or not. There is no way you would take orders from anyone to go purge yourself of me. You might do it of your own volition, but not because someone else told you to. You do whatever the hell you want. Always have. Always will."

He shifted uncomfortably under her too-accurate analysis.

"Why are you here? Really?"

He felt himself flush as he sat up and faced her.

"Frank begged me to come."

✦

Dale Earnhardt had nothing on him. . . .

Later that morning, Veronica and Jake were in the backseat of Frank's Mustang convertible, barreling down Route 9 toward Barnegat.

She was practically peeing her pants with fright.

Jake was laughing his ass off.

Flossie, in the passenger seat, watched as her scarf whipped off and flew away. With a cry of distress, she lowered her head toward her lap.

Rosa and the two Mafia dudes were tailing them in a big, black Lincoln with tinted windows.

And what was her idiot grandfather doing?

Singing! Along to "Cemetery" polka, which was blasting from the CD player. Something about Uncle Bill having a tumor as big as an egg and a Puerto Rican mistress with a wooden leg. Besides puffing on his smelly cigar and belting out the horrid lyrics, Frank was racing down the road, foot pressed to the accelerator, oblivious to all their protests to slow down. He hadn't stopped for one single blessed stop sign or red light so far.

Not to worry, he'd assured them the one time they'd been able to make themselves heard over the polka music, roar of the engine, and the wind, which was, incidentally, blowing her hair forward into her face. Apparently, he had some kind of police sticker on his rear bumper that pretty much ensured no cops would pull them over.

It wasn't a ticket she was worried about. It was death, as in crashing into a tree or some other immovable object.

And the bugs. And dust. Somehow, Frank had managed to find the only swarm of springtime gnats and dust clouds in New Jersey and drove right through them. Veronica had eaten three bugs before snapping her mouth shut. *Remind me never to buy a convertible. Moon roofs suit me just fine.* At least it wasn't locusts, she consoled herself.

After telling her grandfather this morning in no uncertain terms that she would not get involved with Jinx, Inc., he'd somehow talked her and Jake into staying long enough to have lunch at some nearby restaurant. A place that Frank boasted had the best soft-shell crab sandwiches on the East Coast. He'd offered to drive them across Barnegat Bay to the restaurant in a motorboat, which Veronica had, of course, vehemently declined.

And wasn't that odd? He was in dire financial straits, and yet he hadn't sold his Mustang or the motorboat. Well, maybe they were the next to be sold.

Still, her grandfather made her so mad. Like always.

First of all, this wasn't "nearby." Secondly, she hadn't signed on for Frank's Great Adventure Ride. Third, had no desire to eat fully intact crabs with legs and guts, thank you very much! Fourth, she suspected the foxy old fool was up to no good.

That last misgiving soon proved true.

With a screech of brakes, the car fishtailed into the parking lot of the Lighthouse Inn, raising a cloud of crushed clam shells in its wake. There was a collective sigh of relief and one "Whoo-ee, baby!" Plus "Dontcha just love a good polka?"

Not only was he acting like a madman, but he also resembled one now. His hair now looked like Don King's combed with a mixer. At least he'd shaved.

Frank opened his car door, practically skipped around the front, and opened Flossie's door. Flossie jumped out and punched Frank in the stomach. "Don't you ever do that to me again!" Flossie wore the same outfit she'd had on earlier. The only difference was now her bouffant hairdo looked like bouffant on steroids, thanks to the wind.

Veronica popped her fifth Pepto of the day. She could only imagine how she looked herself.

She soon got her answer when she unclipped her seat belt and turned to her ex-husband, who continued to laugh hysterically as he undid his own seat belt. Except now his mirth was directed at her. She couldn't see his eyes behind his sunglasses, but, too cracked up to speak, he kept pointing at her hair and saying, "You, you, you . . . !"

She did the only thing any sane woman would. She followed Flossie's suit and punched Jake in the stomach. He pretended to be really hurt as he crawled out of the backseat. Pulling a compact from her purse, she checked herself out and screeched, "EEEK!" The knot on top of her head had come undone and hair was sticking out every which way. Think bed head in a wind tunnel. A dusting of dirt covered her face, and she could swear she saw streaks of dead bug juice. She had two long runs in her stockings from grabbing for the seat when Frank had first taken off, but she'd missed her mark and her fingernails had clawed her knees.

Jake, of course, looked just fine.

"What? What did I do?" Frank asked Flossie.

Flossie gave him a disgusted once-over, then said, "Oh, land's sake!" when he kept on blinking innocently at her. With a last glower, she stomped ahead of him toward the inn, her high heels wobbling in the clam shells.

Veronica saw Rosa and her sons already entering the inn, seemingly nonplussed by the ride from hell.

Just then, a young man came peeling into the parking lot in a cherry-red Chevy Impala, probably 1960s vintage. It was about the size of a small bus.

"Hey, John." Frank waved.

"Yo, Frank!" A very nice-looking guy, probably early twenties, waved to all of them as he got out of the car. He wore a T-shirt that proclaimed, "Cajuns do it better . . . and better . . . and better." Judging by his long, lean body, he probably lived up to his T-shirt.

"That's John LeDeux, an assistant diver for the Pink Project," Frank explained. Then he yelled out to the young man, "What are you doin' driving a gas-guzzler like this?"

"At my age, cars are moving motels," he replied. "Besides, everyone knows that hot cars are babe magnets." Then the young stud had the audacity to wink at her, as if she might be a babe, before walking toward the inn.

"I think he likes you," her grandfather remarked.

"No, he doesn't," Jake countered.

The idiot! Both of them!

Her grandfather grinned, pleased with himself. Then he turned and asked Jake if he could talk to him in private.

Jake shrugged, and the two men walked a few yards away. Frank was saying something to Jake, who nodded several times, then reached into his pocket and pulled out his wallet. He handed something to Frank.

"Why are we dawdling out here in the parking lot?" Frank snapped. "Let's go join the party." Before she could say anything, Frank walked briskly toward the inn.

Veronica and Jake gawked at his back, especially when they noticed that Frank's denim shorts were so worn his white underwear was visible. He had changed into an equally ragged T-shirt with the logo "I AM JINXED!" and a pair of purple suspenders.

"What party?" she asked Jake.

"Hell if I know!" He took her arm. "But I damn sure need a drink. Maybe two."

"Just so it's not tequila," she blurted out before she could bite her tongue.

Jake took off his sunglasses and turned slowly to scrutinize her. He was clearly surprised that she would bring up something intimate from their past—like the two of them having a contest in a Mexican cantina over who could drink the most tequila margaritas. He'd won hands down. At least, that's what he'd said when they woke up in an upstairs bedroom, married again. He'd been wearing only a sombrero. Shades of their cowboy marriage! She must have a thing for men with hats.

But now she ignored the questioning tilt of Jake's head and continued walking.

"No tequila," he agreed, catching up with her.

His agreement annoyed her, contrary woman that she was.

She and Jake walked side by side through the door. It was a really nice restaurant—not an inn at all—with one glass-fronted side giving a magnificent view of Barnegat Bay. She'd half-expected some dive that smelled of beer and grease. On one wall were lovely framed prints showing the famous Barnegat Lighthouse through the years.

The hostess, standing before a tall lectern, waved them in. "The Jinkowski party is in the back room." Her grandfather must have warned her they were just behind him.

"What happened back there?" she asked Jake. "With my grandfather? What did he want?"

"He asked if he could borrow my credit card. Said he forgot his own," he replied somberly. "I hate to say it, but you might be right about the money situation. I've never known Frank to go anywhere without a wad of cash or plastic."

"I hate to see him like this. No matter what I think, Frank has always been so proud. This must be demeaning for him."

"I wonder . . . ," he started to say, then stopped.

"What?"

"I wonder if we were right, if that's why he turned over all his property and the business to you? Maybe he knows he's in too deep but is too proud to ask for your help."

It was a far-fetched idea, but it made sense.

"Knowing that, does it change your mind about taking over Jinx? Temporarily?"

"No way!" she snapped.

Then, "Maybe."

Then, "No, no, no! I am not being suckered into his wily net."

Then, "He *is* my grandfather, after all."

Then, "He wouldn't do it for me. Would he?"

Then, "If he really is nearing bankruptcy, how can I just turn my back?"

Then, "But deep-sea diving? Me?"

Then, "My grandmother would have a fit."

The whole time she argued with herself, Jake remained silent, a little half-smile on his face. They stopped before entering the small room in the back of the restaurant.

Finally, she groaned. "Oh, my God! I'm seriously considering joining Jinx, aren't I?"

"Yep." Jake's half-smile became a full smile.

"Deep-sea hell." She popped another Pepto. By the time the day was over, she could very well be overdosing on the antacid.

Both of them took a deep breath, started to enter the room, then stopped in their tracks. No one had noticed their arrival yet, except for Anthony and Stefano, who were standing guard inside, one on either side of the entrance.

Her grandfather was by the bar talking to a short gentleman with pure white hair on his head and in his impeccably trimmed mustache and goatee. He held what appeared to be a boat captain's hat in his hand.

Flossie and Rosa stood close by talking to a thirty-something, blonde woman who wore coveralls and a baseball cap with prominent NASCAR emblems. Veronica thought she heard them discussing menopause, of all things. She was sure when she heard Jake mutter, "This is just effin' wonderful!"

Most surprising of all, Veronica recognized the little red-haired elderly woman she'd bumped into in Atlantic City last night. She was shaking her finger and talking a mile a minute to a young man—the young man of the moving motel outside. It must be the nephew she'd been searching for, the male stripper. Veronica couldn't help but give him a quick once-over. *Uh-huh! Male-stripper material, for sure.*

Maybe the white-haired gentleman was the cousin the elderly woman had mentioned, the one with prostate problems. *How nice that I know such an intimate thing about a perfect stranger!*

The old lady went over to talk with the other ladies while Mr. Chippendude—that's what the old lady had called the troupe—joined two thirtysomething men by the far window. They were examining what looked like state-of-the-art diving equipment. One had long hair and appeared to be Hispanic. The other had short brown hair, sort of a military cut. All three of them were tall, over six feet, tanned, lean, and drop-dead gorgeous.

The Hispanic guy glanced up, saw her, and smiled.

Jake growled beside her.

Anytime she could make Jake growl was a good day in Immaturity Land. So, of course, she smiled back at the hot tamale.

"This is payback for my engagement, isn't it?"

"What? You don't think I could attract a handsome hunk like that? Or be interested myself?"

"Are you kidding? He is *not* handsome. He looks like a bad clone of Antonio Banderas. And he is not your type at all."

"And my type would be?" Quickly, she added, "Don't answer that."

The guy turned his attention back to the other two men.

Just then, the old lady spied Veronica and yelled, "Yoo-hoo! Remember me?"

How could I forget?

"It's the hooker from the casino," Granny Clampett told the other ladies. "Holy catfish! What happened to your hair, honey? You sure could use a day at Charmaine's beauty salon."

Everyone in the room turned to stare at her.

Jake was back to laughing hysterically. *The jerk!* Between guffaws, he inquired, "So, baby, how much do you charge for . . . ?" And in a hushed voice only she could hear, he mentioned something so unspeakably explicit, she, who'd thought she'd heard or tried every sexual trick in the world with him, grew red-faced.

She lifted her chin high and walked away from him, heading to the bar. She told the bartender, "Tequila margarita, please. And make it a double."

Chapter
5

His boots were made for walkin'....

Two hours later, Jake sat on a bar stool, nursing a long neck and wondering why he was still here, treading the fine line between insanity and stupidity.

Never mind that he was missing appointments with his stockbroker to invest his latest winnings, with a real estate agent about a beachfront cottage he was about to purchase, and with his literary agent who wanted him to write another how-to poker book.

Meanwhile, Trish was back in Brigantine, probably bawling her eyes out, even though she was the one who'd given him the boot. She probably hadn't meant it. She'd probably expected him to say, "No, babe. You're the only woman in my life. I don't give a rat's ass what Ronnie does anymore." He hadn't protested Trish's ultimatum at all, dumb shit that he was. Yep, he was becoming insaner and stupider by the minute.

On the other hand, Trish might be in the parking lot of his condo, making a pyre of all his clothes and personal belongings. Trish was no pushover. He would worry about that later. He had to survive this "party" first.

He and Ronnie had become acquainted with all the others over a great seafood lunch. Some of the folks had left—Henri Pinot, Flossie, and the Mafia trio. Those remaining were mingling and still discussing the plans to start working together the following week. Not that he had agreed to anything. Far from it. And yet . . . he seemed to be hanging around for some demented reason. His brain said, Walk away. Another body part said something entirely different—and, no, it wasn't his cock. He was pretty sure his heart couldn't stand another round with Ronnie.

Speaking of whom, the bane of his life, his bleepin' ex, the boulder in his future, the thorn in his ass, uh, heart was doing her best to piss him off by continuing to flirt with Adam Famosa, the Cuban dude with the ponytail. Famosa, a college professor of oceanography and a skin-diving expert, told him he'd worked for Jacques Cousteau when he was a grad student. *La-de-da! I once worked for Jimmy the Goon.* The jerk looked like something off the cover of one of those romance novels Ronnie used to devour. Ronnie and Famosa stood in front of the bay window chitchatting and laughing like old friends. *Ha, ha, ha!* Jake was thinking about puking.

Frank came up and sat on the bar stool beside him. They both glowered at Ronnie and the Fabio wannabe for a second. Then Jake took a long swallow of beer, and Frank puff-puff-puffed on his big cigar. *What a pair we are! Pitiful and his brother, More Pitiful!*

"So, you gonna help me out on this project?" Frank never was one to beat around the bush.

"It's not a good idea."

"I think it's a damn good idea."

"You have enough members on your team. You don't need me."

"The hell you say! Don't bail on me, boy. I need you more than any of them."

Jake laughed. "And why would that be?"

Frank's face turned red, and his lips quivered.

Oh, great! I'm about to make an old man cry.

"To do the computer crap. Isn't that what you did before you went pro with poker?"

"That is such a load of crap." Jake laughed again. "You got along without me before."

Frank slammed his fist on the bar, causing the bartender to jerk with surprise and everyone in the room to turn toward them for a moment before resuming their conversations. At least Frank had the sense to speak below a roar when he asked, "Can't you just do it because I'm asking you? As a favor?"

Frank has balls. I gotta give him that. "With no questions asked?"

Frank nodded.

Yeah, that's gonna happen. Tilting his head in question, Jake studied Frank. There was something really strange going on here . . . and not just Frank's empty pockets. Still, Frank had never really asked a favor of him before. And the old guy had been there for support after each of his divorces, especially the last one following the Insanity Marriage, which just about did him in. And if the Pink Project was Frank's last chance, who was he to begrudge him a little time?

No, no, no! We're talking Ronnie here. Jake was a gambler, but this bullshit drama with Ronnie was a

game he would not play again. He'd taken his chips off
that table two years ago. The stakes were too high.

"What are you mumblin' about?"

"What are you doing with the Mafia?" he countered.
"Talk about making a pact with the devil."

Frank puffed on his cigar for a bit, then said, "I'm
not sure Rosa can be called Mafia."

"Her sons can."

"Yeah, I know. Don't worry. I'll watch my back."

"I wonder . . ."

"What?"

"Could there be more in that wreck than diamonds?
My gut instinct says yes. Either Rosa's gang intends to
take all the rocks, including your share, or they're looking for something else."

"Hmmm. Could be."

"My instincts say be careful." Jake studied people
for a living, one of the requirements for being a professional poker player.

"Duly noted," Frank replied; then he added, "See?
All the more reason for you to join the project, another
set of eyes. C'mon."

Jake was spared having to answer because the red-
headed old lady, Louise Rivard, joined them, along
with her great-nephew, John LeDeux. They were Cajuns from some bayou in Southern Louisiana. She was
about a hundred and ten and batty as they come, and he
was a young, full-of-himself stud who'd recently graduated from Tulane University with a degree in criminal
justice. Apparently, he was going to be a backup diver
on the project.

John picked his great-aunt up by the waist and set
her on a bar stool so she wouldn't get a crick in her neck

talking to them. "Here you are, Tante Lulu. A Pink Penguin . . . your favorite." He handed her a pink drink in a tall glass with an umbrella, and she slurped appreciatively for a few seconds.

"Hey, I saw y'all playin' yesta-day in AC," John said to Jake in his Southern drawl. "You're really good."

Jake inclined his head in acknowledgment of the compliment.

"Playin' what?" the great-aunt asked Jake. "Holy crawfish! Doan tell me yer one of them strippers, too, jist like Tee-John. A Chippendude." Tee-John, meaning Little John, was the nickname given to the nephew when he was way shorter than he was now.

But Chippendudes? Stop the presses! I would definitely be a dud if I had to dance and strip at the same time.

"Tante Lulu rescued me last night from The Oasis casino, where I was part of a dance troupe," John explained, an unrepentant grin on his face. "A summer job before hitting the job trail."

"Dance troupe, my hiney! You was takin' yer clothes off fer money. Talk about!"

"Not all my clothes. My . . . uh . . . privates were covered." John winked at the rest of them, as if sharing a private joke.

I hope he doesn't think I care one way or another if he's putting his family jewels on display.

After harrumphing at the boy's nonsense, the old lady gave Jake a thorough head-to-toe survey. "Yer a little old ta be shakin' yer bare tush, ain't ya?"

Oh, good Lord! "I am not a stripper. And I'm not old, either. I'm only thirty-five." *Now why do I feel the need to defend myself to a lady as old as God's mother?*

She arched her brows to indicate that thirty-five was definitely old. "Doan get yer bowels in a twist, boy. Tee-John said you was playin'. I figgered dancin' buck nekkid is one way of playin'."

"Hey, while I think it might be cool to strut my stuff, I am not a stripper." He couldn't wait to tell Ronnie that the same person who thought she was a hooker thought he was a stripper. *The hooker and the stripper ... Sounds like a good name for a fifth marriage—The Hooker/Stripper Marriage.* Jake's eyes widened with incredulity at his own dangerous musings. No surprise that he discovered himself working the worry beads in his pocket. *I did not just think the word* marriage *in connection with my ex-wife. Definitely not! Never ever again! Oh, shit! I've gotta get out of here.*

"Tante Lulu, Jake is a professional poker player," John said patiently, giving his great-aunt's small shoulders a squeeze.

That went over just as big as the stripper occupation. "You plays cards fer a livin'?"

Jake nodded, still reeling inwardly over the marriage brain blip he'd just had.

"Thass like sayin' a person jump-ropes fer a livin'. Or plays Ping-Pong fer a job. Tsk, tsk, tsk! It mus' be a Yankee thang."

"Now, Auntie," John said, "that's a bit harsh. Remember how you put food on the table during those lean years? Weed. Need I say more?"

"Oh, oh, oh! Someone needs to have his mouth washed with lye soap. The herbs I gave out in my healing was always legal."

"I was just teasing."

"Some things are not funny." She glowered at her

nephew. "You ain't so big I caint paddle yer be-hind, boy, and doan you fergit it."

Everyone just smiled at the old lady.

"So, you're from Louisiana?" Jake asked Tante Lulu and Tee-John. "Were you affected by Hurricane Katrina?"

Tante Lulu rolled her eyes. "Does a gater stink?"

Jake guessed that meant yes.

"Everyone in Southern Louisiana was affected in one way or another," Tee-John said. "We were luckier than most, being so far inland, but still, most of my family lives on the bayou. So there was plenty of wind and flood damage."

"Not as bad as most, though. Thass fer sure," Tante Lulu added. "I gots friends who'll never be the same. Specially those that fish fer a livin'."

Tee-John laughed then. "We practically had to hog-tie my great-aunt here to make her leave for shelter. She wanted to ride out the storm on her back porch. We probably would have found her body in the middle of the Mississippi if she had."

"Pfff! I woulda been fine."

"As it turned out, my great-aunt single-handedly ran a shelter for the disaster victims in the basement of Our Lady of the Bayou Church. What a gal!" He winked at her, and she beamed back at him.

Brenda Caslow joined them then. Brenda, a blonde who hailed from Savannah—a real Georgia peach, if there ever was one—had been a NASCAR mechanic. She was probably Ronnie's age, or a little older, but that's where the similarity ended. Of medium height and average build, she seemed to have been poured into her coveralls, which clearly showed her hips and ass straining at the seams. Brenda was going to be the cook/mechanic on the project.

"Give me a grapefruit juice on the rocks," Brenda told the bartender. Frank had told them earlier that Brenda was often on one fad diet or another. This week it was grapefruit. That should make for an interesting menu on board.

"What? Why are you all gawking at me?" Brenda asked.

"They's all lookin' at yer butt, bless their hearts," Tante Lulu said. "My buns usta look like that before they disappeared."

The rest of them just about choked on their tongues.

"So, did you ever work with Dale Earnhardt, Sr.?" John asked quickly before Brenda clouted the three of them.

"Sure. I was in his pit crew for three years."

Brenda could have just as easily said she used to be God's right-hand angel, so impressed was the boy. He sidled up closer to Brenda, who eyed him like a bothersome gnat.

Tante Lulu harrumphed in disgust, knowing her nephew better than the rest of them. "She's too old fer you, boy."

"Hey, I'm only thirty-three," Brenda said, even though she obviously had no interest in the young man.

"*Chère*, I always did like older women." John waggled his eyes at Brenda.

Brenda gave John a full-body survey, which was not complimentary. "Honey, I would crush you if I sat on you."

John shook his head sharply. "No, no, no! You can sit on me anytime."

"That'll be enough of that kind of talk," Tante Lulu scolded her nephew, slapping him on the upper arm.

"You and every other man in this room couldn't keep up with me," Brenda said, walking away.

"Hey!" Jake and Frank and John said at the same time, just a little bit insulted. Then they all watched Brenda's very curvy butt sway from side to side.

"Mercy!" John drawled.

They all burst out laughing.

"Men!" Tante Lulu said, which just about summed up the situation.

Soon after that, Tante Lulu and John left for Newark, where the old lady was taking a plane back to Louisiana. It was a given that on the drive the boy's ears would be blistered about behaving himself while working on the Pink Project. It was also a given that the boy would have a wild time anyhow. Apparently, Henri Pinot had gotten the diving job for John as a way to keep him out of trouble. Jake suspected that was a losing battle.

Ronnie continued talking to the jerk Adam Famosa. They'd been joined by Caleb Peachey, the tall guy with the military haircut, who, it turned out, was a former Navy SEAL and a former Amish. If that wasn't an oxymoron . . . An Amish SEAL. There had to be a story there.

Ronnie had cleaned herself up after their ride from hell, and the two dudes were clearly as aware as he of how well Ronnie cleaned up. Occasionally, Famosa would put a hand on her forearm as he talked to her. Peachey kept his hands to himself and was mostly quiet, but Jake could see how much the guy was attracted to Ronnie, too.

He stuck a hand in his pocket and frantically rubbed the beads between his fingertips.

I have got to cut this out. It's like I've got a death wish. Ronnie is not mine anymore. I have no right to be jealous. She and I have gone our separate ways—happily. Get a life, dimwit!

"What are you mumbling about?"

The soft ring of his cell phone saved Jake from answering.

"Jensen here."

"Jake, it's Trish. We need to talk."

Oh, great! When a woman says, "We need to talk," it usually means she has a bug in her ear. "Baby, this is definitely not the time. I'm in the middle of ... something."

"I don't mean over the phone. I meant ..." She paused as if something just occurred to her. "Where are you?"

"Barnegat."

A telling silence followed.

She probably thought he was buck naked in bed with Ronnie. That's the way women's brains worked. He put her out of her misery by disclosing, "With Frank. At the Barnegat Inn."

"Oh." He heard the relief in her voice. But then she asked, "Is ... is Ronnie there?"

Women! Why can't they just let things ride? Why do they have to prod and prod and prod till there's an open wound? Then they wonder why men do stupid things, like tell them what they really think. "Yes, Ronnie is here. Right now she's on the other side of the room flirting with two deep-sea diving studs."

Frank choked with laughter at his side. It must have been obvious that Jake was covering his ass.

He ignored Frank and told Trish, "You're right. We need to talk this thing out."

"I love you, Jake."

He hesitated, which he knew instantly was a mistake, and said, "I love you, too." It was a millisecond too late. "I'll see you in an hour or so." Taking a last swig of his beer, he told Frank, "I've gotta go."

"Where?" Frank snapped, clearly not pleased.

"Home."

That raised Frank's eyebrows, but he didn't ask where home was or who he shared it with, thank God.

"Tell Ronnie I had to go . . . home."

Frank guffawed. "Tell her yourself."

Not in a million years am I going near her.

"How you gonna get out of here? You left your car back at my house."

"I'll hitch a ride by boat." Frank's Long Beach Island house was just a short jaunt across Barnegat Bay.

Ever persistent, Frank asked, "Will you be coming back to help with the project?"

"Hell, no!" he said, immediately followed by, "Hell if I know!" as he slapped some bills on the bar. And that was the God's honest truth.

Ronnie glanced up then, noting his handshake with Frank and apparent leave-taking. Their eyes held for a long while.

He broke the stare first and told Frank, who was watching closely, "I can't come back. I mean, I shouldn't come back. Son of a bitch! I just don't know. It would be pure hundred proof insanity to . . ." His hand moved through the air with uncertainty.

Frank chuckled, then muttered under his breath as Jake walked away, "You'll be back."

✦

Sometimes blood is not thicker than
water. . . .

"If you leave now, the door will not be open for you
when you come back," Lillian Satler said in her corner
office at Boston's Satler, Satler, and Dilroy, Esq. "And
you will come back. You always do."

Veronica stared at her grandmother, who was sitting
ramrod stiff behind her pristine mahogany desk, like the
queen of bloody England. Wearing the same tailored
gray suit she wore every day—she must have a dozen in
her closet—the Boston Lawyer of the Year, four times
over, could have passed for sixty, not the seventy-five
she was. Her figure was as trim as when she'd been a
teenager. Her perfectly dyed, short brown hair was the
same as it had been when Veronica was a toddler, not a
strand out of place or one single hint of gray. Her face
was smooth, thanks to plastic surgeries and collagen in-
jections. She wore pearls at her neck and pearl studs in
her ears.

With dismay, Veronica realized she was wearing
identical pearls, both family heirlooms.

Despite her fine outward appearance, Lillian was as
hard as nails inside. Many an unsuspecting company
lawyer had learned that fact over the years when they
met her in court. Veronica had personally learned the
lesson at a young age. She was sent off to boarding
school when she was eight, never knew physical affection, was told what to do about everything right down
to her brand of toothpaste. *No wonder I'm a mess!*

She'd told her grandmother that she wanted to take off for a month to get her head straight, to decide if she wanted to continue practicing corporate law or some other related field. She had not mentioned—yet—why her grandfather had put all his property in her name.

"Why is this coming up now? Why, every time you see your grandfather, do you come back distressed? What did he say? Why do you give him so much power?"

"One, I hadn't seen him in three years, so your use of the words *every time* is a misrepresentation. Distressed? I'm not distressed. Tired is more like it. As for power, hah! If he had power over me, I would have jumped at his offer to run his treasure-hunting company."

Uh-oh! She hadn't intended to give her grandmother all that information. With good reason.

Lillian hissed in indignation. "How dare he? You do not have the talent to run such a crackbrained enterprise. You are much too smart to even consider such lunacy. You carry Satler blood in your veins. You would not demean our name. Of course you refused."

Actually, she had refused, but Lillian's assessment of her capabilities rankled. And why did she always ignore the fact that Veronica had Jinkowsky blood in her veins, too? "Not necessarily," she lied. "I told him I would think about it."

"Unacceptable!"

"It might be fun to try it . . . for a few weeks . . . a month at most." *The salt air must have infected my brain. I could not actually be considering . . . No! Never!* Still, she blundered on, pride driving her. "I could clear my calendar to accommodate the absence.

Besides, I haven't taken a vacation in years. Since my last wedding, if you must know."

Not surprising that the suggestion went over like baked beans at a Boston society wedding. Her grandmother's face turned red. "I should have known when you said you wanted a few weeks off that it was more than that. Well, that justifies what I said earlier. Leave this job for even a few days and you won't have a job."

Veronica hadn't seriously considered taking her grandfather up on his offer—until now, when her grandmother egged her on. To say that her job was on the line if she took off for a few weeks was outrageous. "I think Frank needs me." That was as much as she would disclose about her grandfather's problems. Lillian would pounce on that weakness and flog it to death. Even the obnoxious old coot didn't deserve that.

"So that's why he put all his property in your name. A ploy to get you into his camp."

Camp? This is not a battle of exes. I am not some prize for them to fight over. "Be reasonable."

Her grandmother's steely expression told Veronica loud and clear that there would be no concessions. "Veronica, please, think about this. You are not a risk-taker. You are a serious businesswoman. At heart, you are just like me."

"I am not!"

Instead of taking offense at Veronica's vehement denial, her grandmother gave her a sweeping glance. And, yes, Veronica was wearing a trim tailored suit with a white blouse, just like Lillian, except hers was navy blue, not gray. Veronica's hair was long—something Lillian had always objected to—but she'd pulled it back off her face in a neat coil. *Am I really turning into my grandmother? No! That's impossible. I won't stand for it.*

"You would be such a fish out of water on a treasure hunt. It's laughable."

Suddenly, Veronica recalled an argument she'd had once with Jake. *During the Cowboy Marriage, I think.* He'd accused her of becoming a clone of her grandmother, that she never took chances, that she wanted guarantees in life. In other words, she was boring. *I am not boring. I'm not.* Her fingers touched the pearls at her neck. *Oh, shit! I'm going out and buying a red dress after I leave this office. And maybe even a bikini. And a thong. Yeah, a thong. Victoria's Secret, here I come.*

Veronica was making jokes with herself, but she really felt like crying.

"Are you paying attention to me?"

You'd think I was twelve instead of thirty-two the way she talks down to me.

"Call the bum's bluff," Lillian persisted. "Take the business, house, and personal property and run. Sell them first chance you get. You don't owe the bastard a thing."

Oh, that would be ethical! "I have no plans to take over his business or anything else. It would only be a temporary arrangement." *I don't believe it. She is forcing me to do something I never intended to begin with. Me? A treasure hunter?*

"It's a goddamn trap. He'll turn you into a bimbo just like that slut girlfriend of his."

"Flossie is not a slut."

Her grandmother threw her hands up. "See? You're already siding with your grandfather."

"This is not a competition between you and Frank."

Lillian raised her eyebrows a fraction.

Veronica was accomplishing nothing, arguing with her grandmother when the subject was her grandfather. It was surprising that Lillian had even given her son—Veronica's father—the Jinkowsky name when he was born. Veronica suspected her grandmother had been forced to do so for legal reasons or because of a bribe from her grandfather.

"I mean it, Veronica. Go to work with your grandfather, and you lose your job here."

Veronica blinked rapidly to avoid tears. Her grandmother hated crying. To her, it was the supreme act of feminine weakness. "I can get a job elsewhere."

Lillian refused to budge.

Well, stubbornness ran in the family. Therefore, Veronica replied, "So be it."

That shocked the old lady. She'd expected Veronica to tuck tail and do her bidding, as usual. "You would risk your career, risk a chance at full partnership, to work with that . . . that good-for-nothing?"

"You've been holding that partnership apple over my head for three years now. The only way I'm ever going to get a bite is over your dead body."

Lillian inhaled sharply with shock. "That is not true."

"Yes, it is, Grandma."

Her grandmother inhaled sharply again, but this time with disgust. She hated being called Grandma. "Yes, ma'am" and "No, ma'am" were the preferred replies.

"I'll never be awarded even a junior partnership while you're still actively working here. You like too much the prestige of being the only female partner in a firm your great-uncle founded."

"I find your attitude offensive." Lillian stood and leaned forward, her hands braced on the table. "You should be grateful for all I've done for you, young lady."

I've been on my own for ten years, and I'm still "young lady" to her. Yeah, I'm going to be made partner real soon. Next will come the guilt trip: "I raised you when your mother died. I stood by you through all your divorces. I've been the only steady anchor in your life." Yada, yada, yada. "I've worked hard for this firm, *Grandma.* Every perk I've received has been earned and deserved."

"I know you've done a good job, Veronica." Lillian sat back down and visibly tamped down her temper. "That is not the point."

"What is?"

"Your association with that . . . man." She couldn't have said it any plainer.

"Why do you hate Frank so? It's been fifty years, for God's sake. Did you ever love him? What did he do to make you so bitter?"

"Everything." Her grandmother's voice was so sharp it could have cut ice.

"Did you ever love him?"

Lillian, who had never remarried, drew herself up even straighter. "I will not discuss that man or my personal history with you. Not now. Not ever."

"Well, then, I have no choice but to help him." *She is backing me into a corner. She could very well force me to do the thing she does not want me to do.*

"Don't you dare blackmail me."

"It's not blackmail. I'm just laying all my cards on the table." *It's just me seeing the light.*

"Cards! That's the kind of thing your ex-husband would say." Her grandmother narrowed her eyes at her. "Is Jacob involved in this disaster?"

God! She's got to be the only person in the world who calls Jake Jacob. Veronica would have liked to deny Lillian's suspicion, but her heated face gave her away.

"Oh, God! Will you never learn?"

"Apparently not," Veronica said as she turned and walked out the door. With alarm, she realized that she'd just made a decision. God help her!

I. Am. Going. To. Be. A. Freakin'. Treasure. Hunter. Aaarrgh!

Chapter
6

Don't let the door hit you in the . . .

A week had passed since Jake's meeting with Frank and Ronnie, and his life couldn't get any worse.

He prided himself on the fact that he hadn't gone back to Frank's place, but little else.

Sitting in the La-Z-Boy recliner in his Brigantine apartment, he watched a NASCAR race on his wide-screen plasma TV. And he watched Trish as she made a big production out of moving out to live with a fellow pre-med student in Cherry Hill.

It was a very modest apartment, considering his means these past few years, but he intended to change that soon with the purchase of a beachfront cottage. It would cost a small fortune but was a really good investment. Plus, being on the ocean would pretty much preclude Ronnie ever being there, with her water phobia. Sort of an insurance that he wouldn't ever talk her into a fifth marriage. *Hmmm. I wonder if my engagement to Trish is . . . was . . . the same kind of insurance.*

Cutting off all avenues for me to lose my head over Ronnie again. But I digress. Digress? What kinda high-brow word is that for talkin' to myself in my head? Yikes! I better not smile.

Humor was the last thing he needed to display right now. That didn't mean he couldn't get a little male revenge. Every time Trish slammed the front door, he turned the volume up louder on the TV. She was in the process of carrying boxes filled with her belongings out to her car. To say she was pissed would be like saying sex was a little bit fun.

Slam, bang.

Vroom, vroom.

Slam, bang.

Vroom, vroom.

He didn't know who was being more immature. Okay, he'd probably win that contest hands down. So, he decided to take the high road. The next time Trish came storming back into the apartment, he turned the volume down, stood, and tried to talk to her. "You don't have to do this, honey."

"Yes, I do."

There was fire in her blue eyes, which should have been a warning to back away and shut up, if he was smart. Which he apparently wasn't.

"Listen, all I said was I need some time to get my head straight."

"Why don't you stick your head straight up your you-know-what while you're at it?"

Okaaaay! "You're the one who said I should go get Ronnie out of my system."

"And you thought I meant it?"

Well, yeah. "Be reasonable. All I said was—"

"Screw you."

"That, too," he tried to joke.

She snarled. He was pretty sure that meant she was not amused.

"You're still wearing my ring. You should stay."

"I moved the ring to my right hand."

Uh-oh, there must be some hidden female message that I missed here. "And that means . . . ?"

"We are not engaged anymore until you prove I'm the only one."

"Right, left, what's the difference?"

"Pfff! You are such a stupid prick."

"I may be stupid, but not stupid enough to hook up with Ronnie again. Just because I was stupid four times doesn't mean I'm going for five. Give me some credit." He reached for her, and she swatted his hands away.

"Don't you dare touch me—not while you've got your ex-wife on your mind."

"Who says I have Ronnie on my mind?"

"Jake, you've had a hard-on ever since you saw her last week."

"How do you know it's not for you?"

"Give me a break."

Time for a new tactic. "I thought you loved me." *For chrissake, that's the kind of thing women say—or wussy men.*

"I do love you, but not enough to play ménage-a-Ronnie."

"I never suggested any such thing," he protested. He'd been with Trish for more than a year. He'd finally gotten over his last round with Ronnie. He couldn't let his life fall apart . . . again. "I do love you, Trish. Honest, I do. But—"

"But you love your ex-wife, too," Trish finished with a sigh.

"I think I'll always have feelings for Ronnie, but I won't willingly jump off that cliff again. Give me some time." He figured *willingly* gave him a bit of wiggle room if he should somehow be dumb enough to succumb. Thank God for the artful dodge.

"Will you be fucking Ronnie while you're taking that time?"

He cringed at her crudity, not because the word offended him. He used it often enough himself, but Trish didn't.

"Listen, Jake, sooner or later, you are going to leave me—*unless* you resolve your issue with Ronnie. Consider this a preemptive breakup."

"Preemptive?" he sputtered. "What is this, a baseball contract or something?"

"Or something."

She was so angry, her nose was flaring like a draft horse, not that he would mention that fact.

"Excuse me," someone said behind them. "I've been knocking."

Saved! he thought.

He and Trish both swiveled and saw his friend Grace O'Brien standing in the open doorway.

A reprieve! Hallelujah! He walked over and gave her a hug. Grace was an Irish redhead, an ex-nun and a world-class poker player. Grace sometimes played in the same tournaments that he did, including last week in AC. She had come in a respectable fourth.

"Another woman!" Trish exclaimed, throwing her hands up in disgust.

"Huh?" he and Grace said.

"Oh, no, you don't understand—" Grace started to say.

"This is Grace. You've heard me mention Grace before. Grace *was* a *nun,* for God's sake," he explained, as if that was any kind of explanation. Trish had never met Grace before, but she had to have seen her at the tournament yesterday. She just wasn't thinking clearly; that was the only explanation Jake could imagine.

Trish gave him a look that pretty much accused him of wanting a ménage-a-four, or whatever it was called in French. With a nun yet! Or ex-nun . . . same thing.

Before he or Grace had a chance to further protest Trish's assumption, Trish picked up one of the three suitcases left in the hallway and walked out the door in a huff.

"What's going on?" Grace asked him, retrieving a couple of towels from the floor, which Trish must have dropped on one of her Road Runner trips through.

"Trish's dumping me."

"For good?"

"It depends, I guess."

"On what?"

"Me."

"Uh-oh. I smell wife in this picture."

Although Grace no longer belonged to any religious order, she still retained some of the Catholic church's values, including the sanctity of marriage. She'd told him on more than one occasion that Ronnie was still his wife, despite all the divorces.

"No, Ronnie is not in the picture," he said, which wasn't really a lie. "Trish thinks she is, but she's not."

Grace arched her eyebrows at him.

"Listen, there's a saying that applies perfectly to me:

'Marriage is a three-ring circus—the engagement ring, the wedding ring, and the suffering.'"

"What's your point?"

"I've had suffering up to my eyeballs."

"Oh, please! Do you want balloons for your pity party?"

Grace did have a way of grounding him at times. Good friends did that, he supposed.

With a sigh of resignation, he walked into the kitchen and got himself and Grace a beer. "What brings you here? Not that you need an excuse."

Grace followed him and took a glass out of the cupboard. She poured carefully to avoid too much foam. After taking a taste and licking her lips, she said, "It's a beautiful day, and Angel stopped by to take me for a ride on his motorcycle. He's down in the parking lot now, checking his crankbox or crank-something."

That accounted for Grace's hair and outfit. Her hair was short and bright red, usually combed back neatly off her face. Today it stood up in spikes like a rocker's. Plus, she wore jeans, boots, and an oversized Harley-Davidson leather jacket—probably Angel's.

"I'm thinking about getting a tattoo," she told him.

He grinned. "Where? On the butt?"

"No. That's too much of a cliché. Maybe the back of my neck."

"Ouch!"

"Angel says I really should do it—throw caution to the wind, be a free spirit."

"Figures that Angel would have something to do with this. Just so you don't get a piercing anywhere near . . . um . . . erotic zones."

It was hard to embarrass Grace, even though lots of

people tried, her being an ex-nun and all. Then again, he'd heard stories about Grace back in her nun days. Grace had not been a typical nun, by any means. Now, she tilted her head, trying to picture those piercings in erotic zones.

Everyone knew that Angel Sabato had had his cock pierced. Talk about insanity! But Angel claimed it enhanced sex. Jake couldn't imagine how, and he didn't want any graphic explanations.

"Okay. No piercings," Grace replied belatedly.

He and Grace walked into the living room. She sat down on the sofa, and he went to the window. Angel was down there, talking to Trish. Rather, Trish was doing all the talking, gesticulating wildly as she spoke. Probably cutting Jake to pieces while Angel just nodded and patted her on the shoulder occasionally.

Within minutes, Trish was gunning the motor on her Mazda Miata with its small U-Haul trailer, and squealing out of the parking lot. She would probably come back later to get the rest of her stuff. He hoped. Maybe he hoped. Yep, he hoped.

Angel came in a few minutes later, shaking his head at Jake. "Man, you are in such deep shit, they oughta name a fertilizer after you."

"Tell me about it," Jake said after he went into the kitchen and came back with a beer for Angel.

"She's really hot . . . and nice," Angel remarked as he settled his butt into the La-Z-Boy and turned the volume up on the NASCAR race.

"Don't tell me you were hitting on Jake's fiancée." Grace tsk-tsked her disapproval to Angel.

He just grinned. "She told me she and Jake aren't engaged anymore." Then he turned to Jake. "Do you mind if I date her?"

"Hell, yes!"

Angel and Grace both smirked at him.

"Trish and I have hit a rough patch. That doesn't mean we're through for good."

"Couldn't you have talked her into sticking around so you could work things out?" Grace asked him.

He could feel his face flush.

"Uh-oh!" Angel and Grace said at the same time.

"I might not be around for the next few weeks," Jake surprised himself by saying. When had he come to that decision?

"Uh-oh!" Angel and Grace said again.

They probably thought he was hooking up with Ronnie again. They'd certainly witnessed it before.

"This is not about Ronnie."

Angel laughed and made a mooing sound.

"What does that mean?"

"I'm suffering from a bit of déjà moo," Angel explained. "As in, I've heard this bullshit before."

Jake rolled his eyes and Grace did the same.

"Dear St. Anthony, come around," Grace prayed. "Something's lost and can't be found. Jake's sanity."

Grace was like a dog with a bone when it came to him and Ronnie. According to Grace, St. Anthony was the patron saint of lost things—a lesson she'd taught them in the past when things had come up missing, like an earring or a poker chip. It was a stretch to ask St. Anthony to find his sanity.

"I *might* be going treasure hunting," he announced before they could ask more questions about Ronnie— or Trish. He should have kept his trap shut because he really hadn't made a decision. Really. Not.

"No shit!" Angel exclaimed.

"What kind of treasure?" Grace asked, equally impressed. "Pirate treasure?"

He shook his head. "Mafia treasure," he blurted. His trap must be stuck in yap mode. "I can't say anymore," he added. "In fact, I haven't made any decision. But if I did, I'd be working for a few weeks with my ex-grandfather-in-law, Frank Jinkowsky. He operates a treasure-hunting business."

"Wow!" Grace was staring at him as if he'd suddenly turned into Batman and had just driven up in his Batmobile.

"And here I was planning to talk you and Grace into a cross-country motorcycle trip. It's either that or let my agent book me for a nude calendar."

Jake and Grace gaped at Angel.

"You know that *Playgirl* spread I did? Well, apparently, some poster company wants me to do a calendar." He shrugged, indicating it was no big deal.

It would be a big deal to me.

"Can I attend the photo shoot?" Grace stared at Angel in total seriousness, as if trying to picture him without clothes. She was probably kidding, but then, maybe not.

"Honey, I will give you a private viewing," Angel told her.

"Promises, promises."

"Back to this road trip . . . ," Jake prodded Angel.

"Oh, yeah. I was thinking about a cross-country road trip, with a few stops along the way for poker tournaments. We would end up at the World Series of Poker in Las Vegas. But, man, that would be tame compared to treasure hunting."

Instead of scoffing at the suggestion, Grace said, "That sounds great, but I don't own a motorcycle."

Jake gaped at her, then clicked his mouth shut. "Me neither." He added a silent prayer of thanks that they'd gotten off the subject of him, Trish, and Ronnie.

"I rode my bicycle across Ireland one time," Grace said.

"Not quite the same thing, Red." Angel smiled at Grace in an indulgent manner that caused her to stick out her tongue at him. If Jake didn't know better, he would think they had something going on.

"Actually, a road trip would be a great way to clear your head about Ronnie and Trish," Grace offered.

"Yeah," Angel agreed. "There's this shop up in Asbury Park where you two could buy bikes at a discount. Hey, we're all flush after that last tournament. Are you game?" He looked at Jake and then Grace.

Hmmm, not a bad idea! Get away from Trish—and Ronnie. Forget treasure hunting. What better way to clear my head than being on the open road? Maybe I'll get a tattoo, too. "Free at Last!" That's what it would say. And a piercing . . . but only in my ear.

Another part of his brain had a different opinion. *You're running away again, just like Ronnie says. Maybe I should stick around this time. See what happens.*

No, no, no! That is the road to disaster.

So it was that four hours later, the three of them were tooling down the Garden State Parkway on their hogs. The next morning, they were packed and on their way to the West Coast.

He'd called Trish's cell phone and left a message

saying she could move back into the apartment since he would be gone for several weeks—on a bike trip to Vegas. He didn't want her to think he was off somewhere with Ronnie, boinking himself into a stupor. She'd called back and left a message on his cell phone: "The gray matter in your head must have turned to sludge. You don't need to clear your mind. You've already lost it."

So, now the three of them were on their way, wind in their hair, good vibrations under their asses. Life couldn't get any better.

Chapter
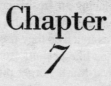
7

New leaves are sometimes hard to turn. . . .

After two days in Jinx, Inc.'s, Barnegat warehouse office, Veronica was finally making headway with the paperwork. The actual search would begin the day after tomorrow—if there were no more problems with the boat's motor.

It was only nine-thirty, her third day in the office, and thus far she'd organized the files in a rudimentary fashion. She'd paid bills from a dismally small business account, something she needed to discuss with her grandfather, but he was steering clear of her on that subject—and a few others. After the argument they'd had the first day she came back, when he'd been showing her around the place, he was probably afraid she'd ask more questions—not just about the business but about his personal finances as well. Thus far, he'd managed to evade explaining the missing bank statements, mortgages, deeds, that kind of thing. She didn't even know if he outright owned the diving boat, the warehouse, or his home. All she'd seen were general office files and Project Pink data. It was a start, anyhow.

She'd managed to handle her aversion to salt water and its scent by placing air freshener cones around the office. When she went outside, the saltwater breezes didn't bother her as much as they used to; even so, she was popping Peptos like peanuts from a quart-size jar she'd bought at Wal-Mart. Forget pink diamonds; she should invest in the company that made pink Pepto.

Henri Pinot, the man hired to captain the boat, had been forced to drop out at the last minute. It appeared the prostate trouble that Tante Lulu had alluded to was more serious than he'd originally thought. He was scheduled for surgery in Baton Rouge on Friday. Her grandfather had commiserated with Henri and told him not to worry, that there was a treasure-hunting venture he wanted to try in Louisiana in the next few years. Henri should be on his feet again by then. Besides, her grandfather said, he could take over the captaining job himself, which made Veronica reach for the Pepto yet again.

Aside from Henri, everyone else was here, raring to go. Except Jake. But then he'd never promised Frank, or her, that he would participate. She was better off without Jake here, she told herself, although she could use his help with the ancient computer. Well, it was ten years old, but that was ancient in computer land.

She decided to put all her concerns aside because, frankly, she was enjoying herself. And that was a surprise. She should have felt out of her comfort zone, but she didn't. She wasn't an auditor, but she had a little accounting experience from college. It was a sign of her sorry life that she got satisfaction out of balancing the books, much the same as she used to feel after a successful legal battle. She wondered if Jake felt the same when he won a a poker tournament.

"Va-va-voom! You are lookin' hot, hot, hot today, darlin'," John LeDeux said. Strolling into the office, he laid an ink-toner cartridge on the desk. She'd asked him last night to buy it while in town.

Her face heated at the young Cajun's blatant perusal of her body, clad in what was the first stage of a wardrobe makeover. The new Veronica Jinkowsky. When she'd awakened this morning, just past dawn, she had donned tight, low-riding jeans and a midriff-exposing, stretchy black T-shirt that proclaimed, "I GOT STUNG." She'd put on and taken off the cropped shirt three times this morning before murmuring with self-loathing, "Get a grip, girl." Not her usual style. At all.

"What's with the 'Stung' T-shirt?"

"Jake is a huge Sting fan. He must have given me a dozen Sting—or Police—concert shirts over the years."

"Yeech! Sting is an old codger," John said with a grin, dropping into one of the office chairs in front of the desk. "Now Trent Reznor from Nine Inch Nails, that's another story."

Sting an old codger? He better not say that around Jake.

"I do like your jeans, though, chère. Very, very sexy!"

Give me a break! Actually, she'd had to lie on the floor to get into them this morning. It should be interesting when she had to use the restroom today.

"And I really like that watch. Where'd you get it? I'd like to buy one for Tante Lulu."

Veronica glanced down at the only jewelry she was wearing—a smiley face watch, another gift from Jake. During the painful tail end of their Insanity Marriage, he'd put the gift in her lap with a hug and a whisper in her ear: "You need to smile more, honey." Wearing the watch now was certainly . . . timely.

"It was a gift," was all she replied. Then she laughed and added, "I'm not sure whether these new clothes make me look hot or hilarious. The big question is, Do I look like Martha Stewart trying to be Pamela Anderson, and failing? Don't answer that. It was a rhetorical question."

He grinned. "I like the new you."

"I do, too," Veronica admitted, also with a grin.

It was silly to place so much importance on apparel, but after the unpleasant confrontation with her grandmother, Veronica had gone immediately to her apartment in downtown Boston and made all the preparations for a one-month absence. Paying bills in advance. Notifying the doorman. Clearing out the fridge. Canceling appointments. She'd wanted to take care of everything right away before she changed her mind, or her grandmother tried to change her mind. It never happened.

Then, she'd done the silly thing . . . well, silly for her. The drive back to Long Beach Island had been well under way when she'd stopped at the behemoth Woodbridge Mall. If she was leaving her old professional life behind, she'd decided she was going to change her personal life, too. Her grandmother's remark that Veronica was just like her had cut to the quick. Inside, Veronica was not prissy and boring like her grandmother. At least she didn't think she was.

So, a whole new nonboring wardrobe completed her transformation. She hoped. That meant jeans, bright-colored tops, a few daring dresses—and not one single suit. Some cute hair clips. A gold lamé one-piece bathing suit, with black squiggles edging the rounded top and the leg holes, a signature of Daphne, an up-and-coming designer. The suit was cut high on the hips, very conservative in front, but exposed her back all the way to her buttocks. It wasn't a bikini, but it was racier than anything she'd ever bought before.

Every purchase she'd made had been decided with one question in mind: "Would my grandmother ever wear this?" If the answer was no, she had tossed it in her bag. She wasn't going for the bimbo look, but she was definitely avoiding the lawyer-with-a-pole-up-her-butt look, which her grandfather had insinuated was her style during one of their arguments.

"So, what're you doin'?" John asked her, jarring her back to the present. She already knew he had time to kill before meeting Adam and Caleb at ten for some practice diving in the bay to test their equipment.

"Inputting Project Pink data into the computer. Employees, job descriptions, salaries, equipment needed, fixed and variable expenses, assets, liabilities, along with research details about the enterprise. The only thing missing is the exact site location. My grandfather says it has to remain secret."

"Oh, yeah! Every salvager knows to protect his numbers."

"That's what Frank says: 'Trust no one, or else pirates will steal the site.' I mean, really, pirates? He must be delusional . . . or trying to scare me. More likely he's been OD'ing on old Errol Flynn movies again."

"It's not as wacky as it sounds. Deep-sea treasure hunters always worry about someone stealing their wreck sites. If even the scent of a new site gets out, boats within a thirty-mile radius would use directional finders to zero in and steal the discovery."

"Couldn't Frank get a government order protecting the wreck from rival treasure seekers?"

"Hah! That would be like trying to kill a shark with a flyswatter. Nope, Frank is right to be tight-lipped about this." John stood and ambled over to the wall to study some pictures. "Wow!" he said.

That had pretty much been her reaction when first entering the office. The grungy walls were a testament to a lifetime of respected work. Awards and thank-yous from many quarters—everything from local historical societies to the Museum of Natural History. From different countries, too—Italy, Greece, Spain, and various parts of the United States. Despite all her grievances about Frank, she had to give him credit for his achievements in a career she had always considered just a step below, well, poker playing.

"Well, look at that. Jacques Cousteau." John pointed to one of the many framed photographs, this one a picture of a younger Frank in a diving suit with the famous ocean explorer. "And President Friggin' Reagan. Oops, 'scuse my language." Yep, there was Frank in a suit and tie with President Reagan, for heaven's sake!

"Who's that?" she asked. In this picture, her grandfather stood with another man of similar age, their arms looped over each other's shoulders, grinning at the camera.

"That's Mel Fisher."

"And I should know who Mel Fisher is?"

John laughed. "He's famous in wreck diving as the guy who discovered the *Nuestra Señora de Atocha,* a Spanish galleon that sunk off the coast of Florida in the 1600s."

Veronica moved on and noticed a framed diploma from Princeton University dated 1953, the same year Frank and her grandmother had presumably married. She'd never seen or heard any reference to their marriage anywhere, not even a wedding picture. *How sad!*

"Yo! That is so cool!"

Veronica looked at the photo John was admiring. Only a young man like John would think it was cool for Frank to be photographed sitting on Mussolini's gold toilet. She shook her head at his misplaced admiration.

"And is that really Mel Gibson shaking Frank's hand in that photo?"

"Seems to be."

"Do you think Mel might have been considering a movie about Frank's life?"

Veronica chuckled. Wouldn't that be the last straw on her grandmother's back? "I sincerely hope not."

After John left, Veronica continued, perusing the wall. She'd had no clue about Frank's reputation, her opinions probably colored by her grandmother's hatred of him. Still, she was a grown woman and should have formed her own opinions.

That didn't mean she'd suddenly developed a great affection or admiration for Frank. He was still the same ornery old man who'd made her life miserable on more than one occasion. Like their argument last night, when he'd inferred that she had the same judgmental pole up her ass as her grandmother, just because she'd lectured him about not marrying Flossie. So much for a new wardrobe and new image! To Frank, she was the same as always. Okay, in his defense, she'd also thrown in his smoking smelly cigars, his failing to get a real job with retirement benefits or a good IRA, and his never growing up in general.

She sat down at the desk then and started to work at the computer again. It made a funny whirring sound, and the screen went black. "Oh, no! No, no, no! Dammit!" she yelled, trying desperately to bring the machine back to life by punching various buttons.

Stefano, one of Rosa's sons, rushed in, handgun raised. "What?" Before she could blink, he was in a crouched firing position, surveying the room.

"Omigod!" She ducked to the floor, behind the desk. Her tight jeans strained their seams. "What's the matter?" she yelled from her hunched-over position.

After a long silence in which Veronica could swear she heard her heart beating, Steve said a foul word. Then, "You can come out now." He still had the gun dangling from his fingertips when she emerged.

"Why do you have a gun?" She practically screeched as she crept warily from behind the desk.

He gave her a look that pretty much put her in the idiots class. "Why did you fuckin' scream?"

"Nice language! Because the computer crashed—for the fifth time in two days."

"Un-be-fucking-lievable," he muttered, oblivious to her complaint about his swearing.

She stood and dusted off her behind—actually, she was checking for splits in her jeans.

He put the gun back into a shoulder holster, hidden under an open denim shirt, which he wore over a white wife-beater T-shirt and jeans. Actually, he didn't look

half bad in a dangerous sort of way. At least that had
been her opinion before he'd done his Rambo imper-
sonation.

"I thought you were in danger," he grumbled.

"Jeesh! What did you think, that I'd been attacked
by some cybercrook . . . or a dust ball?" she joked.

His face didn't crack even a sliver of a smile.

Steve and Tony had been standing guard outside the
office and Frank's house every day, all day, being relieved occasionally by some cousin or other. What they
were guarding, she wasn't sure. Maybe they thought
Frank and his crew were going to run off with the diamonds. Or maybe—ha, ha, ha!—they feared pirates.

Steve continued to glare at her.

"I wish I had a new computer," she said, trying to
break the silence. "But Frank doesn't want me to spend
any more money than I have to and, really, I can probably get it to reboot, but holy cow, what did you—"

Steve turned and stomped out the door in the middle
of her nervous blathering. *Well, so long to you, too, Mr.
Manners!* She was lucky she hadn't peed her pants.

She worked till noon, saving her data every five minutes just in case the computer crashed again. Flossie
and her grandfather showed up with a "little" lunch
Flossie had prepared.

Her grandfather grumbled to Flossie, "It's cheaper
to make the food ourselves, but did you have to make
so much?"

Flossie just elbowed Frank in the side. "Stop being
so stingy."

While her grandfather went aboard the *Sweet Jinx,*
his diving boat, to help Brenda work on the trouble-
some motor, Flossie enlisted Veronica's help to set up

folding tables in the warehouse where the office was located.

On the way out the door to get the boxes of food from Frank's truck, Veronica almost ran into a big, chest-high carton that had been placed near the entrance. "Who put this here?" Veronica asked.

Flossie shrugged.

Veronica read the print on the box: "MACINTOSH." She was pretty sure it wasn't a carton of apples. *Could it be? I don't believe this!* It was a new computer—a super-dooper computer with all the bells and whistles. "Did my grandfather buy this?"

"No. Definitely not. He would have told me if he had," Flossie said, her brow furrowed just like Veronica's.

"That's odd. Just this morning, I wished for a new computer and . . ." Veronica's words trailed off as she saw Steve standing nearby, leaning against a piling on the bulkhead, arms folded across his chest. Could it be? Did Steve—did the Mafia—get a computer for them? Just because she'd wished for it? Uh-oh! Did it "fall off a truck"? Was it stolen?

For now, she decided not to question Steve. After all, her grandfather might have bought it, without Flossie's knowledge. Yeah, Frank probably bought it and didn't want Flossie to know about such an extravagant purchase in light of their diminished finances.

Soon there were two folding tables covered with tablecloths and enough food to feed a school of sharks. Her grandfather and Brenda stood at a utility sink, washing away the grease from their hands from tinkering with the boat's motor.

And in stumbled Adam, Caleb, and John, all of them resembling monsters in their neoprene deep-sea diving attire. They quickly shucked the fins, fitted hoods, and goggles, and unzipped the suits—which must have been terribly hot—down to their waists, exposing their sweaty chests. Dry suits, which were big and bulky, were a necessity for deep-sea diving. In the cold, bottom waters of the East Coast Atlantic, where the deep wreck diving would be done, the temperature could plunge as low as forty degrees; therefore, hypothermia was always a concern.

Steve was there, too, though he kept to the doorway, standing with his Styrofoam plate in hand. He answered questions from anyone who approached him, but he kept mostly to himself.

At one point, with polka music blasting away, her grandfather explained to them all the recurring problem they were having with the motor. "I wish we could buy a new one, but that's just not feasible on such short notice. Don't worry, though. Brenda and I will putter with it."

Translation to Veronica: *He can't afford a new one.*

There were stacks of delicious chicken salad sandwiches cut into crustless, whole-wheat triangles, and several homemade salads—potato, crab, pasta, and fresh fruit. For dessert, there was baklava, still warm from the oven. Plus, Flossie had provided a bowl of grapefruit slivers for Brenda, who was on a grapefruit-only diet. Flossie must have been busy all morning. For some reason, Veronica had never pictured her as the domestic type. Probably because of the way she looked. Today, she wore blue capri pants; a matching blue and white sweater tucked into the pants that sported a wide silver chainlink belt; and high-heeled, silver slingbacks. And of course the big, blonde hair and makeup out the kazoo.

Flossie was probably another example of Veronica's misjudging people, à la her grandmother, she decided.

At one point during lunch, Veronica thought back to her grandfather's complaint to Flossie about bringing so much food. She wondered why Flossie, usually sensitive to her grandfather's every wish, would be so careless when money was tight. Frank looked at her, as if reading her mind. "It's cheaper than the caterer Floss wanted to hire." He sighed dramatically.

Just then, Flossie went, "Eeeek!"

"What? What?" Frank grumbled. "Did you see another mouse? I swear those exterminators don't know what they're doing."

"No, silly," Flossie responded. "I broke one of my sculptured nails opening the pressure lock on that plastic container."

"Shiiiit!" Frank exclaimed while the rest of them stifled a grin. "Why dontcha just cut them all off?"

Flossie's expression of horror was priceless. You'd think he had suggested cutting off a limb.

"Don't start cryin', for chrissake," he interjected quickly. Everyone knew Flossie was going through menopause, and her mood swings were horrific. "Just go over to that nail place and have it fixed."

"I wish I could." Flossie sniffled. "But Vivian is out with the flu, and no one else at Nail You does manicures like her. Good heavens, it's hot in here. Did you turn the air conditioner down again?"

Meanwhile, polka music continued to blast away on Frank's tape player. A scene right out of a Fellini movie.

"Uh, any chance we could turn the music down?" Veronica asked Frank.

"What? You don't like polka?" The amazement on his face was almost comical, as if everyone should like accordion music.

"I don't mind polka, but it's too loud. And, jeesh, I didn't even know there was such a thing as disco polka. There ought to be a law or something."

"There's no such thing as a too-loud polka," her grandfather said stubbornly, and walked away.

The disco polka music segued into "The Last Polka." She could only hope.

Nevertheless, excitement rippled throughout the group, the crew talking excitedly about the upcoming diving expedition and what they might find. Everyone seemed to be on an adrenaline rush. Veronica assumed it was the same at the onset of every new treasure-hunting project.

"Nice outfit," Flossie told her.

Oh, that's just great. I'm fond of Flossie, but she really has horrible taste in clothes. "Thanks. The food is delicious. Did you prepare it all yourself?"

Flossie practically beamed at the compliment. "Yes. It's the first time I've tried baklava, though. Was it okay?"

"More than okay. I had three pieces."

"That's what I like to hear."

"Flossie, do you mind if I ask you a question?"

Flossie immediately went stiff, bracing for what she thought might come.

"What's wrong with my grandfather? I mean, how bad is the money crunch?"

"I have no idea what you're talking about." Flossie's face bloomed with a blush.

She's lying. "He won't even show me his check-book."

Flossie's blush deepened to crimson under her heavy makeup. "He doesn't show *me* his checkbook, either. We have separate accounts."

Hmmm! That could be another sign of his money problems. "I can't help him if he keeps me in the dark. Can't you make him be more forthcoming with me?"

"Do you honestly believe I could make your grandfather do something he doesn't want to?"

"You've been with him a long time."

"Yeah, well, you've been with Jake a long time, too. Off and on. Does he follow your orders?"

Veronica laughed. "Point taken."

"Where is Jake, anyhow? I thought he'd be back here by now. Frank keeps getting an answering machine when he calls Jake's condo."

"Oh, I forgot that he was supposed to help with the project," Veronica lied. "I have no idea where he is." *Actually, I can guess. He's with his fiancée. Maybe even off somewhere, like Las Vegas, getting married.*

Flossie squeezed her hand with understanding.

Well, that certainly brought my good mood down to the pits. Next I'll be having a crying jag, like Flossie. I've gotta stop this. Change the subject. Anything. "Let's cut to the chase here. Is Jinx, Inc., on the verge of bankruptcy?"

Flossie's pink face went bright red. "You'll have to ask Frank about that." Turning abruptly, she said over her shoulder, "I need to clean up."

Okaaay, Veronica thought. *Flossie refuses to answer my questions. Hmmm.*

Frank was clapping his hands, calling everyone to attention. "Back to work, guys. We'll meet here again tomorrow morning, hopefully with a firm departure time. See you then."

The three divers were putting on their dry suits again when her grandfather came up and handed her a big box. "Here. This is for you," he said gruffly.

"For me? A gift?"

"Why shouldn't I give you a gift?"

"Maybe because you never even sent me a birthday card in the past thirty-two years."

Frank jerked back as if she'd slapped him. "I sent cards . . . and presents, too." Under his breath, he muttered, "The bitch!" Then he stomped away, over to Flossie, where he began talking and gesticulating wildly.

Really, the man had the disposition of a bear. Could it be true, what he said about having sent her cards and gifts? If so, her grandmother had a lot more to answer for than giving her the boot from the law firm. But she couldn't think about that now. She set the large box on the floor and saw the imprint on the top: "Elmer's Dive Shop, Brielle, NJ."

He wouldn't.

She opened the box and dropped the lid on the floor.

He would.

Inside was a complete neoprene diving outfit, a wet suit, not a dry suit like the men had on, which meant it would be very tight. "Noooooo!" she screeched, and looked toward her grandfather, who, surprise, surprise, had already left the premises. "I'm not going to be deep diving," she yelled, hoping he could hear her from where he was probably hiding.

"Of course you won't be deep diving. You need to

practice in shallow water first," he called back, his voice getting progressively fainter as he walked away.

Her skin felt clammy, and her head hurt as she stared down at the "gift." It was another way in which her grandfather hoped to torture her. She had enough problems breathing in the salt air, let alone diving. No way! The man must have lost his mind.

She decided she needed to find the miniature St. Jude statue that Tante Lulu had given her and everyone else on the team before she'd left last week. Patron saint of hopeless causes, she was pretty sure the old lady had explained. The problem was, in this situation, she wasn't sure if it was her or her grandfather who fell into that category.

"Oh, definitely you," a voice in her head said. Whether it was St. Jude or her subconscious speaking, she couldn't say, but it gave a whole new meaning to the expression "talking heads."

Veronica started to walk back to the office, then turned around, walked back, and picked up the box. Maybe she'd try it on to see how ludicrous she looked in such a revealing suit.

The voice in her head was laughing.

Chapter

8

How long can a woman suck in her stomach without exploding . . . ?

"Hey, Ronnie," Adam Famosa called out as he walked into the Jinx, Inc., office a short time later.

Veronica was in the restroom, where she had done the most ridiculous thing. She'd actually shimmied herself into the skintight diving suit. Chalk it up to female vanity. Well, she'd found out how revealing it was when she checked herself out in the long mirror on the back of the restroom door.

The "rubber" suit, which pretty much amounted to a full-body girdle, was so revealing, she was pretty sure the mole on her left breast was evident, not to mention the cellulite on her thighs. A woman would have to be a flat-chested, perfect size five to feel comfortable in this thing, and Veronica hadn't been a size five since she was, oh, let's say, ten. And while not supersized in the bust department, she was not a pancake, either.

"Ronnie?" Adam called out again. His persistence

would have been admirable under other circumstances. But right now, jeesh, you'd think he would take the hint that maybe she didn't want to talk with him since she wasn't answering his call. Men. They were all clueless—even when they were well educated, which Adam was.

Incredible! she thought, and walked out.

Adam's face broke into a grin. It was unclear whether he was grinning at the prospect of her as a diver, or because he was happy to see her, or because she resembled a sausage and was making a spectacle of herself.

A second passed, though it seemed like an hour, as Adam continued to grin, despite having to know perfectly well that she was embarrassed to be seen in the revealing garment. His dark eyes roamed her body at will. Adam was the type of guy girls like her avoided in high school—one with experience in his eyes and one thing on his mind. He was no teenager, and Veronica was no schoolgirl, either. The implications were frightening . . . and tantalizing, at the same time.

"Hey, Ronnie," he said lazily, but only after he'd looked his fill.

"Adam," she replied, which was not easy to do when sucking in her tummy. Slowly, she eased her breath out, and—*Thank you, God!*—her stomach stayed flat. No water retention today. Still, she stood extra straight, just in case. "Don't you dare say a word, or you are dead meat," she warned, waving at her attire.

He indicated his lips were sealed, but his eyes were laughing. "Are you going to be diving with us?"

"Hardly. This is my grandfather's idea of a joke." At least, she thought it was. Frank couldn't seriously think she would go diving, not with her fear of the ocean. "I've never done any diving."

"I could teach you," he offered. His words said he was referring to skin diving; his eyes said something entirely different. "I'm free later today."

Oh, boy! He is not going to give up. "No, thanks."

"C'mon. Diving with you would be fun."

Not in my dictionary. "Maybe another day," she lied. "I'm tied up this afternoon." *Or I will be if I can get out of this glove.*

Adam was a Cuban expatriate, having escaped to this country with his parents when he was only eleven. When he wasn't teaching oceanography at Rutgers, he was enjoying his hobby as a diver on deep-sea-wreck diving expeditions. His long black hair, which contained a few white threads, was tied with a leather cord at the back of his neck and hung down his back. His skin was dark, a combination of genes and sun, she supposed. While not handsome—his mouth was too thin and his nose too strong—he *was* attractive, in a beware-I-am-a-wolf-and-I'd-like-to-eat-you sort of way.

"Are your classes over?" she asked casually, and stepped behind the desk, which provided a little bit of cover, at least up to her thighs. She thought about sitting down, but she was afraid something might rip.

"Yep. Semester ended yesterday. I submitted grades last night."

"Will you be teaching this summer?" *Oh, God! I feel as if I'm bare naked, and I'm standing here chitchatting. Is this a woman's worst nightmare, or what?*

He shook his head. "I'm free till August. After the Pink Project, I'm going to explore the *Titanic* again with a group of advanced divers."

"No kidding! Gee, I'd imagine the *Titanic* has pretty well been explored to death by this time." *More chitchat. Why won't he just go away?*

"Actually, it's not. Most people don't realize that artifacts are still being recovered from the *Titanic,* even after all these years and despite that goofball movie." He was walking around the office, looking at the pictures on the walls.

Veronica felt a bit more comfortable with his back to her. She had already learned that serious divers and students of wreck history despised the portrayal in the James Cameron movie. Adam apparently shared that sentiment. "What made you decide to join the Pink Project? Surely there are more historically important expeditions."

"Frank." He turned to look at her as he spoke.

"My grandfather? You're doing this because of my grandfather? Not because of the treasure involved?"

Adam smiled at the disbelief in her voice. "Frank Jinkowsky is a legend. One of the best treasure hunters in the business, better even than Mel Fisher. Most divers, myself included, consider it a privilege to work with him."

"I had no idea," she admitted. "I guess, being an outsider, I never saw him that way." That sounded dumb even to her own ears. How could a family member be called an outsider?

He stared at her for several moments, then asked, "Would you like to have dinner tonight?"

"Me?" *Could I sound any more dorky?*

Adam winked at her. "Yeah, you. What do you say?"

Veronica could see the interest in his eyes, especially when they perused her from face to toes, then back up again. *He likes what he sees. Holy moly! A sexy, eligible man finds me attractive. Oh. Is he eligible?* Her eyes shot to his left hand. Okay. No ring.

He saw where she had glanced and laughed. "No, I'm not married."

"Ever been?"

He shook his head. "Almost. Once."

"Sure. I'd love to have dinner with you," she said before she could bite her tongue. "I'm staying at the Starlight Motel. What time should we meet?"

"Hey, I'm staying at the Starlight, too."

She might be rusty at dating, and she'd never been that good at understanding men (otherwise, she wouldn't have been married and divorced four times), but she knew exactly what was on this man's mind.

Oh, boy! He's thinking more than dinner now. I can tell. Maybe that was his agenda all along. Can I handle that? Yes. I've got to handle that, if I'm going to change my life. Jake's not here. He's apparently gone on with his life. I need to do the same. "Eight o'clock, then?"

"Great! We'll go to Dirty Doug's, unless you object. It's a local bar that serves great grilled oysters and good music."

"Dirty Doug's, huh?" *My grandmother would choke if she knew I was going to a place with that name,* she thought. *Good!* "I take it casual attire would be appropriate?" *Body armor and a chastity belt come to mind.*

"Yep. See you about eight, then. I'll come to your room?" His eyes arched in question.

"No, I'll meet you there," she replied quickly. "I have a little . . . uh, shopping to do first . . . on the way . . . at Wal-Mart."

He wasn't buying her hedging at all. Still, he nodded

his agreement. But, just before he left to return to diving practice, he turned and said, "By the way, Ronnie, you look hot in diving gear."

Veronica smiled for the next five minutes, relishing his compliment. But then the usual reservations set in.

What am I doing?

Getting on with my life.

But . . . am I ready for a new relationship?

More than ready.

I don't know how to act around anyone but Jake.

Learn.

But what if . . . ?

Stop questioning every little thing. Go with the flow. Relax.

Relax? Hah! I'm so nervous even my toes are shaking. What if he wants to have sex? Who am I kidding? He wants sex, all right.

Why am I making rash judgments about the man? Where did the sex idea come from?

My libido, of course. My rusty libido.

When was the last time?

One year since a date. Two years since sex.

Am I pathetic, or what?

Jake wasn't the only man Veronica had slept with, but she could count them on one hand. There was an expression, "Once burned, twice shy." Well, she'd been burned four times, and *shy* didn't begin to define her hesitation to be involved with men.

But, son of a gun, I'm going on a date.

I better shave my legs.

No, no, no! It's just a date. No sex. Just a friendly dinner with a nice man.

Ha, ha, ha!

Then her traitorous thoughts turned once again to Jake. She shouldn't feel guilty about dating other men—even having sex with other men. But she did. Would Adam be the one to help her finally put Jake in her past? A fling, that's what it would be. Nothing serious. Her heart simultaneously wept and rejoiced at the possibility. It was for the best. She knew that. Her heart didn't, but it would . . . in time.

Brenda walked in then, gave her a head-to-toe survey, and said, "Girl, you've got more nerve than I do."

They both burst out laughing. And continued to laugh while they struggled to get Veronica out of the tight garment. She was covered with sweat by the time they finished, and sweat acted like glue in a rubber suit.

"I need to buy some food supplies for the trip," Brenda said over a cup of coffee that Veronica had brewed on the ancient coffeemaker. She planned to buy a new one before she came in tomorrow morning. "Can you give me some cash or a card?"

"How much do you need?"

"Hmmm. We'll be out at least a week. I figure at least five men—Frank, Adam, Caleb, John, and Steve or Tony—and three women, if Flossie comes along. She told me she might, just for the fun of it. How about five hundred? There's a pretty good-sized freezer on board, and I already have lots of canned goods."

Veronica did a quick calculation and decided there would be enough in the business checking account to cover that amount. She handed her the Jinx, Inc., debit card, then asked, "Did you get the motor fixed?"

"Nope. I sent Frank into Manahawkin to get some parts. Looks like we might not be able to head out till Wednesday."

"Is it safe? I mean, will it be safe to go out on the ocean with a patched-up motor?"

"Oh, it'll be safe enough. Worst thing that could happen is the motor won't turn over and we'll have to call the Coast Guard for a tow. Of course, that would be disastrous in terms of keeping the site secret. Every deep-sea treasure-hunting boat on the East Coast tuned in to the Coast Guard radio will head there then like a swarm of sharks."

"How much would a new motor cost?"

"For a boat that size, I'm thinking ten thousand or more. I haven't priced them lately."

Out of the question, then, Veronica decided. With Frank's reduced circumstances, she couldn't see any way to manage that kind of money. Besides, she still needed to ask Frank how he planned to pay all these people—or if he planned on paying them at all. Maybe they just got a share of the profits.

All these people. A thought niggled at Veronica. Then she knew what was bothering her. "You said three women. I sure hope you mean Rosa is going along. And not—"

Brenda grinned. "Yep, you."

"Oh, no!"

"Frank said you'd be going, that he needed you."

"For what?"

"Computer work. Deckhand. Assistant diver."

"I do not know how to dive."

"No problem. You cook, and I can help dive. Maybe I could lose a few more pounds that way." Brenda was a medium-height blonde, about five-six. She was not overweight, but by the standards set by women's magazines, she could lose ten to fifteen pounds. As a result,

Brenda, like many women over thirty, was always on a diet.

"I don't know how to cook very well, either," Veronica said. "Certainly not for a group that size."

"Make sandwiches. They won't be fussy."

"I am *not* going out on a boat," Veronica emphasized, "and definitely not for five days." *I wouldn't be able to carry enough Pepto or Dramamine to last that long.*

"We'll see," Brenda said with a laugh. "Frank can be persuasive."

Yeah, like a sledgehammer. Time to change the subject. "Are you married, Brenda?"

Immediately, Brenda stiffened.

"I'm sorry. I didn't mean to get personal."

"No problem," she said, relaxing her shoulders. "I'm divorced. Three years now. And I'm still healing the wounds."

Veronica knew how that felt. "Do you see him . . . ever?" Of course, Veronica would ask such a dumb question, with her history.

"Not if I can help it. Lance Caslow was the husband from hell."

"Lance Caslow? The race car driver?" Veronica wasn't a NASCAR fan, but even she recognized that name.

"None other. Have you ever met any race car drivers?"

Veronica shook her head slowly. "I don't think so."

"Aside from being miserably moody when on a losing streak, Lance doesn't understand the word *fidelity.* I suspect he's nailed every groupie within a five-mile radius of every racetrack in America."

"Nice guy!"

"Hey, his favorite expression is, 'NASCAR drivers know how to jump-start a car—and a woman.'"

"Modest, too."

"Drivers are the most narcissistic men in the universe. They think their dirty underwear ought to be bronzed. Do you know, Lance once made me give him a blow job while in his car going a hundred twenty miles per hour?"

Veronica's eyes widened at that image.

"Defies believability, doesn't it?" Brenda said with a laugh. "And he didn't even reciprocate. Not that I would have wanted him to, especially not in a car. Well, anywhere for that matter. He was a lousy lover, or at least that's what I like to tell people. Plus, he has a needle dick. I tell everyone that, too, just to annoy him." She grinned impishly.

Way more information than I need to know!

"I've embarrassed you. I'm sorry. Sometimes I'm too candid. It's just that Lance makes me so mad."

"No, no, that's all right. I wasn't embarrassed." *Much.*

"Yeah, right. How about your ex?"

I should have known this conversation would lead to Jake. Can I talk about him? Hah! Why not? "It wasn't a sex problem with us," Veronica revealed with more candor than usual. "Sex does not a marriage make, though."

Brenda appeared unconvinced about that. "Even so, girl, what were you thinking, marrying and divorcing the same man four times? If he was good in the sack, he must've been a world-class two-timer."

"Actually, I don't think Jake ever cheated. While we

were married, anyhow. He had plenty of women in between, though."

Brenda tilted her head at her. "Who left who?"

"Jake always leaves. Yeah, I do a bang-up job of provoking arguments and prolonging them, but, dammit, he should stick around until we can resolve things. The arguments were mainly about his poker. But also about me and . . ." Her words trailed off. She really didn't want to talk about Jake.

Brenda seemed to understand and dropped the subject. "Anyhow, I have a five-year-old daughter, Patti. So, one good thing came out of all that pain."

"A little girl? How wonderful!" Veronica frowned then.

Brenda read her silent question and answered, "She stays with my mother in Perth Amboy when I'm out of town."

Veronica was seeing Brenda in a new light, and she liked what she saw.

"Gotta get back to work," Brenda said, draining the last of her coffee and standing up. "By the way, did I see Famosa coming out of here a while ago?"

"He asked me to dinner tonight."

Brenda wagged a forefinger at her. "Be careful, toots. Famosa and my ex come from the same hound dog mold. Womanizers to the bone. And you know exactly which bone I'm talking about, don't you?"

Yeah. She did.

Chapter
9

Laying it on thick, Cajun style . . .

John LeDeux sat in a booth at Dirty Doug's with Adam Famosa and Caleb Peachey, trying to be heard over the three-piece band blasting out country rock ballads.

He and Caleb were drinking cold beers and inhaling roasted oysters—a house specialty cooked on the barbecue pit out on the deck. Adam was waiting for Ronnie to arrive for their dinner date. Brenda had gone home to be with her daughter overnight.

While Adam and Caleb—also known as Peach, a nickname from his Navy SEAL days—talked about some diving expeditions they'd been on in the past, John looked around the tavern and sighed. *What the hell am I doing here?*

John was a Southern boy, Cajun to the core. He felt out of place, disoriented, here in the North. Anywhere, for that matter, when he was away for long from the bayous he loved. Oh, there was a good reason for his being this far North; well, not so good, but a reason just the same. He'd lost a bet with his best friend from college, Harry "Hoot" MacTavish, who had demanded as his prize that John take a job as a stripper for two weeks. Since Hoot lived in Jersey, he had a friend of a friend with connections to a casino in Atlantic City. Never one to back down, John had agreed.

He was there two weeks as one of the "Ten Dudes from Dallas," not that any of them were from Dallas, except the manager of the group. To his surprise, he had already become bored, despite the female attention, something he usually lapped up whenever he could get it. Hey, he was twenty-two years old; *testosterone* was his middle name.

Then Tante Lulu had shown up, with great timing, to drag him off the premises. When he'd seen her in the Oasis club walking through all the women waving five-dollar bills, he'd about swallowed his tongue. Tante Lulu was a real corker, and he would do anything to please her; everyone in his family felt the same way. So it wasn't a shock that he'd gotten this summer job on a diving boat due to her contact with Henri Pinot, who had been hired as captain, until he had developed some medical problems.

Which all led to his point of confusion. He had graduated recently from Tulane with a degree in criminal justice. But he had no clue what he wanted to do next. Get a job on a police force somewhere in Southern Louisiana. Apply for the FBI's training program. Or go to law school, like his half brother, Luc. The stripping had been only a lark. The diving would be a fun diversion. But his future . . . ah, his future . . . That required a serious decision. And yet he was currently buried in a cloud of uncertainty.

Everything moved too fast here in the North. The music, for example, was nothing like the Cajun and zydeco songs of his culture. Yankees didn't understand ordinary daily expressions like "Sit a spell" or "Over yonder" or the bawdy "Shuck me, suck me, eat me dry," which everyone knew referred to crawfish. The people were always in a hurry, unlike his Southern comrades who knew there was no point in rushing. The food was bland, not enough spices or Cajun lightning. And they talked too fast. A slow, Southern drawl was much more attractive—and effective, with women, in his experience.

"Rhett, you are so full of it," Famosa said, jabbing him with an elbow. "Like a drawl is going to get you jack shit with a woman . . . any woman over the age of sixteen, anyhow."

Apparently, he spoke that last thought aloud, which was a mistake, of course. These two guys, who were ancient—in their thirties, he would guess—liked to tease him about his age and his Southern roots. At least, Famosa did. Peach probably thought it.

"Enough with the Rhett jokes. I live in Louisiana. *Gone With the Wind* took place in Georgia."

Yankees, Famosa in particular, couldn't care less whether he came from Tara or Tallahassee; it was the same thing to them.

"You guys think you know so much just because you're older than me. Well, let me tell you, we Cajuns know stuff from the time we grow hair in our armpits, stuff that makes us more virile than the average Yankee man."

Peach just shook his head, but Famosa asked, "Yeah? Like what?"

"Most men don't like to dance. We Cajuns do. Women love men who can dance."

"I'm not so sure about that," Peach remarked. "I used to be in the Navy SEALs. Women are drawn to them like ants on a"—he grinned—"peach. Didn't matter if the men could walk straight, let alone dance." Peach didn't talk much, and John was surprised that he'd volunteered so much information.

"If dancing is all you Southern boys know how to do well, Bubba, I'm not impressed. Besides, Cubans aren't bad dancers." Famosa was speaking now.

"Tsk-tsk-tsk! Bubbas come from Texas."

"Redneck, then," Famosa razzed him. "Or cracker."

John shook his head. "Nope, those are usually from Arkansas or Alabama," he replied with a straight face. "Anyhow, back to Cajun expertise—I didn't want to say anything, but there is other stuff we Cajun men have that the rest of you don't."

"You're pulling our legs," Famosa scoffed, but then repeated his previous question, "Like what?"

"Like JuJu tea. Whoo-ee, a daily dose of that and you are one happy stud."

"I'll probably regret this, but what is JuJu tea?" Famosa asked him.

"It's a secret. Honest, ask anyone south of the Mason-Dixon line if Cajun men are sex personified. Some people claim it's 'cause we eat so much crawfish, fat and all, but we know better. You'll never find a Cajun man taking Viagra, I'll tell you that. Yep, JuJu tea." He sat back, took a long swig of beer, and just waited.

"Are you bullshitting us?" Peach piped in.

He grinned. "My sister-in-law's family mass-produces

the stuff. Ships it out by the truckloads. I can get you some if you want."

"I don't need it," Famosa bragged.

"Me neither," Peach added.

But John could tell they were interested. They'd probably Google it on their computers when they got home tonight.

"Actually," Peach offered, "I've always thought the best aphrodisiac for a man is a naked woman."

They all agreed on that.

"Let me ask you this," John said, and took a long draw on his beer to make sure he had their attention. "Do you know what a woman says after her fifth orgasm?"

Peach stifled a grin, sensing what was coming next. But Famosa said, "What?"

"You have to ask? You mean, you don't know?" John laughed. "My point exactly. Yankee men could learn a lot from us Cajuns."

Famosa and Peach both groaned.

After taking a long drink of beer, Famosa said, "I saw a guy wearing a T-shirt yesterday that said, 'Most women fake orgasms; most men don't care.'"

John's mind was boggled by that idea. Then he shook his head. "He couldn't have been a Cajun. We know better."

"I was just joking, for chrissake."

John wasn't so sure about that.

Just then, John noticed a girl who was standing near the bar with her girlfriends. She wore tight white jeans, a fringed shirt, cowboy boots, and bright red lipstick. Plus, she was blonde. His kind of girl!

"Learn from an expert, boys," he said. Shoving

Famosa to let him out of the booth, he stood, then pretended to crack his knuckles in preparation. Once he walked across the short dance floor and cut the girl from her girlfriends' herd, he stood in front of his target and said, "Hey, darlin'."

She smiled like a cat who'd just been offered a saucer of cream.

Yep, a good drawl would do it every time.

✦

Jumping headfirst into the deep end of the dating pool . . .

It was dark by the time Veronica arrived at Dirty Doug's, where Adam was waiting for her in a booth with Caleb Peachey. She saw John LeDeux out on the small dance floor with a cute blonde, and holy cow, the boy could dance!

She was a little late, having tried on five different outfits, finally settling on black jeans; low-heeled shoes; and a filmy, almost transparent, gold metallic blouse that tapered at the waist and floated over her hips, providing a hazy view of her black bra and bare abdomen. Vacillating over clothing choices was a new experience for her, which pretty much proved her grandmother's contention that they were alike. Tailored suits had been the garment du jour for them both. Not anymore for Veronica, though, she promised herself.

Loud country and rock music, provided by a three-piece band on a dais, filled the room, making it difficult for people to carry on a conversation. Although she much preferred groups like Aerosmith—being from Boston, that was almost a given—Veronica liked some country songs, much to her grandmother's consternation and Jake's amusement. If it wasn't classical music, her grandmother considered it trash. If it wasn't Sting, Jake wasn't interested. In particular, she liked Kenny Chesney and K.D. Lang. And Sheryl Crow's version of "The First Cut Is the Deepest"—a concept Veronica didn't entirely buy. She knew from experience that all cuts went deep . . . all four of them, in her case.

Adam stood when he noticed her walking toward him. *Good heavens, are those leather pants he has on?* While he waited with a smile on his face, his eyes traveled over her body. *Yep, the gold slut blouse had been the right choice.*

"Hi, Adam," she said.

"Hi, gorgeous," he replied, which was a too-obvious line she found distasteful. Caleb must have, too, because he cringed.

"I'm really glad you came," Adam added, squeezing her shoulder.

She slid into the booth, and he followed after her, his hip pressed deliberately against hers. Across the table Caleb just watched the two of them, a serious expression on his face.

"Hi, Caleb," she said.

"Ronnie."

She saw Adam give Caleb a look, which she interpreted to mean, "Get lost."

Caleb pretended not to notice, and studied his beer bottle when he wasn't studying her.

Adam tried to get the waitress's attention then, but

the place was so busy, it didn't look promising. "I'll go to the bar and get our drinks. What would you like, Ronnie?"

"White wine?"

"Sure." Adam glanced at Caleb and asked, "Wanna come with me?"

Caleb didn't even blink when he answered, "No."

She and Caleb were left alone then.

Veronica was kind of glad that Caleb had stayed. Adam came on a bit too strong, and she might need a "chaperon." The thought made her smile. A Navy SEAL chaperon? Oh, yeah!

"Are you and Adam an item?" Caleb asked, stone-cold serious.

Did the man ever smile?

"An item?" She laughed.

"Exclusive," he explained.

She realized something in that instant. Even though Caleb hadn't said anything or acted in any obvious way, she sensed that he was interested in her . . . as a woman. *Two men in one day. Do wonders never cease?*

"I don't even know Adam. This is just a first date."

"So, the answer is no?"

"Yes, Caleb, the answer is no."

He showed no expression at that news, not pleasure or distaste. But the interest was definitely there.

Possible involvement with Caleb scared her . . . almost as much as reinvolvement with Jake. Adam she could handle, because she knew it would be a fling. Not so with Caleb. The guy had red neon signs flashing "Danger" all over him. Same with Jake.

"Do you ever smile?" she blurted out.

Her question caught him off guard. But then he did smile, and Veronica almost reeled at the impact. The man was drop-dead, come-here-baby gorgeous. She'd known he was attractive before, in a silent, brooding sort of way, but when he smiled . . . whew! The temperature in the room went up a few degrees. She needed to change the subject, quick, lest she do something foolish, like ask him for a date.

"Is it true that you're Amish?"

"Not anymore."

"Is your family still Amish?"

"Yes, well, I assume they are. I haven't seen or heard from them in fifteen years."

She tilted her head, confused. He said the words flatly, as if they didn't matter, but something in his whiskey brown eyes said different.

"I'm being shunned."

Veronica thought she knew what that meant. "Your family can't be in contact with you?" Reflexively, she reached across the table and squeezed his hand in sympathy.

He just stared at her hand on his, as if it was something he did not understand or was unaccustomed to.

There were so many questions she wanted to ask. Why are you being shunned? When did you leave the clan? Is there some girl you left behind? What made you become a SEAL? Aren't Amish pacifists? Why did you opt out of SEALs?

But he was clearly annoyed at her intrusive questions. That was proved true when he pulled his hand out from under hers and asked, "How is it that you married and divorced the same man four times?"

She felt her face heat with embarrassment. "Touché!"

He nodded at her backhanded apology.

The silence that followed was uncomfortable, so she rattled on. "What do you do for a living now? Wreck diving?"

He shook his head. "I've only been out of the teams for six months. I do a little commercial diving—oil rigs, bridge abutments, that kind of thing. Not sure what I want to do next. I'm sort of drifting." That was a long spiel for Caleb, and his face reddened as a result.

"I know what you mean . . . about drifting. I'm between jobs, too."

"I thought you were a lawyer."

"I am. An unemployed lawyer, at the moment."

Their conversation was cut short by Adam's return.

For a while, Veronica just sat back and listened while Adam and Caleb discussed with much enthusiasm the upcoming wreck operation. Occasionally, she commented or responded to a question put to her, but mostly she enjoyed eavesdropping on their excitement.

"This is my twentieth deep dive," Adam said. "How about you, Peach? I would imagine you did a lot of deep diving in SEALs."

"Nah. I've only gone below two hundred feet a few times. The teams do more underwater demolition in shallower waters than that."

Veronica had already learned that two hundred feet was the dividing line for deep diving—where special breathing equipment was required; where decompression was essential to avoid narcosis, or the bends; where only the most accomplished or adventuresome divers dared venture. "Will the Pink Project wreck be down that far?" she asked when there was a break in the back-and-forth conversation.

"Probably," Adam said. "We've prepared for that eventuality."

"Is it dangerous?"

"Any dive is dangerous," Caleb replied. "But deep diving has its own particular risks, and an ill-equipped or ill-prepared team can be snagged at a hundred feet. We lost a SEAL trainee at Coronado last year because he hadn't checked his equipment before going down. There was a leak in his air hose, and he wasn't able to get back up in time."

"That's nothing. If you ever see a diver come up with narcosis, bleeding through the nose and ears, you never forget it. On that gruesome note"—Adam turned to her with a laugh—"are you ready to eat?"

"Yes. I'm famished."

"Well, I'll shove off," Caleb said, standing and slapping a few bills on the table. "I'll see you later." He was looking at Veronica when he spoke.

"What's going on?" Adam asked once Caleb left.

"What do you mean?"

"Peach. Was he hitting on you?"

She smiled. "No. I think he was trying to pull your chain."

"Ah," he said, understanding.

Veronica ordered a medium-rare black and blue burger, a blackened ground sirloin patty topped by blue cheese, with Boardwalk fries. Adam got a well-done steak with mushrooms and a baked potato dripping with butter and sour cream. They shared a Bananas Foster for dessert.

While they ate and then danced several sets of slow songs, they talked and talked and then talked some more.

Adam was a very interesting man. Full of himself, sure, but he lived a fascinating life, full of adventure. He was probably unmarried because he was having too much fun, even at age thirty-seven, taking advantage of the sexual favors women gave him freely. But he was intelligent and attractive. A girl could do worse for a fling. Not that Veronica had decided on a fling—with him or anyone else. Still . . .

Adam followed her back to the motel since they'd both driven to the tavern. He walked her to her door and leaned an arm against the door frame. He was so close, she could smell his deodorant. He probably expected her to invite him in. Actually, Veronica considered it and rejected the idea. For now, at least.

"Good night, Adam."

He arched his eyebrows, then shrugged, getting her silent message that the evening was over. "Thanks for a great evening." He leaned down to kiss her.

Veronica returned his kiss. "That was nice," she murmured.

"Nice?" he hooted with disappointment. Then he really kissed her, putting his arms around her and pulling her sharply forward so they were pressed together. His one hand was at her nape, holding her head in place, and his other hand locked around her waist.

She had no choice but to put her hands on his shoulders.

When the kiss ended, he leaned back and asked in a husky voice, "How was that?"

"Much nicer," she said, but what she really thought was, *Just nice.*

A short time later, when she was in her motel room, alone, she heard a knock on the door. *Good Lord! Does the man not take no for an answer?*

She walked, barefoot, over to the door and opened it a crack, then wider. "Caleb? What are you doing here?"

"Couldn't get you out of my mind."

Oh, my God! Now that gets my attention. "Are you staying here, at this motel?"

"No. I'm at the Hampton . . . down the road a ways."

She leaned against the door frame. "And?"

"And I was driving past, saw your car, and thought, what the hell!" With that, he pulled her into his embrace; backed her up against the door, which slammed against the inner wall of the motel room; and kissed her. Really. Kissed. Her. Kissed her so good and so long that her toes curled. For sure, there was a certain part of her body melting. His erection pressed against her stomach. His one hand slipped under her gauzy blouse and kneaded her breast till a nipple blossomed against his palm. He used his other hand to caress her behind. No subtlety here. No "Can I?" or "Please, baby?" This was hard-core sex he was offering.

Then he stepped away from her, surveying her with dark, smoldering eyes.

The one word that came to her mind was not *nice*.

"Make a list, Ronnie," he said in a voice smokey with desire, "of everything you like in bed. I'll do all of them, and then we'll hit my list."

Without another word, he left, closing the door behind him.

Veronica sank to the bed, weak with surprise and, yeah, a little bit of arousal. And for the first time in, oh, let's say forever, she giggled.

Just before she fell asleep a short time later, it wasn't Adam or Caleb she thought about, though. It was Jake. And his kisses. *Night thoughts,* that's what Jake always called them. Those passions or forbidden yearnings that could be pushed aside during daylight hours came back to haunt in the still of the night, in that ethereal moment just before sleep.

Much as she would have liked otherwise, her dreams were of Jake that night. As always. *Am I a sap, or what?*

Chapter
10

THE SAPPY WEDDING

Thirteen years ago . . .

They were running away from their own wedding reception.

"Shhh," Jake whispered to her.

Veronica giggled.

She wore a white gown and veil; he had on a black tux. From down the hall in the banquet room, they could hear the musicians begin to play big-band songs for dancing—her grandmother's choice, though not objectionable to her and Jake. "Sentimental Journey" wafted out to them.

"My grandmother will have a fit," she said.

"Yep," Jake agreed with a grin. Her grandmother didn't approve of Jake and didn't mind showing it every chance she got. She would blame Jake for their early, unannounced departure.

The elevator ping-pinged, then opened. Jake took her hand and they rushed in, repeatedly jabbing the CLOSE button in their impatience, then using a key to take them to the penthouse bridal suite. Once the elevator door swooshed shut, Jake leaned back against one wall and smiled at her, a lazy smile so full of heat she felt herself melting, bit by bit, from head to toe and some interesting places in between.

What a beautiful smile he has, dimple and all, *she observed. It was the first thing she'd noticed when she met him three years ago on the Boston U campus. She'd probably fallen in love with him on sight. He'd always claimed the same about her.*

She leaned against the opposite wall and smiled back at him. "So, what do you think we should do, now that we're an old married couple?" *They'd married five hours ago at St. Jerome's Cathedral.*

"Oh, I can think of a few things." *He crooked his forefinger at her, beckoning her to come closer.*

"Oh, no!" *she said with a laugh.* "Now that we're married, I get to call the shots."

"Is that a fact?" *he asked as the elevator doors swooshed open directly into the entryway of their suite.*

Seeing the gleam in his blue eyes, she picked up the skirt of her gown and started to run. He caught up with her in a few long strides, put his hands on her waist, and lifted her high, then swung them around in a joyous circle.

They gazed at each other in wonder. They were so wildly in love. Even though she was only twenty-two and he was twenty-five, they sensed how special their love was.

From the open balcony doors, they could hear the band segue into The Police's "Every Breath You Take." It was Jake's favorite song, by his favorite band.

She arched a brow at him.

He laughed. "I gave the band leader a twenty."

"My grandmother will have a fit," she repeated.

Jake grinned and tightened his arms around her waist, pulling her close against his body. She looped her arms around his neck.

He kissed her then, a kiss that went on and on. So gentle that it spoke volumes. She touched his hair. His thumb outlined her jaw. And all the while they continued to kiss. She would remember that kiss till the day she died.

Against her mouth, he whispered, "Hello, wife."

A thrill ran through Veronica at his words. Even though they'd been married for five whole hours, it was the first chance she'd had to really register that she was now Mrs. Jake Jensen.

"Hello, husband," she said, and laid her cheek against his shoulder. They danced then, slow, slow, slow. She could feel his heart beating and fancied that they were both breathing in unison. One heartbeat.

It was a moment out of time, to be cherished forever. A memory they were creating, like a picture in an album, to be taken out over the years to remind them of how perfect things had been on that one day and that one time.

The band must have taken a break, because the only sounds in the room now were the rasp of a zipper and the swoosh of her gown falling to the floor—followed by the sweet sounds of skin against skin, the clicking of her great-grandmother's pearls, and softly murmured endearments.

Later, Jake leaned over her and whispered, "I love you so much." There were actually tears in his eyes.

Which caused her to choke up, too. "Forever," she said back. "I will love you forever."

It was all so sappy . . . and wonderful.

Chapter

11

Grumble, grumble, grumble . . .

Frank was in a rip-roaring bad mood.

It hadn't helped that wacky Vivian, the manicure lady from Nail You, showed up at ten last night to fix Flossie's broken nail. Coughing up a storm, Vivian had left her flu deathbed to help Flossie with her dire emergency—a broken nail, of all things. She never said how she'd found out about Flossie's dilemma and seemed terrified when asked.

He got up at dawn, as was his custom these days, but a little more tired than usual due to the late-night visitor. Hey, he was seventy-five years old; he didn't want to waste a minute of the time he had left. Besides, he needed to get into the office before Ronnie arrived so he could hide more of his financial papers. His granddaughter was way too smart, and she was relentless in pursuing the location of every single dime of his.

Out on the deck, while the sun rose over the ocean and the seabirds awakened loudly, he did a series of push-ups. Not as many as he'd done in his younger days, but he still managed a set of fifty halfway decent ones. He inhaled the fresh sea air, which he loved, and saluted the lighthouse, which was his daily ritual, too. But his mood got worse instead of better. By the time he was on his way to the office at seven A.M., smoking cigar firmly planted in his mouth, zipping across the bay in his speed boat to the Barnegat wharf, he was hunting for someone on whom to vent his frustrations.

He was tired of pretending to be poor.

He was tired of arguing with Ronnie over every little thing . . . and her threatening to quit every other hour.

He was tired of waiting for Jake to arrive.

He was sick and tired of Jake's frickin' answering machine. Whoever invented those contraptions ought to be drawn and quartered.

He was tired of being nice. Well, nice for him.

He was tired of Rosa making one demand after another. The latest was that she wanted to go out on the boat with them, along with her two sons. She'd already bought a boating outfit, she'd told him, whatever the hell a boating outfit was. He'd told her she might break a nail; she'd told him he might break a leg. There was a hidden warning in that, he'd decided. They'd compromised on one son, period, going out with them. Even that rankled.

He was tired of Flossie's hot flashes and mood swings. Their bedroom felt like an igloo these days. She was turning into a psycho. Lovey-dovey one moment, Hannibal Lecter the next. Last night she'd burst out crying just because he said he'd never liked Elvis.

He was tired of fabricating reasons why Ronnie's

presence on the boat during the search was essential. If he didn't convince Ronnie to come along and experience the thrill of treasure hunting, he would never get her to take over Jinx, Inc.

Flossie, on the other hand, who'd had only a passing interest in his treasure-hunting projects in the past, had come up with the bright idea that she was coming along. Rosa had probably put that bug in her ear. But neither hell nor high water nor his bursts of temper were going to stop Flossie. He'd briefly considered telling her she might break a nail, but refrained when he contemplated the body part Flossie would threaten to break. It wouldn't be a leg, for damn sure. Before Frank left the house this morning, Flossie told him she would be gone all day, probably off to some mall buying a "boating outfit."

He was tired of all the postponements of the Pink Project. He was leaving for the wreck site tomorrow if he had to row the damn boat.

And he was low on Cuban cigars. Maybe Famosa knew someone who knew someone.

As he pulled into his designated slip before the warehouse, he took in the scenic picture of his diving boat, *Sweet Jinx,* which was anchored right next to him. God, he loved that boat. She was more than twenty years old and had more patches and renovations than an aging movie star. Formerly named *Down & Dirty,* she was a sixty-five-foot former tramp steamer that had been gutted and refitted to become a diving vessel with all the latest bells and whistles. The old lady could accommodate fifteen people in a pinch, ten comfortably. The boat was perfectly suited for treasure hunting on the high seas. Not that all his treasure hunts were aquatic ones, but when he did hit the deep waters, *Sweet Jinx* had all the latest technology and gear to make the operation safe and efficient and comfortable.

Just then, he noticed something. Ronnie and several of the crew members stood on the wharf, talking excitedly. Why were they here so early? And what had them so excited? More problems? He thought seriously about turning his boat around and going to the Anchor for a double shot of bourbon—a little hair of the dog, except that he hadn't had the pleasure of the "dog" last night.

"What's going on?" he grumbled once he climbed onto the pier.

The group—Ronnie, Brenda, Adam, Caleb, and John—parted in the middle, and he had an open path to the shiny *motor.* He glanced from one to the other, asking, "Where did this come from?" It was a brand-spanking-new luxury model of a Vanguard motor, a perfect fit for the diving boat. The thing had to have cost at least ten thousand dollars.

"Did you buy this?" he accused Ronnie. When her mouth dropped open, he remembered his poor man act and added, "We don't have the cash for this."

"Not me," Ronnie said. "Besides, how would I know what kind of motor to order—or get it here so quickly?"

"You?" He looked at Brenda. The woman knew more about motors and how they worked than anyone else in the team.

She would know exactly what kind of motor they needed and how to get it.

Brenda put up both hands and shook her head.

The others were shaking their heads as well.

He thought for a couple of seconds, then told Brenda, "We might as well use it."

The three guys picked up the motor and followed Brenda over to the boat. This new motor would ensure that they started the search by tomorrow morning, as planned.

Finally, my bad mood has a reason to lift.

He turned and saw that Ronnie was still standing there, frowning at him.

Maybe not.

"I think I know where the motor came from."

"Where?"

She motioned her head toward Rosa's son, Tony, who was sitting on a piling, throwing a crab line into the bay. Jersey had some of the best blue-claw crabs in the world, after all. Tony scowled at Frank and Ronnie, then turned away.

Frank frowned. "Are you saying Tony—rather, Rosa—is responsible for this?"

"All I know is that yesterday I wished I had a new computer, and hours later, I had one sitting in front of the office. Then, yesterday afternoon, I heard you wish that you had a new motor. Steve, or Tony, was there each time."

Was that why Flossie's manicurist had shown up last night? Had one of Rosa's sons made Vivian an offer she couldn't refuse, just because Flossie had wished it? He grinned.

"It's not funny. They're probably stolen property. Mafia loot."

"Oh, I don't know about that."

"Why don't you ask him?"

"A person shouldn't look a gift horse in the mouth."

"A person could end up with a gift horse's head in his bed."

"Did anyone ever tell you that you can be a pain in the ass? Don't answer that." He turned and yelled over to Tony, "Hey, Tony, did you bring this motor here today?"

Tony didn't even look up from his crab line. He just shook his head.

"Ask him if his brother or mother brought it here. You asked if *he* brought it *today*. Maybe he brought it last night. Go ahead, ask him." Ronnie gave him a look that pretty much said he should do her bidding . . . pronto.

Not bloody likely! "Your nagging is really starting to bother me. Maybe I should just drop you in the bay. That would shut you up."

She gasped, and an expression of hurt flashed on her face, immediately replaced with anger.

"Lighten up, girl. I was just kidding," he said, which pretty much amounted to an apology for him. "Listen, Ronnie, why don't you go into the office and call Jake? See why he's not here yet. We're leaving first thing in the morning, and he's not answering my calls."

"What makes you think he would answer my call?"

"Oh, he would answer your call, all right. Jake gets loopy just looking at you. All you'd have to do is crook your finger, and he'd be tripping over himself to get here."

"You are so wrong." She inhaled and exhaled to tamp down her temper. "Why are you so determined to have him here on the project? Me, too, for that matter?"

Questions, questions, questions. "Because I want a great-grandchild," he said before he had a chance to bite his tongue. Oh, well, it *was* part of the reason. He didn't reveal *that* much.

"From me and Jake?"

"No. You and Captain Hook. Of course you and Jake."

Her mouth gaped open with disbelief. "You want me and Jake to have a baby?"

"Yes, dammit!"

"You're as bad as my grandmother. She wanted us to have a baby, too, so that she could control the baby's life like she did mine."

He could tell she regretted mentioning his ex-wife and admitting that maybe, just maybe, Lillian hadn't been the perfect role model. But he couldn't let the comparison of him and Lillian stand. "I'm in no way like your grandmother."

"Why are you so insulted? You keep telling me that *I'm* just like her."

"That's different. You are. But there's hope for you yet. Stick around me long enough and you'll lose some of that starch in your undies."

"Aaarrgh!"

"Get movin', girl. Call Jake. Have a baby. Maybe two. But help me find the goddamn pink diamonds first. Treasure now, baby later."

He began to stomp toward the boat, anxious to get this project on its way, anxious to get out of Ronnie's way before she hit him.

To his back, she yelled, "Not a chance!"

He just laughed.

Oh, ho, ho, and a bottle of . . . Pepto . . .

Early the next morning, the Pink Project crew got ready to take off.

Veronica watched from the wharf as the gear and supplies were packed on board. Last-minute checks were being made of everything from the new motor to the diving apparatus. All the team members were so excited that a small part of Veronica—the part that fancied walking on the wild side—wished she could be an actual member of the team. With a sigh, she gave a last wave and went back into the warehouse office, determined to find all the missing financial papers while her grandfather was gone.

A few minutes later, Frank rushed into the office, panicked. "You gotta come on board. It's . . . it's about Jake," he told her, then rushed off.

Despite her aversion to water, Veronica followed him, never hesitating to step on board in her concern over Jake. She caught up with Frank down in the spacious cabin, where he was getting a bottle of water from the fridge. "What? What about Jake?" she practically shrieked.

"Uh . . ." He took a long swig from the icy bottle.

"I'm going to dump that water over your stupid head if you don't tell me right away."

"Tsk-tsk-tsk! Got ants in yer pants, girlie. Hey, that's a good one. Ants in yer pants, an itch in the you-know-where, you and Jake, babies. Ha, ha, ha. Okay, okay, don't be lookin' all witchlike at me. I finally got in touch with Jake last night." He paused, indulging in another swig.

"And?" she prodded.

"He's in New Orleans."

New Orleans? The Insanity Wedding. Veronica could never think about the Big Easy without remembering her Insanity Wedding there. Elation, and dismay, swept over her at the same time. Apparently, Jake was safe, but he wasn't coming back. Not that he'd said he would. Not that she wanted him to. Still . . .

"He's gamblin' on a riverboat there."

"Here's a news flash, Frank. One, that's nothing new—gambling is what Jake does. Two, I don't give a hoot where he is. Three, why did I have to board this blasted boat to hear this spectacular news?"

"Just thought you'd like to know."

A motor turned over then. Very loud. And fine hairs stood up on the back of her neck. "You wouldn't!"

"Yep, I would," Frank said, pleased as an accordion player at a Polish wedding.

"You . . . dumbass moron. I swear, I ought to . . . to . . . punch your lights out. And I would, if I could."

By the time she got up on deck and made her way to the wheelhouse to scream at Brenda to turn the boat around, it was too late. The Pink Project was under way.

"Turn around!" she ordered, first her grandfather, then Brenda, then each of the crew members, who had followed, not wanting to miss the show, even Steve who just peered at her through his dark sunglasses, saying nothing. No one would listen to her.

"It's for your own good," Frank said.

"Old man, you are delusional."

"It's bad luck to turn around right away," Brenda contended. A blush belied her words.

"I've heard enough about good luck and bad luck to last me a lifetime. I was married to a gambler, remember?"

"It's gonna be fun, *chère*," John said.

"Fun is dinner and a Broadway play. Fun is winning a difficult case in court. Fun is a hot fudge sundae. Fun is *not* puking my guts out on a freakin' boat." She hated the shrillness in her voice.

John just grinned at her.

"Since Jake's not here, you can be the computer tech," Adam offered. "I'll show you how to track the site with the computer mapping system. Every aspect of a dive is recorded on camera; then we study the tapes over and over, like football coaches before the big game."

Like I care! She gave him a look that said loud and clear what he could do with his proffered help.

Adam just grinned, too.

"How about you, bozo?" she said to Caleb. "Do you have something asinine to say, too?"

"Not a thing." He put his hands up defensively and laughed.

"You planned this all along, didn't you?" she accused her grandfather. "Oh, God! That's my luggage over there, isn't it? And that diving suit you gave me. I swear, I have fallen into Alice in Wonderland's garden hole, and you are the Mad Hatter."

He shrugged, lit a smelly cigar, and walked away.

Meanwhile, the boat chugged its way out to sea. There was no turning back. It appeared as if she might be trapped for as much as a week on the high seas. It was enough to make a grown woman cry.

A short time later, despite all her protests and against her will, Veronica accepted the fact that she was not only on the *Sweet Jinx*, but was also a full-blown member of the Pink Project team. Just the idea boggled the mind! And her stomach.

Standing on the bow, fortified with Dramamine and Pepto, she watched the boat part the ocean, and, once she calmed down, she had to admit it was a wondrous sight. With the endless horizon of water, she could see why men had such respect for the sea. The ocean scared the bejesus out of her, but that didn't mean she couldn't see its beauty.

"It's beautiful, isn't it?" her grandfather said, coming up to lean his elbows on the rail beside her.

"No, it's not," she replied contrarily.

"You still mad at me?"

"Of course I'm still mad at you, you lunkhead. You tricked me."

"Well, now, it depends on your definition of *trick*."

"Don't play Clintonese with me."

"All I did was mention Jake and you took off like a chicken with its head off."

Now that's a picture!

"Tells ya somethin', doesn't it?"

Like I'm pathetic. She refused to fall into his trap of discussing Jake again, or his desire for great-grandbabies.

That didn't stop him. "Sooner or later, you two are gonna figure a way to live together."

I've skipped down that yellow brick road way too many times. "Don't bet the boat on it."

He chuckled, insinuating that she was going to fall into the Jake trap again.

"The first time we spot another boat, hopefully the Coast Guard, I'm going to flag them down and have you arrested for kidnapping."

"No, no, no. Whatever you do, it can't involve the Coast Guard. Boats within a fifty-mile radius listen in on their radio. Treasure hunters from all around will be on our tail if they get wind that I'm out here."

It was useless arguing with her grandfather. She

never won. "Go away. I'd rather be miserable all alone."

"It would be nice if you could view this all as a great adventure."

"You've got to be kidding."

"Lotsa women would give their eyeteeth to be on board a pleasure boat with five men—not that I want you foolin' around with any man besides Jake. Nosiree. But see how happy the other two women are here?" He referred to Brenda, who had made her way down to the galley kitchen to prepare lunch, something involving sauerkraut by the smell of it, and Flossie, all decked out in capri pants and a nautical-motif halter top, reclining on a lounge chair under an awning reading—could it be?—the *Wall Street Journal*.

She homed in on something else her grandfather had said. "Pleasure boat?" It was a refurbished tramp steamer with all the charm of a rusty tin can—on the outside. The decrepit boat from the old Humphrey Bogart movie *African Queen* came to mind. She had to admit that the inside was spiffy, though, with sleeping accommodations for all of them—cramped, but sufficient—and a complete kitchen, toilet facilities, and a stationary table and benches for eating.

In addition, the boat had a computerized mapping system. Also, a wireless side-scan sonar connected to a laptop took pictures of anything sticking up out of the murky bottom; it mapped the sea floor far below where divers and global positioning system equipment could go. And there was a magnetometer to detect iron and steel, even when well buried in the sand. A water blower powered by wash from the boat's propellers pushed away sand while sending clearer surface water down to aid the divers.

New devices were being invented daily to allow for deeper ocean recoveries, such as a robot that could be dropped to unheard-of-before depths, her grandfather had explained last night. Such robots cost as much as two million dollars, an expenditure her grandfather obviously could not afford.

Despite the lack of a robot, Veronica was impressed with the Jinx, Inc., operation, though she wouldn't tell Frank that. At least she now knew where some of the money invested by Rosa and Jake had gone.

"It would be a pleasure boat if you'd give it a chance," her grandfather persisted. "Why not give it a chance? Why do you always prejudge?"

"I'm getting tired of you always saying that I misjudge people and things."

"You do ... sometimes," he said in a surprisingly gentle voice—gentle for him, anyway.

She frowned her confusion, then shook her head; it didn't matter. "Why did you have to use underhanded methods to get me here on this boat? In fact, why did you have to use underhanded methods to get me to Long Beach Island in the first place? Why couldn't you have just asked me? Nicely. For a change."

"Would you have come?"

"Probably not."

Frank raised both hands in a "So there!" manner.

"I don't understand you."

He arched his eyebrows in question.

"Always, even when I was a child, you pushed me. 'Learn to swim.' 'Don't you have any normal clothes?' 'What do you mean, you never went on a roller coaster?' 'Why don't you go to a public school like everyone else?' 'Why do you have to go to a fancy-pantsy school like Cedar Hill?' 'Didn't your father ever take you to a baseball game?' 'Do you ever get dirty?'"

Frank winced at her mimicking him. "Listen, your grandmother and I were like two cats in a room full of rocking chairs for years after our divorce. When she was pregnant with your father, she earned her full membership in the Bitch of the Month Club. At first, I steered clear of her, which proved to be a mistake. I ended up not seeing Joey, your dad, while he was a kid, before she had a chance to poison him against me. Then, when I got my act together and tried to be a father to him, she made every little request a bargaining tool. The measliest overnight visit cost me big-time—not in money, but other things." He coughed and turned away from her. After a long moment, he turned back and said, "By the time you came along, and after Joey died, the only communication I had with Lillian were battles. So, when I did get to visit with you, my temper was already riled, and I could see how much you hated being around me."

Veronica practically gaped at her grandfather. That was the most personal information he'd ever disclosed to her, but he raised a million other questions. There were big, big holes in his story, important things she could tell he'd left out. She wasn't about to let him off so easy. "And that's your excuse for being a miserable, crude bully to me over the years?"

"Yeah." He laughed. "I better go over and help lay out the diving gear."

He left with a cloud of cigar smoke following in his wake.

Veronica decided to go down below and help prepare lunch. The first thing she saw was Brenda, stirring a pot while dancing in place to the music coming from the radio on the cabinet next to a restaurant-quality range. It was the old Bob Seger version of "Old Time Rock & Roll."

"Can I help?" Veronica asked.

Brenda jumped and almost dropped her wooden spoon. "Oh, I didn't hear you come in. Yeah. How about setting the table? Eight, I think. Me, you, Flossie, Frank, Steve, Adam, Caleb, and John."

"What are you making?" Veronica asked as she took out the plates and cutlery.

Brenda laughed. "As if you couldn't tell! Sauerkraut." She pointed with her spoon at the commercialsize kettle holding what had to be two gallons of sauerkraut. Already on the counters were hot dogs and baked beans, coleslaw, and a tossed salad. Glancing in the freezer, she saw several cartons of ice cream—her grandfather's choice for dessert, she supposed.

When Veronica made no comment on the menu, Brenda laughed again. "I'm on a diet. Nothing but sauerkraut and baked beans. The rest of the stuff is for everyone else."

"Uh . . . how long do you have to be on a sauerkraut and bean diet?"

"Four weeks . . . or until I lose twenty pounds."

Twenty pounds in four weeks? Good luck! "You don't look overweight," Veronica remarked. And Brenda didn't. Truth to tell, she was just right. "With you, I would think losing twenty pounds would be kind of drastic."

Brenda shook her head vehemently. "I have a fifteen-year high school reunion coming up and a slinky, siren red, size seven dress I intend to wear, or die trying. I weigh one hundred and fifty friggin' pounds." Just then, Veronica noticed the scale in the corner. "I weigh myself three times a day," Brenda admitted.

"But, Brenda, you've got to be, what, five foot six?"

"Five-six and a half, but no woman in the world wants to weigh that much."

Veronica had to admit one hundred and fifty had a distasteful sound to it. "So, are you hoping to hook up with some old high school sweetheart at the reunion?"

"Hell, no. I just want to show my ex-husband—the only boyfriend I ever had as a teenager—what he's missing. He'll be there with his latest bimbo; she weighs no more than one hundred pounds, and twenty of that is in her boobs."

They both smiled at that image.

"It's probably silicone," Veronica offered.

"Definitely. Lance probably thinks they're real, though. Men! Clueless slimeballs, all of them."

"I'll second that," Veronica said. "My ex is engaged to Casino Barbie. When she's not being Ms. Premed Barbie."

"God, I hate Barbie," Brenda said. "Do you know there's even a NASCAR Barbie? Like those breasts would fit inside a race car harness! Not!"

They laughed again.

"You ought to bring some handsome guy with you to the reunion," Veronica suggested. "No strings. Just for show."

"Now where would I find one of those on such short notice?"

"There's probably some agency called Studs "R" Us."

"If there was, they'd make a mint."

"Or try eBay. They have everything there."

"I heard what you said about eBay," Flossie remarked with excitement. She was coming down the steps, followed by Frank, Adam, and Caleb. Steve had probably volunteered to man the wheel while everyone ate lunch. "I have a friend, Ginger, a divorcée, who bought a weekend date with a celebrity on eBay. It was all for some charity. Eye candy, and then some! Well, he wasn't really a celebrity. I think he came from one of those male escort places, but who cares! He looked like Johnny Depp."

"Is that the guy who put ten thousand dollars on her Visa card?" Frank inquired snidely.

"I love eBay," Flossie continued, ignoring Frank as she helped put the remaining dishes on the table, along with pitchers of ice water and iced tea. "I bought a sable coat on eBay last week. It was only five thousand dollars."

"Whaaat?" Frank roared. "You spent five thousand frickin' bucks on a rat skin? Are you nuts?"

Veronica fully expected Flossie to burst out crying, as was her pattern lately, menopause having turned her into a pendulum of moods. Instead, she lashed out. "Yeah, I spent five thousand dollars. Of my own money. And maybe I'll spend another five thousand dollars next time I log onto the Internet. Betcha there's a one-day spa treatment I can bid on at Manhattan Magic. I'd bid up to two thousand, even. eBay has everything."

Frank looked as if he might choke but thankfully held his tongue for once.

But only for a minute.

After everyone had washed their hands in the tiny bathroom and sat down on benches bracketing the galley table, he took one long look at the dishes placed in front of them. He especially went wide-eyed over the stainless steel bowl, probably a washbasin, filled almost to overflowing with sauerkraut. That and a slightly smaller bowl of baked beans held center stage.

"What the hell is this?"

Brenda immediately stiffened and put a hand on each side of her curvy hips. "I'm on a diet, a sauerkraut and bean diet. Wanna make something of it?"

Everyone at the table knew enough to keep quiet, although the men barely stifled grins as they studied their plates, then began to help themselves to the food.

Except for Frank. "A sauerkraut and baked bean diet? Holy crap!" he said. "What? You gonna fart the fat off?"

It didn't help matters that Frank's tape deck launched into the rowdy "Too Fat" polka. What a coincidence!

"At least you coulda thrown some kielbasa in. What? Don't tell me. You didn't bring any kielbasa? That does it. I am definitely depressed."

Brenda glowered at Frank, then picked up a pitcher of ice water and dumped it over his head.

It was something they'd all wanted to do at one time or another.

Chapter
12

Catching the fever . . .

By midafternoon, they were anchored at the designated site.

It was a perfect day for diving. The ocean was calm, like a sheet of glass. Underwater visibility should be great.

Frank basked in the pitch of excitement. Everyone was chomping at the bit to get started, even his granddaughter. Ronnie was in the wheelhouse with Famosa, learning how to use the computer mapping equipment. Oh, Ronnie tried to pretend she was here against her will and that she couldn't care less whether they found anything or not. But, hot damn, Frank could see by the gleam in her eyes and her eagerness to help that she was catching the fever. That had been his goal all along.

LeDeux was running the side sonar scan while Brenda showed Steve how the magnetometer worked. Even Flossie—slathered head to toe with sunscreen and wearing rhinestone-studded sunglasses—had been put to work, watching the fishing lines that had been cast over the other side of the boat. Dinner, they expected optimistically. He hoped she didn't have one of her hot flashes in the middle of reeling in a big ol' fish; she might just scare the fish, he thought with a grin. *Not that I would tell her that. I am not that dumb!*

"You got everything?" he asked Peach, who was gearing up. He would be the first diver to splash down today.

Peach nodded, adjusting his face mask and doing a last-minute check on his dry suit, flippers, and, most important, the twin tanks on his back.

"If everything goes according to plan—"

"Which it rarely does," Peach quipped.

"And assuming we find the wreck site on our first try—"

"Which pretty much never happens," Peach interrupted again.

Frank glared at Peach for his smart remarks. "Then we should have enough time, before dark, for two more dives—first Famosa, then LeDeux."

They had drawn up a grid, a one-mile square, of where the wreck *should* be. It was impossible to be more precise. Any number of factors could have affected the location, including faulty human reporting, currents that could have moved the debris, and hurricanes over the years. Right now, they sat over one corner of the square. If that didn't work out, they would move forward about a quarter mile and dive again. On and on till they reached the opposite corner, which would probably be tomorrow morning, if Frank's guess was correct. If that row on the grid didn't pan out, they would start on the next quarter-mile down, over and over till they got to the exact wreck site. It was pretty much like mowing a lawn.

The problem was, the dives were deep, below two hundred feet, which meant that a diver could spend only about twenty-five minutes down below and an hour coming back up, stopping at intervals to decompress. The bends or narcosis was always a concern, even with modern equipment. Once the diver came back up, he couldn't return to the water for two or three hours because he continued to decompress. That meant that another diver would make the next dive. That would be Famosa. Then LeDeux. Then they would start all over again with Peach. Slow, methodical, but necessary for the safety of all concerned.

Once they hit pay dirt, the first diver would case the site, foregoing any treasure retrieval and just gaining knowledge. The next diver would secure the grapple to the wreckage and take some videos. The third and subsequent divers would actually bring up the artifacts, or in this case, diamonds.

Frank wished he was going down himself. He had on many occasions. But his age and physical condition precluded that now; divers had to be in top form.

"Good to go?" he asked Peach.

Peach bit down on his regulator, gave a little wave to him and the others, then allowed himself to roll backward over the gunwale and into the water.

Veronica and the rest of the crew came down to stand beside Frank at the rail. The tension in the air could be cut with a knife. "This is really exciting," she admitted.

"Yep," he agreed without an "I told you so," as she would have expected.

"Remember that trip, Frank, two years ago off the North Carolina Outer Banks?" Brenda said from Frank's other side. "We were looking for that sunken Spanish galleon, but, man, we didn't know what we were going to find down there, the *Sea Witch* or any one of the hundreds of wrecks in that area."

"Yeah, that was a good one. Paid for itself tenfold," Frank replied. "Even after we gave half the artifacts to the state for museums and the like. Definitely exciting."

Veronica frowned with confusion. "Hundreds of wrecks? Just off the Carolina coast? Really?"

"Oh, yeah!" Brenda answered. "Of all those gold-laden sailing ships from England and Spain, many of them never made it through the rough Atlantic waters, especially during hurricane season."

"Hey, I've researched this. It's my area of expertise," Adam added. "If you count all the shipwrecks over the past three thousand years, three million, or more, still lie at the bottom of deep waters around the world. Three million! During a five-year period in the nineteenth century alone, one thousand of the ten thousand ships insured in England went down and have never been found. Some are down too deep. Some have deteriorated over time. But most are in unknown spots."

Veronica smiled at Adam's little spiel. He sounded like the professor he was.

"The Florida Keys are supposed to be paradise for us treasure hunters since there are so many lost ships there. But, really, they're everywhere," Frank elaborated.

John leaned forward to address Brenda. "Like you said, *chère,* there are thousands of wrecks here on the East Coast. But we have our share off the Gulf of Mexico, too, especially Spanish and French. Oil drillers find evidence of them all the time. Divers even uncovered a Nazi sub there years ago."

"That's nothing," Frank added. "Just a decade ago, two young divers on a Brielle boat discovered a German U-boat. Off the New Jersey coast, for chrissake! Now, some Mafia don, wrapped in a concrete suit, that I could see. But an actual U-boat? Unbelievable. Neither the U.S. government nor the Germans had any idea it was there."

Steve gave Frank a dirty look for the Mafia remark, but of course he said nothing because that would acknowledge his connection to the mob. Besides, it was hard to take Steve seriously at the moment since he was wearing that skimpy black Speedo, topped by an unbuttoned Hawaiian shirt, presumably to cover his shoulder holster. What he was going to shoot on this trip, Veronica had no idea. Maybe a shark.

"That is incredible," Veronica commented, referring to the shipwreck information. She would bet that most people, like her, didn't know what treasure the world's oceans and seas still held. "Millions of shipwrecks still down there? I'll need a little time to register that."

Her grandfather checked his watch. "Peach has been down there twenty minutes, and he hasn't blown a cup yet. My guess is there's nothing there."

Brenda quickly explained to her that divers took a couple Styrofoam cups down with them. If they located the wreck, they let a cup float to the surface, as a signal.

Everyone, except her, Frank, and Flossie, wandered off then to do their various jobs. Adam started putting on the rest of his diving gear, assuming he would be going down once Caleb came up and they moved anchor a quarter mile away.

Suddenly, Veronica thought of Jake and wished he was here. Not just to share in the excitement—he would get such a kick out of the adventure, deeming it the ultimate gamble—but so he could see how she was handling being out on the open sea. To her amazement, she was hardly nauseous, probably because she kept downing Pepto and Dramamine. And she was hardly afraid. In fact, she was thinking about letting Adam give her some diving lessons once this project was completed. Jake wouldn't think she was just like her grandmother now. Nope, she was well on her way to being, if not interesting, at least not boring.

"I wish Jake was here," Frank said, breaking the silence.

Veronica's head shot up. *Is the old man reading my mind now?*

Flossie, misinterpreting the expression of dismay that must have been on her face, squeezed her hand and said, "He'll come, honey. Something must have held him up."

Yeah, like a poker game. Or his fiancée. Without acknowledging Flossie's sympathetic comment, Veronica turned and went to the galley to help Brenda prepare dinner.

It's not that I miss the jerk. Nope. It's just that we've always shared things. And this is important. To me. Oh, hell!

The sunny day had turned suddenly gray.

✦

Would you please be my stud . . . uh, date?

Dinner was late that night, and, yes, it was fish. Lots of fish—sea bass, flounder, and even steaks from a small shark. Flossie made twice-baked potatoes that oozed cheddar cheese, and Veronica made her specialty, a wilted lettuce salad. For vegetables, there was more of the sauerkraut. Plus beans. For dessert—what else?—ice cream. Brenda might be subsisting on only sauerkraut and beans, but the rest of them feasted royally.

"So, we start tomorrow right after sunrise," Frank said. "We should be able to get five or more dives in, if we don't find the site right away."

"The ocean in this area is great for diving," Caleb remarked. "Calm, with no strong currents. And it has exceptional viz."

"That will change once we work the wreck. It's inevitable that silt will be raised," Adam contributed.

"Hope the weather holds up," John said. "Nothing like a storm to churn up the waters. Where I come from, the bayous are stained brown, like iced tea, from all the tree bark. Talk about a viz problem!"

"Is that when you wrestle alligators?" Adam teased John.

"Make fun of me. Go ahead. But I *have* wrestled gators, guar-an-teed. Come down and I'll show you."

Adam just rolled his eyes.

"Guess you and I are bunking together," Adam told Caleb. "Do you want top or bottom?"

"Top."

"I saw your duffel bag in there," Adam continued. "Are you a neat freak, or what?"

"What do you mean?"

"I've never seen anyone pack so perfectly. You probably color-coordinate your tighty whities."

"They're all black."

Okaaay!

"I don't wear any," John pronounced with an exaggerated leer at Brenda. He wore a T-shirt that said, "Rap Is Crap."

The boy sure does have a wicked sense of humor.

"Neither do I," her grandfather said, and all heads turned to him.

Eew!

"You are such a liar." Flossie leaned her head playfully on his shoulder.

"You're a liar, too, LeDeux," Adam said to the boy.

"Listen, Yankee, going commando is a fashion statement where I come from."

"You are so full of it," Caleb said, shaking his head at John's nonsense.

"Hey, I've got to have a bunkmate, too." John looked pointedly at Brenda.

"Don't even think it, boy." Brenda smacked him on the side of the head as she refilled his water glass. "Even if I was a cradle robber, which I'm not, I've had it up to my eyeballs with egomaniacs."

"I'm insulted," John said with a grin.

"Unless . . ." Brenda tapped her chin thoughtfully.

Everyone waited to hear what she would say next.

"I don't suppose you own a suit."

"Mais, oui!" the Cajun boy replied. "And I look mighty fine in it, too."

"We've got a date, then," Brenda said. "June fifteenth. My high school reunion. Maybe you could tell everyone you're still a stripper. That would sure impress my ex-husband—that, along with your age. He'll be all worried that someone might outdo him in the sack, not that it would take much. Have I mentioned that Lance Caslow has a small dick?"

Everyone's jaws dropped at Brenda's crudity, except Frank, who took the opportunity to tell a joke. "How are a cobra and a small dick the same?" When several of them only groaned, he answered himself: "No one wants to fuck with either of them. Ha, ha, ha!"

Dirty jokes from my grandfather! I think I'll go kill myself.

"I don't get it," Flossie said.

"Never mind, sweetie, I'll explain later. When we're alone." Frank gave Flossie a big kiss on the mouth, then a big wink that promised more than an explanation of a joke.

Eeew!

"So, you'll go to the reunion with me?" Brenda said to John. "And you'll dress nice . . . and behave yourself . . . and act like you think I'm hot stuff?"

This is a disaster in the making.

"Whatever you want, *chère,*" he said, reaching to put his hand around her waist.

She slapped his hand away.

"Man, there is nothing sexier than a woman on the make," John proclaimed to the other men at the table, his dark eyes dancing mischievously.

"Dream on, boy," Brenda said.

"Does that mean we're not bunkmates?"

"You could say that."

"Will it be okay if I ask your ex-husband for an autograph?"

Brenda snorted her disgust. "Do that, and I'll cut your balls off and feed them to those alligators you keep bragging about."

"I think she likes me," he confided in a loud whisper to the others at the table.

"You can't be that dumb," Frank said. "Nobody is."

"Well, actually," Adam said, his lips twitching with fun, "he's a Southerner. So, maybe . . . Did you hear about the Southern boy who was asked to spell *Mississippi?* He said, 'The river or the state?' "

John laughed good-naturedly with the rest of them. "Did you hear about the dumb Northern man? When his girlfriend asked to feel his muscle, he rolled up his sleeve."

"I don't get it," Flossie said.

"Oh, shush!" Frank told her.

"That'll be enough," Brenda proclaimed, standing.

"Oh, sug-ah," John told her in his deep Cajun drawl, "there ain't no such thing as enough."

Amusement flickered in Brenda's green eyes.

At least John had gotten the last word in, as he'd no doubt planned.

To get laid or not to get laid, that is the question. . . .

After dinner, Adam asked her, "Do you want to go up on deck for a breath of air?"

"No!" Frank roared. When Veronica raised her eyebrows at him, he said, "I need your help with . . . something."

Veronica understood the old coot. He honestly believed she and Jake still had a chance.

Later that night, as she lay staring up through the darkness at the ceiling of her small bunk room, where Brenda slept soundly above her, Veronica contemplated the incredible day she had experienced. She hadn't developed a sudden affection for her grandfather, far from it, but she was learning so much from him. And it was a good feeling not to be afraid on the water. She might be about to embark on a relationship with a new man—Adam or Caleb, she wasn't sure. Not once had she thought about her old job and what she would do next week or next month. It was as if she were on a slow-moving roller coaster, chug-chug-chugging to the top of what promised to be a thrilling adventure. This trip was going to change her life; she just sensed that it would. In what way, she didn't know. But her whole body was on high alert, waiting for something important to happen.

In the midst of all this weighty contemplation, a tear slipped through her eye and rolled down her cheek. There was something missing in this picture.

Jake.

Why aren't you here?

I miss you. I know I shouldn't, but I do.

Oh, Jake.

Giving up, Veronica quietly eased herself out of bed, trying not to awaken Brenda. Slipping on a pair of running shorts—she'd been wearing a T-shirt and panties to sleep in—she crept out of their small room and made her way up the steps and out onto the deck. The old Veronica would have needed Peptos and a lot of courage. The new Veronica just plowed ahead.

There was a full moon out over the very still, black water. The only sound was the gentle lap of the waves against the side of the boat. She walked over and leaned her elbows on the gunwale.

Remarkable! She stood here, on a boat, in the middle of the ocean, for heaven's sake, and she didn't feel nauseous or terrified. And she hadn't even taken a Pepto since this afternoon. The aversion to sea air and water had been mostly in her mind, she realized.

Just then, she heard a soft noise and realized she wasn't alone. Caleb sat in one of the two swivel chairs at the back of the boat, which were normally used for fishing. His bare feet were propped up on the rail. He wore only sweatpants, even though it was a little chilly. In fact, she clasped her hands against her upper arms and shivered.

"Hi," she said.

"Hi," he said back, eyeing her scanty attire.

Grabbing a soft beach blanket Flossie must have left after her bout of sunbathing today, she wrapped it around herself, then walked over and sat down in the other chair. "You couldn't sleep either?"

"I rarely sleep much. Three, four hours a night, usually."

"Really?"

"I've never been a long sleeper, but especially in SEALs, we did a lot of short naps—sometimes standing up, with our eyes open. It's become a habit, I guess."

"Why did you leave the SEALs, if you don't mind my asking?"

He didn't immediately answer, and she wondered if her question had been too intrusive. But then he said,

"Burned out, I guess. I got too good at killing, and that started to scare me."

A chill swept over Veronica's body. She'd known that SEALs were America's silent heroes, going into terrorist countries, fighting the wars others pretended were unnecessary. Still, to have a man admit to killing was jarring, to say the least.

"Is there some woman in your life, Caleb?"

She could see that her out-of-the-blue question surprised him. But then he smiled—the man did have a very nice smile—and said, "Not anymore."

She tilted her head in question.

"There was someone . . . once . . . a long time ago, but nothing since has lasted very long. I'm not a good risk for meaningful relationships."

Veronica suspected that the one-time love had something to do with his leaving the Amish and his being shunned. Changing the subject, she said, "You could always go back to being a farmer. That's what Amish do mostly, isn't it?"

He laughed. "I've shoveled more horse manure and milked more cows and plowed more fields than I ever want to. No, I'll never be a farmer."

They sat in companionable silence for a while.

"How about you and Jake? Do you think you'll ever get back together?"

She stiffened at the personal question, then relaxed her shoulders when she admitted to herself that she'd been just as nosy. "I don't think so. No, I know that we won't. Neither of us could go through that again."

"You still love him." It was a statement, not a question.

She sighed. "I'll probably always love him in some

ways, but I—we—can't live together. And he's engaged to someone else . . . I think. But, really, I don't want to talk about Jake."

She sensed his unspoken "Why?"

Because it hurts so bad.

Caleb stared at her for a long moment; then he surprised the spit out of her by saying, "I want to make love with you."

Oh, jeez. Oh, jeez, jeez, jeez! "You don't beat around the bush, do you?" Her voice had a strange wobble to it.

Instead of replying, he extended a hand to her.

She stared at the hand.

I am tempted. I am so freakin' tempted.

But I don't do casual.

Yeah, but maybe it's time to try something different.

But, whoo-boy, making love with this particular guy? I don't know. It's like going from the kiddie dating pool to the Olympic diving event, all in one swoop.

Jake wouldn't hesitate.

That last thought triggered her decision. She dropped the blanket, laced her fingers with his, and let him pull her over; he settled her astride his lap, facing him.

Caleb was a well-built man. Probably had zero body fat. And there was a part of him that was particularly impressive. She shifted to confirm that fact.

He jerked against her, then framed her face with his hands, pulling her down for a kiss. As kisses went, it was great. Slow at first. Urging. Then hungry. Then his hands slipped under her T-shirt and weighed her breasts in both hands, thumbing her nipples into sharp points.

He was aroused.

She was aroused.

And it just didn't feel right. That fact was emphasized by the quiet tears that slipped from her eyes.

"Hey, sweetheart," he said, pulling back and wiping away the moisture with his fingers. "What's the matter?"

"I'm not ready for this."

He looked as if he wanted to change her mind, but then he kissed her lightly and set her back on her feet. "I understand. Maybe some other time?"

She nodded, started to walk off, then turned back. "I don't usually do this kind of thing."

He quirked a brow.

"You know . . ." She waved a hand at the chair they'd been sitting on.

He still didn't seem to understand. "Do you mean impulse fucking?"

Okaaay! With a weak laugh, she said, "Not quite the words I would have used, but, yes."

She went back to her bunk. Alone.

It was a long time before she fell asleep.

Chapter
13
THE COWBOY WEDDING

Nine years and three months ago . . .

She was in Aruba for a vacation.

Her marriage had lasted three years. It had been nine months since the divorce.

Jake showed up wearing a cowboy hat, cowboy boots, and a dimpled grin that said "I dare you." Why that attire? Some kind of themed poker tournament, of all things.

They decided to have a drink for old time's sake. Her first mistake.

Jake happened to mention he was studying tantric sex.

There was a wedding chapel across the highway from her hotel, flashing a neon sign that said, "Quick Weddings."

Cowboy and sex.

Enough said!

Suffice it to say that she and Jake ended up in her hotel suite a few hours later, married again.

They were sitting on the floor in the lotus position, facing each other. Naked, except for the cowboy hat Jake wore at her insistence. And her grandmother's pearls, which she wore at his insistence.

Yippee-kay-ay-aye . . . and then some!

"Stop giggling," Jake told her. *"You're supposed to take this seriously."*

Hard to do when your you-know-what is pointing at me. *"And the point of all this is . . . what?"*

"To prolong ejaculation so the woman can have unending orgasms."

"I like the sound of that. But poor you!"

"No, it's great, or it's supposed to be. No-penetration sex."

"You've got to be kidding," she said, then homed in on one word he'd used. *"Supposed to be great. Don't you know for sure?"*

He waggled his eyebrows at her. *"You're the first woman I've been able to talk into this crap."*

"You!" She launched herself at him, but he caught her in his arms and rolled them both over so that she lay on top of him.

"So, lady," he said then, *"did you come to my ranch to ride, or what?"*

"I didn't bring my saddle."

"No problem. I can show you how to ride bareback . . . uh, I mean, bare-assed." He walked his fingers up her leg, bringing long-dormant nerve endings to life, like flowers after a spring rain.

She smiled at her fancifulness.

He smiled back at her.

As his eyes roamed her body, something pulled deeply inside.

Jake jackknifed into a sitting position with her still straddling his lap. He held her tight, as though he never wanted to let her go. "I missed you so much!" he said against her neck.

"You broke my heart," she told him, holding on just as tightly to him. "Don't leave again."

"I love you, I love you, I love you," she said over and over. Or was it him?

All she knew was, frozen places were melting in both of them. They would make it work this time. They would.

Chapter

Aliens invaded his brain ... or God's big toe ...

Jake was having the time of his life. Not!

The first day was a blast. The wind in his hair, good vibrations under his butt, just like he'd predicted at the beginning of this road trip. And freedom. Precious freedom. Not to mention good friends on either side of him, tooling down the highway.

No lingering regrets over Trish. No yearnings for Ronnie. He was his own man. He didn't need no stinkin' relationships.

That mood lasted about half a day.

Then they passed through the Poconos, and he recalled the time he and Ronnie had gone camping. She'd lost her panties to a wily squirrel, and he'd lost his cool over what she'd done to him with s'mores.

He and Angel and Grace stayed in a motel on the Ohio border that first night. As he lay on the lumpy mattress, his arms folded under his neck, he was reminded of the first apartment he and Ronnie had rented. The box springs under the lumpy mattress made so much noise when they made love that a tenant downstairs complained to the landlord: "They're like a bunch of fuckin' rabbits up there." They'd put the mattress on the floor after that.

The next day, the three biker musketeers, the self-proclaimed holy trinity of poker idols, decided to make a detour to Louisiana before heading to Las Vegas. *Some detour!* They ended up in Nashville. And, no offense to Elvis, but all Jake heard was country music I-Can't-Live-with-You, I-Can't-Live-without-You love songs. *Yep! That about sums it up for me.* Grace tried to talk him into a visit to Graceland, which he politely declined. Before he fell asleep that night, music floated up from the bar downstairs. Ronnie wasn't a huge country music fan, but she did like some of it, and the Patsy Kline classic "Cryin'" was one of her favorites. *Which is precisely what I feel like doing.*

For lunch the next day, in Mississippi, he ordered a black and blue burger. And he wasn't even thinking that it was the way Ronnie liked her meat cooked. *Hah!*

They hit New Orleans on the fourth day, which just happened to be the site of his fourth wedding—the Insanity Marriage. *I need this reminder like I need another couple of weddings under my belt. Shit!*

They were now on their second day in the Big Easy. The gambling was good in the steamboat casino. The food melted in their mouths—piles of spicy crawfish, oyster po'boys, gumbo, jambalaya, and sweet pralines. The rowdy Cajun music put a smile on everyone's face, and the French Quarter jazz was out of this world.

So why am I so miserable?

"Why are you so miserable?" the seemingly clairvoyant Angel asked him. They were eating breakfast on the terrace of their French Quarter hotel, crawfish and eggs, of all things, seasoned with Cajun lightning, or Tabasco sauce. The young waitress was doing everything but stand on her head to get Angel's attention; he did have a way of attracting everything in skirts, especially the young ones who sensed his bad-boy aura—or so Angel kept telling them ad nauseam.

"I'm not miserable," he lied.

"You are the most piss-poor liar in the world." Angel laughed.

Grace laughed, too, then put a hand on Jake's forearm. "What's the matter, Jake?"

He thought about telling them to mind their own business. He wasn't about to open a vein for them. But then he decided, *These are my friends. They care.*

"Something strange is happening to me. I'm in the middle of some kind of emotional fallout," he admitted. "Maybe I'm going crazy. Maybe aliens have invaded my body."

Angel and Grace looked at each other. They must have been discussing him.

"This is about Ronnie, right?" Angel tipped his chair back against the hotel wall and sipped at a cup of thick Creole coffee. The gloating expression on his face made Jake want to kick the leg of Angel's chair and land him on his laughing ass.

"What else!" he replied with self-disgust. "Though why, after two years of not seeing her and my getting engaged to another woman, it should hit me again . . ." He shrugged. "I just don't friggin' understand it."

"God is giving you a nudge with his big toe," Grace diagnosed.

"Say what?"

"God has plans for you. I've told you all along that Ronnie is your wife, despite all the divorces. God's getting tired of the way you keep mangling things. So, he's giving you a push."

Jake's mouth dropped open with shock. Yeah, she had been a nun at one time, but she had to be kidding about this religious bunk. "So, that's your story?"

"And I'm sticking to it."

"You should listen to her," Angel said. "She has an in with the Big Guy."

"I do not," Grace protested. "Some things are just obvious."

"Not so obvious to me," Jake grumbled. "I can't go through this again. I'm still raw from our last divorce."

"Doesn't that tell you something?" Grace shook her head at his defeatist attitude.

"Ya do what ya gotta do." That was Angel's half-assed advice, which was almost as bad as the God's toe business.

"Listen, Jake, you love Ronnie; she loves you." This from Grace. "That's more than most marriages in trouble have to go on. It's a foundation, for heaven's sake. Build from there." Grace was getting exasperated with him. He was exasperated with himself.

"Easy for you to say."

"No, it's not easy for me to say. I wish I had someone in my life to love me the way you and Ronnie love each other."

Grace was getting riled up, and Angel didn't help matters when he offered, "I'll love you."

"Get a life," Grace said. "Like I'd ever stand in your sex line."

"I beg your pardon." Angel really appeared to be offended.

Jake laughed, glad to have the attention away from him. But that didn't last long.

"I never did understand what keeps breaking you and Ronnie up," Angel said. "Bad sex?"

It was just like Angel to think about sex. The horndog.

"No, sex has always been great with us."

"Holy crap, what's wrong with you two, then? Love and sex, what more do you want?" Angel gazed at him as if he were a peculiar bug under a microscope.

"Angel, sometimes you are a world-class jerk. *Bad sex?*" Grace mimicked. Then she turned to Jake. "Is it the poker?"

"Partly. Correction, it was a big reason with our first marriage. I was doing extreme stuff in the beginning. Putting a second mortgage on the house to fund my gambling, that kind of thing."

Grace and Angel understood. Lots of professional gamblers took foolish risks at first. Angel, for example, lost his auto body shop. Grace did some nutty things while still in the convent.

"Are you addicted? Are you low on cash? Do you even enjoy the game anymore? Do you *need* to gamble . . . for the money, I mean?" Talk about cutting right to the bone! Angel should know better, though.

"This last tournament, on top of my last book deal, put me over the million-dollar mark. I've salted most of it away in safe stocks and won't touch that for gambling—ever. I still have a hundred thou in seed money for poker." He wasn't telling them anything they didn't know. In truth, the three of them had done extremely well the past two years.

"Have you told Ronnie that?" Grace asked.

"No." He'd be damned if he tried to get her back that way. If she didn't want him with all his warts, well, screw her. "Besides, that wasn't our only problem."

"If you offered to give it up—don't look at me like that—would she come back to you?" Grace asked.

"I doubt it. And, dammit, yes, I could walk away. But I don't want to. I think I'll always want to play, at least occasionally."

"There are two sides to every story. What does Ronnie do to contribute to your breakups?" Grace sure was being persistent today.

"She can be so priggish sometimes. She picks fights with me. She thinks poker is worthless, which pretty much means she thinks I'm worthless. Her grandmother gives witches a bad name, which means Ronnie probably has witch genes. Her grandfather is a nutcase, which means she probably has nut genes, too. Other than that, she's perfect."

They both smiled at his portrayal of Ronnie, not believing for one minute that he thought so little of her.

Just then, his cell phone rang. He opened the lid, hoping it wasn't Trish again. She kept calling, and he didn't know what to say to her. But, no, it was a strange number, with a New Jersey area code.

"Jensen here," he said into the phone.

"Jake, is that you?" It was Frank. He must be using someone's cell phone.

"Yeah, it's me. Where are you?"

"Out on *Sweet Jinx*. We started the Pink Project on Monday."

"Out? You mean on the ocean?"

"Where else, dumbbell? Did you think we took the boat to the mall?"

Frank's sarcasm annoyed him, but he put that aside. "Uh, who's there with you?"

"Brenda, Flossie, LeDeux, Peachey, Famosa, and . . ."

Jake held his breath.

"And Ronnie."

"On a boat? Ronnie's out on a boat?"

"Yep. And she's lovin' it."

Jake couldn't believe his ears. Ronnie had this real fear of water. She could swim but preferred not to. And there was her nausea when near water. "Bet she's inhaling Pepto by the gallon."

"She was at first, but now she's okay."

"Really?" That irritated him. Ronnie shouldn't be changing while he wasn't around to see it. Good thing he didn't say that aloud. Even he could see how immature that would sound.

"Listen, the battery on Brenda's satellite phone is runnin' low. I just called to tell you that you better get your ass here pronto. Ronnie's about to make a big mistake."

The fine hairs rose on the back of his neck. "What kind of mistake?"

"Sex."

"Whaaaat?" *Should I ask him? No! Yes! Dammit, how does he always trap me like this?*

"These two guys are sniffing around her, like hounds on a poodle."

"What two guys?" *Like I don't know.*

"Famosa and Peachey. She already had a date with

Famosa, but Peach is the one about to score . . . I think."

Score? Oh, shit! Does he mean . . . What else could he mean? "Uh . . . what exactly do you mean by 'score'?"

Frank said something so crude and graphic that Jake felt his face turn red, and he hardly ever blushed. "How do you know? They're probably just friends."

Frank snorted into the telephone. "I'm old, not dead. Don't you think I can tell when a guy's got sex on his mind? And that Peach, he could give you a run for your money. Flossie says he has a butt you could crack walnuts on, and Brenda says she heard SEALs can last like two hours in the sack."

I do not friggin' believe this. "What do you want me to do?"

"Do you still love her?"

He refused to answer. But he began to finger the worry beads in his pocket.

"This might be your last chance."

The line went dead.

He was clutching those beads so hard he would probably have dents in his palm.

Angel and Grace looked at him with interest.

"Frank says Ronnie is out on a boat in the middle of the ocean, and you know how scared she is of water. Plus, the old fart says Ronnie is about to get it on with some guy who has a butt that could crack walnuts. And he has the staying power of a . . . Navy SEAL."

Both their jaws dropped as they gaped at him. Then they burst out laughing.

"I should probably go back and help her. She's probably terrified, being on the open seas and everything."

They continued to laugh.

"And, really, Ronnie is naive when it comes to men. She needs me to check the guy out."

They weren't buying his motives one bit and went on laughing like hyenas. He thought about throwing his worry beads at them.

"He says this is my last chance."

They stopped laughing.

He left for home that night.

✦

YMCA, YMCA . . .

Three days later, they still hadn't located the exact site. Frank sensed they would soon, and his instincts were always good.

He got up before dawn and checked all the equipment that would be used on board once the divers went down, even though they had been checked and rechecked before. A person couldn't be too careful on a diving operation.

He decided to do his morning push-ups before everyone else awakened. The sun just came over the horizon when he began. A small orange ball against a pale blue palette. Scenes like this convinced him there was a God. "One, two, three . . ."

"Oh, good Lord!" someone shrieked, and he fell flat to the deck like a pancake.

He got up on all fours, clumsily, then managed to sit down, even though his knees and other parts of his body protested. Turning, he saw Ronnie. "What the hell's wrong with you, girl? Now I have to start over."

"Are you crazy?"

"Probably."

"You're exercising with a cigar in your mouth," she pointed out, as if he didn't know.

"It's not lit."

"You're seventy-five years old."

"So?"

"It isn't safe for you to exert yourself that way. Is it?"

"Now you're going to worry about me? Pfff!"

"I just don't want to deal with a dead body here at sea."

"I promise not to die until we get back to Barnegat."

"That is not funny."

"I'll tell you what's funny. You worrying about me. If I didn't know better, I'd think you care."

She snorted.

That snort hurt a bit, so he retorted, "You could use a little exercise yourself. I see some dimples on those thighs of yours."

Ronnie gasped. If there was anything that was universal to women, it was concern about their thighs. Flossie even bought some $200 cellulite cream one time. He'd instinctively gone for the jugular with Ronnie. In truth, she looked fine . . . more than fine. Jake should be here to see her in that gold bathing suit with the black squiggles around the edges. He'd never let her go then.

"You are a nasty old man," she said.

"Yeah."

She dropped down to the floor beside him.

"What are you doing?" he asked suspiciously.

"If you can't beat them, join them."

"Well, that's as clear as fog."

"If you can do push-ups, then so can I. Besides, as you said, I need to work on my cellulite."

So it was that five minutes later, they were still doing push-ups side by side. He had to admire his grand-daughter. She was keeping up with him just fine.

Then Peach came on deck. "Those are sissy push-ups. You're doing them wrong."

He and Ronnie flattened themselves on the deck with a groan. They would have to start over.

"Well, big shot," Ronnie said, "wanna show us how the big boys do push-ups?"

"Sure." He smiled at Ronnie in a way Frank did not like. Not one bit. And did he have to walk around in only a bathing suit, showing off all those muscles? It was indecent for a man to be that fit.

"You need to prop yourself on the toes of your shoes and don't go all the way down. Make your body parallel with the deck when you drop."

They did several of those, and Frank's heart about gave out. Then they changed to another "rotation," this time one-arm push-ups. Peach was yelling, "Push 'em up! Push 'em up! Down! One! Down! Two! Down! Three!" like a badass drill sergeant. That was when Frank said to himself, "Forget this!" and resumed his regular push-ups. Ronnie kept up with Peach as best she could; he was probably doing them easier than he normally would.

Brenda walked up to them then, a coffee cup in her hand. Apparently, coffee was okay on her frickin' fart diet. "Can I lose weight doing those?" she asked Peach. He and Ronnie sat up and took a breather, resting their forearms on their bent knees.

"Sure, but better yet, you'll tone your muscles,

especially if you add sit-ups and butt crunches to your routine. You'll definitely lose inches."

Brenda set her cup on the side and said, "I'm in. I need to look like Pamela Anderson without the boobs in six weeks."

"I wish I had some weights," Peach said. "They're the best for toning and muscle definition. Even ankle weights would be good."

"I wish I had one of those high-velocity fans," Brenda said, as she huffed and puffed during her push-ups.

"There's an air conditioner," Frank pointed out.

"Yeah, but it's not powerful enough. It's hotter than Hades down there when the range and oven are both going full blast."

"Well, if we're talking about wishes, I wish I had a Starbucks double mocha latte with whipped cream. Yeah, I know, Brenda, there are way too many calories in the whipped cream. But it's the best pick-me-up in the world."

Only women could continue to yammer away when they are working up a sweat, Frank thought.

"Coffee isn't good for you," Peach told Ronnie.

Peach, on the other hand, could probably bench press a whale and still keep talking.

"Lots of things aren't good for a person, but they're delicious," Ronnie replied.

Is there some innuendo in what she just said? I hope not. Frank stood and wiped his brow with a forearm. The three of them were going gangbusters. Jake would shit a brick if he could see Ronnie with her rear up in the air like that. And Peach! He glared at Peach, who paid him no attention; he was too busy ogling Ronnie's rear in the air. Flossie was right. You could crack walnuts on his ass. Frank didn't like that one bit. Females tended to be attracted by that kind of crap, and he didn't want Ronnie attracted to anyone but Jake.

All three of them were sweating like hogs by then. He knew for sure that he was out of his league when Peach gasped out that old SEAL motto, "Pain is your friend, ladies. Welcome the pain."

Frank snorted his opinion of that. Pain was a sign that your body couldn't take any more, in his opinion. But what he said, instead, was, "I wish Jake was here."

No one reacted to his wish. Not even Ronnie.

Jake better get here pretty soon.

If he's coming at all.

Maybe he better go find that St. Jude statue that Louise Rivard, LeDeux's great-aunt, had given him and all the other members of the crew. He was starting to panic; things were a little bit hopeless.

What if Ronnie discovered he wasn't poor as a church mouse before Jake got here? Once she was reunited with Jake, he figured she would be too happy to care. But if Jake didn't show up first . . . whoo-boy!

St. Jude, are you up there?

✦

Making my way back to you, babe . . .

Jake flew into Newark that evening.

Angel had agreed to ship his bike back for him. Grace had hugged him and promised to pray for him.

Scary, that, someone praying for him. But, truthfully, he didn't know how Ronnie would react to his coming back. Would she welcome him or tell him to hit the road, for good?

But first things first. He had to go down to Brigantine and break things off for good with Trish. It wasn't fair to her, leaving her hanging in the wind, using her as a backup in case Ronnie gave him the no-go. Easier said than done when he got there. Trish cried. A lot. He felt lower than shark shit, as Frank would say, because he did care about her. Just not enough for a lifetime commitment.

Ronnie was another story altogether. He had no clue why he was here or what he hoped to accomplish; he just knew that he had to try . . . something. It was a bit like flying into the mist, letting happen what happened. Putting himself in fate's hands—or God's. *Grace must be rubbing off on me.*

But that was all behind him now. He drove into the parking lot of the Barnegat wharf where Frank had his warehouse. He didn't know what he was going to do next since *Sweet Jinx* was presumably still out to sea, but it seemed like a good starting place.

Right away, he noticed Anthony Menotti lounging against one of the piers, standing guard, he supposed, though there wasn't much to guard. His brother was probably out on the boat.

He walked over. "Hey, Tony. You heard anything from the boat today?"

He nodded. "They still haven't found the site. Maybe later today."

"Any chance you know where they are?"

He gave him a look that pretty much said he was a dunce if he thought otherwise.

"What say we ride out and see what's happening?"

Tony didn't immediately say that it would be impossible, which led Jake to think they could, if he did a good enough job convincing his Mafia friend. "Why?"

Think quick, buddy. Think. "You could relieve your brother. I could pick up some fresh food supplies; they must be dying for fruit and a good steak, rather than fish. And, dammit, I need to see my wife . . . my ex-wife."

Grinning at the last, only honest explanation Jake had given, Tony pointed out, "Frank is obsessive about keeping the site secret. He thinks other wreck divers would sniff out his site and steal the treasure."

Jake reluctantly agreed that was a possibility. But then he thought of something. "I'll bet you could lose a car chasing you, right?"

"Right."

"There you go!"

"What does that have to do with . . . oh, I see. You're challenging me to a boat chase, if necessary, to get us out there?"

"Bingo!"

Rubbing his chin thoughtfully, he looked at Jake, then out to the watery horizon, then back at Jake. "I'll do it, but not for any reasons you mentioned."

"Oh?"

"I'm bored out of my skin here. It's so bad I've been thinking about buying a paint-by-number set."

Humor from the morbid mob brother? Amazing! "You go hire a boat. I'll go to the store," Jake suggested. "But be careful who you rent from. They might pass the word to one of Frank's pirates."

"I'll just buy a boat. Meet me here in an hour."

Just buy a boat? And have it ready to go in an hour?

Okaaay! I do not want to know how that's going to happen.

Just then, a taxi drove into the parking lot, and who climbed out but Louise Rivard, that young buck John LeDeux's great-aunt. The one he'd met at Frank's luncheon two weeks ago. The one who mistook Ronnie for a hooker and him for a stripper.

He smiled widely. "Hey, Ms. Rivard, what are you doing here?"

"You kin call me Tante Lulu. Everyone does. I decided to be a treasure hunter. Been a landlubber too long. Time fer a change," she explained while the cabdriver, clearly overwrought—who wouldn't be after a considerable time in the dingbat's company?—took her bags out of the car; there were a lot of them.

"Treasure hunter, huh?" He grinned because, yep, over the blonde shaggy haircut, she wore an Indiana Jones–style hat. Plus, she had on a suit that came right out of a Banana Republic catalog and leather boots that probably came from the kids' department at Wal-Mart. She also had an ammunition belt crisscrossed over her nonexistent bosom. He hoped to God they were blanks.

"Does your nephew know you're here?" he asked.

"Nope. It's gonna be a surprise."

Oh, yeah! Jake smiled with anticipation.

"Are you nuts?" Tony had the misfortune to ask her.

"Listen heah, young man. I doan know what flew up yer chimney, but I ain't in the grave yet, and if I wanna be a trapeze artist or hula dancer or treasure hunter, thass my bizness. Now, how do we get out to that boat?"

Her use of the word *we* resonated in the air.

"Is that a gun yer wearin' under that shirt?" she asked Tony, blinking with surprise.

"What of it?"

She put her hands up in surrender. "Hey, I gots no problem with a man protectin' hisself, or a woman. In fact, you kin borrow some of my bullets iffen you wants to."

Tony's eyes about bugged out at that suggestion.

"I gots jambalaya in the cooler, and I doan want it to spoil. Cripes, what a time I had talkin' the airline into bringin' it on the plane! You boys wanna share my sunblock? It's a special mix I made up with crawfish fat and gator poop. Ha, ha, ha. Jist kiddin' 'bout the poop. It's crawfish fat and mashed aloe. I'm a *traiteur,* you know—thass a healer—so I know 'bout potions and such. Holy sacralait! It's gonna be hot out there on the ocean. Do ya think we'll see any sharks? I hope so. I ain't never seen a shark before. Plenty of alligators, but no sharks. Well, what are you standin' there for? Dawdlin' doan make the gumbo boil."

Tony looked at him, and he looked at Tony. Then they both smiled. Trying to talk to this ding-a-ling was like trying to nail mashed potatoes to the wall. But it appeared that he and a member of the mob were about to go out to sea with the world's oldest, and no doubt only, midget explorer.

Did life get any better than this, or what?

Chapter
15

He was a knight in shining bass boat . . .

They had already completed two dives today and were about to start another with both John and Adam going down in tandem when they heard the sound of a motor in the distance.

"Oh, shit!" Frank said as the boat came into view. It was one of those big sport-fisherman-type motorboats. "That's all we need. Someone to steal our site."

Veronica had learned that Frank was suspicious of everyone, even the Coast Guard. "They're probably just out fishing," she tried to assure him.

"Maybe it's the news media," Adam offered unwisely. "Maybe that *Asbury Park Press* reporter we saw last week has sniffed us out. Pete Porter, that was his name. He was asking lots of questions."

"Either way, pirates or reporters, it's a disaster," her grandfather remarked dolefully. "But, if it's Porter, I'm personally gonna throw him overboard. He'll be swimmin' with the fishes, for sure." Her grandfather winked at Steve.

Steve did not wink back. Instead, he pulled his gun from its holster and checked the barrel. If the doofus dared to shoot at *anyone,* they would be in big trouble.

They all grew serious as they waited for the boat to get closer. The springtime sun was beating down fiercely. Slathered with sunblock, Veronica wore only a bathing suit. They all did, except for the two divers.

Like everyone else, Brenda had succumbed to the heat, daring anyone to make a remark when she donned a modest two-piece white suit. Frankly, she looked pretty good, despite her concerns about her weight. Veronica could tell that the men thought so, too. Even Steve, who might just toss her over his shoulder and carry her off somewhere to do who-knew-what to her Mafia-style.

Her grandfather, white zinc oxide on his nose, wore red, baggy swimming trunks and had white suspender marks on his deeply tanned skin, accentuated by wild gray chest hairs matching the mop on top of his head. He made a fashion statement all his own. Not a GQ one. More like Wild Old Buccaneer Looney Bird.

Flossie was all spiffied up with full makeup; a blue floral, skirted bathing suit with a sheer cover-up; and blue wedgie sandals. Her big hair was so lacquered that it didn't even stir in the breeze. Rhinestone-studded cat sunglasses shaded her eyes.

And, of course, there was Steve-o in his Speedo.

But that was neither here nor there. The boat was getting closer.

John put a pair of binoculars to his eyes and said,

"*Dieu!* I should have known. I really, really should have known." He exhaled with disgust, then handed the binoculars to Steve. "Great!" Steve smiled. "I was ready for a break. He must have got my message that Brenda was running out of sauerkraut and that Flossie wished for some Purple Passion nail polish."

Frank glowered at Steve, who might or might not be kidding, and took the binoculars next. He didn't say anything. He just did a little Snoopy dance around the deck and went over to put a polka on the CD player. She thought she'd hidden all the polka CDs, but he must have a backup stash.

Caleb looked next and muttered a foul word under his breath.

Finally, it was Veronica's turn. "He wouldn't!" she exclaimed.

"Yes, he would," her grandfather said gleefully behind her.

It was Jake standing at the front of a huge powerboat, the kind usually seen on ESPN Outdoors engaged in big fish tournaments, marlin or bass or something, she told herself with hysterical irrelevance. He wore a black baseball cap, a black T-shirt, black sunglasses, and black jeans.

Just like a cat burglar. Where that idea came from, she had no clue, except he was in a boat driven by Anthony Menotti, who certainly must have engaged in a burglary or two.

"Why now?" she asked herself.

But her grandfather heard. "Better late than never."

She turned abruptly and speared him with a glare. "Did you have something to do with Jake being here?"

"Yes. No."

She put her hands on her hips. "Which is it?"

"I kinda kept asking him to come. But that's not why he's here. You're the reason he's here."

"I think it's sweet," Flossie said. "It's like a knight in shining armor comes to save his lady fair." Everyone turned to gape at Flossie, who raised her chin and said, "It's true."

Caleb repeated the same expletive he'd used on first recognizing the riders in the boat.

Is he jealous? Why? All we shared was a kiss. Hah! That was more than a kiss, and we both know it.

"Except that her knight is riding a bass boat, and the only thing he's saving her from is getting boinked by Peach." That was Brenda's witty opinion.

Veronica gasped. "Brenda!"

Caleb flinched at Brenda's insight.

Adam said to Caleb, "Hey! Have you been hustling my girl behind my back? You scuzzball!"

"She's not your girl," Caleb defended himself.

"I am not your girl," Veronica said at the same time.

Brenda was laughing so hard she bent over at the waist.

Unhappy with all of them, Veronica turned back to the water. Tony was putting some ropes around an air conditioner and big fan, which John and Adam proceeded to pull up to *Sweet Jinx*. After that, a set of dumbbells and weights were sent up. Then, Tony sent up a white cooler and some boxes of groceries. In the cooler she saw a plastic container of food and a cool Starbucks coffee.

Oh, my God! I wished for a Starbucks double mocha latte with whipped cream, and here it is, even if the cream is a bit flat. And Brenda wished for the air con-

ditioner and fan. And Caleb said he wished for some weights to help Brenda with her exercises. And my grandfather, the louse, wished for Jake. These Mafia guys were either telepathic or wish fairies.

It was then that she noticed the third rider on the boat. A small person. She squinted to see better. Yes, it was a small person . . . wearing an Indiana Jones–type hat. *Good grief!* It was Louise Rivard, John's great-aunt, the one she'd met in that Atlantic City casino.

She looked at John.

"What can I say? Tante Lulu is her own person."

"Did you invite her?" Frank asked John, not appearing overly concerned.

"Mercy, no! She probably came to check up on me. To see if I'm doing something naughty." He said *naughty* as if it were something delicious.

Brenda laughed. "Does she think you're out here on the boat stripping?"

"Tsk-tsk-tsk! Stripping isn't the only naughty thing I do," he told Brenda. "Want me to tell you about my other naughty doings?"

"Get a life!" Brenda told him.

Everyone scrambled then to make sure the boat was secured to *Sweet Jinx* to prevent it from drifting away. But Veronica just stood in place.

My life isn't screwed up enough; now I have Jake to screw me up even more.

Aren't you even a little bit glad to see him? a perverse part of her brain asked.

Veronica didn't even have to answer herself. Her rapidly beating heart and heated blood did all the talking.

You could say she was a bayou Ann
Landers. . . .

Could a man go from sane to insane in one hour?

That was the question Jake soon pondered. And the
cause of his insanity? A constantly talking, outrageous,
interfering midget of a woman who claimed she was
sent by St. Jude to help them all because they were so
hopeless.

Tony went off to buy a boat, leaving him with the
Cajun dingbat. *Smart guy!* During that one-hour wait
till Tony came back, Jake had had the pleasure of Tante
Lulu's sage advice all to himself.

"Whaddaya mean, you ain't been to confession in five
years? I knew there was a reason St. Jude sent me. I jist
knew it. And doan you be tryin' to tell me you ain't sinned
in all that time. I know what men like you are up to. I
wasn't born under a dummy rock, you know. Well, not to
worry, we'll get you back to the church once we come
back from treasure huntin'. Meanwhile, you could make
yer confession to me, iffen you wants."

He didn't *want,* he told her.

Then she'd started in on his poker playing. "Are you
an attic?"

"Huh?"

"Are you an attic? Caint ya hear, boy? A gambling
attic. You know, like a dope attic or a sex attic. I heard
'bout those sex attics on *Jerry Springer.* Didya know
some peoples gotta have sex like twenty times a day?
The mens mus' have sore wee-wees. And the women . . .
whew, betcha it hurts when they pee."

Jake's jaw dropped for about the tenth time by then.
"No, I am not an addict," he'd said finally.

Tante Lulu wasn't buying that one bit. "They hold AA meetings at Our Lady of the Bayou church every other Monday, before bingo. I could introduce you to Father Bernard, iffen you wants."

He didn't *want,* he told her again.

After that, it was all downhill. "How come you and Ronnie keeps gettin' divorced? I never did hold with divorce myself, 'ceptin' where a man beats up on his woman, or she's doin' the hanky-panky with every man in sight. Or if he's a mean drunk, which that rotten Valcour LeDeux is. He was my dead niece's husband, bless her soul, John's papa. I know it's a sin to hate anyone, but I do hate that man. So? Answer my question."

He hadn't had a clue what her question was by then. But that didn't stop her from continuing.

"People today think marriage is disposable, like diapers or tissues. They doan wait around long enough to make it work. What you two needs is to be locked up somewhere for a few weeks. Then you'd work yer problems out, guaranteed. Naked. Yep, you should be locked up naked. Works every time."

He wasn't about to ask how she would know that.

"Do you have a hope chest?" she asked out of the blue.

"A what chest?"

"Hope, boy, hope. You deaf or sumpin'?"

He rolled his eyes and bit his bottom lip to restrain himself from saying something foul. Or giving a woman the age of Moses the finger. "What's a hope chest?" he asked with as much politeness as he could muster, which wasn't much.

"Usually it's young girls what gets hope chests.

From the time they's fourteen or so, they starts to collect things they'll need once they get married. Like towels and bed linens and doilies and such."

Luckily, I'm not fourteen or a girl. And doilies are not quite my style, lady.

"But I gives them to my nephews, too. Soz they can get started on the way to happy marriages."

Jake had a sneaky suspicion where this was headed.

"Yep, I'm thinkin' you need a hope chest to get yer next marriage on the right track. I'll get you one after I get back home. I have 'em made special by a carpenter in Lafayette."

"Lucky me!"

"Doan give me any of yer sass, boy. Ain't my fault you made a mess of yer life. But not to worry, I'm here to help you get it back on track."

That's what I'm afraid of.

Fortunately, Tony returned then with one of those big-ass sport fishing boats that kazillionaires bought for a couple hundred grand to go out and catch fifty dollars' worth of fish. He'd probably paid cash for the thing . . . unless it had fallen off a truck. *Ha, ha, ha! Yep, loony bin, here I come.* Another strange thing. Tony brought with him an air conditioner, a high-velocity fan, and a Starbucks coffee with whipped cream that he stashed in the cooler. But strangest of all, he carried a full set of dumbbells and weights onto the boat.

Tante Lulu immediately started in on Tony. Even over the roar of the motor as the boat danced over the waves, he could hear her yammering on and on.

"Are you Eye-tal-yan? I makes a real good chicken cacciatore. And ravioli. 'Course I spice it up with Cajun herbs and use andouille, thass Cajun sausage, instead of ground beef. Didja ever make Eye-tal-yan jambalaya? Yum!"

At first, Tony just ignored her, but the lady had a way of working her way under your skin till you had to respond.

"Are you in the mob?"

"Everyone thinks all Italians are in the Mafia. Those are just rumors," Tony remarked.

"Hah! I know about rumors, 'specially those on the bayou grapevine. Rumors multiply quicker 'n jackrabbits on Jack Daniels."

Tony was surely regretting having actually spoken to the woman, but it didn't matter, really, because she just kept blathering.

"I nabbed some of the Dixie Mafia one time. They was stealin' gold and hiding' it in the bayou. Well, I dint catch 'em all by myself, but I helped. Do you know any of the Dixie Mafia? I had a neighbor down the bayou named Georgio Pioli. Everyone thought he was in the Mafia, but turns out he was jist a gay hairdresser who shortened his last name from Pissomme 'cause you kin imagine why."

Tony looked as if he'd like to bury her in some bayou.

"You ever killed anyone? When? How? How many? Did ya ever put a horse's head in anyone's sheets? Ever meet Marlon Brando? How 'bout Frank Sinatra? Now, there was a man to make a woman's belly button melt. I even shaved my legs when I went to one of his concerts back in 1965 ... jist in case, ya know what I mean? It's not polite to ignore an old woman. By the way, did I give you a St. Jude statue yet?"

Jake thought he heard Tony groan, but he might be mistaken. It could be the motor.

"When was the last time you went to confession?"

This time Tony's groan was loud and clear. "You want to take over the wheel?" he yelled to Jake.

"Not a chance!" Jake yelled back, even when Tony's eyes pleaded with him. Jake pretended not to notice. *Better him than me.*

"You got a hope chest?" Tante Lulu asked Tony then.

Jake couldn't help but let out a hoot of laughter at the old bat's good-hearted lunacy.

Now they were approaching *Sweet Jinx,* which was anchored up ahead. As they got closer, he saw everyone lined up along the rail. His heart hammered against his chest as he tried to pick out Ronnie. Nothing unusual there. Even after more than a decade, it was his standard reaction. That, and a hard-on.

There were two guys in diving suits, Famosa and LeDeux. Frank and Flossie were waving wildly at him. At least someone was glad to see him. Then there was Brenda, who was talking to Steve.

And—son of a bitch!—was that Ronnie in a gold bathing suit, with her hair piled atop her head in a pigtail, like one of those Pixie dolls, and with all that bare skin sporting a nice, healthy tan? He started to smile, then stopped. Peachey stood next to her, an arm on her shoulder—all six-foot-four of him with his twelve-pack abs and Popeye muscular arms. *Show-off!*

Frank had been right. Ronnie was about to make a big mistake. Well, he was here now. He would set her on the right course.

He hoped.

That funny voice in his head was laughing.

Or maybe it was Tante Lulu, standing next to him. She shoved something into his hand. "Here, honey. I think yer gonna need this."

It was another one of those plastic St. Jude's statues. He was about to tell her that she'd already given him one when she was here last, but then he decided a double dose of St. Jude might be a good idea, in case hopelessness entered the picture.

Once the boat was secured, he and Tony climbed up the rope ladder after Tante Lulu, who almost fell trying to carry her purse, which was so big she could hide a pig in there; knowing her, maybe she had.

After vaulting over the rail, Jake shook hands with Frank.

"Ahoy, matey," he joked.

"Welcome aboard, you scurvy dog," Frank joked back.

"Hey, all this pirate lingo makes me think we should be belting out some sea chanties," LeDeux said. "Like, 'Hey, ho, blow the man.'"

"You, idiot!" Famosa shook his head at LeDeux. "It's supposed to be, 'Hey, ho, blow the man *down*.'"

LeDeux tapped his chin thoughtfully, then grinned. "I like my version better."

Enough of this nonsense! Jake headed for Ronnie, who was glaring at him. Not a good sign. "Hey, baby," he greeted her. "Nice bathing suit."

"Shut up," she said.

Whoa! That's a little extreme, dontcha think? What he said was, "Aye, aye, cap'n."

She looked like she might like to see him walk the plank or swab decks indefinitely. For sure, he didn't think she would be hoisting any tankards with him anytime soon.

"Am I sensing a little hostility here?" he asked.

"If I had a gun, I'd probably shoot you."

Steve said, "Uh, I can—"

"Don't even think it," Ronnie said quickly, shooting daggers at Steve. Then she turned and was about to stomp away from Jake. That's when he got a view of the back of her suit. First of all, the whole one-piece suit was made of some shiny gold material with black squiggles along the edges—not Ronnie's style at all. The front was fairly conservative, except for being cut high on the hips, making her long legs seem even longer. It was the back that made him almost swallow his tongue. It was cut so low that the top of her buttocks were almost exposed. He raised his sunglasses on his head to get a better look.

What is going on here? Unfortunately, he made the mistake of speaking his thoughts aloud. "What's going on here?"

She spun on her heels and caught him ogling her butt.

It had been his experience that women did not like men to stare at their butts, and Ronnie was no exception. Not that women didn't wear clothes to accentuate said butts, but he was no fool. He wasn't about to mention that female illogic, not in her present mood.

"What are you doing here?" she demanded.

Hello to you, too, darling. "Come to work on the Pink Project."

"You're a little bit late, aren't you?"

He shrugged.

"Does Frank have something to do with this?"

"No," he lied.

"You liar!"

"Just a little bit."

She put her hands on her hips, waiting. Which called attention to her bathing suit. "Jesus, Mary, and Joseph! Call me crazy, but are those sperm?"

"What?"

"Those black squiggles on your suit look like sperm. Yep, sperm chasing each other's tails."

She glanced down at her chest to check out the decoration on the neckline. Then her nicely tanned face turned beet red. "You moron! Only you would think something like that."

"I thought it, too," her grandfather piped in, then had the good sense to let Flossie lead him away.

"What does Frank have to do with your being here?"

He shifted from foot to foot. This was not turning out like he'd expected. Yeah, he'd anticipated that she'd be a little miffed. But after that, a hug at least would have been nice. "He might have mentioned that you were about to make a big mistake, but that's not why I came. Not really."

"A big mistake?" She frowned with confusion.

Jake's eyes shot to Peachey, who was standing there, way too interested in their conversation. Jake glowered at the jerk, but did he get the hint and take a hike? Nope.

"You are a real piece of work," she said, coming up to him and wagging a finger in his face. The wagging finger was a sure sign she was about to go on a tear. "You don't want me, but you don't want anyone else to have me."

"No, no, no! That is so not true." Jake noticed everyone standing around listening to them. So, he took her by the hand. "Let's talk in private." He proceeded to pull her toward the other end of the boat, but she balked.

Peachey stepped forward and said, "The lady doesn't appear willing."

Mr. Amish SEAL is challenging me? "Stay out of this. It's none of your business."

"I'm making it my business."

Okay, the guy is probably a little more physically fit than I am. Okay, a lot more. Okay, he could probably beat me to a pulp, or crush me by sitting on my chest with that walnut-cracker ass. Navy SEALs know secret ways to kill people, don't they? But I can't just stand here. I have to stand up for my woman. He thought about saying, "You want a piece of me?" but settled for, "I. Don't. Think. So," through gritted teeth.

"Stop it! Stop it, both of you!" Ronnie shouted. To Peachey, she added, "I'll talk to you later." To Jake, she said, "Come with me."

Jake gave Peachey a gloating look, but Ronnie spoiled the effect by kicking him in the shin with her sandals, which hurt . . . a little.

When they were somewhat out of sight, Ronnie turned and confronted him. "Why are you here? I thought you were off somewhere gambling."

Jake winced at the sneer that accompanied *gambling,* but then that was nothing new. "I reached a point where I had to ask myself, Do I want to slit my wrists or jump off a cliff?" When that didn't bring even a crack in her evil glower, he went on. "Life is like a poker game . . . ," he began.

She put her face in her hand for a moment. Ronnie never did appreciate his poker metaphors.

"Life is like a poker game," he barreled on nonetheless.

"As long as the river card is still in the deck, there is always hope."

"Oh, Jake! I gave up hoping a long time ago."

"Listen, Frank told me how great you've been doing out here on the water. No seasickness. No fear of drowning. If you can change, so can I."

"It's not the same thing."

He couldn't let her go without a fight. He just couldn't. "I've been miserable." He stepped forward, reaching for her. "I want to kiss you so bad, my lips ache."

She jumped back, putting some distance between them. He knew without a doubt that if he kissed her, the game would be over. He and Ronnie had a chemistry that defied logic and description. By stepping back, she was making sure they couldn't touch.

"I'm always miserable when I'm not with you, but this time it's worse than it's ever been."

"Couldn't have been too bad. You managed to have sex with, live with, and get engaged to another woman during that time."

She has a point there. "I was kidding myself. I think it was my lame effort to get over you once and for all. It didn't work."

"And Trish?"

"I broke it off with Trish—for good. None of this ring-on-the-right-finger bullshit, either."

Not even a hint of a smile.

"I told her yesterday. There's no turning back. Please, honey, I am so fucking lonely without you."

"I've heard that song before," she said.

"So have I," he reminded her gently. He couldn't resist then; he reached up to tweak her cute top-of-the-head ponytail.

She slapped his hand away. "Don't you dare give me that look."

"What look?"

"You know exactly what look. You have it down pat. The I-love-you-so-much-baby-I-can't-live-without-you-let's-go-have-makeup-sex look."

Which made her glare even more.

"I love you," he said, as if that said it all, which it did, but it wasn't cracking any . . . walnuts . . . with Ronnie.

"What's different now than the other four times?"

I shoulda had a plan. I shoulda thought this out more. Ronnie always wants to have details. Think, buddy, think. And make it good. He stuck a hand in his shorts' right pocket and fingered his worry beads.

Her eyes shot to his pocket. She knew exactly what he was doing. The witch.

"Okay, here's the deal," he started, gulping a few times. "I'm staying this time. No running when you jerk my chain. No running when I feel the walls crowding me in. No running when it seems like our marriage doesn't have a shot in hell. No running when your grandmother bitch-slaps me, figuratively speaking. No running when you tell me you hate poker. No running when you roll your eyes at my Sting CD collection. Tante Lulu told me that people today give up too quickly, and I'm thinkin'—"

"You're taking advice from that woman?"

"She's not so bad." *I can't believe I am defending her. God would be proud of me; no, St. Jude would be proud of me.* "She's gonna get me a hope chest."

That made her jaw drop practically to her sperm-chasing chest.

"And we could study tantric sex together." He waggled his eyebrows at her, trying to lighten the mood.

"Dream on," she said.

"That's an Aerosmith song," he continued to joke. She wasn't buying his humor. "Listen, Ronnie, I'm going to do anything I can to make it work this time. Anything. It may have taken me forever, but I surrender. I can't live without you."

"Anything?"

"Yep." *Practically.*

"Would you give up gambling?"

"Yes." *Probably.*

"And get a real job?"

"Absolutely." *Eventually.*

"And buy a house with a white picket fence?"

"I'll even throw in a dog." *But no picket fence.*

"And babies?"

That stopped him. Ronnie had never yearned for children—at least she hadn't in the past. But she knew how much *he* did not want kids, considering the zoo he'd grown up in—a single child raised on a farm by ex-hippie parents who resembled the Osbournes more than the Cleavers. Vicious arguments had been the norm in their household. They'd been so loud he had sometimes hidden under the bed when a child; then they would be all lovey-dovey afterward. No wonder he always left before Ronnie's arguments with him reached that level. Still, as he had in the past, he told her, "If you want." But then he made the mistake of going too far. "In fact, I think we should have five kids."

"You are weirding me out." She stared at him for a long moment, then laughed. "You are so full of it. Honest to God, you almost had me there."

"I was telling the truth," he protested.

"Stay away from me, Jake. I don't want you within ten feet of me on this boat, and then I want you out of my life when we get off this boat."

That hurt. Bad. "Sorry, honey, but there's no going back for me now. You are my mission."

He heard her mutter something as she walked away. It was either "mission impossible" or "miserable idiot."

Hah! She didn't know about his secret weapon. He fingered the item in his other pocket.

St. Jude.

Chapter
16
THE TEQUILA WEDDING

Blame it on the tequila, baby . . .

Three years had passed since their second ill-fated marriage, which had lasted only two years, and it would soon be the seventh anniversary of their Sappy Wedding. He was in Tijuana for a poker tournament, drowning himself in tequila. Tequila margaritas to be precise. Lots of them.

It was either fate or God playing a practical joke, but, unbeknownst to him, Ronnie was registered at the same hotel for a lawyer's conference. Who knew stiff-necked attorney types did their boring legal stuff in Tijuana, of all places! You'd think they'd go somewhere like Boise or Akron.

Anyhow, he was sitting there, minding his own business, getting pleasantly crocked, when in walked Ronnie with a group of her colleagues. They were all dressed like librarians, even the men, with business suits, no-nonsense shoes, and expressions that pretty much amounted to sucking lemons as they viewed the other lowly occupants of the hotel bar.

Two things happened to Jake at once: his heart squeezed with the pain of their separation, and another part of his body squeezed, then burst into life again.

She took one look at him, then did a double take. She probably groaned then, but he was too poleaxed to notice. All he knew was that, within minutes, she was sitting at his table and, by her third tequila margarita, no longer looking librarianish. In fact, her hair was half in and half out of its bun. She ditched the suit jacket and unbuttoned a few buttons on her silk blouse. The heat, dontcha know. Ha, ha, ha!

He was no better. Somehow, he'd found a sombrero. Better that than a lamp shade, he supposed.

Then, after her fourth tequila margarita—they were having a contest—she got up on the dance floor, by herself, much to the amusement of the small band and the customers, and did her own version of Ricky Martin's "Livin' La Vida Loca." A mighty fine version, he had to admit. When he told her so, she admitted, "I've been taking belly-dancing lessons. That's why I'm so limber."

He choked on his drink, then developed an overwhelming desire to see just how limber she was—up close and personal. Like, naked.

"Why belly dancing?" he asked with a surprisingly casual voice, even though his dick was doing its own belly dance. "I mean, it's not your usual style."

Her head shot up, and her honey-brown eyes glared at him with affront. "My usual style? Do you mean boring?"

He made the mistake of laughing.

"If you must know, I heard that belly dancers have better orgasms." She licked the salt off her lips with the tip of her tongue. She might as well have been licking

his cock for all the effect it had on him. He had to re-strain himself from leaping over the table to help her out with the licking. Luckily, or not so luckily, he con-trolled himself. Otherwise, he would have missed her follow-up. "I'm planning on having lots of those—or-gasms, I mean—with other men." She topped that off by bursting into tears.

The weeping blindsided him. Ronnie was usually so in control of her emotions. She knew exactly what she wanted and how to get it. Even at their divorce hear-ings, one and two, she'd sat there stone-faced while he'd felt like broken glass inside.

He slid his chair around the table and put an arm over her shoulder, pulling her close. She proceeded to wet his skin with her tears. "Ah, Ronnie, don't do that. Please, honey, don't cry."

"I . . . I . . . can't . . . help . . . it," she sputtered. "You make me so mad. It's all your fault."

Isn't that just like a woman? Blame it on the man. *"Why?"*

"I miss you so much."

He shared her emotion. And, dammit, he felt like crying himself.

He knew how this woman looked when she climaxed. He knew how she sometimes snored softly when she slept. He knew she had a mole on her left breast. He knew where her G-spot was and her eight other most erotic spots. He knew she got sick from red wine and drunk on just three glasses of wine. He knew her, period.

And she knew him equally well.

Taking a napkin off the table, he used it to wipe away her tears, all the time murmuring, "Shhh, don't cry. Everything's going to be all right. I promise."

Finally, she settled down and apologized for her outburst. He slid his chair back to his position, opposite her. His heart was thudding madly, just waiting... waiting... waiting. Both of them stared down at the table, too overwhelmed with emotions they had tamped down for one long year.

Finally, Jake raised his head and looked at Ronnie. She looked back at him. Their gazes held for several heart-pounding moments. And they knew in that instant that they were going to kick the marriage bucket a third time.

Two hours later, married again, they could barely keep their hands off each other. In fact, he had dry sex with her against the wall at the back of the wedding chapel, a knee-trembler, for sure. Then, wet sex on the floor of the hotel bathroom. Even wetter sex in the shower. And then—God bless his amazing dick, they ought to have a special spot for it in Ripley's—they had hotter-than-hot wet sex on the bed in the middle of the night.

The best part was when Ronnie moaned and said, "I love you, dammit."

The second best part was when she'd shown him some of her belly-dance moves. Naked.

The third best part... Okay, there were so many best parts, he could hardly name them all.

The next morning, sober again, they blamed it on the tequila. But, personally, Jake thought they just used that as an excuse. They loved each other too fucking much to stay apart forever.

Chapter
17

Welcome to the Crazy Cruise . . .

By the time they sat down to dinner that evening, Jake concluded that this was one hell of a looney-bird party Frank was hosting on his boat.

Ronnie was still so pissed that she wouldn't speak to him. He really would have liked to check her out some more in that sperm-chasing suit, but she'd put a T-shirt over it, probably due to his unfortunate observation. He still couldn't get over the fact that his unflamboyant wife—or ex-wife, if you want to be picky—would have bought a shiny gold, revealing suit like that. She must have turned a leaf, or something. A gold leaf, he joked with himself. *Yep, I fit right in here with the looney birds.*

He tried to decide whether her new leaf was good or bad. *I like it,* he concluded. But then he recalled the way Peachey and Famosa had been ogling her earlier when she bent over to pick up the Starbucks coffee, which Tony had placed on a low deck table. *I sure didn't like it then.*

On the other hand, the T-shirt she'd put on was from a 1998 Sting concert. He'd given it to her. For some reason, that made him feel all warm and fuzzy inside. *Like a looney bird?*

He wanted to ask her how her grandmother was taking her association with Frank, how Frank had talked her into participating in the venture, why she was no longer popping Peptos, and, most of all, if she still loved him. All these questions would have to wait till the smoke stopped coming out her ears.

It had been late afternoon by the time they'd gotten here today. Now, after another unsuccessful dive, the last one of the day, they sat down to dinner. Famosa and Peachey beat him to bench seats on either side of Ronnie in the galley kitchen. He sat opposite her, next to LeDeux, who was assigned to be his bunkmate. *Oh, joy! Not!* Jake had already announced that he would sleep alone up on deck. Maybe Ronnie would sneak up and join him. *Delusional, man, delusional!*

Frank was on his other side, beaming like an idiot. You'd think he would be upset about all the unsuccessful dives so far, but, no, he was happy as a lark because Jake had finally arrived. Frank claimed that Jake would bring them good luck, guaranteed.

To which Ronnie had snickered.

Tante Lulu's arrival was also a good omen, in the world according to Frank, because of her "in" with St. Jude. That remained to be seen, although John had already regaled them with stories of her famous St. Jude "miracles."

The air conditioner and high-velocity fan made the entire below-deck area cool and pleasant, something it apparently hadn't been before their arrival. He wondered how Tony had known to bring them, but then recalled seeing him using his satellite phone.

Everyone was tired after the day of diving, so there was a companionable silence at first. Steve and Tony, ever the loners, chose to stay up on deck and eat some Italian submarines that Tony had brought from a favorite delicatessen.

Then, out of the quiet, Ronnie flashed him a glower and said, "For your information, they're not sperm. They're commas."

Every head in the room swiveled to gawk at her. He had to put a hand over his mouth to stifle a laugh. *Come on, baby, rise to my bait. I'd rather have you screaming at me than ignoring me.* "I'm no fashion expert . . . ," he began.

She guffawed at that.

Someone ought to tell her that guffawing from a woman was not attractive. Maybe he would tell her, later. For now, he resumed his statement. "I'm no fashion expert, but I find it hard to believe that someone would put commas chasing commas on any clothing."

"It's the trademark of that new designer Daphne." Ronnie's face was pink with embarrassment as she realized she'd stepped into a hole of his making.

"Come on, sweetie. That is a streeeetch." He knew he shouldn't push the teasing, but, dammit, it annoyed the hell out of him to see her bracketed by those two homely studs. *Homely, I wish.*

"It's like little alligators on golf shirts." Brenda was showing her friendship colors, coming to Ronnie's defense. "And NASCAR is the worst. They've got so many company emblems on them, it's a wonder they can even walk."

"I never could understand how some wimmen spend hundreds of dollars fer handbags with someone else's name on 'em. 'Specially when you kin buy practically the same thing at Wal-Mart fer twenty bucks." That was good ol' Tante Lulu's opinion, bless her down-to-earth soul.

Flossie's face lit up like lights on a Las Vegas strip. Apparently, this was a subject close to her heart. "I like to go on eBay and buy designer handbags, like Gucci or Coach, and they're only a hundred dollars there."

"eBay again!" Frank exploded. "A hundred dollars!"

Flossie gave him a glare that could cut concrete. "Do. Not. Tell. Me. What. I. Can. Do. With. My. Own. Money." Flossie's tone was pure ice, a bit of an overreaction to Frank's remarks, in Jake's opinion.

Ah! The money issue. Jake had forgotten that Frank's financial problems were the reason Ronnie was even here. Flossie must be grating under their tightened circumstances.

Everyone quieted under the strain of Frank and Flossie's open quarrel.

But then the talking picked up again as Tante Lulu helped Brenda put some large bowls on the table—the jambalaya, which the old lady had brought in a cooler all the way from Louisiana; some beaten biscuits; okra— yeech!—and a green salad. The odd thing was, though, when Brenda sat down, there were two bowls, one of sauerkraut and one of baked beans, in front of her.

Brenda glanced at him, saw his question, and said, "I'm on a diet. I need to lose twenty pounds this month."

"Whoo-boy, let me tell you about her diet . . . ," Frank began with a snort of laughter.

Brenda swatted Frank on the shoulder with a wooden spoon. "Say it again and you are dead meat."

Everyone laughed. Jake figured it must be some private joke.

"I can't believe Charmaine let you come back here, all by yourself," LeDeux said to his great-aunt once she sat down.

"Hah! Charmaine ain't my mother. I kin do whatever I want to, without my niece's permission. Talk about!"

LeDeux gave her a suspicious look. "Does Charmaine know you're here?"

"Mebbe she does, and mebbe she doesn't."

"Tante Lulu!"

"Oh, all right. I left a message on her answering machine . . . once I got here."

"There'll be hell to pay," LeDeux remarked to no one in particular.

Tante Lulu ignored his comment and asked, "What you been up to, Tee-John?"

LeDeux brightened. "I have a date with Brenda. We're going to her high school reunion. She wants to make her ex-husband jealous."

The old lady just nodded, as if that made perfect sense. "Is that why yer eatin' sauerkraut and beans?"

"Yes, I only have twenty-seven days to lose twenty pounds, and, merciful heavens, that jambalaya smells divine."

Tante Lulu continued to nod. "Charmaine was on that diet one time, but had to stop 'cause it gave her too much gas."

"Hah! How come she's allowed to say it and I'm not?" Frank asked.

"She didn't say it quite the way you did, dear."
Flossie patted Frank's hand.

"Anyhow, I gots some herbs that can melt the fat
away," Tante Lulu said. "Put it in yer tea in the morning and before you know it, pfffft!"

The ears of each woman in the room perked up at
that.

"Maybe she'll get some for you," Frank told Flossie.

Even though Flossie had appeared interested in the
herb, she bristled at his mentioning it. "You think I'm
fat," she wailed.

"Huh?" Frank said.

"You think I'm fat and ugly and I hate you." With
that, Flossie tossed her napkin on the table, stood, and
ran out of the room.

Instead of rushing after her, Frank told the rest of
them, "It's the menopause . . . more like mental-pause.
She's got a split personality these days. Sometimes she
reminds me of Bette Davis in *What Ever Happened to
Baby Jane?*"

Good thing Flossie had left. She probably would
have choked Frank if she heard him talking about her
like that.

"I don't suppose you brought some of those herbs
with you," Brenda said to Tante Lulu.

"Sure did. I allus carry herbs with me, jist in case.
Those people at the airport were mighty testy about it,
too."

"Tante Lulu is a famous *traiteur*," LeDeux explained.
"That's a healer. Lots of people in the bayou come to
her before going to a doctor."

"Did she ever give you a hope chest?" Jake asked

LeDeux. *Frank's foot-in-mouth disease must be contagious. Note to self: shut up!*

Ronnie grinned at his discomfort.

"Yeah, but we have a pact to fill it slooooowly. I'm not gonna be ready for marriage for a spell." LeDeux elbowed Jake under Tante Lulu's radar as if they were good buddies. "Did she give you one, too?"

"No, but I'm gonna. That boy needs a hope chest to get his love life back on track." Tante Lulu looked directly at Ronnie when she said that.

Ronnie's face went white. "Whaaat?"

"Usually I gives my family hope chests when I think they's ready for the thunderbolt to hit, even the men."

Way to go, lady!

"The thunderbolt of love," LeDeux interpreted for her.

I love it! Batten down your hatches, sweetheart. My thunderbolt is a comin'.

"But it's clear as a bayou sky that you two already been hit by the thunderbolt so many times it's a wonder you ain't got 'lectricity comin' out yer ears."

Jake grinned. *There is that smoke.*

Peachey and Famosa frowned.

Ronnie made a harrumphing sound, just like her grandmother did sometimes, usually at him, and said, "That was about as clear as a Starbucks cappuccino."

"You mus' be thick or sumpin', bless yer heart. Girl, you look at this boy like he's some kinda eye candy."

"I do not!"

Jake continued to grin. *I am starting to love the old bat.*

"And you," the old bat said, pointing her finger at him. *Uh-oh!*

"You look at her like she's a cone of sweet praline

ice cream you wanna lick up one side and down the other till she melts."

Yep! I couldn'ta said it better myself. Jake winked at Ronnie, whose jaw had dropped practically down to Sting's forehead.

"Speaking of ice cream," Frank said. Ronnie's grandfather always had been an ice cream aficionado. Apparently, that at least hadn't changed.

While everyone, except Brenda, sat eating various flavors of ice cream, Jake told Frank, "I have an idea how you might perfect your computer mapping."

"Really?" Frank put his spoon down and waited for his explanation.

"I brought my laptop with me. I had a three-hour layover in Chicago. While I sat in the airport lounge, I thought of a few new programs that might allow me to overlay your grid with the magnetometer and sonar readings."

"Do tell," Famosa remarked sarcastically.

Condescending snooty prick college professor! I'll show him. "I hit a WAP and downloaded fresh GODAR sets to overlay the GrADS. So I'm thinking if we can collect some virtual biological sludge for the GCMS, we might just be able to sniff out the wreck site. I downloaded some software, and, you know, it isn't intended for this purpose, but it just might work."

"Huh?" Mr. Snooty Prick Professor looked like he'd been poleaxed.

Everyone else just stared at him as if he'd sprouted three heads. Jake loved computers. Sometimes he forgot that not everyone shared his passion, or expertise. Other times, like now, he took immature delight in deliberately putting an asshole in his place.

"Repeat that in normal language," Ronnie advised him with a small smile.

How many times has she said that to me in the past? Starting over, he explained, "I used a wireless access point and downloaded the latest data from the Global Oceanographic Data Archaeology and Rescue project to match up with the Grid Analysis and Display System. Once your divers are down there, it's possible to take some samples near the ocean floor and run them through the gas chromatograph mass spectrometer, where any differentiation in microscopic sea critters and their chemistry that doesn't match up with the climatological conditions could suggest the presence of the wreck, which might not have been noticed before."

"Is he speaking some foreign language?" Tante Lulu asked Flossie.

"Geekspeak." Ronnie sort of smiled again, which he took as a good sign.

"Whatever he said, it sounds great." Turning to the others, Frank added, "Jake is a computer genius."

Peachey and Famosa didn't appear all that impressed, and Ronnie, no longer smiling, still put him in the same category as, oh, let's say, a snake's belly button. Tante Lulu was more interested in the long red fingernails sported by Flossie, who had slipped back into her seat a few moments ago, oblivious to the fact that she'd just thrown a hissy fit.

"By the by, I have some herbs that'll help yer condition," Tante Lulu mentioned.

"Condition?" Flossie accused Frank.

He pretended innocence.

"Oh, doan go gettin' yer knickers in a twist." Tante Lulu patted Flossie on the shoulder.

"Back to that plan of yours, Jake." Frank wisely changed the talk away from menopause. "How 'bout we go up into the wheelhouse where the computers are. Ronnie can show you what we've done so far, and you can explain your ideas to her."

"Whoa! Why do I have to be involved?" his contrary ex-wife protested. "Now that Jake is here, I'm no longer needed to handle the computers. In fact, Steve, or Tony, can take me back to Barnegat."

Jake felt a momentary panic that she would leave before he had a chance to make his moves. Not that he had any specific moves. But he was planning on getting some.

"You're needed, all right, missie," Frank told his granddaughter. "Two sets of eyes are better than one when it comes to treasure hunting. Can't tell you how many times one diver overlooks something another diver sees right off the spot."

God bless Frank's badass version of Cupid!

Ronnie probably would have resisted some more, except Tante Lulu asked, "Where'm I gonna sleep? It's past my bedtime."

Everyone gawked at the old lady because, hello, it was still daylight.

"You can sleep in the same bunk room with Ronnie and Brenda, I suppose," Frank offered. "Ronnie, would you be willing to give up your bunk to Louise, I mean, Tante Lulu? You could put a sleeping bag on the floor."

Jake raised a forefinger in the air. "I have a suggestion."

Ronnie, Famosa, and Peachey all exclaimed, "No!" at the same time.

Methinks she doth protest too much.

On the other hand, methinks I better work on those moves, real quick.

"Hope I doan wake you when I get up." Tante Lulu was addressing Ronnie and Brenda. "I likes to get up afore dawn to do my jumpin' jacks. Kin I use yer music player, Frank? I allus exercise to 'Sweatin' to the Oldies.'"

Frank looked horrified at the prospect of anything other than polka blasting from his CD player.

The rest of them were horrified at the prospect of a woman as old as Tante Lulu doing jumping jacks.

"Tante Lulu has a thing for Richard Simmons," John explained. He pulled her to his side for a quick squeeze, then kissed the top of her head, which only reached his chest. But then, LeDeux turned to Frank and added, "Hey, if we're gonna change the music on occasion, I vote for Cajun. We need a little zydeco to liven things up here." He shimmied his shoulders to demonstrate. "I just happen to have a CD in my bag."

"Hah! Sting all the way."

Ronnie ignored him while everyone yelled out their choice of music.

"Nobody's touching my CD player," Frank said. "You folks can exercise to polkas or whistling for all I care."

"Speaking of exercise," Brenda interjected. "Some of us have been working out on deck right after dawn. Peach has been showing us SEAL exercises. You could join us, Tante Lulu."

"I ain't doin' any jumpin' jacks without Richard." She glared at Frank.

Jake shook his head to clear it. This whole scene had taken on the aura of a slapstick comedy. The Three Stooges and then some.

But then he realized that Peachey was addressing him. "What?"

"I asked what kind of program you're on. You're reasonably fit." He said *reasonably*, but he said it condescendingly.

Well, news flash, bozo, anyone would look pitiful next to Your Royal Rambo. "I run." *Sometimes.*

"Oh, great! I run, too. Maybe we can do a morning run together sometime."

"Sure." *When hell freezes over.*

"I like to do twenty miles to loosen up, but I can shorten it to ten for you."

WHAT? "Oh, don't do me any favors. I can do anything you can do." *Did I really just say that? Shit! I'm acting like a teenager facing off with the school bully.* He noticed the grin on Ronnie's face. She knew exactly what Peachey was doing . . . goading him. And she liked it. "Maybe you could join us on the twenty-mile run, honey."

She nodded her head at him in a touché manner.

"Anyone like to play a game of poker before bedtime?" *Come on, big shot. Welcome to my arena.*

Not surprisingly, Peachey and Famosa begged off. In the end, no one played. By the time he and Frank and Ronnie went over the computer data and new programs, it was eleven. They all turned in.

Because of everything that had happened that day, he was wide awake as he lay on his sleeping bag on deck, under the stars, arms folded under his neck. Good thing the weather was holding. If it rained, he'd be forced to sleep on the galley floor.

What am I doing here? he asked himself.

Taking back my life, he answered himself.

Ronnie asked me how it is different this time.

I'm older, wiser.

That's debatable.

Sometimes a man needs to reassess his life. Mine has been life with Ronnie and life with poker. There's no question which one is more important. Somehow I lost the reality of that.

I'm not buyin' it. And neither will Ronnie. Gotta do better.

But what?

I need some grand gesture. Something so spectacular Ronnie will know I mean it this time.

He thought for a long while. Staring up at the stars, he wondered if there really was a God up there, or St. Jude. He wondered how he could have screwed up his life so badly. And he prayed. He honest-to-God prayed for the first time since he was a boy back in Omaha.

Then a grand idea came to him—a true-blue ace in the hole he'd forgotten he had—and he did a mental high five.

In the pink . . .

The next morning, they hit pay dirt—or, you could say, pink dirt.

Adam was the first diver splashing down to a site Jake had suggested last night after studying all the data they had collected before. He really was a statistical computer genius, she had to give him that. The new site was north and a quarter mile west of where they had been diving.

About twenty minutes after Adam's splash down, two Styrofoam cups came floating to the surface, the signal that a wreck had been located. "Shiver me timbers! We got it, me maties! We got it!" her grandfather shouted, so ecstatic that his cigar flew from his mouth and went overboard. One less cigar was a good thing, in Veronica's opinion. Frank gave Flossie a big, loud buss on the lips, then swooped her up in his arms and polkaed her around the deck, despite her feeble protests that he was behaving like "an old fool."

Veronica surmised that all treasure hunts resulted in this kind of exhilaration, but Frank must be feeling particularly ecstatic because this would solve his financial woes.

Tante Lulu was jumping up and down, too, as she held on to her straw sun hat. "I tol' you so. I knew I was gonna be good luck. I jus' knew it. I prayed to St. Jude las' night."

John reached down and lifted her into a warm hug. "That's right, Auntie, you always were good luck." Then John turned to Brenda and gave her a quick kiss and a pat on the rear of her tight jeans, which caught her by surprise; otherwise, she probably would have belted him one.

Tony and Steve were already on their satellite phones, presumably calling their mother to inform her of the news.

Jake looked at her speculatively.

She raised a halting hand. She knew that look.

He ignored her, wrapping his arms around her and yanking her against his body. Even though she tried to push him away, he held on tight, burying his face in her neck. "Congratulations, honey, you are now a full-fledged treasure hunter."

"No. I'm. Not." She wanted to tell him that her contribution to this project was minimal, but she barely got those few words out over the overwhelming pleasure of being in Jake's arms. He smelled like Jake. He felt like Jake. She stopped struggling and put her arms around his shoulders.

Jake inhaled sharply.

She knew exactly how he felt.

He drew back, but only a little. He wasn't letting her go; that was evident. As he stared at her through ocean-blue eyes, only one thing stuck out to Ronnie: He had tears in his eyes.

She moaned. *I am lost.*

He didn't kiss her. That was a line neither of them was ready to cross. Well, she wasn't ready. He probably wasn't, either, despite his claims to the contrary. But his face was so close their lips almost touched. She could feel his breath. He could feel hers. She felt his arousal brush her belly, even through his jeans and her shorts. Her arousal must have been evident in her eyes; Jake always said her eyes were a giveaway. Right now, she didn't care.

The people and activity around them dwindled to nothing. They were aware only of each other. That's the way it always was.

"Hey, you two. Get a room," someone yelled with a laugh.

Slowly, she and Jake parted. Her brain was fuzzy. His eyes were glazed over with passion. He licked his lips, as if to savor her flavor, even though he hadn't actually kissed her. Then they turned slowly to see everyone staring at them. Most were smiling, except Caleb, who was frowning. And Steve and Tony; they weren't frowning, but they weren't smiling, either.

Ever so slowly, he released her with a whisper. "I'm sorry." For what, she wasn't sure. The near kiss, his presence here on the boat, or the past ten or so years? Then he turned without a word, and walked away.

Everyone resumed their assigned jobs then, but now with a sense of excitement. Flossie and Tante Lulu went down to the galley to prepare a special celebratory lunch. Jake was up in the wheelhouse working the computers and preparing for the videotape of the wreck that Adam would bring with him; she would join Jake shortly, once her still-raging hormones were under control. Caleb and John were putting on dry suits for the next dive. Brenda was checking the anchor line that Adam would use to guide him back up. Frank was supervising it all with a professionalism and expertise that shouldn't have surprised her, but it did. Most of the time he came across as an ignorant oaf, crude and offensive. But she was beginning to suspect it was an act. For what purpose, she wasn't sure, but she promised herself to find out.

"Is this the most exciting moment in treasure hunting, locating the site?" she asked her grandfather when he came over to stand at the rail beside her.

"The second best thing." He talked around the new cigar in his mouth. "Best thing overall is when they first bring up the treasure. Even in the best-planned salvage operations, you never know for sure what you'll find."

"Are you expecting any surprises with this project?"

"Oh, yeah!"

"Why do you say that?"

"Because I don't trust the Menottis any further than I can throw 'em."

"I thought Rosa was your friend."

"More like a close acquaintance. Don't think for one minute that Anthony and Stefano are here to guard their mother's interest—at least not totally for that reason."

"What do you mean?"

"There are diamonds down there, I'm sure, but my instincts tell me there's something more, and my instincts are rarely wrong." She must have looked skeptical because he continued, "Jake thinks so, too. You know that Jake has a talent for reading people, has to when he's playing poker. He's been suspicious from the get-go, I expect."

Nice of Jake to let me know. The jerk! "Good gravy, Frank! Why are you involving yourself with such dangerous people? And Flossie and the rest of us, too?"

He blinked at her, surprised at her attack.

"And is that the real reason Jake is here? He thinks I am in some danger?"

"Girl, surely you know why your husband is here." Frank refused to acknowledge that Jake was her exhusband. "None of you are in any more danger than you would be at home. And we're prepared for any violence."

"Would you please explain how?" She pretended to be looking around the boat for something. "Nope. Not a cannon in sight."

Frank didn't laugh at her lame attempt at humor, which should have alerted her to his next words. "Most everyone's armed on this boat, except for you and Flossie."

Oh. My. God! "Do you mean guns?"

"No, slingshots. Shiiit! Of course, guns."

"I did not sign on for any *Indiana Jones/Romancing*

the Stone kind of half-baked adventure." She put her hands on her hips and stamped her foot with irritation. "Actually, I didn't sign on for anything, when you get right down to it."

"Now, now—"

She stamped her foot again. "Dammit, I'm not a kid. Stop treating me like one."

"Okay, you're right. We're on a treasure hunt. There is always some danger on these projects, whether they're at sea or on land, whether they're here in the U.S. of A. or off in frickin' Casablanca. It's the nature of the beast—money. Anytime things of value are involved—translated, money—there's always gonna be someone who's greedy and wants it all, or someone who wants the treasure without the work."

"Translated?"

"On Project Pink, we've got to watch our backs in two directions—the Menottis and the pirates."

Pirates again!

"But I don't want you to be concerned. Everything is going according to plan."

Aaarrgh! She had lots more to say, but she clamped her mouth shut for now, especially since Caleb, in full diving gear, came up to stand beside them, and her grandfather scurried off. Resting her arms on the rail, she stared over at the anchor line. "How long before Adam will be back up?"

"At this depth, he can stay down only twenty minutes, but he needs to take an hour to decompress on the longer journey back up." At her questioning expression, he explained, "At intervals, as he ascends, he stops and waits a certain number of minutes before moving up again. It's painstakingly slow, but necessary to avoid narcosis. Believe me, the bends are not a pretty sight. And a horrible way to die."

"Why are you and John gearing up so soon?"

"Famosa's job was to attach an anchor line to the wreck so *Sweet Jinx* won't drift away and to videotape the wreck from all angles. No excavations at this point. Everything slow and cautious. Famosa won't be able to dive again for a couple hours, more decompressing on board. So, LeDeux and I will go down next and begin examining the wreck hands-on and continue videotaping. We might not actually bring up artifacts, or diamonds, for two or three more dives."

"Are you excited?"

He gave her a look loaded with double meanings, but then he said, "Yeah. We all are. I can't wait to see the video and hear what Famosa reports."

"Me, too," she admitted.

"Are you going to stick it out till the end or go back with the Mafia brothers?" He must have overheard her making that threat to her grandfather.

She thought for several moments. "Good sense dictates that I get out of Dodge ASAP, but the treasure fever has hit me, too, I suppose. Oh, not the treasure itself, but the lure of the unknown. I know there are risks and no guarantees, but that's what makes it appealing, isn't it?"

Caleb raised his eyebrows at her.

Before she could elaborate, Jake walked by and interjected, "Tsk-tsk-tsk! Ronnie, a risk-taker. Before you know it, she'll become a gambler."

"You . . . you . . . you . . . ," she sputtered, but he was gone, heading toward the anchor line where everyone else was gathering. How soon he'd recovered from their near kiss!

Within seconds, Adam's head popped up out of the water. He swam over to the boat's side, dipped his head underwater, and came up the ladder.

He had a broad smile on his face. "There's good news, and there's bad news," he said, breathing heavily as he removed his tanks and pulled off his head gear.

Frank took the bag with the video camera from him. Silence reigned as they waited for Adam to elaborate.

He soon did, and the news was surprising, to say the least. "I found the *Sea Witch,* and it probably contains the diamond cache. But surprise, surprise"—he held in his open palm an ocean-encrusted iron cross with what appeared to be a swastika in the center—"it's a Nazi ship."

Chapter
18

Could this treasure be *verboten* . . . ?

Pandemonium broke loose then.

For a long moment, it appeared to Veronica like the showdown at high noon, except it was only ten A.M.

Steve and Tony took out pistols, probably because everyone was glaring and yelling questions at them. Which caused Caleb to pull out a pistol and what she knew was a lethal K-Bar knife from a Discovery Channel program on special forces. Presumably he could slit a terrorist's throat and disappear before the terrorist could say *Osama*. Famosa and Brenda were reaching for weapons as well, rifles, for God's sake. *How did I miss those?* John went into his great-aunt's huge handbag and pulled out a pistol big enough to blast an elephant to smithereens.

Veronica had no further chance to observe the chaos around her because—*"Ooomph!"*—Jake flung himself forward and tackled her to the deck. He lay on top of her, presumably to protect her from the gunfire.

She screamed, "Get off me," but he wasn't budging.

"Lay low till everyone calms down," he said into her ear. "I don't want you hurt by any side action."

"And what do I do if you get shot and bleed all over me?"

She felt the ripple of his soft laughter against her cheek. "Then you collect on my million-dollar insurance policy."

That stopped her short. Jake had her listed as his beneficiary on an insurance policy? And not Trish? Why? *Enough of such morbid thoughts at a time like this!*

Through her peripheral vision, she could see Tante Lulu coming up from the galley with a butcher knife in her hand. *Is she going to filet the two thugs?* Flossie looked like she was about to faint, but, no, she pulled a pair of manicure scissors from her beach coverup's pocket. *Yeah, that'll make the Mafia Dumb and Dumber quake in their Speedos.*

"Put the goddamn weapons down!" Frank bellowed. "I mean it. We need to talk, not kill each other."

Jake kissed her neck, then slowly lifted himself off her. She couldn't help but notice that his first thought in a moment of danger had been to protect her. Not that she needed his protection. Or wanted it. Still . . .

Everyone proceeded to lower their weapons, although Steve and Tony appeared most reluctant, being outnumbered as they were.

"Everyone, shut the hell up and listen." Frank's face grew florid with anger and the stress of his hollering. If his financial problems didn't give him a heart attack, this latest crisis just might. "We need to know the situation first. Famosa. Speak."

"It's the *Sea Witch* down there, all right. You'll see

that on the video, but you'll also note that there's a swastika on other objects, too, like the dinnerware. And the remnants of some of the bodies have iron crosses, probably decorated S.S. officers."

"Shit!" Caleb said, which was repeated by some of the others.

"And there's more of those Nazi emblems down there, on everything from medals to plates."

"What does it mean?" Veronica asked.

"I suspect that when the Nazis were pushed out of Italy in 1945, some of the Nazis tried to get their private plunder out of the country," Adam speculated. "I rather doubt they were headed for the U.S., though. Probably Argentina. And the ship was blown off course. That's just a guess, of course."

Frank looked at Steve and Tony. "Well? Are there diamonds down there? Or was that a lie to get us here for some crackbrained reason? And, son of a bitch, what's the Mafia doing with the Nazis?"

"Yeah, the diamonds are down there, and some other stuff. And, yeah, it was Nazi plunder, but it was plunder taken from my family in Sicily," Steve answered, which was more words than he usually put together at one time.

"Wait for our mother. She'll explain," Tony added, equally terse.

"We need to decide *now* what the frickin' hell to do with a Nazi vessel. We need to act quick, or we're gonna have the U.S. Park Services on our tail, not to mention the Italian and German governments, who will all claim jurisdiction." Frank was combing his fingers through his hair with agitation. "Bottom line, bozos, we can't wait to meet with Rosa back on shore."

"Actually," Tony said, motioning his head toward the horizon.

In the midst of the chaos, no one had noticed the speedboat approaching. It must be Rosa, who had already been informed of the discovery.

"You folks are crazier than a bayou hermit with a bad case of the heebie-jeebies." Tante Lulu, surely the poster girl for crazy folks, was making tsking noises at the mental state of the rest of them. "All I wants to know is iffen this big lunch me and Flossie is preparin' is fer a celebration or a funeral?"

No one was sure.

✦

She made him an offer he couldn't refuse. . . .

Lunch was postponed till after the Cosa Nostra Jinx Summit.

That's what Jake chose to call the meeting between the Jinx project members and the Cosa Nostra dudes and dudette. He told Ronnie that as they walked toward the wheelhouse.

Ronnie was not amused, but then she was still pissed over his self-appointment as her knight in not-so-shining armor. "How can you joke at a time like this?"

He shrugged. Sometimes, all a person could do was laugh. "If you keep frowning at me like that, your face is gonna freeze. That's what Grace told me a couple days ago when we were in New Orleans: 'Get happy or get lost.' Those were her exact words."

Ronnie still wasn't amused. "I wish you *would* get lost."

Immediately, her head shot up to see Tony and Steve standing in the doorway. "I didn't mean that. Do you hear me? I. Did. Not. Make. That. Wish."

They both nodded at her.

"What was that all about?" he asked her.

"Every time someone wishes for something around those two, the wish is magically granted."

"Like Mafia fairies?"

He could see a smile twitch at her lips, but she held it back. *But, whoa, this must mean Ronnie doesn't want me riding in a concrete boat back to Barnegat.* He, on the other hand, smiled widely. *Hey, I'll take my good news in small doses.*

First, they all crowded around the computer in the wheelhouse to study the video Famosa had just made. It was a little murky, but here and there among the boat's disintegrated wood frame, they could see bones—human bones; mixed in among them, presumably worn on long-rotted uniforms, were various types of Nazi medals. By the looks of them, these were not rank-and-file Hitler soldiers, but higher officers, probably fleeing Italy with their looted treasure.

After viewing the tape several times, they all moved down to the galley to discuss the situation over cups of Tante Lulu's Cajun coffee, which was thick enough to float a boat. Jake sat on one side of the long galley table with Ronnie on his right and Frank on his left. Famosa and Peachey held down both ends of the bench. The ex-SEAL was sticking to Ronnie like a burr on *his* backside; Famosa was, too. But Jake had managed to squeeze himself between the two of them, much to Peachey and Famosa's consternation and Ronnie's amusement. *Sometimes it pays to be immature.*

Every once in a while, he pressed his thigh against Ronnie's, then stared ahead with innocence. She wasn't fooled, of course. But she didn't move. *A good sign.*

On the table's other side sat Rosa, who had indeed arrived by speedboat, wearing a dress even he recognized as fancy-pantsy; medium-heeled shoes—designer something or other that Ronnie, while still on deck, had told Flossie cost about six hundred bleepin' dollars; and a wispy scarf over her helmetlike hair. On either side of Rosa were her two sons and two cousins, Tony and Guido Menotti, who had brought her out on the boat. Guido was a Newark lawyer. Standing back by the stove were Brenda, Flossie, LeDeux, and Tante Lulu, who kept bemoaning the fact that her crab étouffée was going to spoil if they took too long.

Frank was the first to speak, addressing Rosa: "You told us that the wreck took place in the 1950s."

"No, I did not. I said a boat carrying my family property went down about fifty years ago. The *Sea Witch* was lost in a storm the autumn of 1945. Fifty years, sixty years, what is the difference?"

That was splitting hairs five ways to Sunday, but Jake zipped his lips and waited for the whole story.

"Since when were your family members Nazis?" Leave it to Frank to be blunt.

Rosa stiffened and her nostrils flared with outrage. She put out her arms to prevent her sons and nephews from rising to physically fight the insult.

"The Menotti family, and the Lambini family—my maiden name is Lambini—were never allied with the Nazis or with the fascist government in Italy under that bastard Mussolini. If you knew your history better, you would know that thousands of Italian soldiers were *forced* to fight alongside the Nazis in Italy or on the Russian front, but most of them and the citizens of Italy opposed the fascist regime. Whatever rumors or falsehoods people like to tell about the Cosa Nostra, know this: they were never Hitler lovers."

Frank nodded his acceptance of that part of her story. "Why did you tell me that your family heirlooms were on that boat?"

"Because they were . . . *are*. Before the war, my family had many holdings in Italy. When the Nazis arrived, they evicted my grandmother and all her family, allowing them to take nothing with them, including the *Sea Witch,* which belonged to my family. Those jewels belong to me now." Rosa pounded her chest for emphasis.

"Why didn't you tell me about this before?" Frank asked.

"Would you have agreed to the project?" Rosa countered.

"Probably not."

"See, Franco," she told him. "I had to do it this way."

"Well, I for one have no intention of profiting off Nazi memorabilia, no matter how valuable," Famosa said, tossing the iron cross onto the table as if it were something foul, which of course it was. God only knew what atrocities that particular officer had committed to earn that medal.

Everyone else in the room agreed, including Rosa.

"Hey, I got enough crap over Mussolini's toilet," Frank added, pun probably intended. "The press would crucify me if I added insult to injury by salvaging Nazi items, no matter how historical. And speaking of history, this puts our Project Pink in a whole other arena.

I got permits to salvage this ship on the basis that it was a private concern. But if there is any historical significance—and, yes, Nazis fleeing Italy has historical significance—I have an obligation to notify the government, and—"

"And that means the items, including my family jewels, would be confiscated by the government," Rosa finished for Frank.

"At the least, the whole mess would be tied up in courts for years. You might get them back eventually." What Frank didn't say was that, even if Rosa had proof that the treasure had once been her family property, it would be hard, if not impossible, to convince a court that a Mafia family had gained anything by legal means.

"This is a freakin' cluster fuck," Peachey muttered.

Ronnie was more polite in her language. "What a monumental mess!"

That about summed it up for all of them, though Jake was leaning more toward Peachey's assessment.

"There is a way to handle this," Guido, the lawyer, offered. The guy was short and slim, fiftyish, and wore a suit that was probably worth a small car. On his fingers were four rings, two on each hand—forefingers and pinkies. This bit of vanity was balanced by dark eyes that flashed with intelligence. "Wait a few days to notify the government. Take out the family property and then let the government have the rest. What Uncle Sam doesn't know won't hurt him. That way we get what the Menotti family wants. Your project members profit, too. And the historical objects remain untouched."

"Phew! I don't know. If the Park Service got wind of this . . . ," Frank said.

"They won't," Guido assured them in a steely undertone steeped in hidden warning.

"The mob would put a hit on anyone who dared breathe the secret to authorities," Jake whispered in Ronnie's ear.

Her eyes shot to his in alarm.

"What if I refuse?" Frank asked.

"You won't," Guido said, still with that steely undertone.

"Hits "R" Us," Jake whispered to Ronnie again. He loved finding excuses to get so close to her. And he saw her do a little shiver, which meant that she liked it, too. He knew her tells like a poker playbook. He hadn't been married to and divorced from the same woman for nothing.

Frank was no fool. He had to recognize that they were virtual prisoners here now. One way or another, the Menottis were not going to let them leave the site till their family jewels were up on deck. Never mind that they had the Amish Terminator and the Cuban Rambo on board. Mafia boats were probably circling within a ten-mile radius of this site.

Jake raised a hand. "Can I say something?" When no one objected, he said, "Life is like a game of poker." Ronnie groaned beside him, but he didn't let that deter him. "You can either play aggressively or let what happens happen. A rounder or a grinder." He cut a quick glance at Ronnie, a grinder to the core. Then he continued. "I say we play aggressive. Do the dives. Collect the treasures or artifacts. Inform the government as soon as possible. And keep a few secrets, as long as no ethical boundaries are crossed."

"I'll do it, but how do I know you'll keep your end of the bargain?" Frank asked Rosa, not Guido.

Rosa reached into the pocket of her dress and pulled out a silver object—a ladies' switchblade. Laying her white-skinned arm on the table, palm up, she made a light slit across her wrist, then motioned with her head for Frank to do the same. Incredibly, he did. Once they both had thin red lines on their wrists, Rosa pressed hers against his, melding their life fluids. "Blood brother and blood sister we are now. There will be no betrayal."

All of them on the Pink Project side of the table and those standing by the range gaped at the spectacle they'd just witnessed, then released the breaths they'd been holding.

"Now," Rosa said, standing, "what is that wonderful smell?"

"Crab étouffée." Tante Lulu handed her a damp paper towel to wipe her wrist.

"Wonderful! Tony, bring some of that wine I brought with me today," Rosa said, then turned to Tante Lulu. "What can I do to help? I could make some garlic bread."

Unbelievable! The Godfather—rather, Godmother—one minute, and Betty Crocker the next.

As everyone got up and shuffled out to do their various jobs related to the next dive, Frank stopped midway up the steps. "One more thing, Rosa. Anything else you haven't told me?"

Rosa's olive complexion turned red. "Well, there is this itty-bitty thing. It's about those pink diamonds I mentioned. They happen to be set in my grandmother's heirloom necklace. It's gold, heavy gold, and its rare pink diamonds are arranged around a large center stone with decreasingly smaller gems on each side. The Pink Teardrop Necklace it is a called. And . . ."

Oh, shit! A necklace with a name. That surely spells big trouble, Jake thought.

"And what?" Frank prodded.

"It once belonged to Queen Isabella of Spain, the one who sent Columbus on his journey."

Big, big trouble!

"Which means it's worth a fortune," Flossie, their eBay expert, said; although, he didn't imagine they got much Queen Isabella crap on eBay. But then, who knew! If they could sell a grilled cheese sandwich with the Blessed Mother imprint on it, why not ol' Isabella's bling-bling?

Frank put his face in his hands.

Jake saw a gleam of maniacal menopause madness in Flossie's eyes and elbowed Frank as a warning not to criticize Flossie's eBay passion right now. It would take only one jab by Frank to set her off. In that schizo mood, she could probably take down the whole Mafia mob herself.

"It's worth more than a fortune to my family, and don't be telling me it has historical importance and therefore belongs to the government. It was honestly my great-grandmother's property, passed down through the generations by a Lambini ancestor who did a favor for the royal family of Spain."

Probably offed some enemy of the queen.

"I can prove it with photographs." Rosa whipped out a sepia-toned photograph that showed a dour-faced Italian woman—*she was probably in the throes of menopause*—staring at the camera. On her neck was a heavy necklace with a pigload of diamonds, just as Rosa had described.

"What else?" Frank demanded.

"Five Fabergé eggs and an antique snuffbox collection; although they may not have survived underwater all these years, even if they are in protective cases."

Flossie started to say something about eBay and Fabergé eggs, but Frank cut her off, still glowering at Rosa. "And?"

"That's all." Rosa beamed.

Frank, who rarely drank hard liquor, said, "I need a shot . . . or five."

"I have some tequila in my duffel bag," Jake announced.

Ronnie practically got whiplash as her head jerked in his direction.

He winked at her.

"And I need a good lawyer," Frank added.

Ronnie and Guido raised their hands at the same time—a match made in heaven.

✦

The best-laid plans . . .

That afternoon, Frank looked around the *Sweet Jinx* deck at all the carefully choreographed professional treasure-hunting activity going on around him related to the dive, and he was pleased.

"Well, Frank, everything going according to plan?" Flossie asked him in a tone dripping with sarcasm. She was lying on a lounge chair in the shade of the wheelhouse overhang, reading a romance novel, something about virile Norse Vikings.

Hah! He could show her a thing or two about virile Polish Vikings. Especially if this dive was successful today. Man, there was nothing better than adrenaline sex, even better than makeup sex, in his opinion. He must have grinned because Flossie made that tsking sound women throughout time have perfected. Eve probably tsked at Adam the same way.

"Yes, honey, everything is going according to plan," he replied after deciding to ignore her sarcasm. "Looks like we're going to recover some treasure. I've got my granddaughter on the boat, and she's excited about the project, really excited. I think I'm gonna be able to convince her to stay on with Jinx, Inc., even after the Pink Project is completed. And, best of all, she and Jake are together again . . . or they will be once the two of them realize they can't live without each other."

Flossie laughed. "You can't interfere in people's lives like this. It's going to come back and bite you in the butt."

"Why are you being such a Negative Nelly? Be a little more positive here, sweetie. Just think, three months from now, you and I could very well be on the first leg of our trip around the world."

"I hope that's the case, but you need to be realistic. Ronnie is going to find out that you tricked her, and all hell is going to break loose then."

Tante Lulu, who had been sleeping, in fact, snoring, on the lounge chair next to Flossie, sat up abruptly and almost fell off the chair. Once she righted herself, she said, "What you needs is a love plan."

Frank wet a new cigar with his lips, cut off the tip, and lit it. He inhaled deeply and exhaled with a sigh of satisfaction and a cloud of smoke. Then he addressed the old lady—not that he wasn't an old man, but it was hard not to regard her that way. "A love plan? I like the sound of that."

"Oh, for heaven's sake!" Flossie scoffed, but she was all ears, too.

"I'm all for plans," he said, giving Flossie a knowing leer.

"I would like to see Jake and Ronnie back together, too," Flossie explained to Tante Lulu. "But I think we should all stay out of it and let things happen naturally."

Tante Lulu reached for a glass of iced "sweet tea" sitting in the built-in cup holder on the arm of her lounge chair. She'd made a pitcher of the Southern beverage for them all after lunch. Then she asked Flossie, "How's that workin' for you so far?"

God bless her. She's a regular Dr. Phil. And, man, she thinks the same way I do.

Flossie's shoulders sank with resignation. "What can we do?"

"In my family, we have a tradition of all the family members ganging up on the couple to get them together in the end, iffen they caint manage to get together themselves. Once, we all dressed up like the Village People and did a Cajun version of them. Once, Remy got up on stage at the Women's Club banquet in his air force uniform and pretended like he was Richard Gere carryin' off Debra Winger in that movie *An Officer and a Gentleman.* Once, Rusty rode down the streets of Houma on his horse and carried Charmaine off with him. And once we held a surprise wedding."

Frank's jaw dropped, and Flossie said, "Are you for real?"

" 'Course I'm for real. We Cajuns got a good imagination. And our men are romantical—once we give 'em a good shove in the be-hind."

"I just can't picture myself dressing up like a cowboy

or a construction worker and shaking my ass around, unless the band was playing a polka." Frank grinned to himself at the image.

"Yeah, but I wouldn't mind you pretending to be Richard Gere and carrying me off to have your way with me." Flossie giggled, batting her eyelashes at him.

He loved when he could make Flossie giggle like a schoolgirl. "Maybe tonight . . . or when we're back home. I can get out my old Navy uniform and—"

"Would you mind?" Tante Lulu interrupted. "We were talkin' about getting Jake and your granddaughter together. Here's what I think. I already suggested to someone—caint recall who; my memory slips sometimes; guess I gotta get me some of that ginkgo stuff. Anyways, I suggested that we lock them up someplace alone together for a few days. Naked. That would do the trick, guaranteed."

He and Flossie exchanged smiles.

"I like the way you think," he told Tante Lulu.

"I do, too," Flossie surprised him by saying.

Hallelujah! She must be loosening up about my plans.

"Hmmm. The problem is, where could they be locked up? I mean, some desert island would be good, but there's no way I could get the two of them there; maybe Jake, but Ronnie's too suspicious." Frank puffed on his cigar a bit, thinking. "It has to be someplace where they couldn't get out right away."

"I know, I know." Flossie was practically jumping up and down in her chair. "The boat." She tossed her hands out to indicate the boat they were on.

"Yer a genius," Tante Lulu said. "Are you sure you ain't Cajun?"

At first, Frank didn't understand, but then, little by little, he saw the possibilities. "After the project is over, we lure them out to this boat, maybe even at this site. Then we have Brenda tinker with the engine and the radio. And somehow we take their clothes. And, ta da, two naked people on a boat in the middle of nowhere with nothing to do but . . . whoo-ee!"

"More like whoopie," Tante Lulu quipped.

They all nodded their agreement to the plan.

"We better remember sunscreen," Flossie joked.

"We'll make a list," Tante Lulu suggested. "Lotsa food, mebbe some wine, no books—we doan want them doin' any readin' fer entertainment—and music."

Tante Lulu and Flossie looked at each other and said at the same time, "No polkas!"

He was in a generous mood, so he agreed, but he might slip a polka or two in, anyway.

"Jake loves Sting and the Police. Ronnie likes some country," Flossie informed them. "I'll take care of the music."

"Can I play?" Rosa asked tentatively, peeking around the corner.

Frank hadn't spoken to Rosa since the big discovery and her subtle coercion to get them to continue. But he wasn't really mad at her. "Sure, come sit down."

Rosa had changed from her dress and high heels and was now wearing white sneakers, black slacks, and a white short-sleeved T-shirt that said, "You Gotta Love an Italian."

"Hey, I gots a T-shirt jist like that." Tante Lulu motioned for Rosa to sit down next to her. "'Cept mine says, 'You Gotta Love a Cajun.'" They smiled at each other like old friends.

Good Gawd!

"I love matchmaking," Rosa began, "and I'm thinking that you will have trouble keeping them on this boat and getting them naked. I have some little knockout pills—"

"I don't think that's a good idea," Frank interjected quickly. *Of course the Mafia has knockout pills. Knockout for good, most likely.*

"Oh, you!" Rosa swatted him on the arm playfully. "These aren't illegal drugs or anything. These are just pills that make a person real sleepy, and they last only a short time. Once they wake up, they won't know what happened to them." She smiled brightly as if she'd just discovered spaghetti or something.

"I have herbs that'll do the same thing. No problem." That came from Tante Lulu, of course.

"And candles. We should have lots of candles for atmosphere," Rosa said.

"Good idea," Flossie said. "I can get a good deal on eBay for dozens of scented candles."

Frank was about to say "eBay again!" but he'd learned his lesson. Flossie hadn't had a menopausal maniac mood swing in a couple hours. He wasn't about to trigger another one by criticizing her buying habits.

"Of course we gotta involve St. Jude," Tante Lulu added. "Mebbe we should save him fer later. Like after they's together again, ask him to make sure they doan go separatin' again."

"We might not have to do all this. Maybe they'll get together on their own." Flossie was ever the hopeful one.

"Sounds like a plan to me," Frank said.

The four of them reached their right hands out and made one fist to seal the plan.

They had no chance to discuss more because Peach and LeDeux were coming up from the second dive. And they didn't look happy.

Chapter
19

Where's a safecracker when you need one . . . ?

Veronica's stomach roiled with nausea.

It wasn't her old sea phobia coming back. More likely, this seasickness was caused by this project's seesaw action, up one minute, down the next. But she popped several Peptos, just to make sure.

"What's the problem now?" she asked John and Caleb as they came up onto the deck. Their negative expressions were bellwethers that told everyone gathered that bad news was coming.

"Okay, here's the deal," John said, once he got his breathing under control. "There's a safe down there the size of a Volkswagen. It resembles those old-time bank safes. Must weigh five hundred pounds."

"The problem is," Caleb picked up where John left off, "under normal circumstances, we would use a water-resistant blowtorch to open the sucker, then remove whatever's inside. I do it all the time in underwater construction work, like bridge abutments."

"I thought you SEALs could do anything," Jake remarked. "Cracking a safe should be child's play."

"Fuck you," Caleb retorted.

"No, thanks."

"Okay, okay now." Frank stepped between the two men. "Everyone's nerves are on edge. Let's cool it."

John stepped between the two of them as well. "We can't use a blowtorch or anything else to open the safe down there. First, it would take too long, probably an hour, and our air supply would be depleted. More important, it would be obvious to authorities who examine the site later that we removed something from the safe."

"Can we lift the safe up?" Frank asked.

"Sure we can," Brenda said. "We'll bring a crane out here and hoist the bugger up. A cinch, if handled properly."

"But won't the authorities notice a space in the wreck where the safe had been?" Rosa wanted to know.

"That might not be a problem." Frank was tapping his chin and puffing on a cigar as he pondered this latest development. "A heavy storm is heading in tonight, and it could very well make some changes in the ocean floor. Besides that, the sand churned even in normal ocean currents is quick to cover whatever lands on the bottom."

As everyone talked at once, offering their opinions on how to handle the retrieval, the only thing Veronica could think of was, *a heavy storm?* Her head jerked up, and she peered into the distance where, yep, dark clouds were forming. Now, it was one thing for her to have adjusted her physical reactions to the open waters on temperate days, but the middle of the ocean during a storm? No way!

"Don't worry. I'll make sure you're back on land." Jake put his arm around her shoulder and squeezed her against him.

How did he know what I was thinking? she thought. Then, *How does he always know what I'm thinking? He's an expert at reading people. He's an expert at reading me. Why wouldn't he be? We've been married, like, forever.* "Thanks. I'm sure everyone will want to go onto dry land, at least till the storm runs its course."

Just to make sure, Jake said in a loud voice, "Hey, Frank, how about we take this rust bucket into Barnegat for the night. No one wants to be out in a storm." Frank was about to protest, but Jake continued, in a steely voice now, "You and Brenda can pick up a crane tomorrow. Those chemical toilets can be emptied. All of us could do some laundry and take more than a one-minute shower."

"Plus, I need to get on my home computer to—" Flossie started to say.

But Frank drew himself to his full height—six foot two of burly man—and towered over Flossie. "I've had it up to my eyeballs with your eBay crap."

Flossie, to everyone's surprise, did not burst into tears. Instead, she rose up on the tiptoes of her sequined shoes and jabbed a forefinger into his chest. "Know what I've had up to my eyeballs? Your stupid polkas. And your equally stupid suspenders. And your snoring. And your constant criticism. And those smelly cigars." With those words and Frank's slack jaw, she stomped away and slammed the door leading down to the galley.

Frank shook his head to clear it. "Must be the menopause," he said to everyone standing around, gaping at him.

Flossie poked her head out the door then and added, "And by the way, I was going to check my stocks on my home computer, but now I definitely will be going on eBay. Hold on to your wallet, big boy." She slammed the door again.

After that, everyone began to make preparations for the return trip.

Frank stayed behind and asked Veronica, "Will you be coming back?" He obviously feared that once on land, she would hotfoot it back to Boston and her law practice.

That should have been her plan, but what she said was, "I'll see this project through to the end. But then I'm done."

He smiled so brightly that you'd have thought she handed him the moon—or a new polka CD.

"That was nice," Jake said, coming up to her side. He'd already donned a sweatshirt, and he handed her his Windbreaker, which had "World Texas Hold 'Em Poker Tournament" on the back. She hadn't realized that the wind was already picking up.

"I wasn't being nice. I was being truthful. I'm not a quitter."

He winced at her jab but remained surprisingly silent. The old Jake would have said something equally snide back. He stared at her for a long time, saying nothing. It wasn't "the look"; it was something else.

"What?" she finally asked.

"Will you go out to dinner with me tonight?"

That was a shocker. "Are you asking me on a date?"

He blushed, which was kind of cute. Jake rarely blushed. "Yeah. A date."

"No."

"What do you mean, no? No, not tonight? Or no, not ever?"

She should have said "not ever," but a part of her wasn't ready to be that emphatic. "Brenda and I are going out tonight . . . dancing."

Jake smiled with relief.

Brenda, who was winding some rope in front of them, turned to face them. "We are?"

"Yep. You can stay overnight with me in my room at the Starlight Motel. I know this little place where they have great food and live music. Dirty Doug's."

Jake snorted his opinion of her going to a place with that name, then smirked.

She ignored his snort, and his smirk.

"The place where Adam took you to dinner?" Brenda asked.

"Yes."

Jake was no longer smirking. His face went stiff. In fact, he looked hurt, even though he had no right to be. They weren't married anymore. "You went on a date with Fabio?"

"Fabio?" she asked, even though she knew who he meant.

"Yeah, the Cuban cover boy."

"So what? You go on dates. And, hello! You're engaged."

"I am not engaged anymore. Did you have a date with the Amish commando, too?"

Veronica smiled at his choice of words, and Brenda snickered behind Jake. He didn't seem to notice, or care.

"No, I didn't have a date with Caleb," she said; but then, just because she had a mean streak in her somewhere, she added, "But I kissed him."

"You did?" Jake and Brenda said at the same time.

"Yeah, and it was really hot. So, Mr. Poker Man, what do you have to say about that?"

Jake stared at her for a moment. She knew the instant he moved that she'd miscalculated.

He pulled her into his arms, then gave an additional yank so she was on her tiptoes, aligning her tight against him, breast to chest, belly to belly. No question how much he still wanted her. Then he kissed her, and he kissed her good. There was tongue involved, but she wasn't sure if it was hers or his.

Just as quickly as he'd pulled her into his arms, he set her away from him. "You and I are not finished, babe, not by a Vegas long shot." Then he walked away.

She realized belatedly that there was complete silence on the boat. Everyone had just witnessed the kiss.

✦

Beware of men with plans . . .

Jake was sitting on the aft deck of the boat, arms around upraised knees, watching the storm clouds chase them on the return trip to Barnegat. In his headset, Sting blasted out "Roxanne," the epic Police song, but today, even that couldn't soothe his soul.

The kiss shared with Ronnie less than an hour ago had shattered something inside him. He was afraid of what he might do or say next, so fragile were his emotions. In fact, he kept clenching and unclenching his fists to settle himself down, to no avail.

So, of course, Ronnie came up and sank down beside

him. For what seemed like an eternity, she just stared forward, as he'd been doing.

"Are you okay?" he asked. "The waves are getting kind of rough."

"My stomach's queasy, but I took a couple of Peptos. I should be all right." She was still avoiding eye contact with him. "Is that 'Roxanne' I hear?"

He nodded and removed the headset, clicking the OFF button on the CD player.

"Remember the time, back at college, when you played that song for me? You couldn't believe I wasn't a Sting fan; you thought the whole world should be, even back then." She smiled wistfully. "We were on that grassy knoll by the river, and—"

"I remember," he cut her off, more abruptly than he'd intended. Then, more softly, he said, "That was probably the day I first realized that I loved you."

"Oh, Jake." Out of his side vision, he could see that she still stared ahead, but he could also see that there were tears in her eyes.

"I didn't mean to make you cry."

"I'm not crying. That was a good memory."

He turned his head and looked at her directly. "Yeah, it was, wasn't it?"

They were both quiet for a while.

"That was some kiss," he said.

"Yeah."

"What are we gonna do about it?"

"Nothing."

His heart sank like a rock.

"That's why I came to talk to you. Jake, we're killing each other with these on-again, off-again relationships. It's got to stop."

"I thought I had stopped. I made myself go out with other women. I got myself engaged, for chrissake. And see what happened? One second in your company and I was back to step one."

She nodded. "I've dated some . . . not nearly as much as you, I'm sure."

Don't be too sure.

"But in the back of my mind, I don't think I have really let go. That's why I've been thinking about dating Caleb."

"Caleb?" he growled. "Why him? Why not the Cuban Fabio?"

"I had one date with Adam and knew he was not my type."

"But Peachey? Shit! He's not your style, either."

She grinned at him, knowing there wasn't any man whom he would consider her style. "I think I'm going to try finding out for myself."

Jake's hands fisted and unfisted reflexively. *I am not going to picture her naked with that steroid stud. I can't let myself. I just can't.* "Maybe we could find a way to make it work this time. That's why I came back. I had to try."

"Nothing's changed, Jake."

"Yes, it has. I don't play nearly as much as I used to. I'm financially secure. You wouldn't have to worry." Suddenly, he remembered his "grand gesture" and dug deep in his pocket, pulling out a check and placing it in her hands. "See. That's how much I've changed. Take that and put it in a separate account with your name only. Never to be touched for gambling. Ever. It's proof that my gambling won't ever be a problem for us again."

Ronnie stared down at the paper in her hands. He could tell she was surprised. "One million dollars? You're giving me one million dollars?" Then, surprise changing into anger, she stood abruptly and stared down at him.

He stood, too.

Then she ripped the check into tiny shreds and let them blow out to sea. There were more than tears in her eyes now. "You jackass! You don't know me at all if you think our marriages failed because of money."

"I know that. Dammit! This was supposed to be a grand . . . gesture."

"I give up. You are insane." Shaking her head with a lack of appreciation for his grand gesture, she left.

She probably thinks I'm going to give up now. Hah! I just rattled her big-time. She doesn't know it, but the odds are in my favor. Plan B, here I come.

As he put his headphones on and sank back down to the deck, he smiled. *So she thinks I'm insane. Well, I'm not. I was insane when we got married the last time . . . we both were. But this time we're going to be clear-headed, no rush to the altar. Hold on to your briefcase, my lawyer wife. The jury is still out on us.*

He closed his eyes then, and while Sting crooned "Don't Stand So Close to Me," he remembered.

Chapter
20
THE INSANITY WEDDING

He was in Monaco for an international poker tournament. She, coincidentally, was in nearby Nice, basking in a South of France vacation with a few of her friends. They met up in the posh restaurant of the Riviera Hotel, which overlooked the Mediterranean Sea.

He was dressed up for the occasion . . . well, dressed up for him. A navy blue blazer, light blue Oxford collar shirt, a tie, and khaki slacks with loafers. But she was really dressed up, in a backless, short, black silk dress and rhinestone-studded black high heels. Her brown hair was piled on top of her head in one of those loose styles meant to convey that the woman had just crawled out of bed after getting laid. Pearl earrings were her only jewelry.

It had been one year since their last divorce, since the last time he'd seen her, and almost nine years from their first Sappy Wedding, but it could have been yesterday, as far as he was concerned. His heart constricted, and blood rushed to all the important places in his body. With a sigh, he made his way to her table; he couldn't help himself.

"Ronnie," he said, coming up behind her.

She jumped in her seat, then turned. "Jake. Ohmigod, Jake! What are you doing here?" She was not happy to see him, but then he understood because she had to be feeling the same adrenaline rush he was experiencing.

After introductions to her friends, who had knowing smiles on their faces—he'd met two of them before— and after making some forgettable chitchat about why each of them was there and what they'd seen, he took Ronnie by the arm and led her outside to the terrace so they could talk in private. Big mistake!

They stood facing each other, neither knowing what to say. Maybe it was time for some honesty.

"I can't breathe when I look at you," he said, and that was the truth.

"Me, too."

"Have you missed me as much as I've missed you?"

"I can't tell you how many times I picked up the phone to tell you something, little things, like a case I'd just won, an interesting woman I met at a shelter, the cat that keeps trying to adopt me, a new Thai recipe I found."

"I've drunk-dialed you more times than I can count. Sometimes I even waited till you picked up just to hear your voice before hanging up. How juvenile is that?"

"But then I remember that you're not mine to call anytime I want."

"I'm always yours . . . for whatever reason."

She was looking at him like a weary traveler in the middle of the desert dying of thirst, and he was the tempting oasis. Heady stuff, that.

Suddenly, she flung herself at him. He caught her in

*his arms. What happened next was raw, hard-core sex,
no embellishments . . . well, unless you call crazy-in-
love an embellishment.*

*In hindsight, they shouldn't have gone behind that
mass of potted plants at the end of the terrace, beyond
the lights. In hindsight, she shouldn't have caressed his
lower back, just above his butt, his special erotic spot.
In hindsight, he shouldn't have said, "I want to screw
your brains out for all the pain you've caused me." In
hindsight, she shouldn't have said, "Ditto." In hindsight, he shouldn't have banged her silly against the
hotel wall with her dress hiked to her waist and his
pants around his ankles. In hindsight, it probably
hadn't been a good idea to nail her again in the storage room on the way to the elevators. By morning, he
had banged her so many times his cock felt like a drill.*

Bang, nail, screw, drill? I'm turning into a bloody
carpenter, *he joked with himself.*

*Her mouth was kiss-swollen, and there were chafe
marks on practically her whole body. He had a few bite
marks he would have liked to freeze in place to remind
him later how wild she'd been.*

*They'd said the words "I love you" so many times,
they became a litany. Their lovemaking had a frantic
nature to it, as if they had to do it all, every which way
they could, as well as they could, in case they never got
another chance.*

*All that banging had probably affected his mind, and
hers, too, because by the next evening they were married again. The Insanity Marriage.*

Unfortunately, the insanity ended three months later.

Chapter
21

It was the best of times; it was the worst of times. . . .

Veronica was having a wonderful time, more fun than she recalled having in a long, long time.

She and Brenda had done their laundry this afternoon, after running through the rain to a nearby Laundromat. They'd both basked in long hot showers and indulged in late-afternoon naps in the motel's two double beds. Afterward, they came to Dirty Doug's, where they dined on fresh beer-batter haddock with angel hair pasta au gratin and a luscious balsamic vinaigrette salad. Brenda had dropped her diet for the evening.

Over the years, Veronica had maintained friendships with a few of her old college roommates, but she couldn't remember the last time she'd actually seen or talked to any of them. Their interests had changed, being more into country clubs, children, and subjects that did not interest Veronica. Her life didn't interest them, either. So it was refreshing to have girl-to-girl time with Brenda, whose sense of humor kept her smiling.

"Are you really going to your class reunion with John?"

"Yep, assuming I lose those twenty pounds. I've already lost twelve, but I'll probably gain two tonight."

"Why is it so important to you? Do you still love your ex?"

"No. Yes. I don't know. He is such a prick, really. He let celebrity go to his head years ago and is still basking in the glow of mass female adoration. He wasn't always like that. I've known Lance since we were kids back in Perth Amboy, driving our tricycles up and down the sidewalk in front of our houses. Lance, ever the speed freak, managed to get his tricycle to go twice as fast as mine."

"It's hard to break old . . ." Veronica was about to say "loves" but instead said, "habits."

"Tell me about it. And, hey, I get back at the jerk every chance I get. Everyone I meet gets to hear me say that his family jewels are more like peanuts and his dick hasn't grown since he was two years old. It gets back to him, too." She grinned mischievously.

"Does he see his daughter . . . Patti?"

"Oh, yeah. I can't criticize him in that department. He has regular visitation. I live with my mother in Perth Amboy, but Patti spends a lot of time with Lance in the off season at his home outside Houston. Last winter he took her to Disney World. I manage to be out of sight every time he comes for her, though. I'm afraid my rancor will show in front of Patti."

At least Jake and I didn't have kids to subject our misery to. Somehow, that fact didn't make her feel better.

Caleb and Adam showed up then, and she thought she saw John over by the bar, but the place was so packed, with the rain pounding down on the metal roof, that it was hard to tell. But, yes, there he was out on the dance floor doing his thing with the same blonde who had been here last time.

Veronica went to the ladies' room, and on the way back, a guy asked her to dance. The fact that she was surprised was an indication of how sparse her social life was these days. She hesitated, then said, "Sure."

It was sort of a slow, fast dance—"Hit Me with Your Best Shot." He didn't do any fancy steps that would make him look ridiculous or embarrass her. Over the music and loud conversation, he yelled, "Ethan . . . Ethan Dale."

"Veronica . . . Ronnie . . . Jinkowski," she said when the dance steps moved her closer to him.

"What do you do?"

For one second, she thought about telling him that she was a treasure hunter. But instead, she said, "Lawyer."

He nodded and pointed at himself. "State trooper."

She smiled. He looked like a trooper. Tall, short hair, good build, sort of stoic demeanor.

Adam and Brenda came out and danced next to them. Then John and the girl, who was named—surprise, surprise—Tiffany, a student at Monmouth College. John, who wore a shirt that proclaimed "Your Castle or Mine," was trying to teach them all the Cajun two-step to that song "Boot Scootin' Boogie." By the time three more songs went by, they were all laughing and dripping with perspiration.

Ethan danced with Brenda after Veronica begged

off. Adam steered her back to the table where Caleb sat, brooding over his beer.

"You don't dance?" she asked Caleb while taking a long drink of her frosted Long Island Ice Tea.

"I dance . . . some."

She arched her eyebrows.

"Slow dances. You wanna dance?"

Oooh, I don't know if that's a good idea.

A flash of humor crossed his face, as if he suspected what she was thinking.

They slow-danced to two songs, and she liked it. Well, who wouldn't? With her arms linked around his neck, his arms linked around her waist, and her face against the hard tendons of his neck, she felt, well, tingly inside. *What a teenagey kind of word to use!* She almost giggled, which was also a "teenagey" kind of thing to do.

Caleb smelled of some spicy soap or deodorant, maybe just the detergent or fabric softener in his soft navy T-shirt. The strong heartbeat she felt against her breasts was anything but soft.

But then everything changed.

Her eyes opened lazily at the end of one song to gaze over his shoulder and see . . . Jake! He was leaning back, his elbows resting on the bar, with a bottle of beer in one hand, watching her. He had his impassive, poker face on, which gave her no clue as to his mood. But she could guess.

She stopped and told Caleb, "I've had enough dancing . . . for now."

He raised his eyebrows at her abrupt change of mood, then turned to see where she was staring. "Crap!" he said, and steered her back to their table.

Veronica couldn't feel comfortable after that. She answered questions as others at her table talked, mostly Brenda and Adam. Caleb remained quiet and brooding. It wasn't that Jake did anything overt. Just the fact that he was there put a damper on her fun. As if she had been doing something wrong, which she hadn't been, of course.

They were joined by unexpected company then— her grandfather, looking spiffy in slicked-back white hair, blue jeans, a white Jinx, Inc., T-shirt, and white-on-red polka-dot suspenders. Flossie wasn't too shabby, either, in a pink, short-sleeved spandex dress with high-heeled matching slides. Chandelier earrings comprised of various-sized tiny bells jingled as she moved her head, which was covered with its usual big, blonde hair. She arrived in a cloud of Shalimar perfume, noticeable even in the tavern's heavy air.

"Don't scowl at me like I'm a party crasher," Frank said as he pulled chairs over for him and Flossie. "Flossie made me come, even though I told her they don't play polkas in this dump."

"Tsk-tsk-tsk!" Flossie said, giggling and giving each of them at the table a little wave.

Her evening of fun was not turning out as she had planned.

Frank ordered a beer for himself and a piña colada for Flossie, who told the waiter, "And don't forget the umbrella!" Frank then turned to Veronica and said, "So why aren't you over there with Jake?"

She felt herself blush as Brenda and Adam swiveled in their chairs to see Jake, still at the bar, though now he was talking to the bartender, handing him a bill, and pointing at the band. He was probably telling him to ask the band to tone it down. It was so loud in here, a person could develop a hearing problem. "I think he just came in," she explained, as if it was her fault he hadn't joined them.

Frank nodded.

"Let's dance," Flossie said to Frank.

Instead of balking, as most men did till they had a few beers under their belts, he stood and took her to the dance floor, where he surprised all of them. He steered Flossie around the dance floor in a sweeping old-fashioned waltz, even if it was to Neil Diamond's "Sweet Caroline."

"That is so neat!" Brenda said, mirroring Veronica's own thoughts.

My grandmother would have a fit if she could see how good they look together. But then another thought occurred to her. *Did he and my grandmother dance like this at one time? Did they love each other as passionately as Jake and I once did?* Her eyes immediately shot to Jake to see if he was watching the pair . . . and having the same emotions.

Instead, she saw with delight that life was throwing a speed bump on Jake's plans as well—assuming he had plans—because a small figure climbed up onto the bar stool next to him and tapped him on the shoulder.

It was Tante Lulu.

❉

Dumb no more . . .

"You are such a dumb cluck!"

Jake had been sitting on a stool, leaning against the

bar on his left side, which gave him a good view of the dance floor . . . and beyond. He was nursing a long neck, minding his own business—okay, minding Ronnie's business, too, dammit!—when he heard that familiar voice behind him, making that probably accurate assessment of his mental state, immediately followed by a tap-tap-tap on his shoulder.

It was the new bane of his life, Tante Lulu, looking like a midget on the bar stool, with her white sneakers only reaching halfway to the floor. She had a greenish tint to her white hair today and was wearing a matching bright green jogging suit. *The Jolly Green Dwarf.* "Dint ya hear me, boy?"

"I heard you," he said, turning around to face her.

"Then why are ya standin' here like yer butt's Krazy Glued to the stool, lettin' that stud make moves on yer woman? *Stud* is a word Charmaine taught me. It means hubba-hubba handsome."

"First, I know what a stud is. Second, Ronnie isn't *my* woman anymore. We're divorced."

"Pffff! Iffen she ain't yer woman, ya oughta tell yer eyeballs and yer heart. 'Cause I'm tellin' ya, sure as sunshine in the bayou, ya got yer heart in yer eyes ever' time you look at her."

That's just great. I'm gawking at Ronnie like a lovesick dork.

Actually, *gawking* was a good description of what he'd been doing. He'd known from their short jaunt on the boat that Ronnie had turned over some kind of leaf, and not just quitting her job. Her clothing choices had undergone a dramatic transformation, too. First, there was the gold sperm-chasing bathing suit, and now this sheer blousey thing she wore over low-cut black jeans.

She looked mighty fine. Too fine. *She shouldn't be dressing like that in front of other men. Just me.*

"You could be a stud, too, ya know." The old lady's words brought him out of his brain blip with a jolt as she took a long slurp from a straw in a big red drink, then continued. "The thunderbolt caint do it all itself. Ya gotta work with the thunderbolt, sonny."

I'm going to regret this. I know I am. "How do I become a stud?"

She surveyed him from head to toe as if she were that guy on *Queer Eye for the Straight Guy* and found him lacking. "Get yer jeans a size or two smaller."

Maybe one size smaller. Two, and I won't be able to walk.

"Pump up them muscles in yer chest. Ya oughta try workin' out with Richard and me . . . 'Sweatin' to the Oldies.'"

Oh, yeah, that's gonna happen. Me and a lady with more wrinkles than time working out with Richard Simmons.

"Mebbe ya need to polish yer moves, too," she suggested. "Yer sexual moves, iffen ya know what I mean."

Oh, no! She's going to give me sex advice.

"I got this movie, a dee-vee-deedy that I took from under Tee-John's mattress one time. It's called *The Dummy Guide to Hot Sex.*"

Unbelievable!

"'Course, I also took *On Golden Blonde, Star Whores, Crocodile Done Me, Intercourse with a Vampire,* an *Diddler on the Roof,* but them was pure trash. I doan think you wanna learn anythin' from those movies, 'ceptin' mebbe that one move where the man gets a tongue erection."

Jake could feel his eyes practically bug out. "Does Tee-John—or any of your family—know you've got this stuff?"

"No, and why should they? I'm old enough to do whatever I wanna."

I should say so!

"Doan be thinkin' I'm watchin' these films to turn myself on."

Oh, God!

"My wild oats turned to bran flakes a long time ago. Nope, I watch 'em to get ideas soz I kin edjacate my fam'ly members when they's actin' stupid."

Jake pinched the bridge of his nose to keep from laughing out loud. "Listen, sex is not our problem."

"Yeah, but it can always be better."

"I'm thinking about trying tantric sex." *I'm thinking that I'm losing my mind to discuss this subject with a woman who was around when Iraq was called* Mesopotamia.

"Tantric, smantric, whatever works, honey." She patted him on the arm as if he were a little boy she was advising on the right way to ride a skateboard.

To hell with it. I might as well get advice from her as flounder along on my own because that ain't working. "She doesn't want to be with me anymore. I mean, she wants to be with me, but she won't try again because we've failed too many times."

"No rain, no rainbows."

"That helps. Not!"

"Wear her down, boy."

He grinned. "I'm trying."

"So, what's your plan?"

"Uh . . . I don't have a plan, exactly."

She shook her head as if he was a hopeless case, then proved it by saying, "I'm gonna say a prayer to St. Jude fer you. But ya gotta do some work yerself. Caint ya think of anythin' the girl likes about you, or somethin' that would tug at her heartstrings an' give you a chance to wheedle yer way back in?"

Wheedle my way back in? I don't give a rat's ass about wheedle. I need a way to plow back in, big-time, before someone else does. He thought and thought, and then he smiled. Still smiling, he called the bartender over, handed him a twenty, then gave him his order. And the order wasn't for a drink.

Tante Lulu smiled now, too, after giving him a high five.

Tee-John, wearing a T-shirt that proclaimed, "Your Castle or Mine?" walked up with some blonde chick, looked at him, looked at Tante Lulu, and said, "What are you two up to?"

"Nothing," he and Tante Lulu said at the same time.

And then—*I'm keeping my fingers crossed here*—the band began to play the old Police favorite, "Every Breath You Take."

✦

The dance . . .

Frank might be a polka fanatic, and he might be as old as Moses, but he knew a Sting song when he heard one, and he knew how much those songs meant to Jake, and therefore to his granddaughter.

Kudos to you, Jake, my boy.

First, Frank watched Ronnie, who appeared a bit

shell-shocked before she put her head on the table and muttered, "Damn, damn, damn!" After that, he watched Jake, who took a long drink from his long neck and placed the empty on the bar behind him. Then Jake pushed himself away from the bar and started to walk across the dance floor toward them. Instead of a self-satisfied look on his face, he appeared overly serious and a bit shell-shocked himself.

All the others at the table, not understanding the significance of the song, were staring at Ronnie with concern. Brenda kept saying, "Are you all right?" Adam told Flossie that he thought Ronnie might have had too many glasses of Long Island Ice Tea, on top of the excessive heat in the place. But Caleb was wiser than the rest. His eyes were narrowed at Ronnie, then Jake, who was closer now.

When Jake got to the table, all he said was, "Ronnie."

She groaned and raised her head. "Ooooh, that song . . . that is not fair."

Jake shrugged as if to say, "All's fair in love and war," and just held out a hand to her.

The usually contrary Ronnie stood, without hesitation, and walked toward him, zombielike. He took her hand and led her out onto the small dance floor.

Then the most magical thing happened, and Frank wasn't much into magical crap. Jake pulled Ronnie into his arms. They gazed at each other for one long moment, a gaze so thick with emotion that it brought tears to his eyes. He heard Flossie and Brenda sigh loudly at the scene unfolding before them. Caleb and Adam looked like kids who'd had their candy stolen.

Ronnie buried her face into the crook of Jake's neck,

and he yanked her so close they could have been one. Then they danced. But, son of a gun, Frank had never seen anything quite like it before. He and Flossie had been together for a long time, and they anticipated each other's moves when dancing like lots of old couples did, but this was different. Way different.

They swayed, they dipped, they twirled, never releasing their death hold on each other. Her eyes were closed. His were, too. In effect, it was like two people making love while doing nothing more than dancing. And even though their moves weren't anything spectacular, something about their movements spelled, well, magic.

People on the dance floor slowed, then stopped, to watch them. LeDeux brought his great-aunt, who resembled a broccoli, with her green hair and green outfit, over to their table and seated her. Then LeDeux, who was supposedly quite a dancer himself, studied Jake and Ronnie, and all he said was, "Wow!"

"She doesn't stand a chance," Tante Lulu told the other ladies. "I gave that Jake some sex advice. Plus, he's got St. Jude sittin' on his shoulder."

Brenda and Flossie stared at Tante Lulu, slack-jawed for a second. You never knew what the old bird was going to say.

Her nephew laughed out loud, accustomed to her outrageousness. But Brenda said, "How about giving me some of that advice?" And Flossie added, "Me, too."

"Hey, you don't need sex advice," Frank protested.

"There's no such thing as too much sex advice," Flossie told him with a sweet smile. The sweet smile was a sign that this was one of Flossie's good nights.

No menopausal freak-outs . . . so far. He wasn't about to tempt the hormone fates by disagreeing with her. "Yes, dear" seemed to suffice.

"What's he got that I don't?" Adam griped as he threw back a shot, followed by a beer.

Frank, John, Brenda, Flossie, Tante Lulu, and even Caleb said as one, "Ronnie."

Chapter
22

Sweet temptation . . .

Ronnie drifted on a cloud of sensuality.

The sight of Jake as he looked at her before pulling her into his arms . . . oh, God, it was a sight that had been repeated thousands of times over the years but was no less precious for its repetition. There was yearning in his eyes and hope and love—definitely love. As dangerous as it was, she would never tire of seeing him like this.

She made a small whimpering sound, the sound of surrender.

He blinked, the only sign that he'd heard her.

Her left hand wrapped around his nape; his right hand circled her waist. He held her right hand in his, against his chest. All this, while their gazes remained locked.

The music was just a backdrop. First, The Police's "Every Breath You Take." The song was a poignant reminder of all the good things about her and Jake. He had undoubtedly prompted the band to play their song.

As loud as the band was, the peripheral noises were muted by the thunder of her heartbeat, by Jake's sigh as he drew her nearer, by a dulling of the sense of sound while all other senses took over.

Forget Caleb's spicy smell. The scent of Jake's skin, unadorned by aftershave, was pure ambrosia to her. Even though she couldn't put a name to his unique scent, she could recognize it anywhere.

And the feel of his arms around her, the feel of his heart beating in counterpoint to hers, the feel of the music's rhythm, which caused them to dance so well together—she would never tire of these feelings. Never. "In spite of logic, in spite of all the reasons why this is a foolish, foolish thing to do, it feels so right to be in your arms, at this moment," she told him.

He put his cheek against hers. Sometimes Jake's silence meant he was in his poker "no tell" mode, but sometimes, like now, he was too filled with emotion to speak; that's how well she knew this man, who was a master at "no tells."

The only sense missing was taste, and Veronica knew she would be lost if she got that taste now. Already her defenses were crumbling bit by bit. *If I put my tongue to his neck, if I lean back and dare to kiss him, if I take the hand holding mine over his chest and sweep his palm with a soft butterfly kiss . . . if, if, if. Am I crazy to be thinking like this?*

Crazy in love, that blasted voice in her head said.

"I love you," Jake said against her hair.

She groaned and said nothing, which said everything. With the greatest of discipline, she tried to pull away.

He held on tight. "Shhh. Don't, baby. We don't have to think about tomorrow or forever . . . just now. One step at a time. No harm in that."

No harm in that? Hah! One step is all it ever takes for us. However, idiot that she was, Veronica listened to Jake and relaxed. She was so tired of fighting her love for him. While the band segued into Aerosmith's "Dream On," another Jake request, guaranteed, she asked, "Do you remember the Aerosmith concert we went to?"

"Which one? The one during the Sappy Marriage? Or the Tequila Marriage?"

She laughed against his neck and luxuriated in the feel of her lips against his skin. She also relished the shiver that ran through him. "The first one. Definitely Sappy. It was outdoors. And we brought a blanket and wine and French bread and cheese."

"And we stayed long after the crowds left."

She nodded. Both of them were remembering what happened. *Sweet memories.* After a second, she chuckled. "We were covered with mosquito bites in some unmentionable places."

"Yeah, but the fun we had slathering calamine lotion on those places! One of my top ten favorite memories!"

Leave it to Jake to mention that!

They danced in silence for a moment, but Jake interrupted the silence with a change of mood. No more teasing. "I've made so many mistakes, but marrying you, even four times, was not a mistake. I can't think of it that way. I . . . I just wanted you to know that."

"I know." *And I feel the same way, no matter what I say to everyone, no matter what I say to you.*

The second song ended and another started—"Summer Nights," a little faster this time, but they continued to slow dance, oblivious to the beat. They were setting their own delicious rhythm.

When he drew his head back finally, she knew that he was going to kiss her. She saw it in the slumberous haze in his eyes and the droop of his lower lip. She saw it and could do nothing to stop the inevitable.

At the first press of his lips against hers, pleasure passed through her in waves so intense that her knees buckled. He caught her with both hands at her waist. It was a fleeting kiss, no tongue, no deep hungry pressing, but it was potent just the same. So potent that they both knew a line had been crossed.

Wrapped in the cocoon of that kiss, they didn't realize till after the fact that people throughout the tavern were staring at them and smiling. Her grandfather most of all. You'd think he had just found King Tut's tomb.

But she couldn't think about that right now. Jake had his arm around her shoulders and her tucked at his side.

"I want to make love to you so bad my teeth hurt," he said, pressing a soft kiss to the top of her head.

Okay, this is the moment. I can walk away, or . . . or I can stay. No question what I should do, but what do I want to do? Hah! She tried to make light of her momentous decision. "Poor baby! I wouldn't want you to get a toothache."

He tilted his head in question. Sometimes men were so dense. When understanding seeped into his thick skull, he asked in a husky voice, trying for light, "Do you have any idea how good your chances are with me?"

She raised her eyebrows with amusement. "Uh, yeah. I felt it against my belly when we were dancing."

He laughed. "Hey, don't rub the bottle if you don't want the genie to come out." It was an old joke between them.

"So? Are you expecting me to make the first move?"

He squeezed her tighter against his side with a smile. And Jake had a killer smile.

"Knock yourself out, big boy."

And did he ever!

And neither of them listened to the laughter in their heads, accompanied by the words, "Here we go again."

✦

I forgot to remember to forget you. . . .

They were back in his hotel room, and Jake was as nervous as a boy about to get laid for the first time.

Plopping down into an upholstered chair, he tented and untented his hands several times. Ronnie looked so damn hot with no bra in a red sequined tank top she must have borrowed from Flossie, over glove-tight black jeans. This was so *not* her style. To him, Ronnie would be sexy in a burlap sack.

How did he know she was braless?

Because he knew Ronnie's body better than his own.

Jake kept inhaling and exhaling to settle down, but his nerves had him jittery as a kitten in a room full of pit bulls. It was so important that he not screw things up. As a result, he felt as if he was walking on eggshells. He, who prided himself on his emotional control, was fragile as glass inside.

Ronnie wasn't too calm, either, as she fiddled with her purse, trying to find a hairbrush.

"You know, honey, life is like a poker game . . . ," he began.

She groaned. She'd never been a big fan of his poker metaphors, but at the least they could usually get her to crack a grin. Yep, her mouth was twitching in her effort to suppress her amusement.

"No, listen. Life is like a poker game for us. We've just forgotten the first rule of holes, a rule all gamblers know. When in a hole, stop digging."

"Your point?"

"We've been in this damn hole way too long, and we keep trying to solve our problems by digging and digging. Maybe we need to crawl out into the light and look for other solutions."

"Jake," she said then, walking over to him and lifting one denim-clad leg over his thighs so that she straddled him.

Huh? His eyes practically went cross-eyed as she adjusted her ass on his lap, thus aligning his cock right where it wanted to be. "Works for me," he choked out.

He put one arm around her waist and cupped her nape with the other hand, pulling her head down for a kiss . . . the first of many, he hoped. "I promise—" he whispered against her open mouth.

She put her fingertips over his lips and shook her head. "No promises," she murmured, and lay her lips on his. She didn't have to say she loved him; her kiss told him. "And absolutely no talk about marriage."

I can live with that. "You're calling the shots, baby."

"Hah! That'll be a first." She studied his face for a

minute, then told him, "Do you know what Caleb said to me?"

Now? Now she wants to discuss some other man? "Do I want to know?"

"He told me to make a list of all the things I'd like him to do to me."

The temperature of Jake's already-heated blood inched up to a boil.

"After that, Caleb said we would work on his list."

His blood was boiling now. "I'll kill him. With my bare hands. Slowly."

She shook her head. "Don't you want to know what I put on that wish list, for him to do?"

Hell, no!

"Nothing."

It took a torturous moment for understanding to seep into his thick skull. When it did, he smiled. "Just so you know, I can do lists, too."

She smiled back at him. "I know."

He wanted to stand with her then and carry her to the bed and make love to her till every erotic fantasy on her list was checked off. *Restraint, boy. Restraint.*

Quiet now, she used her forefinger to trace the line of his jaw and then his lips. Then she repeated the path with small nibbling kisses.

He waited . . . with restraint.

The wonder in her eyes as she gazed at him was precious beyond belief to him. "Can I tell you that I love you?"

"As often as you want." She kissed him again, this time with a devouring hunger and a tongue so hot he thought he would explode from spontaneous combustion.

Her eyes misted.

"We don't need any friggin' lists, sweetheart. Just tell me what you want, and it's yours," he told her, once she came up for a breath. He meant that in all ways, but it was enough if she thought he meant just now.

She swiped the tears from her eyes with both fists, then lifted her chin belligerently. "Fuck me."

Whoa! Talk about blunt. But I am not about to argue. And, hey, I know exactly where she's coming from. If she uses the word fuck *instead of* make love, *our hooking up again won't seem so significant, just a fly-by fuck. Boy, is she kidding herself! It's significant, all right. And I'm not flying off this time.* "Anytime, anywhere, babe." With that, he stood with his hands on her ass, holding her up, and walked to the king-sized bed, tossing her to the middle. He immediately followed after her, crawling over her till he lay flat on top of her with their linked hands raised above her head.

"You think you've won, don't you?" she asked.

She didn't appear peeved as she asked that question, so he replied, "I feel as if I've won the World Series of Poker, the brass ring on the carousel, the Masters, the Triple Crown, and the Wheel of Fortune, all together."

"That good, huh?"

Suddenly somber, he closed his eyes and nestled his face in the curve of her neck and shoulder. Inhaling the scent of her skin and a light floral/spicy scent, he recognized her favorite perfume, Chanel No. 5.

"Are you smelling me?" she asked with a laugh.

"Yep, and you smell good enough to eat."

"Promises, promises." She arched her groin up against his groin and wiggled from side to side.

He was the one who laughed then. "Baby, you are tossing out a lot of raw sex talk—raw for you."

"I feel raw," she said, trying to pull her hands from his grasp, probably so she could take over this love play, which he was not going to allow—not this time.

"I can do raw." *I can do hard-core, soft-core, upside down, inside out, any type of sex you want with the adrenaline pumping through my body right now. Not to mention a ton of testosterone.*

It took a half hour for him to get naked and to remove her blouse and sandals and unzip her jeans. It took so long because they'd both had to stop at so many familiar places on each other's bodies to touch and kiss. By the time she was down to just her jeans, they were both worked into a sexual frenzy.

"Can you shimmy out of those jeans?" he gasped.

She laughed. "Honey, we're going to need a crowbar to get me out of these jeans."

"Hah! Never underestimate the determination of a man with a mission," he said, beginning to tug down the low waistband of the tight jeans.

"More like a man with a hard-on," she countered, peering down at him.

"That, too," he agreed. *And, man oh man, look at me!* It was one of those rare, hard-as-a-rock blue steelers that men knew were as special as, well, a royal flush.

Soon he had her naked, and he was embedded in her as far as he could go.

"I love you," she said, and skimmed her palms up and down over his lower back at the curve just above his buttocks, his unique erotic zone.

His cock lurched. "I love you, too," he whispered, nipping at her ear.

"How much?" she rasped out as she tilted her head so

he had better access to the whorls of her ultrasensitive ears.

"Oh, sweetheart, I thought you'd never ask."

With those words, he showed her just how much he loved her. And then he showed her again. And again.

✦

Yeah, but how long would it last . . . ?

At the wreck site on Monday afternoon, everyone waited, in their own way, for the safe to be hoisted up.

Steve and Tony, the good fairies of the Mafia, had shown up in Barnegat yesterday with a crane that fit on top of *Sweet Jinx*. When Frank had asked how much he owed them for the equipment—probably worried how he was going to afford the expenditure in his dire straits—the two men declined to answer. Since no one questioned them further, deciding it was better not to know, Veronica assumed it was another object that "fell off the truck."

Adam had splashed down a half hour ago with chains that he would attach to the safe for the hoisting, and Caleb splashed ten minutes ago, timing it so that he could complete the job once Adam's twenty minutes on the ocean floor were maxed out. It would be more than an hour before they were back on board. John was geared up, too, minus the flippers, fitted hood, and gloves, so that he could finish the job, if necessary; or if the salvage was complete, he would go down and attempt to put the site in order so authorities wouldn't know something had been retrieved.

Adam had taken the Nazi cross with him. He was

going to return it to the soldier to whom it belonged, not out of any respect for a Nazi commander, but to maintain the historical integrity of the site.

Tony was in the other boat, weapon at the ready, in case some pirate treasure hunters, or the Coast Guard, showed up. Not that he was going to shoot at the Coast Guard. She hoped.

Brenda, after greasing and testing the crane apparatus, went down to the galley with Tante Lulu to make what they hoped would be a celebratory feast for dinner. Tante Lulu had soon shooed Brenda away, stating, "Go fix a motor or sumpin'. I kin make a meal faster without you interferin'." Flossie and Rosa were down there, too, playing pinochle; by their hushed voices, she suspected they were planning some mischief.

As for her and Jake, well, they were in the wheelhouse with Frank, working on the two computers and a series of maps laid out there. They'd decided to keep their new relationship secret; well, as secret as anything could be with this gang. No sleeping together or fooling around on the boat. Everything was too tentative and, yes, shaky between them to risk outside interference, like from her grandfather or Tante Lulu.

"Come look at this, honey," Jake said, motioning her away from her laptop, where she'd been recording data that Frank fed her, much of it material that existed only in his head.

Frank's head shot up at Jake's use of the word *honey* and her failure to call him on the endearment.

Veronica ignored Frank's questioning stare and sat down next to Jake. He wore a baseball cap, flip-flops, a gray Boston U T-shirt with the sleeves ripped off, and black bathing trunks. And he smelled delicious, like shaving cream and minty soap. She probably smelled minty, too, since they'd showered together this morning and used the same shampoo and deodorant. She'd also shaved her legs with his razor, and he didn't even complain like he usually did. In fact, he helped her.

Without thinking, Jake put an arm around her shoulders and tugged her closer, kissing the top of her head. Then he pointed to the screen of his laptop, which was super techy compared to what she'd been working on.

Veronica was about to shrug out of Jake's "embrace" but decided, *What's the use?* Besides, she missed him. Hard to believe when they must have made love a dozen times since they'd hooked up Friday night.

Out of her side vision, she noticed her grandfather's gaze latched onto Jake's arm. Then he grinned and sat down to read the data that Veronica had been inputting.

Once again, she thought, *What's the use?* She would have to set her grandfather straight later.

Jake showed her a montage of frames he was making of the treasure hunt, like a slide show of people and their activities, but interspersed were map grids of the shipwreck site, techy charts showing the software program he'd used to pinpoint the exact location. All this he'd put together in a matter of hours. Perhaps it was his talent with computers that frustrated her so. In her opinion, his genius was wasted on poker. But that was something she refused to think about now.

Veronica had been compiling the text that would accompany his work, making for a good narrative account. At this point, no one was thinking about a TV documentary, or even press coverage, because of the legal implications. But the history might be important in the future.

"Hey, Frank, I want you to see this, too."

Frank stood and ambled over, then leaned on Jake's shoulder. Today Frank wore faded jeans so worn they threatened to shred in the least wind, spiffy yellow suspenders, and a flashy Hawaiian shirt about fifty years old by the looks of it, or at least twenty-five years old since she recalled seeing him in it when she was a child. His usual cigar hung from his mouth, unlit, thank God! And polka music played in the background.

Jake exited the program he was in and showed Frank a series of folders, which he said might be useful if he ever did any other deep-sea hunts. "This one marked 'Dive Profiles' is a calculation of dive times and depths, cross-referenced. This one marked 'Tremix' gives your divers accurate proportions for the combinations for mixing the gases." Tremix—an oxygen-helium-nitrogen cocktail—was the modern replacement for compressed air in some divers' tanks. For deep diving, it was safer and longer-lasting than pure oxygen.

Veronica got up and let Frank take her seat. While Jake explained all the work he'd done so far, located in various other folders, her grandfather asked questions and made approving sounds. She stood behind Jake for a second, then decided to go out on deck and see what was happening.

Sensing her movement, Jake reached up over his shoulder. Without turning, he took her hand, tugged it forward, and kissed her wrist. It was a whispery promise kiss, as in "See you later." That kind of kiss had always been their signal, when in public, that they would pick up later where they'd left off . . . as lovers.

With no more words but in a dreamy state, she went out on deck to watch all the activity. Brenda was with John and Steve, working on the hoist that had been rigged to the boat deck on the starboard side. It made a loud, grinding noise as the three worked to lift up the safe, which must have already been secured by Adam and Caleb.

Brenda glanced up, while still straining to help pull up the heavy safe, and grinned. "Looks like someone got some."

Veronica couldn't help but grin back at Brenda's bluntness.

But Caleb's head shot up. While his muscles were *really* straining—and *really* impressive—he tilted his head in question at her. She didn't need to respond. She could see that he got the message. "Crap! Are you a glutton for punishment?"

"Guess so."

Steve just shook his head . . . at her hopelessness, she supposed.

"Hey, do we all get to attend wedding number, what, Five?" John asked. "I know this great Cajun band; my brother René plays in it. The Swamp Rats."

"There is no wedding being planned."

"Yeah, right," Brenda commented. Then, "I could be your maid of honor . . . unless you have someone else in mind."

"There is no wedding being planned," she repeated.

With a gleam of mischief in her eyes, Brenda added, "And Peach here would make a great best man."

"Fuck that," Peach said with his usual succinctness.

"You know what happened, don't you?" John threw in. "My great-aunt has you on her short list of love connections. She's the Chuck Woolery of the bayou. Really, bachelors run when they see her coming. Plus, Tante Lulu prayed to St. Jude all weekend for you two."

"It's a losing battle, then," Veronica murmured. And that appeared to be the truth.

❋

Sometimes all a guy can do is pray. . . .

"Congratulations!"

"For what?" Jake asked Frank, who was sitting beside him, happier than a player with a nut flush. "Working with computers is what I do, when I'm not playing poker. No big deal!"

"Not that, dummy. You and Ronnie. Congratulations for getting back together."

"We're not back together. It's just tentative, at this point."

"Well, make it untentative, boy."

"Stay out of this, Frank. It's none of your business."

"It's my business, all right. I can't stay out of it."

"Why, for chrissake!" He turned to look directly at the old man. The crafty expression on his face caught Jake's attention immediately. He wondered what it was, then laughed when an idea came to him. "You aren't having any financial problems, are you?"

Frank waved a hand dismissively.

"Ronnie's gonna kill you."

"I don't care what she does to me as long as you two are together and running Jinx, Inc."

Jake noticed how Frank was including him in his

grand scheme but decided to shelve that issue for later. "I repeat, why?"

"You and Ronnie belong together. Everyone can see that."

"And?"

"And I don't want the same thing to happen to you two that happened to me and Lillian."

"Which was?"

"It may come as a surprise to you, but Lillian and I loved each other just as much as you two do. We were wild about each other."

"What happened?"

"We were too stubborn to bend. Both of us. I wanted to have an adventurous life, taking risks; she wanted a normal life, no risks."

The unspoken message was that he and Ronnie were the same way. "Okay, I accept that you want us back together, but why go to the extreme of getting Ronnie out on a boat? And why manipulate her into running this business?"

"I'm seventy-five years old. I promised Flossie a long time ago that we would give up the business and spend a couple years just cruising around the world. We even bought a little boat."

"A little boat?"

"Okay, a big boat, dammit. A sea cruiser."

"That's practically a friggin' yacht."

"A big boat," he insisted.

"Ronnie's gonna kill you," he repeated. "In fact, I might take a number myself, because I notice you've included me in those schemes of yours. Me, a treasure hunter?" Despite his words, Jake was smiling. God bless Frank and his schemes. At least he'd gotten him and Ronnie back together, even if only temporarily.

Maybe I oughta check out that St. Jude character. Maybe he can help me figure out what to do different this time.

Sure, a little voice in his head said.

Chapter

23

A Polish rainbow . . . ?

The safe, covered with rust, lichen, moss, and small sea creatures all fused together, was lifted over the ship's rail by the crane.

All the men, along with Brenda and even Ronnie, helped to set it in place. They handled it as though it were the Holy Grail. If they were going to save the safe, which they probably wouldn't, it would take a strong chemical bath to remove all the crud.

Flossie and Tante Lulu stood off to the side, beaming. LeDeux had stayed below, cleaning up the ocean floor as best he could, where the safe had rested for fifty-some years, but he should already be on his way back up. They were waiting for him, and for Famosa and Peach, to continue decompressing before attempting to open the safe.

These were the moments Frank lived for, the gold at the end of the rainbow. That's how he thought of successful treasure hunts. Jake must get the same rush when he got a royal flush in a high-stakes poker game. This recovery was especially gratifying to him today because he was seeing it through Ronnie and Jake's eyes. Their excitement enhanced his excitement.

The question was whether their excitement, Ronnie's in particular, would be enough to convince them this would make a good lifetime venture. Together. Jinx, Inc., meant too much to him to let it just disappear. But Flossie meant too much to him not to spend their last years together, fulfilling *her* dream of seeing the world from the porthole of an ocean vessel. She'd gotten the idea years ago from that stupid *Love Boat* television show. He'd be damned if he would ever set foot on a wussy ocean liner, though. That's why he'd bought *Last Fling,* the so-called miniyacht.

Brenda did a victory dance around the deck, then opened a bottle of champagne Frank had brought aboard for just this occasion. Soon they all held plastic glasses of the bubbly and were raising toasts to each other.

He watched with pleasure as Jake and Ronnie kissed and embraced, then kissed again, in between sips of champagne. Meanwhile, Peach and Famosa glared at the pair, both of them having had their sights on Ronnie. But then the two men joined in the celebration, too.

Flossie came up and hugged him warmly. "Congratulations, honey. You did it. Again."

He gave her a loud smack of a kiss.

Rosa joined them, tears streaming down her face. "Thank you, Franco. Thank you from the bottom of my heart."

Touched by her emotion, he got a bit choked up himself. "We haven't got the diamonds yet."

"We will," Rosa said, giving him a warm embrace, then going off to hug her son Steve as well.

Tante Lulu was leaning over the rail, waiting for her nephew to come up. When he did, a big ol' rascal grin on his wet face, they all circled the safe, wondering what to do first.

The decision was soon taken from their hands.

※

The great chase . . .

All hell broke loose.

Panic washed over Veronica as satellite phones rang simultaneously all over the ship.

Tony called Steve from his boat about a mile away where he was keeping watch. He alerted Steve that "pirates" were on their way, a competing treasure-hunting company known as Shipwreck Salvagers. Tony said he could hold them off for about fifteen minutes if they used that time to get away from the wreck site.

Veronica worried about *how* Tony would be holding them off. She sure hoped it didn't involve violence.

Then Rosa got two calls from cousins who were manning other boats within a one-mile perimeter of *Sweet Jinx*. *Who knew!* In these cases, it appeared to be a Coast Guard cutter, alerted that Frank might be engaged in some wreck diving that needed investigation. The cousins also said they could hold off the "visitors" till *Sweet Jinx* got a head start.

Ominously, Veronica thought she might have heard a gunshot through the phone. Rosa was standing right next to her. But maybe she was mistaken. *I hope.*

Frank got a call directly from Pete Porter, the Asbury Park reporter, who reminded Frank of the story he had promised him first dibs on weeks ago. He was about to board a boat in Barnegat that would take him out to the site, which he apparently didn't have the numbers on yet because he kept asking Frank to tell him how to get there.

Famosa and Peach were already raising the anchor. Steve, Tony, and LeDeux were dismantling the crane as best they could and laying the parts on the deck. Frank yelled to Brenda to start up the motor and beat it back to Barnegat. Immediately, *Sweet Jinx*'s motor turned over, and then it was full-throttle ahead as Frank and Brenda manned the wheel. There was no danger of the safe slipping off due to its weight, but Adam and Caleb still kept an eye on it. Flossie looked worried, and Tante Lulu looked excited enough to pee her pants.

"Come on over here, honey," Jake said, taking Veronica by the hand and leading her to the front wall of the wheelhouse, facing the bow. *Sweet Jinx* was riding the top of the waves like a speedboat, which it was not. If it blew a gasket or something, they were in big trouble . . . not that they weren't already in big trouble. What she didn't want, or need, was an explosion that resulted in (a) her treading the ocean depths or (b) her death.

"This is crazy. We can't run away from the Coast Guard. They'll arrest the whole bunch of us."

Jake patted her hand. "Don't worry. Frank knows what he's doing."

Which worried Veronica even more because she did not have as much confidence in Frank as Jake did. "Do you know a good lawyer?" she half-joked. "We're all going to land in jail."

Overhearing Veronica's last statement, Tante Lulu let out a little whoop of joy. "I haven't been in the slammer fer a long time. I gots to get material fer the book I'm writing. How's my hair look? I wanna look good in my mug shot."

"You're writing a book?" she and John, who was some distance away but approaching, exclaimed at the same time.

"This is news to me," John told Veronica.

"I doan tell you everything," the old lady boasted.

With hysterical irrelevance, and probably stupidity, Veronica asked her, "What's your book about?"

"My life story, and it's gonna be hot, hot, hot."

"Oh, my God!" Veronica said.

"Way to go!" This from Jake.

John just grinned at his great-aunt's outrageousness, then walked away toward the galley steps with her, warning her that the ride back was going to be choppy.

Choppy? I do not do choppy. Where are my Peptos?

Pulling her down to sit on the deck beside him, knees raised, with their backs to the wheelhouse, Jake extended a hand in front of her, palm up. It was filled with Peptos.

For some reason, it made Veronica feel all fuzzy inside at his thoughtfulness. But then, the fuzziness might be the onset of seasickness.

Jake was worried that Ronnie would soon be hurling. So he tried to distract her from her nauseousness and panic by talking nonstop. Bless his heart, as Tante Lulu would say.

"Did I tell you that I made an offer on a beachfront cottage in Stone Harbor two weeks ago? No? Well, I did, but I think I'm going to rescind the offer. I don't

really see you that close to Atlantic City. Oh, good
Lord, don't look like I just asked you to walk the plank.
We're not talking about forever here, just a . . . uh . . .
mutually agreeable . . . uh, meeting place. I can't believe I said that. *Meeting place,* for chrissake. How
about love nest? Just kidding, just kidding.

"Do you still have your engagement and wedding
rings? Good. Unless you want new ones. . . . No, I am
not talking about getting married again. Just a sign
of . . . something . . . like a friendship ring, but more.
Anyhow, the only reason I asked is because maybe you
want to set one of the diamonds we recover today in a
new ring."

That brought her out of her stupor like a bucket of
cold water. "I do not, ever, want new rings. Ever. You,
or the Mafia Bobbsey Twins, better not show up with
any, either. Do you understand me?"

"Loud and clear." Her vehemence surprised him,
and, yeah, hurt him a little.

"I like the ones I have too much."

Okay. I'm not hurt.

Ronnie went back to being silent and holding her
stomach with one of her hands. He made an effort to
distract her some more.

"You do know that Frank wants you—and me—to
take over Jinx, Inc., and live in his house so that he and
Flossie can cruise the world?"

"Whaaat? Since when? How come this is the first
I've heard about a cruise or me living in his house?"
She narrowed her eyes at him. "What would they be
cruising in, this old boat?"

Jake felt his face flush, and he noticed the way Ronnie was studying him and the determined effort he

made to bluff himself into a no-tell mode. Hmmm. What was the best way to squirm out of the tight spot he found himself in? "Maybe you should ask Frank— about the world cruise—once we get back to Barnegat." He hated lying to Ronnie, but maybe a lie of omission wasn't so bad.

Yeah, right! that voice in his head remarked.

"Ronnie, don't get angry with Frank. Despite his roughshod methods, he's trying to make up for lost time with you."

"Maybe. I am glad that this treasure will enable him to get out of financial trouble."

Now would be a good time to tell her that there is no financial trouble, that it was all a ruse. That Frank, in fact, purchased a half-million-dollar miniyacht called the Last Fling. *But fool that he was, he remained silent.*

Remember your theory about holes, Jake my boy. Keep on digging and you'll never get out.

Shut up!

"What did you say?"

"Nothing, honey. Nothing. As I was saying, we have some decisions to make when we get back. Now, now. Don't get your back up before you hear me out. I'm not talking marriage; we both know our track record in the matrimonial department. But you and I have career choices to make. Then living arrangements."

Her eyebrows shot up.

"I don't care where I live or what occupation I have. Really. I'll do whatever it takes to keep you. You can say whatever you want, push all my hot buttons, make me live in god-awful Boston, although I will probably grind my teeth to nubs if I have to be around your grandmother. And be forewarned, I intend to seduce you upside down and sideways till you can't think any-more. You don't stand a chance."

She smiled softly at his spiel.

I'm making progress. She wouldn't smile if I had no chance. Hallelujah! "Bottom line, babe. I'm in for the long haul this time. I am not leaving."

Tears misted her honey eyes, and he could have smacked himself for pushing too hard, too soon. But he was afraid that she would scoot back to Boston once they hit land. This might very well be his last chance.

"Oh, Jake, I don't see any way it's going to work for us."

"Don't say that. Just don't." He had to stop and work down the lump in his throat. *This is just friggin' great. Next I'll be crying.* "Life is like a poker game, sweetie."

"I can't wait to hear this one." At least she wasn't groaning or glaring at him.

"Life is like a poker game," he repeated. "You don't re-ally know what's going to happen till all the chips are on the table. And, baby, you haven't seen all my chips yet."

He pulled her close to him, an arm looped over her shoulders, and kissed her forehead. After that, they re-mained mostly quiet, each lost in their own thoughts.

All Veronica could think about was the mess she'd embroiled herself in. She had no idea what Jake was thinking—probably ways to convince her to stay with him, which, little did he know, wouldn't take much at this point. She'd felt more alive the past few days than she had in years. She had no intention of marrying him again, nothing permanent, but a temporary fling? No, *fling* was too casual a word for her and Jake. An affair? No, that demeaned what they had between them. In the end, she could think of no word to describe the fragile relationship she was willing to try with him. She wasn't willing to walk a mile with him, but a step or two didn't seem too dangerous.

When she'd come to that decision, she had no idea. Maybe when she'd seen him again after two years in Atlantic City and got the crushing engagement news. That had been a wake-up call of monumental proportions.

The question was, Is a flawed relationship, warts and all, better than no relationship at all? There was no easy answer.

So, she thought and thought. *What should I do?*

Long after Jake had made the remark about all his chips not being on the table yet, in the midst of their silence, she blurted out the answer to her own silent questions: "I'm willing to hang around and see how those chips fall."

His head shot up, and he looked directly at her. Pale blue eyes, starkly beautiful. No explanation was needed for her comment. He knew. He nodded and said, "Deal!" But then he laced the fingers of one of her hands with his and grinned. "One of my chips might involve lists."

"Hey, isn't that a coincidence? One of my chips involves lists, too."

✦

You could say she was the Dingbat Terminator. . . .

Everyone in the world was yelling at Frank on the docks back at Barnegat, and he couldn't care less. Life was good . . . as it should be.

"What the hell is wrong with you, Frank? You must have gotten my radio messages telling you to drop anchor and wait for us," Captain George Wright of the Coast Guard hollered, so angry that spittle foamed at the edges of his mouth.

"Broken radio," Frank lied.

"Broken, my ass! I swear, I ought to take you in."

Frank knew George really well. In fact, they'd downed a few at Charley O's on more than one occasion. He'd met his wife and kids. Helped his oldest son get into Princeton. Despite his outrage, George wouldn't arrest him.

"Arrest the bastard. Arrest him," Buck Ettinger, owner of Shipwreck Salvagers, was demanding of George. "He was out there salvaging a ship without proper notification. Guaranteed he's messed with the historical integrity of a wreck site. He's broken the law."

"Give me a break, Buck. You wouldn't know integrity from that hole in your butt," Frank said with a laugh. "And as for breaking the law, I'm not the one with a criminal record."

Ettinger looked as if he'd like to throttle Frank with his big hairy hands. Frank wished he would try. He wasn't so old he couldn't whip a little weasel like Ettinger. Of course, Flossie would skin him alive if he got in a fight.

"You promised me a story," Pete Porter reminded him. "I kept my end of the bargain. Now, where's my story?" Porter was young and ambitious, but he'd always been fair with Frank.

"You'll get the story before anyone else—if or when there is a story." That was all Frank would say to Porter for the moment.

In the meantime, while everyone continued to shout and make threats and while crowds began to gather, Steve, Tony, and Rosa had driven off with the safe in a van; the vehicle had appeared magically on the dock upon their arrival, thanks to the Mafia good-wish fairies, no doubt. Famosa, Peach, and LeDeux, fully armed, were in the back of the van, making sure there was no shady business from the Menottis or anyone else. Later they would all meet at a designated hideout to open the safe.

Flossie had gone back to the house, at Frank's insistence. Brenda, Ronnie, and Tante Lulu were still on the deck of *Sweet Jinx*, along with Jake. They would oversee the inevitable search of his vessel, which had by now been swept clean of any evidence, including computers, which were in the van with the safe.

Just then, though, Ronnie jumped off the boat onto the wharf. "Gentlemen," she said in an authoritative voice, "I am Mr. Jinkowsky's attorney. Anything you have to say to him can be said through me."

Frank's jaw dropped. *Ronnie defending me? I better pinch myself to see if I'm dreaming.* What was most amazing was that Ronnie pulled off her professionalism, despite her windblown hair tucked under a baseball cap, an "I Got Stung" T-shirt, very short denim shorts (think Daisy Duke), and flip-flops.

"I'm George Wright with the U.S. Coast Guard." Frank could tell that George was trying his best not to ask Ronnie what kind of law she practiced, dressed like she was. Today, a guy could be accused of sexual harassment for lots less. "Your client is in a pigload of trouble, Ms. . . . ?"

"Jensen," she finished for Wright; Frank's jaw remained open.

Ronnie using Jake's name? Wonders never cease!
He glanced up at Jake on the deck of his boat, watching them worriedly. He gave Jake an A-OK sign, although Jake wouldn't know for what.

"Is Mr. Jinkowsky really in trouble? Exactly what are the charges against him?" Ronnie asked Wright in a voice dripping with steely politeness.

Wright's face pinkened, and he blustered, "Well, there are no charges yet, but there for damn sure will be an investigation."

"To investigate what? Mr. Jinkowsky has a permit to salvage . . . a certain site."

"He does?" Wright turned to scowl at Ettinger, who must have been the one who tattled. Ettinger was too busy ogling Ronnie's legs to notice that the Coast Guard was now going to be on *his* case. Then George directed his gaze at Frank again and said, "I'd like to see that paperwork."

"We'll have it in your office tomorrow morning," Ronnie answered for him.

"About that story?" Porter reminded Frank.

"You'll hear from me," Frank replied without turning to the reporter.

Ettinger clenched his fists and told Frank, "You will not get away with this."

"Wanna bet?"

"Exactly what did you find out there?"

"As if I would tell the likes of you."

"Don't think I won't be tailing you. You breathe the wrong way, and I'll be on you like a fly on a dung heap."

"You sweet-talker you!"

All conversation was stopped by a loud bang, followed

by the splintering of a nearby piling. A gunshot, for chrissake! Everyone dropped to the ground. Frank made sure Ronnie was safe beside him. In the silence that followed, all heads turned toward the boat.

"Oh, my God!" was the most succinct response anyone could come up with, and that was from Ronnie.

Tante Lulu stood on the deck of his boat holding a pistol. She was in the police firing position—or at least the police firing position depicted on TV cop shows—with her legs spread, knees bent to a crouch, and both hands aiming the weapon. To complete the picture, she was wearing the treasure-hunting costume she'd worn the day she arrived—a safari-type suit and hat, with a cross-belt of ammunition. Her hair was a mass of black curls today. "Step back, Frank. I'll take care of these varmints."

Jake and Brenda were stunned, too, staring at the shooter as if she was two bricks short of a full load, which she was.

Frank slowly rose, his knees creaking in the process. "Put down the gun, Tante Lulu," he yelled. "Everything's okay here."

"You sure? I smell pirates."

"Really. I can handle this," Frank assured her.

Jake and Brenda were arguing with Tante Lulu, who appeared reluctant to relinquish her firearm. Finally, the old lady lowered her pistol and put it in a hip holster.

To the men still on the ground, except for Porter, who was taking photos of the dingy desperado, Frank said, "You can get up. She's harmless."

"Harmless," George sputtered as he straightened. "Did you see the damage she did to that pole?"

"Is she a midget?" one of the other Coast Guard officers asked as a group of them rushed up. "Is she as old as she looks?"

"Ooooh, she probably doesn't have a permit. And she's on Jinkowsky's boat. You'll have to arrest the whole lot of them now," Ettinger predicted. "Maybe we should call the police."

"I'm not arresting anyone till I get all the facts. And we're not drawing local law into this until I deem it necessary," George told Ettinger. To Frank, in an undertone, he added, "You are making it damn hard for me to ignore all this crap. Can't you control your people?"

"Hah! Wait till you meet Louise. Her name is Louise Rivard, but she likes to be called Tante Lulu. *You* try to control her."

George was soon given that opportunity as they all went aboard *Sweet Jinx*. While some of the Coast Guard officers examined every inch of the boat, with Jake and Brenda and Ronnie showing them around and Ettinger and Porter observing, Frank and George went down in the galley to talk with Tante Lulu. It didn't surprise him that he and George found themselves eating gumbo and drinking iced sweet tea before Tante Lulu gave them a chance to question her.

"Just between you and me, Frank, where's your computers, video players, TV screen, the normal items on a diving project?"

"Fell overboard."

"Bullshit!"

"I'll tell you this. We were outside state waters. It wasn't a registered cargo. We did nothing illegal. Give me a few weeks, then we'll talk in more detail."

"Ummmm," George said then, not convinced but

willing to wait. "This is really good, Ms. Rivard. My grandmother used to make gumbo."

"Jist call me Tante Lulu. Ever'one does. Was yer grandma Cajun?"

"No, she was Scottish, but she had a thing about Emeril—you know, that guy on the cooking channel."

"He's hot, all right."

Frank and George looked at each other in amazement.

"*Hot* is the not the word I would have chosen to describe the guy," George remarked while he scarfed up the gumbo with slices of crusty French bread.

"Hey, you're talking to a lady who drools over Richard Simmons," Frank informed George.

George's spoon was midway to his mouth. "You're kidding?"

Frank shook his head.

"Richard is soooo dreamy," Tante Lulu said. "An' I doan wanna hear any smarty-ass remarks about him, either."

A few moments later, at George's persistence, Tante Lulu sat down at the table and began to empty her purse, which was more like a fabric suitcase, searching for her gun permit.

There was makeup; hair dye; curlers; a romance novel—*THE RED-HOT CAJUN*—a small accordion-style photo album; a porno videotape entitled *Romancing the Bone*, which he wouldn't in a million years ask her about; two cell phones; a tape recorder she said she was using to take notes for her book; a thick wallet overflowing with cash, credit cards, and coupons; a long pointy thing that he was pretty sure was a vibrator but was afraid to know for sure; a dog-eared journal of her herbal remedies along with tiny ziplock packets of the herbs themselves; and, finally, a document folder from which she pulled a photo of herself taken in 1942 (man, she really had been a looker back then) and the gun permit.

"Ma'am," George said with a sigh. "This permit is a hunting license."

"What did you need a hunting license for?" Frank asked her.

"Gators," she replied matter-of-factly. "They kept eatin' the okra in my garden. I lives by the bayou."

"And it was issued in 1985," George added.

"So?"

"So, you were carrying a handgun, not a rifle."

"I upgraded."

George groaned. "And hunting licenses have to be renewed each year."

Tante Lulu threw her hands in the air. "How was I to know that?"

George stood.

"Well, ya gonna cuff me? I needs to go to the bathroom first. And put on some makeup. I doan wanna go to the big house lookin' like I jist woke up."

"You're not being arrested," George said.

Tante Lulu's shoulders slumped. Apparently, she had been looking forward to incarceration.

"But I do have to report this to local authorities. And you will be given a warning, at the least."

"Thass okay. My nephew is a lawyer."

She probably gave her nephew lots of business. Frank patted Tante Lulu on the shoulder as they all walked up the galley steps. "Don't worry. I'll take care of this."

"Take care of what?" Brenda asked.

"A firearms warning Tante Lulu is going to get," Frank answered.

Brenda rolled her eyes.

Jake and Ronnie were on the other side of the deck, looking moon-eyed at each other. Ettinger and Porter must have left.

A short time later, after Brenda drove Tante Lulu back to the hotel where she and John were staying and after Jake went to get his SUV, Frank took Ronnie's arm, stopping her in the parking lot where they would wait for Jake. For once, she was docile and followed his lead, staring at him in question.

"I was really proud of you back there . . . well, proud of the way you've handled being on the boat, too."

He thought she was going to give him a verbal tongue-lashing for embroiling her in his troubles, but instead she grinned and give him a playful shove on the chest. "Way to go, Grandpa!"

Frank was too stunned to react . . . at first.

Ronnie isn't mad at me. And she called me Grandpa. Something important just happened here. Frank wasn't much for examining things to death, though. So, he did what came naturally to him. He pulled his granddaughter into his arms and enveloped her in a bear hug, one of those big jobbies that pulled her up on her tiptoes and her face into his neck, and knocked off her cap. She smelled of salt air and sweat and some soft floral fragrance. It had to be the first time in forever that he'd hugged his granddaughter. How had that happened? How had he *let* that happen? Most amazing of all, she was hugging him back.

Finally, when he got his emotions under control

enough to release her, he didn't even bother to swipe the tears that welled in his eyes. Because she had tears in her eyes, too.

Neither of them said a word as she got into Jake's SUV, and Frank drove his Mustang home. He might just have gained a granddaughter today.

I love you, girl, he wanted to say. *I always have.* But it was too soon for those words. Someday, though, he intended to say them out loud, and he hoped to God it wouldn't be too late.

Chapter
24

Diamonds are a girl's best friend . . . and a guy's, too. . . .

They were all assembled in the basement of Adam's home in New Brunswick, staring at the safe, which was about to be opened. Caleb had already used a blowtorch and some tools to pry the lock. The excitement in the room was so thick you could practically see it.

Veronica looked at Jake, who was standing next to her. He winked and took her hand in his, kissing the wrist. A promise kiss . . . for later. She could see that he was just as excited as she was.

"This is fun," she said to him.

"Yeah. The adrenaline high is similar to poker. Now, don't be raisin' your eyebrows at me. Gambling *is* exciting, no matter what you think."

She conceded that point with a shrug. And, actually, she could see similarities. The risks. The high stakes. Even danger, at times. For just a blip of a second, she wondered if Jake might really enjoy treasure hunting.

She even wondered if *she* might like it as a career. *Impossible!* she told herself, although the notion did linger in the back of her mind.

The first thing Caleb took out of the safe, which emitted a musty smell after being closed for so long, was a once-blue, flat, molded velvet box, worn through with age in spots. Because the box, and other items inside the safe, had been kept in the airtight container, they got moldy but were mostly intact, except for the paper, which disintegrated when it contacted the air. The box appeared custom-made. Caleb handed it to Rosa, who set it on the card table next to the safe.

Rosa opened the case slowly, then gasped. "The Pink Teardrop Necklace."

It was spectacular. Even though the gold was tarnished, the pink diamonds sparkled. The necklace was made of a heavy gold choker from which was suspended a large center diamond, with increasingly smaller diamonds traveling all the way to the clasp. Each of the pink diamonds was in a gold mounting, surrounded by tiny white diamonds. The necklace must have weighed a pound. And, in Veronica's opinion, it was probably worth the five million dollars Rosa had originally estimated as its value, especially with its historical provenance. In fact, it was priceless, Veronica decided.

"Put it on," Brenda encouraged Rosa, who was weeping unabashedly. Once it was on, Rosa preened for all of them. Her scooped-neck, red jersey shirt and black slacks were inappropriate for such adornment—a sleek ball gown would be more suitable—but it was beautiful just the same.

"What will you do with it?" Veronica asked her. "Sell it?"

"Never!" Rosa said, shaking her head emphatically. "Into my safe it will go, to be taken out on special occasions. Then, I expect to bequeath it to my granddaughter . . . if I ever get one." She locked her gaze pointedly on her two sons, Anthony and Stefano, as she spoke the latter.

"Maaaa!" the big bad Tony complained, his face red with embarrassment.

"Give it up!" Steve added, also blushing.

Amazing! The federal organized crime unit would not believe this.

Tante Lulu piped in. "I kin help you find them wives. Cupid is practic'ly my middle name."

Tony and Steve rolled their eyes.

"You should be worried," John told them. "When she sets you in her matchmaking crosshairs, you are dead ducks."

"Yep, I'm gonna get them good Eye-tal-yan girls. I might even know some Cajun Eye-tal-yan girls. But, first, I gotta make Jake his hope chest."

"No!" Jake stiffened at Veronica's side. "No, no, that's not necessary."

"It's necessary, all right. And doan be arguin' with yer elders."

Veronica couldn't help but grin.

"It's not funny," Jake said, squeezing her hand.

"Yes, it is." She was laughing out loud now.

Caleb took another item from the safe. It, too, had a special molded case, but it was square. When he opened it, they saw what was probably a genuine Fabergé egg, with its own gold pedestal, nestled on a satin lining. There were soon four more lined up for their perusal.

They were all silent as they admired the still brightly colored enamel of the eggs, which were once made for the Russian royalty.

"I saw a special on PBS last year, where one of these things sold at Sotheby's for a million dollars," Adam told them.

"These might be worth more since Rosa probably knows where they came from," Frank speculated. "In any case, they'll be sold, and the proceeds divided among the crew."

Each of them nodded at that. Rosa didn't seem to mind. She was still fingering the necklace she wore, staring down at it with pleasure.

Next came an antique snuffbox collection, which was probably valuable, though no one knew anything about them, and some clips that might have once held paper money that had long since disintegrated.

The total value of this treasure so far began to stun all of them.

Finally came a leather pouch, which Caleb emptied onto the table. Out came dozens of white diamonds of varying sizes and colors. Veronica knew nothing about diamond quality and ratings, but she assumed these were special.

After that, they began to look at each other, too dazed to speak.

"Holy Jehosephat!" Tante Lulu broke the silence. "This is jist like that King Solomon's Mine. Or Indiana Jones."

They all laughed and relaxed, then began to speak all at once.

"How are we going to sell these things without alerting the authorities?" Jake asked.

"I know someone who'll sell the diamonds discreetly," Steve said.

"More like *fence* them," Jake whispered to her.

"And there's this guy in Switzerland who buys this kind of egg and snuffbox crap," Tony added. "You don't need to use any fancy auction house. And, by the way, old lady, don't you dare be fixing me up with some redneck Southern Italian belle. I'm from New York City, not some freakin' bayou."

"Who you callin' old lady?" Tante Lulu demanded.

"Who you callin' redneck?" John demanded.

"Tsk-tsk-tsk! I taught you better language than that," Rosa admonished Tony.

Everyone grinned at Tony for his stupidity in arguing with the old lady.

"What are you gonna do with your share?" Brenda asked them all. "I'm going to buy a house for me and my mother and my daughter. And put some money away for Patti's college. Maybe I'll buy an expensive car, too, just to annoy my ex-husband."

"I'm thinkin' 'bout buildin' a cottage on that property next to yours on Bayou Black," John told his greataunt, who stared at him with weepy-eyed adoration. "After I go to the police academy and become a cop. We already have a lawyer, a pilot, a teacher, and a hairdresser in the family."

"Well, I'm going to buy my own skin-diving boat," Adam said. "I still want to work for Jinx, Inc., too, but it might be nice to teach wreck diving."

When everyone looked at the silent Caleb, he shrugged his shoulders with uncertainty. "Maybe I'll send some cash to my family . . . well, not my family. They wouldn't accept it. But my younger sister might.

Maybe I'll start my own business. And a new pickup might come in handy. I don't know. Money doesn't mean much to me right now."

"Ronnie?" Frank looked at her.

"I don't know. This is all so . . . amazing."

She could pretty well guess what Frank would be doing. Paying off his debts. In fact, he stammered out, "I'll pay some . . . uh, bills, and, uh, maybe buy a pleasure . . . uh, boat."

Flossie, who was fanning herself with a magazine, smacked him on the arm and loud-whispered, "You old fool!" Then she mentioned that she wouldn't mind keeping one of the small diamonds to set in a ring.

"Anything for my girl," Frank offered exuberantly, patting Flossie on the butt.

Flossie jumped. "Stop it!" For a moment, they all thought she might morph into one of her menopausal mood swings. But instead, she said, "These are my best capris, and your hands are dirty from touching that safe."

"Jake?" Frank inquired.

Jake, who was still holding Veronica's hand, thought a moment, then answered, "There's a business venture I might be investing in." He held eye contact with Frank as he spoke, and Veronica wondered if he meant running Jinx, Inc. Her heart raced at that prospect because she was pretty sure Jake wouldn't get involved unless she was, and Veronica was not ready to make that kind of decision.

After that, they prepared to go home for the night. It was a sure bet that most of them would be unable to sleep, with adrenaline running through their blood. Steve and Tony put the safe in the back of a van. They would dispose of it somewhere, probably the Pine Barrens.

"I wish this night would go on forever," Veronica said a short time later. Her head rested on Jake's shoulder as he drove them back to her grandfather's home at Loveladies, where her car was parked.

Jake chuckled and took one of her hands in his and kissed her wrist. "Not a problem, baby. I just happened to bring my list, and it's a loooong one."

✦

I'll show you mine if you show me yours— your list, that is . . .

It was midnight, and the four of them still sat around Frank and Flossie's kitchen table, drinking coffee. Polkas played softly in the background. The alarming thing was, she was starting to like the awful music, or at least tolerate it better.

Because it was so late, Flossie had talked her and Jake into spending the night in the guest room. She'd been reluctant, despite her easing of anger toward her grandfather, but having seen Jake yawn widely for the third time, she'd agreed. It *had* been a long day.

They'd already discussed the successful treasure hunt to death. The excitement probably wouldn't fade for weeks . . . or longer.

"What will you do now?" Veronica asked her grandfather. "Take a vacation?"

Frank looked at Jake, then Flossie, before he replied, "Maybe later. Not right away."

Veronica frowned, trying to figure out what the hidden message had been all about. He just shrugged, though she detected a slight blush on his face.

"Do you have another treasure hunt lined up?" She watched as her grandfather yawned loudly.

"I have several possibilities," Frank said, "but I won't be running Jinx, Inc., anymore."

That again! "I am not qualified to run a treasure-hunting business, Frank, if that's what you're implying. I know that you think I—or Jake and I—are capable of the job, but we're not."

"I could stick around to help," Frank offered, staring down at his coffee cup. "What do you think, Jake?"

Jake gave her a quick glance, almost like an apology, then told her grandfather, "Yeah, I think we can do it, with your mentoring. And, actually, I think it would be fun. But will we do it? That depends on Ronnie. Wherever she goes, I go."

They weren't touching or even holding hands, but she felt the heat of his gaze. She wanted so much to believe him, that he would stay this time, but she had been hurt so much in the past.

"At least think about it," her grandfather urged. "You don't have to answer right now."

"It would mean so much to your grandfather," Flossie added, patting Frank's liver-spotted hand.

"I'll think about it," Veronica finally conceded. "Seriously."

That seemed to satisfy everyone for now.

"Don't forget," she told her grandfather, "we have to be at the Coast Guard office early tomorrow morning . . . rather, this morning."

Frank waved a hand in the air dismissively. "No problem. I'll make a few phone calls. We won't have to report to anyone."

She raised an eyebrow, but then recalled that Frank had friends in high places in the Garden State. "Won't you have to inform them about the wreck still down there, the Nazi soldiers and stuff?"

"Oh, yeah, but not the Coast Guard. They would just turn it over to the U.S. Park Service, which has jurisdiction over historically important sites. Nope, we'll go directly to one of the archaeologists I know who works in the Park Service . . . in a few weeks."

Does he have friends everywhere? Hah! A rhetorical question if I ever heard one.

"You asked me about future projects," Frank said then. "Maybe I could show you some of the ideas tomorrow. There's one treasure hunt that's particularly interesting. A privately owned cavern in Central Pennsylvania that legend says . . . Well, we can talk about all this when we're all more awake."

They all nodded. Soon Frank went off to bed, and Veronica helped Flossie clean up the dishes and set the automatic coffeemaker for the morning. Jake said he was going to take a shower before hitting the sack, a sack she expected to share with him.

"Don't be too hard on your grandfather." Flossie dried her hands on a dish towel. There was genuine concern in her heavily mascaraed eyes.

"Why would you bring that up now? I mean, the tension has eased a bit the last few days, don't you think?"

"It has, but there are way too many bad feelings, too much bad history, on both your parts. I just don't want you to judge him too harshly when he makes mistakes."

"Is this all related to Frank's wanting me to take over his business?"

"No. We're going to take off, regardless of whether you get involved in Jinx, Inc., or not, no matter what Frank says. On the other hand, in some ways it *is* related to the business. Frank's methods are sometimes rough, like how he got you to come here."

Veronica snorted to show what an understatement that was.

"He loves you, but he's a proud man. And yes, pride can get in the way of love."

Flossie's words raised a whole bunch of questions, but when Veronica opened her mouth to ask them, Flossie raised a hand and said, "I've said enough for tonight. Tomorrow you can get some answers."

When Veronica went up the stairs to the guest bedroom, she noticed that the walls and rooms weren't quite as "pillaged" as they were downstairs in the library and halls. In fact, the "Red Room," as she'd always called this room because of its burgundy velvet draperies and faded red oriental carpet, still held all its old antique furniture, including the big, raised walnut bed.

She heard the shower turn off in the adjoining bathroom and Jake yelled out, "Can you get me that paper in the back pocket of my jeans?"

She went into the steamy bathroom, redolent of Irish Spring soap, and noted that, despite the modern shower stall, the claw-footed tub still held prominence, along with a pedestal sink reminiscent of the early twentieth century. His jeans were lying on the tiled floor. Jake was just opening the shower door when she pulled out the paper and began to unfold it. It was a list. *Oooooh, boy!* And the first few things she read were so, well, not kinky, but definitely outrageous, even for Jake. She wasn't sure she could even do number three.

She glanced up to see a dripping-wet Jake leaning against the open sliding door of the shower, wearing only that drop-dead dimpled grin that always made her melt. Slowly, he beckoned her with a forefinger.

Chapter
25

The terrible trouble swooped down on them in a gray silk cloud. . . .

It was barely dawn when Jake awakened the next morning, despite not getting much sleep last night . . . not that he was complaining.

Ronnie had been insatiable. Okay, maybe he'd been the insatiable one, but she'd been more than willing to try everything he asked of her. *Everything*. What a girl! And she'd demanded a few things of her own. What a girl!

For a few moments, Jake relished the sounds of the awakening beach, which could be heard through the open windows. The waves hitting the sand. The seabirds squawking for their first food of the day. A dog barking somewhere in the distance. If only he could freeze time; if only he and Ronnie could go on with their lives as peacefully as this; if only . . .

Ronnie was spooned against his back, both of them naked. Her left arm lay on the pillow above his head.

Her right hand lay lightly pressed against his belly. He peered down, liking the possessiveness of her hand on him. His cock liked it, too, because it immediately stood up with interest.

Should he awaken her for a little early morning delight? No. Not yet. Maybe he would go downstairs and make some coffee for them. He could use this quiet time to think . . . and to plan. Ronnie wasn't won over yet, by any means.

He used the bathroom, which pretty much took care of his morning erection, then slipped on his jeans commando. It wasn't a sexual or fashion statement. Frankly, he hadn't brought a change of underwear, because he and Ronnie had decided to stay here at the last minute. Barefoot and barechested, he padded into the kitchen and changed the timer on the coffeemaker. It immediately started perking.

A few hours later, he'd drunk three cups of coffee; walked the beach; fed the seagulls and terns some scraps of bread; and read the *Asbury Park Press*, which, thankfully, had nothing about their treasure hunt . . . yet. Ronnie, Frank, and Flossie were sleeping late, but he chalked that up to the long and exhilarating day they'd had yesterday.

He poured a cup of coffee for Ronnie and was about to take it up, having decided that today was the day for some truths, especially about Frank. But just then, he heard a knock on the front door.

He frowned and looked at the stove clock. *Eight o'clock? Who would be here so early? Oh, shit! I hope it's not the police.* Jake set the cup down and headed down the hallway.

Then he got the shock of his life. It was Lillian

Satler, Ronnie's grandmother and Frank's ex-wife. As far as he knew, she'd never been to this house—at least not in the ten years he'd been married off and on to Ronnie.

She wore a gray silk suit that ended midcalf over a pristine white silk blouse, black medium-high-heeled shoes, and pearl earrings. Her perfectly waved brown hair looked as if it wouldn't move in a tornado, and not because of hair spray, like Flossie. It just wouldn't dare. Lillian had looked the same way forever.

"Well, well, well," he said, leaning against the door-jamb. "Hi, Grandma!"

Her upper lip curled with distaste as she surveyed him, disheveled hair to bare toes. "Don't be impertinent with me. Where's Veronica?"

"Sleeping. In my bed."

Lillian actually gasped with distress at that news, and her lip curled even more. "Go get her."

"Why?" he asked, unmoving.

"I have some news she should hear."

Uh-oh! Alarm bells went off in Jake's head. This could not be good. "Why don't you just give me the message, and I'll pass it on to her?"

"Why don't you move, you worthless bum."

Well, at least I managed to rattle the old biddy's composure. "Ronnie's happy. Can't you be happy for her?"

"Happy? With you?" She made a most unladylike snort. "I won't allow that."

"*You* won't allow that? Man, you are one cold . . ." He wanted to say *bitch,* but he restrained himself, and said, ". . . witch."

"Do you think I care what *you* think of me?"

"Jake? Is someone there?"

Jake groaned as he heard Ronnie coming down the hall behind him. Lillian practically gloated. When Ronnie reached him, she ducked under the arm he had extended across the open doorway. He could smell the Irish Spring soap she must have just showered with.

"Lillian! What are you doing here?"

"I've come to give you some news, and to bring you home."

The bells in Jake's head were clanging like wind chimes. *Bad news, bad news, bad news* . . .

Lillian surveyed, with equal distaste, Ronnie's wet hair, her Daisy Duke denim shorts, braless tank top, and bare feet. "Here," she said, shoving a folder into Ronnie's hands. "You'll find that your grandfather is not in financial straits. In fact, he has a million dollars in his stock portfolio, which his . . . his floozie . . ."

"Her name is Flossie."

Man, she has the curled lip thing down pat.

"Floozie, Flossie, no difference. *That* woman manages his stocks for him. In addition, Frank owns outright this house, two vehicles, the warehouse, and the diving boat; well, he did until he turned them over to you. Oh, and a small yacht, which he did not turn over to you."

Ronnie's jaw dropped lower and lower with each of Lillian's bits of information. "That can't be true."

"Of course it is. Would I step foot on that . . . that . . . man's property if it wasn't? You've been duped, young lady. So, pack your suitcase and let's get out of here. In fact, leave everything. I can send someone for your belongings later."

Ronnie's brow furrowed. "How do you know all this?"

"I hired a private detective."

Ronnie flinched as if she'd been slapped. The frown on her face deepened while she quickly flicked through the folder. "How could this be?" She turned to Jake. Then she dropped the folder and clapped both hands to her chest. A whimper escaped her parted lips. "You knew?"

He hesitated, but then nodded. "Not all along, but I guessed." *I knew it, I knew it, I knew this would happen.*

"When? How long have you known?"

"A week or so, I guess. It doesn't matter, Ronnie. Listen to me—"

"It. Doesn't. Matter?" She stared at him as if he were some kind of slimy creature.

Which was precisely how he felt. He tried to reach for her, but she shoved his hand away. Tears welled in her eyes and began to leak.

He couldn't stand to see Ronnie cry. Usually, his practice in the past had been to leave before the tears flowed. No escape now.

"Do not even think of crying over this louse." Lillian pointed a finger at him. "Or your grandfather, an even worse louse." Lillian reached to draw Ronnie outside with her, but Ronnie shoved her hand away as well and stormed down the hall.

Before he went after her, he said to Lillian, "Are you happy now?"

"Yes," she said with absolutely no regrets.

Frank and Flossie showed up then to complete the "party." Frank wore baggy plaid shorts with a black T-shirt and X-and-O neon orange suspenders. He was barefoot, too, and was sporting his Don King white hair this early in the morning. Flossie, on the other hand, was fully made up and wore a tight white shirt tucked into red shorts and red wedge-type shoes. Her big hair was a testament to the declining ozone layer.

Lillian took a step back and almost fell off the small porch. Her distaste for his and Ronnie's attire was nothing compared to her distaste for Frank and Flossie.

Her expression might work wonders in a courtroom, but Frank appeared undaunted. "Go back, Floss," he said, giving Flossie a soft shove behind him. "I'll take care of this."

Jake left with Flossie, who was alternately weeping and murmuring, "I told him. I told him not to do it."

Flossie went into the kitchen, probably to make a big breakfast; that had been her way of handling stress in the past.

Jake went out on the beach where he saw Ronnie sitting. As he walked out onto the cool, early morning sand, he wondered if this was the end, once again, for him and Ronnie, even before they'd really begun.

No, I won't let that happen.

A little voice in his head said, *Atta boy!*

✦

Her inner bitch was a wonder to behold. . . .

Frank stared at Lillian, the woman he'd once loved.

He hadn't seen Lillian in almost fifty years, since their last court battle over visitation rights for his son, Joey, a boy she'd never allowed him to get to know. She'd almost done the same with his granddaughter. Maybe she'd succeeded now—a final alienation.

Lillian had aged well—on the outside—better than

Flossie, who was a good twenty years younger. Probably plastic surgery. There was a coldness about her, though. He couldn't imagine ever having loved her, and he *had* loved her passionately when they had both been students at Princeton. Hard to believe that this stiff farce of a woman had returned that passion in triplicate. Hard to believe that that prissy pursed mouth had ever gone down on him. Or that those bony legs had ever been wrapped around his waist.

He shook his head to whisk away the unwelcome memories. "What have you done, Lil?"

"I've told Ronnie the truth about you."

"The truth?"

"You tricked her into coming here. You're a liar, like always."

"Don't you care how you hurt your granddaughter?"

"It's for the best. She's strong. She'll get over it."

"When did you turn so mean?"

"I'm just being honest with her."

"What did I do to make you this bitter for so many years?"

At first, she wasn't going to answer, but then her face softened just a little as she admitted, "You crushed my dreams." Immediately, she regretted her words as her expression went cold as ice again. "But dreams are for children. I learned that the hard way."

"I'm sorry," was all he could say.

"I don't want your pity."

It was useless trying to reason with Lillian. He turned away, closing the door behind him. He needed to find Ronnie and try to repair the damage Lillian—no, *he*—had done.

It can't be too late. It just can't.

It's not, a little voice in his head said.

That's just great. Now I'm taking advice from a voice in my head.

Be careful there, old man. I have friends in high places.

✦

Love makes the world go 'round . . . or not . . .

"I love you, Ronnie. Please. Please don't shut me out."

Veronica could not look at Jake right now. She was too angry, too hurt. "I could understand my grandfather making a fool of me, but you? You, I thought I could trust."

"You can."

"No. No, I can't." She turned to look at him beside her on the sand, both of their knees drawn up. There was something odd about his face. *He's scared,* she realized. For just one second, she wanted to comfort him, but she couldn't. Not now. "How long have you known? What exactly do you know? And why didn't he, or you, tell me?"

"I was suspicious from the beginning. I mean, Flossie's a stock market genius, you know. It was highly unlikely that she would have let Frank squander a fortune."

"No, Jake, I did not know that Flossie played the stock market. Another thing to add to my 'Making a Fool of Veronica' list. Not that I want to think about lists right now." She narrowed her eyes at him. "Was last night a game to you, too?"

"Don't you dare demean what happened with us last

night. You know I love you, dammit. Whether we screwed with a list, with a bar of soap, with our toes, or by playing strip polka to the beat of one of Frankie Yankovic's greatest-hit polkas on that old eight-track of your grandfather's, that doesn't make any difference. If our lovemaking was a game, it was a game we both played . . . with love. Furthermore, you are the one, babe, who always said the best lover was a man who could make a woman smile in bed." Jake's face flushed with anger as he clenched and unclenched his fists. He was flashing emotional tells like a blinking neon sign. Next he'd be pulling out his worry beads. Yep, there he went, putting his right hand in his pocket.

Well, I'm angry, too, big boy. And I have more reason than you do. "Okay, last night was . . . what it was. How about my other questions?"

"I was suspicious from the beginning, but it wasn't till I got here and noticed Frank's, well, body language, expressions, eyes. I confronted him about it, and he admitted that he was pretending to be on the skids so that you would feel sorry for him and come to run the business."

"How pathetic!"

"Yeah."

"Why couldn't he just ask me? Why couldn't you just tell me?"

"He feared the same thing I did. You would be out of here like a slingshot."

He was probably right. Still . . .

"I just flicked through my grandmother's detective report"—and wasn't that another kick in the gut—"but I really didn't get a chance to read all of it. Tell me."

"Frank's probably a wealthy man . . . very wealthy.

Yeah, he's done some stupid treasure hunts over the years, but mostly they've been legitimate projects that reaped a profit. He and Floss aren't big spenders, so I imagine he has plenty socked away or invested in the business."

"But you invested a hundred thousand in Jinx, Inc."

"That was more a sound investment for me than to help Frank out. I fully expect to get a healthy return on my stake."

She tried to digest all he said with a clear mind, which wasn't easy. "And the missing artwork and antiques and collector books?"

"I don't know. Probably in the attic."

She shook her head at the outrageousness of it all. "A deliberate ruse to trap me. Lies, all of it."

"Mostly sins of omission, not outright lies."

"And that excuses deception for him or for you?"

"He was desperate." The implication was that Jake was desperate, too, but she would address that issue later. "Don't be so skeptical. The man really loves you."

"He has a sad way of showing it."

"Probably. Your grandmother didn't make it easy. Then he let his pride get in the way. Hell, he's the one who should be explaining this, not me."

Veronica blew out air in a big exhale.

"So what now?" Jake finally asked.

"I don't trust you."

Jake winced at the words and their deliberate coldness.

"Life is like a poker game . . . ," she started to say.

"Whaaat? I'm the one who does poker metaphors, not you."

"Life is like a poker game," she repeated, "you've

gotta know when to fold them, know when to walk
away—like that old Kenny Rogers song."

"I'm not leaving, Ronnie. Just get that through your
head. I. Am. Not. Leaving."

She studied his face, his handsome face that she
loved so much, and said, "It looks like I'll be the one
leaving this time."

✦

Getting advice from beyond, well, the
bayou . . .

A week later, Jake was still back at his apartment in
Brigantine, but only for a short time more. He was not
giving up on Ronnie. Not this time.

To prove how serious he was, if only to himself, he'd
sold his condo in a quick real estate transaction *and*
cancelled the tentative offer on the beachfront cottage.
The movers would be coming in three weeks to put his
furnishings in storage; that's when the new owners
would take over. The next place he lived would be one
he and Ronnie chose together. He hoped.

He hadn't talked to Ronnie in all that time. She'd
changed her cell and home phone numbers. Her grandmother, the one time she didn't hang up on him, told
him Ronnie hadn't come back to work. But that didn't
deter him. She needed time; he could give her that.
Timing was everything, in poker and in life. And he
was an expert at strategy and not acting hastily. In fact,
he was lining up the ammunition for the seductive assault he planned for her. He was prepared for a long-
haul siege, if necessary.

The phone rang just as he closed the door to his condo, so he went back in. He was driving up to Manhattan to meet with his agent about the book deal. He figured that a book could be written anywhere—anywhere he and Ronnie settled. And the poker, well, that was Ronnie's call.

The phone continued to ring, and he quickly opened the door. He hoped it was Ronnie, but more likely it was Frank, who'd been having an equal lack of luck in finding Ronnie. But it wasn't either of those.

"Jake? Holy Sacralait! I been havin' the hardest time findin' yer number. I musta called twenty Jake Jensens this mornin'."

"Tante Lulu? Where are you? I thought you went back to Louisiana."

"I did. Had ta weed my garden, take care of some healing bizness, visit with fam'ly, and—shoo, ya hear me, shoo, you varmint!"

"Huh?"

"Jist a minute. I'll be right back." The phone clanked down on some hard surface, and he could hear Tante Lulu shooing someone, or something, away. She was soon back. "Sorry. I had to get a broom and shoo away that ol' gator. He has a taste fer my okra, of all things. Talk about!"

The old lady has an alligator in her yard, and she shooed it away with a broom. Unbelievable!

"Anyways, I'm callin' ta see iffen you and Ronnie are hitched again yet."

"No, we're not hitched. She's not even talking to me."

"Not to worry. I been prayin' to St. Jude. An' you'll be gettin' yer hope chest soon. Tee-John is comin' back north to go to that prom thing with Brenda."

"It's a class reunion, I think."

"Prom, reunion, whatever. I'll have him cart it on the airplane with him. By the by, whass yer fav'rit color? I wants to finish up the embroidery on the doilies and dish towels. You better get yer butt in gear with Ronnie, boy. Or else me 'n Rosa 'n Flossie'll have to go through with our plan. Hold on. I gots to go stir the gumbo."

It was hard to follow a Tante Lulu conversation. She tended to meander from one subject to another. But several things became clear to him:

She was praying for him. He could live with that. He wasn't too proud to accept help from any quarter.

She was actually making him a hope chest. Bless her heart! How could he refuse such a gift? Angel and Grace would die laughing when he told them about it, though.

She was embroidering doilies for him. Doilies!

Most alarming, the dingbat trio were hatching a plan to get him back with Ronnie. He shuddered to think what it might be.

"I'm back. You and Ronnie wanna have yer second honeymoon here on the bayou? I mean, yer fifth honeymoon. I kin go stay with Charmaine on the ranch, and you two can cuddle here in my cottage."

"I don't think—"

"It's real nice."

"Well, maybe." *Good Lord, I'm planning a honeymoon with a woman who won't even speak to me, and the wedding planner is a five-foot-zero octogenarian dingbat.* Even so, he was grinning when he hung up the phone.

On the way back from the city later that day, he stopped at Loveladies to talk with Frank. Frank looked awful, like he hadn't slept in days. He was out on the deck, alone, polka music playing so loud he was surprised all the birds on the beach hadn't flown away.

Jake turned the volume down on the tape deck and stepped outside, sitting down on a chair opposite Frank at the patio table. "Where's Flossie?"

"Hairdresser."

"I got your cashier's check. For a million freakin' dollars."

"You all got checks. I took my three million, gave you and Rosa a million each for your thousand-dollar investments, and everyone else on the project got a cool million, except for LeDeux, who got five hundred thou. I even gave Tante Lulu, Flossie, Tony, and Steve fifty thou each. The remainder goes into an investment fund for the next project, with all the team members having an equal share."

"Not a bad haul!"

"Especially for two weeks' work; actually, lots more time when you consider the research and preparation we did first. Still . . ."

"It's hard to believe all that money. Especially that buyers were found for all that stuff in less than two weeks."

"Never underestimate the power of the mob."

"Have you notified the authorities about the wreck site yet?"

"Yep. Well, sorta. I called Lyle Jordan, an archaeologist who works for the Park Service outta Washington. He specializes in World War II history. He's the one I worked with on the Mussolini toilet. He'll be contacting the Park Service. I expect to take them out to the site next week. You wanna go with us?"

"Maybe. You should probably invite the other members of the team, especially Adam. He seems to be somewhat of an expert on that era."

Frank nodded. "I'm going to talk to the *Asbury Park Press* reporter next week, too. Gotta be careful how I handle that. Don't be surprised if he calls you." Frank then directed his bleary eyes at him, speaking of the subject they'd both been dancing around. "You heard from Ronnie?"

Jake shook his head.

"Me neither. I've made a mess of things, haven't I?"

"Yep."

"I got her new phone number."

"You did? How?"

"I have a friend from the FBI who knows someone at the phone company."

Why am I not surprised?

"But I think I'll go see her in person, instead of callin'. She might hang up on me, but I doubt she'd shove me out the door."

That was debatable.

"Do any of these friends of friends of yours know what Ronnie's been doing?"

"Not all the time."

"Some of the time?"

"She does some volunteering at a woman's shelter. She eats out. She got a cat. She goes to the beach . . . on Martha's Vineyard."

"Martha's Vineyard?" He and Ronnie used to go there on occasion. Long walks on the beach. Lobster dinners.

"Just day trips. She's been talking to a realtor."

A realtor? Could she be thinking the same way he was? New beginnings all around? "About what?"

"Don't know. What's *your* plan?" Frank asked him.

"I don't have a plan, precisely, but I'm giving her time to sort things out. After that, all bets are off."

"Don't wait too long. You snooze, you lose."

"Tante Lulu called me."

A big ol' grin popped onto Frank's somber face. "She's a lulu, isn't she?"

"Oh, yeah."

"I met her when she was young. She was some looker in those days. And wild."

I do not want to imagine that old lady being the wild thing. "Hey, she mentioned some scheme that she and Flossie and Rosa and you have been cooking up to get me and Ronnie back together."

"It's a last-ditch effort. Probably never happen."

"You're not going to tell me what it is, are you?"

"Nope."

"Would I be happy or unhappy with this scheme?"

"Oh, definitely happy."

On that note, Jake got up to leave. "Keep in touch, Frank. Tell me what she says if you find her."

"I will. Oh, and another thing."

"Yeah?"

"It wouldn't hurt if you and I adopted that St. Jude fellow."

Chapter
26

And the healing begins . . .

"He never beat me."

Veronica couldn't believe this young woman would actually defend the man who had caused her to seek refuge at St. Mary's Women's Shelter in Boston. "Cynthia," she chided.

Her expression must have registered with the twenty-year-old. Still, she made excuses for the man. "Not physically."

"Honey, abuse doesn't always come in the form of a fist. Your husband controlled every aspect of your life, right down to accompanying you to the toilet. He cut off all your ties with your family and friends. He wouldn't let you have a job or a checkbook. You had to fold clothes in a certain way or he would make you fold and refold them a dozen times as a lesson to do it *the right way.*"

"But he never hit me, like my dad used to hit my mom."

"That doesn't make it right. Do you want to go back to that kind of life . . . to him?"

"No!" she replied vehemently. Then more softly, "But I don't want to have him arrested or anything. And I don't want him to take my kids. He has money for lawyers. He says the court would give him Jesse and Jo Lynn in a heartbeat . . . 'cause . . . 'cause I'm not fit to be a mother."

"Don't let him determine your self-image. Is there any chance . . . how about counseling?"

Cynthia shook her head hard.

"Okay, I'll start divorce and custody proceedings. Do not, I repeat, do not contact your husband or tell anyone else who might talk to him where you and your children are."

She nodded, tears streaming down her face.

"Don't worry, honey. Everything will work out in the end. Maybe you'll even find a good man who will appreciate how wonderful you are."

"There are no good men," Cynthia said on a sob.

Veronica was going to let her statement stand, but then she disagreed. "Yes, there are."

And that was the truth, Veronica thought as she drove back to her apartment a short time later. Her grandfather was not a bad man, as her grandmother had led her to believe all these years. Misguided, maybe, but he'd done nothing to be loathed for or frightened of, as far as she could tell. Not to her, anyhow.

Jake was a good man, too; that had never been in question. And he loved her; that, too, had never been in question. There *was* a question, though, of whether she could trust him. Until she resolved that issue in her own mind, she could not talk with him. But she thought about him. A lot.

The bottom line was that she was still angry—well, more hurt than angry—with Jake and her grandfather. But she wasn't so blind as to not recognize they'd both had good motives.

Her grandfather must have hurt her grandmother deeply for her to be so vindictive. Veronica wasn't sure she'd ever be able to forgive her.

Odd that all these thoughts had been prompted by the young woman at the shelter. Oh. Perhaps not so odd. It was all about manipulation, she decided with sudden insight. Her grandmother manipulating her all these years to conform to her image, to hate and fear her grandfather, to toe a line she had drawn. Then this stupid ruse of her grandfather's about being poor—that had been a form of manipulation, too. And Jake had been in on the manipulation; that's what hurt the most, even if his manipulation had been done to get her back.

Luckily—well, luckily for her grandfather—she was in a relatively good mood when she came up the sidewalk from the parking garage and was about to enter her apartment building.

Frank sat on a low brick wall, waiting for her. And what a sight for sore eyes he was. This must be his idea of dressing for a special occasion. His gray hair was slicked back off his face; Flossie had probably put a little hair spray on it. He wore new khaki slacks with sharp creases ironed into them. He even wore a button-down white shirt and docksiders with socks. The only touch of the old Frank was the black suspenders with red tongues all over them. What a handsome man he must have been at one time! Still was. No wonder even a woman as stiff as Lillian had fallen for the rogue back then.

Frank looked worried, as well he should. "Ronnie," he greeted her.

"Frank."

"I need to talk to you."

She motioned for him to follow her into the building. He took the plastic bag from her, which contained cat food, kitty litter, and a frozen Mexican dinner.

Once they were in her apartment, he sat in a wingback chair by the window with Ace, the new coal-black cat she'd rescued last week, sitting on his lap, purring. She'd already made them both cups of tea. She sipped at hers. Frank's sat untouched on the Shaker table beside his chair.

"Nice apartment," he commented.

"Yes, I like it. I've worked hard over the years to collect the antiques and get the colors of the walls and carpets just right." *Who am I kidding?* "I've put the place up for sale."

Instead of asking her why or being surprised, Frank just nodded. "Jake already sold his."

Whaaat? "Why?"

"I'll let him tell you—next time you see him."

If there is a next time. "Okay. Let's cut to the bone. Why are you here?"

Frank continued to pet the purring cat with long sweeping strokes over its back. Finally, he looked directly at her with eyes she suddenly realized were the same honey color as her own. "I love you."

That was the last thing she'd expected him to say, and it threw her off guard. *Why tell me now? What can I say to that? "It's too late"? "Thanks"?*

Because she remained speechless, he continued, "I know I've acted like a jackass over the years, and I'm sorry for that."

"Please. Don't rehash old stuff."

"I have to. I need to explain. I did love your grand-mother, and I had intended to go to law school with her, but at heart I always was a little bit wild. When I was handed all that inheritance, it gave me the opportunity to be wild in a respectable way, if that makes sense."

Like Jake?

"Well, it sure didn't make sense to Lillian. I honest-to-God thought she would give in and come with me. I was wrong. I especially thought she would come back once she found herself pregnant."

She hated that this proud man was humbling him-self. She wished he would stop and be his old obnox-ious self. That, she could deal with. This . . . this stranger wanted something from her she wasn't sure she could give.

"After that, things went downhill like a greased pig on a sliding board. She wouldn't come to me. I wouldn't go to her. She never notified me when Joey was born. I went to court to make sure my name was on the birth certificate. She started calling him by her maiden name. I went to court to fight for joint custody. She promised to give him the Jinkowsky name if I would drop my legal fights." He looked at her through soulful eyes. "For years after that, I said to hell with her! Pretended I didn't care, probably *didn't* care half the time. Booze can numb the heart as well as the brain. By the time Flossie came along and straightened me out, the damage had already been done with Joey. He screamed every time I tried to bring him here to visit. So, I gave up. Isn't that sad? That I would give up so easily with my own son?"

This was all beginning to make a warped kind of

logic. "That's why you tried so hard with me. Well, tried so hard in a way that frightened me."

"Yep. I wasn't used to kids. Never had any brothers or sisters. Every time you were forced to come here for a visit by that court order I finally got, I bumbled around and made one mistake after another."

"Why didn't you ever say, well, what you said before?"

"That I love you?"

She nodded.

"It's hard for me to say those words, even to Floss. Don't know why. Maybe because I grew up in a family where they tended to assume those things and never say them out loud. You know what the second hardest words are for me? And they were for my father, too. In fact, I never heard him say them."

She cocked her head for him to continue.

"I'm sorry."

Veronica began to weep.

Frank set the cat on the floor and opened his arms for her. And, hard as it was to believe, she, a thirty-two-year-old woman, sat on her grandfather's lap, where they hugged each other and wept for all the lost years. Veronica had grown up in a house without physical affection, but she never, ever realized that there was this hole in her life that only a grandparent, Frank, in particular, could fill.

It wasn't a happily ever after, but it was a start.

Until she called Jake in Brigantine that night. She was going to ask him to meet with her, to talk about a possible relationship, to say that she loved him and was too miserable without him.

The phone picked up on the first ring.

It was a woman.

"Who is this?" Veronica asked.

"Trish Dangel. Who is this?"

Veronica stared wordlessly, in shock, at the telephone. Then she hung up.

Jake had done it again. The minute they had a disagreement, he left and took up with another woman. True, she had been the one to leave this time, but the dust hadn't settled before he was hooked up with another woman.

The phone continued to ring after that until she took it off the hook. Jake had probably star-sixty-nined her.

When will I ever learn? Am I a glutton for punishment? There were no tears this time, just utter devastating disappointment.

It was over.

※

Laissez les bon temps rouler—let the good
times roll . . .

John LeDeux walked into the ballroom of the Franklin Hotel in Perth Amboy, where banners announced "Class of 1992—St. Mark's High School Reunion."

He looked damn sexy, if he could say so himself, in a brand-new, dark blue Boss suit, a light blue shirt, and a navy tie sporting little red peppers, the main ingredient in Tabasco, or Cajun Lightning. It was his own hidden message for tonight. These Northerners didn't know how to have a good time. He intended to show them.

On his arm was a woman who was naturally beautiful. He was in his element here, playing the lover to a
beautiful lady, and he was loving it.

"Shoulders up, babe," he advised Brenda. "Show off
that cleavage."

"Behave, you jerk. I want people to believe you're
my date, not my gigolo."

"Tsk-tsk! Not nice to call your lover names, unless
it's 'Oh, baby! Do me one more time.'"

She pinched his arm.

He pinched her butt.

Brenda shot him a dirty look, but not too dirty. She
knew he was prepping her for their upcoming "per-
formance."

"You look great, *chère*." And she did. Her blonde
curls were piled on top of her head, with loose strands
dangling down in a sexy, bed-tossed way. She wore a
low-cut red halter sheath dress, matching stiletto heels,
and red screw-me-silly lipstick.

They walked into the crowded room where a band
was playing nineties music, in this case, Marky Mark's
"Good Vibrations." Oh, yeah. There was going to be
some vibrating tonight, if he had any say. Some couples
were dancing; but mostly people stood around, cock-
tails in hand, reminiscing about old times.

"Oh, God! There he is."

Emerging from a circle of people, Lance Caslow
walked toward them. If John were female, he would
probably think Caslow was handsome in a blond I'm-
a-sexy-race-car-driver sort of way. John was a longtime fan, but he was not intimidated by the guy's
celebrity status.

John wrapped an arm around Brenda's bare shoulders and tugged her closer. She smelled good, like vanilla or something sweet.

"Brenda," Caslow said when he was directly in front of them. He didn't look happy. Especially when his eyes latched onto John's fingers making little circles on Brenda's shoulder.

"Lance." Brenda leaned her head onto John's shoulder, causing Caslow's jaw to clench.

"You've been avoiding me."

"When?" She batted her highly mascaraed eyelashes just the way he'd shown her how.

"For the last two friggin' years, that's when. Every time I come to pick up Patti, you disappear into the woodwork. If I didn't know better, I'd think you're afraid."

Well, by golly! Do I sense a little hostility here?

"Why would I be afraid of you?"

"Not of me. Of yourself. I'm thinkin' you're still in love with me."

"Of all the egotistical . . ." Brenda glanced around and said, "Where's Barbie?"

"Barbie who?"

"Oh, I don't know, the Barbie of the Month, I guess. You know, the bimbo with the big boobs who sat on your lap in the '03 NASCAR race picture that ran in, oh, let's say, every newspaper in the world."

"Are you still pissed over that? Shiiit! I didn't even know her name."

"You knew her well enough to have her ass in your lap and your hands propping up her breasts."

Caslow shook his head sadly. "Arguing with you is like drag racing over a cliff."

John coughed, "Ahem," figuring it was time to liven up this party.

"Who are you?"

John made a slow sweep of Brenda's arm with his palm, wrist to shoulder and back again, just to see Caslow's reaction. John assumed that hissing sound he made was not approval. "I'm John LeDeux. Brenda's date. I've heard a lot about you."

"As a NASCAR driver?"

"Well, yeah, but also from Brenda."

Caslow let out a short hoot of laughter. "What? Is she still telling the small-dick jokes?"

"Only the truth, sweetheart," Brenda said with an exaggerated smile on her face.

"I, on the other hand, am amply endowed," John said, just to needle the guy.

Caslow's eyes about bugged out. "For chrissake, how old are you?"

"Old enough!"

"You have some nerve questioning the age of my date when jailbait is your norm," Brenda spat.

"Dammit, Brenda! Cut it out. I came here to see you, not to fight." He inhaled and exhaled several times to calm himself down. "Do you want a drink?"

"Yeah, we'll both have gin and tonics, light on the gin for my honey here," John said.

Caslow looked as if he'd like to make roadkill of him with a race car. "Are you sure you're legal?" he muttered as he went off to the bar.

"Well, that was fun," John said to Brenda once her ex was gone.

"I'm so nervous I'm shaking."

"You two have it bad."

"I beg your pardon?"

"It's obvious that he still loves you. His eyes devour

you. And you, come on, admit it. He still rings your bell."

"Rings my . . . my . . . ," she stuttered.

"Let's dance," he said. "Time for step two of 'Annoy the Hell out of Lance.'" It was Right Said Fred's "I'm too Sexy." Very appropriate song, in John's opinion.

Dancing came naturally to Cajun men—well, at least the LeDeux men. And John, with all modesty, knew he was the best. Not in a flamboyant way, but slow and sexy; that was the trick.

By the time that song ended and the DJ turned on "Jump," he and Brenda had their moves down pat. She was shimmying. He was coming up behind her, both their knees bent, hips undulating, doing a Cajun version of dirty dancing. People started to stop and watch them, even Caslow, who stood on the edge of the crowd, staring at them with dismay.

The next song was a slow one, that hokey "How Am I Supposed to Live without You?" by Michael Bolton. By then he took pity on Caslow, who'd ditched the drinks and stood frozen like a lovesick puppy. With a jerk of his head, he motioned Caslow to make his move.

Brenda didn't have a chance to protest when Caslow came up and took her in his arms and began to dance. At first, she was stiff as a board, throwing eye-daggers at John and mouthing "traitor," but then she relaxed. John felt a sort of satisfaction watching her link her arms around her ex's neck and laying her face in the crook of his neck, with Caslow tugging her even closer. Both of their eyes were closed. He figured he must have inherited a bit of Tante Lulu's matchmaking genes.

Walking off the dance floor, he picked up one of the three gin and tonics Caslow had gotten for them. As he sipped, he surveyed the room. *Oh, yeah. Twelve noon, straight ahead. Blonde with bedroom eyes scoping me out.*

With a grin, John put his drink down and sauntered over. In his best Southern drawl, he said, "Hey, darlin'."

✦

One party crasher, two party crasher, three party crasher . . .

"I can't believe I'm going to crash a high school re-union. This has got to be a new low in my pitiful life."

Veronica was speaking to Adam and Caleb, who flanked her as they walked into a hotel ballroom where Brenda's class get-together was being held. It was nine o'clock, and the event had to be half over.

"Nothing pitiful about it," Adam asserted. "We're here to offer moral support to Brenda."

"Yeah. She was probably too embarrassed to ask for our help," Caleb observed. "That's why she invited that young pup LeDeux as her date."

Veronica gazed with amusement at the two men, who were looking very spiffy. Adam wore a dark suit with a red and yellow striped tie, and Caleb was in a navy blazer and khakis with a dark tie sporting a bunch of tiny images of the Navy SEAL budweiser. Hey, she didn't look too shabby herself, even though she had been given only a half hour to get dressed when Adam and Caleb showed up unexpectedly at her Boston apartment late this afternoon. She wore a short black, silk, sleeveless sheath dress. She recalled having worn it once when vacationing in the South of France, when Jake . . . well, never mind. Anyhow, she'd dressed hurriedly and pulled her hair off her face with pearl and diamond clips to match her pearl earrings; her only other adornment was her rhinestone-studded black high heels. It had taken them four hours to get here, even speeding in Adam's brand-new Lexus.

"Uh-oh! Looks like we're too late," Adam said.

They all turned to the crowd in the middle of the ballroom.

Brenda was dancing with what must be her exhusband, a blond god in an expensive brown suit. So much for her making him eat his heart out with jealousy. John was dancing, too, with a blonde bombshell . . . what else? And they all appeared half crocked.

"Nah, not too late. Looks like we arrived just in time," Caleb said. "But first, I think we all need a drink after Famosa's driving."

"What? You think I drive too fast?" Adam asked, actually surprised by Caleb's comment.

"No, Sherlock. You don't drive too fast; you fly too fast. For chrissake, you were doing ninety half the time."

"Yeah, but I was doing forty in traffic the rest of the time. So, it all equaled out."

Veronica rolled her eyes.

Once they had drinks in hand—her, white wine; Adam, scotch on the rocks; and Caleb, a beer—they watched the dancers. When the song ended and Brenda and John spotted them, the four joined them at a large, round table.

"Hi, I'm Lance Caslow, Brenda's ex-husband," the

blond god said, offering handshakes to them all. A personable fellow, despite all the things said about him by Brenda, whose face was pink with embarrassment at having been caught with her ex.

"I've heard a lot about you," Veronica, Adam, and Caleb said in unison.

"Needle dick, right?" Lance said with a laugh, shaking his head at Brenda.

"Well, it is," Brenda said.

"Not," he said.

"Don't be thinking that I'm getting back together with Mr. I'm too Full of Myself," Brenda told everyone at the table.

Lance waggled his eyebrows.

"We're not." She spoke directly to Lance. "I was just being nice so you wouldn't be embarrassed in public if I tossed you in the punch bowl."

Lance laughed. "You could try. And as long as you're being nice, how about you and me . . . ?" He said something so explicit then that everyone's jaws dropped.

Brenda's eyes narrowed with fury.

Lance continued to laugh, which infuriated Brenda more. She took a long swallow of her drink, and said, "Did I ever tell you guys about the first time Lance and I made love? If you think his driving is faster than the speed of sound, boy, you should have—"

"Well, this is pleasant," John interrupted. "Guys, I'd like you to meet Sonia Reeder, who probably thinks we're all nuts. Sonia, this is Brenda, Lance, Ronnie, Caleb, and Adam. Brenda and Lance, you must know Sonia from high school." John and Sonia, who wore a red, skin-tight latex short-sleeved dress and chandelier rhinestone earrings, smiled at them all, sat down on the two empty chairs and picked up drinks they must have left there.

"Sonia Reeder?" Brenda's brow was furrowed. "Is that your maiden name?"

"Nope," Sonia said, grinning.

Now Lance's brow was furrowed. "You look familiar."

"Oh," Lance and Brenda said at the same time. "Steve Reeder."

John choked on his drink, and Caleb had to clap him on the back. Everyone was laughing, including Sonia. Before he had a chance to check himself, John blurted out, "I put my tongue in a man's mouth. Eeew!"

"You weren't saying 'eew' at the time, sweetie," Sonia said sweetly.

"You just met her—him—and you were French kissing?" Veronica shook her head with incredulity.

"Hey, I'm a fast mover," John said.

"I can attest to that." Sonia batted her false eyelashes at John.

John groaned.

"I told you he was a dumb Southern boy," Adam told Caleb. "Did you hear about the cracker whose dog couldn't learn tricks?"

John just grinned, not at all offended.

"You have to be smarter than the dog to teach it stuff," Adam finished.

"Not bad," John said. "But do you know how a Yankee man is different than a hot fudge sundae? No? Well, a hot fudge sundae always satisfies a woman."

"I like hot fudge sundaes," Sonia said, licking her lips and staring at John like he was a sweet treat.

"I don't want to hurt your feelings, but I'm not gay," John told Sonia.

"Good, because I'm not a man—anymore," Sonia replied, a teasing twinkle in his—her—eyes.

"Help!" John appealed to the rest of them.

After that, the party went downhill, or uphill, depending on who was talking. Alcohol played a big part. Since the dinner was over and it was a cash bar, no one cared about the party crashers. Or that there was one more late party crasher.

Jake.

✦

The things a guy will do for love . . . !

This had to be the most half-baked, half-assed thing he'd ever done in all his life, but Frank had insisted that he drive up to Perth Amboy for Brenda Caslow's high school reunion if he ever wanted to get Ronnie back.

He should have gone to Ronnie's apartment when she called last night and Trish had answered the phone. Didn't Ronnie trust him at all? Hah! The answer to that question was obvious. Trish had only been there to gather up the last of her belongings. The new owners would be coming next week.

He knew Ronnie was home last night when he'd star-sixty-nined her and called and called and called. He'd been about to go to her place this afternoon when Frank stopped by and told him he better get his ass in gear if he wanted to catch Ronnie before it was too late. "Do the words *Famosa* and *Peachey* ring any bells, boy?"

That's how he'd ended up here, at a freakin' high school reunion.

It was ridiculous, really. He didn't go to his own reunions. And he couldn't remember the last time he'd worn a suit . . . probably his grandmother's funeral three years ago. Furthermore, it was almost eleven o'clock when he got to the Franklin Hotel. Everyone had probably already left.

Well, they hadn't left, he realized with a sigh as he entered the ballroom where a DJ was still spinning old nineties tunes, in this case, Kriss Kross's "Jump." LeDeux was out on the dance floor cutting a mean rug with some blonde in a red tart dress. Even Famosa was making a fool of himself, fast dancing like an arms-flopping idiot with Brenda and, yep, Lance Caslow. The trio were a regular Lords and Lady of the Dance. They all looked a little bit drunk.

Then he saw the backs of Peachey and Ronnie, sitting at a table, watching the dancing. Damn, he'd thought Peachey was out of the picture. They were sitting real close together, and Ronnie was wearing that backless black dress that had pretty much resulted in the Insanity Marriage in Monaco. Well, he wasn't insane now, but he sure was pissed. So this was why Frank wanted him to come. The SEAL-Amish Rambo was horning in on his woman—before he had a chance to make her his woman again.

"Ronnie," he said, coming up and placing a hand on her bare shoulder.

She and Peachey both jumped with surprise.

"Go away," Peachey said.

"Get lost," he said back.

"Asshole!"

"Prick!"

"You are such a loser. Why don't you go play cards or something?"

"Why don't you go blow up a terrorist or something?"

"Both of you, stop it! You're behaving like children." Ronnie stood and turned toward Jake, putting her hands on her hips—with consternation, he supposed.

He could deal with consternation. Now, disgust, that was another matter.

"Where's your latest girlfriend?"

"You're my latest girlfriend."

"You think?"

"Yeah, I think. You look great. Dance with me."

"You've got to be kidding."

"Don't you even want an explanation?"

"No."

"Well, I'm giving it, anyway. The movers are coming next week, and Trish came to pick up the last of her stuff. That's all."

"You are a prime candidate for Liars Anonymous," Peach interjected.

"Butt out, butthead."

"I don't think so."

Jake decided to ignore Peachey and asked Ronnie again, "Dance with me?"

"Hey, she came with me," Peachey said, also standing now. The ex-SEAL had a few inches on him; he was probably six foot four, and his muscles outmatched Jake's two to one. Hell, his muscles probably outmatched Mister Universe.

No matter. Jake had four words for him, "Who the fuck cares?"

"I did not come with you, Caleb. I came with you *and* Adam. This is not a date." The latter she directed at both him and Peachey.

That was nice. She must be glad to see me. Or at least not angry to see me. "Okay. Now will you dance with me?"

"It's a fast dance. You don't fast dance."

"We'll slow dance to fast music. Big deal!"

"What are you doing here?"

"Can we just friggin' dance and get away from Rambo here?"

Rambo grinned, and Ronnie grinned, too.

"You're jealous." She was enjoying his frustration.

"Damn straight I am." His eyes strayed to the dance floor. "Is that a guy LeDeux is dancing with?"

"How did you know?" Peachey and Ronnie both wanted to know.

"It's obvious."

"Not to us," Ronnie said.

"Are you going to make me beg?"

Peachey made a snorting sound before tipping a longneck to his mouth.

Jake didn't care about making a fool of himself. This was too important.

"Would you"—Ronnie studied him with her head tilted to the side—"beg?"

He started to go down on one knee.

Ronnie immediately reached out and pulled him with her. "Idiot! I was just teasing."

"I'm not."

Peachey spoke over them both. "I'm not giving up, Ronnie. Sooner or later you'll get sick of the gambler here. I'll be waiting."

"When hell freezes over," Jake said. He gave Ronnie a quick pass-by kiss on the lips before she could protest or belt him one. Then he led her to the edge of the thinning crowd still on the dance floor. Okay, he didn't lead her, he pulled her. Behind his back, he gave Peachey the finger. Immature of him, sure, but, man, did it feel good!

Luckily, the DJ melded one song into another, and now it was "End of the Road," by that old boy band Boyz II Men. Slow dances he could handle. All you had to do was stand still and sway.

"You left me," he said right off, even though she was tucked up against his chest, her long hair brushing his cheek. He could swear he felt her heartbeat. *Kerthump, kerthump, kerthump.* "There is nothing between me and Trish."

She hesitated, then said, "Okay."

He breathed a big sigh of relief. "Why did you go away . . . and stay away? Why wouldn't you take my calls?"

"I needed time to think, to see where I should go from here."

"And what did you decide?"

"I'm still thinking."

"Maybe I can help you make a decision." He ran his palms over her silky rump, then back to her waist. Hey, he never claimed to be smooth. Besides, she didn't seem to mind.

"Maybe." After a long silence, she said, "I won't marry you again."

That was probably a wise decision. "Ever?"

"I don't know."

"I can live with that—*if* we're together."

"And I think I'd like to have a baby."

Boy, that one coldcocked him. He drew his face back to look at her. She was dead serious. "You want to have a baby *without* our being married?" Was this shades of his goofball flower-children parents or what? They had opposed marriage on some screwy moral grounds! Probably the reason why he did just the opposite and got married so many times.

"No, I meant *if* we ever decide to, you know, again. I . . . we . . . can make that decision later."

Whew! That was better. "I'm going to write another book about poker. So, we can live wherever you want."

"You don't have to give up poker playing."

"Yeah, I do. For a while."

"You won't believe this, but I'm thinking about moving into Frank's house."

Another coldcock. "With Frank and Flossie?"

"No, silly! They're going off on some world cruise."

"And you would live there alone?"

"No! *We* would live there."

His heart skipped a beat, then began to chug like a locomotive. "You and me? Together?"

She nodded.

"You made this decision, even thinking that I was back with Trish?" *Chug, chug, chug,* his heart went.

"After my initial anger, I cooled down. You wouldn't do something that cruel to me."

He swallowed awkwardly at that vote of confidence. "And what would we be doing there, *together,* at Frank's house, other than fucking like rabbits and making babies?"

"Baby. Singular."

He waited.

Finally, she offered the zinger. "We would be partners in running Jinx, Inc. Oh, don't look so shocked. It would only be temporary. One or two projects. To see if we can do it. To see if we're capable of handling it. Besides, we both have plenty of money to get started."

Now that his pounding heart was beginning to slow, he laughed at the absurdity of it all, and at the same time, at the rightness of it all. Finally, when they hugged each other and kissed and hugged some more, Jake said, "Jensen and Jinx, Inc., right?"

"Oh, no! Jinx and Jensen, Inc."

"Whatever!"

A short time later, they were leaving the hotel, about to walk over to the parking lot, about to launch this tentative, temporary life they'd agreed upon, when Steve and Tony, the Mafia twins, approached them. They were dressed all in black, like gangsters. And they were clearly carrying.

"This can't be good news," Jake whispered to Ronnie.

"What are they doing with those handcuffs?"

"Handcuffs? What handcuffs? Oh, shit!"

Ronnie's question came too late because the two thugs already had her and Jake in strangleholds and their hands cuffed behind their backs. The area in back of the hotel was empty, so there would be no help from a passerby. Where was Rambo when he was needed? Probably inside, nursing his bad luck.

Each of the guys did something strange then, even more strange than the handcuffs. They each held out before him and Ronnie small vials of an amber-colored liquid.

"You can either swallow it, or let me whack you out with the butt of my gun," Steve said.

"What is it? GHB or something?" Ronnie asked in a wobbly voice.

"Unbelievable!" Tony remarked. "No, it's just some herb tea Tante Lulu sent to my mother to knock some sense into the two of you."

"Is it our share of the Pink Project money that you want?" Ronnie squirmed, to no avail, as they steered them toward a Lincoln Continental with dark windows.

"I knew you guys were going to renege; I just knew it," Jake told them.

Steve's response was to shove him hard into the backseat. Ronnie fell on top of him when they shoved her in, too.

"Drink the damn stuff," Steve said once they were sitting up beside each other on the bench seat. Then he held Jake's nose and jammed the vial in his mouth, forcing him to swallow. Actually, it did taste like tea. Tony did the same thing to Ronnie.

Soon they were headed down the parkway.

"Where are you taking us?" Jake asked.

"The ocean," Tony, who was driving, answered. "Naked."

"Help! They're going to tie us to cement blocks and drop us in the ocean." Ronnie's eyes were wild with fear. Talk about a nightmare come true for her!

"You two are morons. You watch too much TV," Steve remarked. "We're just following orders. We ain't gonna kill you."

"You're not?" Ronnie whimpered.

"Whose orders?" Jake asked, a sudden suspicion coming to him.

"Our mother, Flossie, Tante Lulu, and Frank," Tony explained.

"I don't understand," Ronnie said. "Why would they ask you to kidnap us? Oh. Oh, no! This isn't part of their scheme to get me and Jake back together, is it?"

"Don't ask me," Tony said. "We're just following orders."

Jake was beginning to feel woozy. Ronnie's eyes were starting to flutter.

"We're already back together. Temporarily," Jake tried to say, but the words came out slurred and faint. In fact, he couldn't pronounce the word *temporarily,* which came out sounding like *tempy.* Ronnie was snoring softly, her head on his lap, the hem of her dress having ridden up to no man's land.

"Then you're going to really like what these ladies have in store for you," Tony said.

And, boy, did they ever!

❦

Not a bad philosophy of life . . .

Days later, out on the Atlantic Ocean, where they were playing not-so-reluctant nudists on *Sweet Jinx,* Jake was heard to say, "Life is like a poker game. Sometimes in life you are dealt a dream card, and, man, you gotta run with it."

"Am I the dream card?" Veronica asked.

"Oh, yeah!"

But then Veronica said, "Life is like a treasure hunt. Sometimes the gold you seek is in your own backyard."

"Are we the gold?" Jake asked.

"Oh, yeah!"

About the Author

Sandra Hill lives in the middle of chaos, surrounded by a husband, four sons, a live-in girlfriend, two grandchildren, a male German shepherd the size of a horse, and five cats. Each of them is more outrageous than the other. Sometimes three other dogs come to visit. No wonder she has developed a zany sense of humor. And the clutter is neverending: golf clubs, skis, wrestling gear, baseball bats and gloves, tennis rackets, mountain-climbing ropes, fishing rods, bikes, exercise equipment . . .

Sandra and her stockbroker husband, Robert, own two cottages on a world-renowned fishing stream (which are supposed to be refuges), two condos in Myrtle Beach (which are too far away to be used), and seven Domino's Pizza stores (don't ask!). One son and his significant other had Sandra's first grandchild at home with an Amish midwife. Another son says he won't marry his longtime girlfriend unless they can have a Star Wars wedding. Another son who is twenty-three fashions himself the Donald Trump of Central

Pennsylvania. A fourth son . . . Well, you get the picture.

Robert and Sandra love their sons dearly, but Robert says they are boomerangs: They keep coming back. Sandra says it must be a sign of what good parents they are, that the boys want to be with them.

No wonder Sandra likes to escape to the library in her home, which is luckily soundproof, where she can dwell in the more sane, laugh-out-loud world of her Cajuns. When asked by others where Sandra got her marvelous sense of humor, her husband and sons just gape. They don't think she's funny at all.

Sandra is a *USA Today, New York Times* extended, and Waldenbooks best-selling author of fifteen novels and four novellas. All of her books are heavy on humor and sizzle.

Little do Sandra's husband and sons know what she's doing in that library <grin>.

"Some like it hot and hilarious,
and Hill delivers both."
—*Publishers Weekly*

The high "jinx" continue in
Sandra Hill's next novel!
Turn the page for
a preview of

Pearl Jinx

AVAILABLE IN MASS MARKET JULY 2007.

Chapter

1

Crazy is as crazy does . . .

Caleb Peachey jogged along the road, scanning the log cabin up ahead. It sat nestled in the thick woods on the banks of the Little Juniata River, almost hidden from view. He hoped to find the crazy woman at home this early in the morning.

Crazy Claire, that's what some of the locals called her. Dr. Claire Cassidy, historical archaeologist, to her colleagues. PhDiva, to him. Actually, he was beginning to feel like the crazy one as he attempted to make contact with the elusive woman. In fact, he was beginning to wonder if she even existed. *Crazy Claire is gonna be Crazy-Friggin'-Dead-Claire if she doesn't stop hiding from me.*

Five miles back and a half hour ago, at dawn, he'd left the Butterfly Bed & Breakfast in Spruce Creek, where he and his team from Jinx, Inc., a treasure-hunting firm, would be staying. He'd arrived here in Central Pennsylvania yesterday morning. The rest of the team would be here this afternoon, but the project itself couldn't start until Dr. Cassidy was on board, as per orders of the National Park Service, which made sure no historical artifacts were disturbed. Now, he could understand the government being worried about metal detecting on a battlefield, trafficking in relics, defacing previously undiscovered prehistoric rock wall art, that kind of thing, but, dammit, they were just going to take some pearls out of a cavern here—a privately owned cavern, to boot. They weren't going to blow up the freakin' place.

Stopping in the clearing before the house, he bent over, hands on thighs, and breathed deeply in and out to cool down, not that he had broken a sweat or anything. Hell, he'd been a Navy SEAL for ten years, up till two and a half years ago, and they ran five times as far before breakfast, wearing heavy boondockers, not the two-hundred-dollar, ergonomically designed Adidas he had on now.

He knocked on the door. Once. Twice. No response except for some cats mewling inside. Same as yesterday, except there was a battered station wagon here now, which he took as a good sign. The woman hadn't responded to the messages he'd left on her answering machine the past few days either. "Hi! This is Claire. Your message is important to me. Blah, blah, blah!" Caleb mimicked in his head. Apparently not *that* important.

A fat calico cat, probably pregnant, sidled up to him and gave him the evil eye, as only a cat could do. Then she sashayed past, deeming him unworthy of her regard.

Through his side vision, he noticed another cat approaching, but, no, it wasn't a cat; it was a rat. Okay, it was a teeny-tiny dog that looked like a rat, and it started yip-yip-yipping at him as if it was a German shepherd, not a rat terrier.

Caleb couldn't fathom people who wanted such itty-bitty things for a pet. But then some people even took slimy creatures into their homes. Like snakes. Having a fierce aversion to snakes, he shivered.

Through its beady eyes, the yipping dog gave him the same you-are-so-boring look as the cat and sauntered off, around the side of a modern addition to the old cabin.

He decided to follow.

The back of the cabin was a big surprise. While the front was traditional log and chink design, the back was all windows facing the river some fifty feet below. Cushioned Adirondack chairs had been arranged on a wide deck. An open laptop sat on a low wooden table.

You-know-who must be home. Ignoring my calls. Son of a bitch! Oooh, someone is in big trouble.

He turned toward the river and inhaled sharply at the view. Not just the spectacular Little Juniata with the morning sun bouncing off the surface, creating diamond-like sparkles. Fish were actually jumping out of the water to feed on the seasonal hatch hovering above. He was familiar with this river, having grown up in an Amish community about ten miles down the road in Sinking Valley. What caused him to gasp, though, was the woman standing thigh-deep in the middle of the river. She wore suspendered waders over a long-sleeved white T-shirt. Her long, dark red hair was pulled up into a high ponytail, which escaped through the back of a Penn State baseball cap. *Auburn,* he thought her hair color was called.

Could this possibly be the slippery Dr. Claire Cassidy?

Crazy Claire? For some reason, he'd expected someone older, more witchy looking. It was hard to tell from this distance, but she couldn't be much older than thirty, although who knew? Women today were able to fool guys all the time. Makeup to look as if they were not wearing makeup. Nips and tucks. Collagen. Boob lifts, ferchrissake!

The woman was fly-fishing, which was an art in itself. Caleb was the furthest thing from a poet, but the way she executed the moves was pure art in motion. Like a ballet. Following a clock pattern, she raised her long bamboo rod upward with her right hand, stopping abruptly at noon to apply tension to her line. Then she allowed the rod to drift back slowly in the forward cast, stopping abruptly at eleven o'clock, like the crack of a whip. The follow-through was a dance of delicacy because the fly should only land on top of the water for a few seconds to fool the trout below water level that it was real live food. Over and over she performed this operation. It didn't matter that she didn't catch anything. The joy was in the casting.

And in the watching.

Dropping down to the edge of the deck, elbows resting on raised knees, he breathed in deeply. The scent of honeysuckle and pine filled the early morning air. Silence surrounded him, which was not really silence if one listened carefully. The rush of the water's current. Bees buzzing. Birds chirping. In the distance, a train whistle. He even saw a hawk swoop gloriously out of the mountains searching for food. Caleb felt as if he'd been sucker punched, jolted back to a time and place he'd spent seventeen years trying to forget.

The Plain People, as the Amish called themselves,

were practical to a fault. Fishing was for catching fish.
No Lands' End angler duds or fancy Orvis rods or custom-
made flies. Just worms. But his *Dat* had been different.
As stern as he was in many regards, he had given Caleb
and his four brothers an appreciation for God's beauty
in nature and the heavenly joy of fly-fishing. Much like
that minister in the movie *A River Runs Through It*,
Caleb's old man had made fly-fishing an exercise in
philosophy, albeit the Old Order Amish way of life.
Caleb smiled to himself, knowing his father would not
be pleased with comparison to an *Englisher*, anyone not
Amish, even a man of God.

And, for sure and for certain, as the Amish would
say, they didn't believe in that wasteful "catch and release" business, which the fisherwoman in front of him
was doing now with a twenty-inch rainbow. How many
times had Caleb heard, "To waste is to destroy God's
gift"? No, if an Amishman caught a fish, he ate it. With
homemade chow-chow, spaetzle oozing with butter,
sliced tomatoes still warm from the garden, corn fritters,
and shoofly pie.

Stomach rumbling with sudden hunger, Caleb shook
his head to clear it of unwanted memories, stood, and
walked down the railroad-tie steps to the edge of the river.

The woman glanced his way, then did a double take.
After a brief hesitation, she waved.

Yep, she must be crazy.

He was a big man, six-four, and still carried the mus-
culature that defined a Navy SEAL. The tattoo of a
chain around his upper arm usually gave women pause.
Plus, he was a stranger. But did she appear frightened?
Nah. She just waved at him. He could be an axe murderer

for all she knew. She was either brave or stupid or crazy, he figured. Maybe all three.

Enough!

He waded into the cold water. It soon covered his shoes, his bare legs, his running shorts, and then the bottom of his T-shirt. Once he reached the woman, whose mouth was now gaping open, he gritted his teeth, then snarled, "Your phone broken, lady?"

She blinked. Tall for a woman, maybe five-nine, she was still a head shorter than him and had to crane her neck to stare up at him. "Ah, the persistent Caleb." Then she smiled and shook her head as if he were not worthy of her attention. Just like her damn fat cat and her damn rat dog.

Taken aback for a second by her attitude, he failed to register the fact that she had, unbelievably, resumed fishing. *She's ignoring me. I don't fuckin' believe this. Three days of chasing my tail, and she thinks she can ignore me. I. Don't. Think. So.*

Without warning, he picked her up and tossed her over his shoulder in a fireman's carry, just barely catching the bamboo rod in his other hand as it started to float downstream. With her kicking and screaming, he stomped through the water, probably scaring off every fish within a one-mile radius.

"Put me down, you goon."

"Stop squirming. I'll put you down when I'm good and ready. We're on my clock now, baby."

"Clock? Clock? I'd like to clock *you.*"

His eardrum was in danger of breaking from her screeching.

"I mean it. Put me down. Aaarrgh! Take your hand off my ass."

"Stop putting your ass in my face."

"You are in such trouble. Wait till I call the police. Hope you know a good lawyer," she threatened to his back.

"Yeah, yeah, yeah. I'm shakin' in my boots . . . rather, my Adidas."

"Ha, ha, ha! You're not going to be making jokes once you're in the clink."

The clink? Haven't heard that expression in, oh, let's say, seventeen years. Once on the bank, he propped the rod against a tree and stood her on her feet, being careful to hold on to one hand lest she take flight, or wallop him a good one.

"What the hell do you think you're doing?" she demanded, yanking her hand out of his grasp, then placing both hands on her hips.

"Getting your attention."

"You got my attention when you failed to complete the Park Service forms for the project—*a month ago.*"

Oh, so that's what has her panties in a twist. "They were fifty-three friggin' pages long," he protested. The dumbass red-tape forms asked him, as Pearl Jinx project manager, to spell out every blinkin' thing about the venture and its participants. There were questions and subquestions and sub-subquestions. He'd used a red Sharpie to write "Bullshit!" across the empty forms and returned them to her. "Okay, my returning them that way probably wasn't the most diplomatic thing to do, but, my God, the Navy doesn't do as much background checking for its high-security special forces as your government agency requires."

She snorted her opinion. "It's not *my* agency. I'm just a freelance consultant, specializing in Native

American culture. You must know that Spruce Creek is situated right along what was once a major Indian path. In fact, Route Forty-five that runs from Spruce Creek to Danville was once an Indian trail known as Karondenah Path. Indian Cavern in Franklinville is only a mile or two away from the cavern you'll be working, and it was loaded with artifacts. We have to be sure nothing of historical value is disturbed by your project."

If I needed a history lesson, sweetie, I would turn to The History Channel. "Yes, I'm aware of all that, but you're changing the subject. I must have put a dozen messages on your answering machine in the past thirty-six hours and God only knows how many before that. Guess how many times you called me back?" He made a circle with a thumb and forefinger. She was lucky he didn't just give her the finger.

"That doesn't give you the right to manhandle me."

"That was not manhandling. If I was handling you, babe, you would know it."

"What a chauvinist thing to say!"

"Call me pig, just as long as you call me."

She threw her hands in the air with disgust, then shrugged her waders down and off, hanging them from a knot on the same tree where the rod rested. Underneath, she wore dry, faded jeans and thick wool socks, no shoes. Only then did she turn back to him. "You idiot. I've been gone for the past week. I got home late last night. That's why I didn't return your calls."

"Oh?" Caleb had been working for two years on various Jinx treasure-hunting projects, but this was the first time he was a project manager. It was important to him that it be a success. Pissing off a required team member was not a design for success. "Sorry," he said. "I misunderstood."

She nodded her acceptance of his apology and offered her own conciliatory explanation. "I like to spend time in the woods."

"How about using your cell phone to check messages?" *There I go, being snippy again.*

"I don't believe in cell phones. Besides, what would be the point of taking modern conveniences into the forest?"

He rolled his eyes. *She doesn't believe in cell phones. What century is she living in?* That's what he thought, but he was polite when he asked, "So, you've been camping?"

"Not exactly." Without elaborating, she started to walk back toward the cabin.

He hated it when women stopped talking in the middle of a conversation, especially when the guy was being logical, not to mention bending over backward to tame his inner chauvinist. He soon caught up with her.

"What was so important that you had to get in touch with me right away?" she asked when they got to her deck.

"'Right away' was three days ago, babe."

She arched her brows at his surliness, and probably at his use of the word *babe,* too.

Tough shit! He tamped his temper down, *again,* and replied, "The Pearl Project starts tomorrow."

"And?"

"We've been told that you have to be there as a Park Service rep from the get-go."

"And?"

"And you haven't confirmed." Her attitude was

really starting to annoy him. Starting? More like continuing. *Behave, Peachey. Don't let her rile you. An impatient man is a dead target.*

She arched an eyebrow at him again. "Since when do I need to confirm anything with you?"

Uh-oh! Are we gonna have a pissing contest over who's in charge? I can guarantee it's not gonna be her. If we have to vet every little anal thing, we'll be here in the boonies for months instead of weeks. He put his face in his hands and counted to ten. When he glanced her way again, he said, "Look, we're gonna have to find a way to work together. Truce?" He extended a hand.

She hesitated, but then agreed, "Truce," and placed her hand in his. Her hand was small compared to his, with short unpolished nails. He could swear his heart revved up at just the feel of her calloused palm pressed against his calloused palm.

Am I pathetic or what?

"Are you hungry?"

That question caught him by surprise. Was her new strategy torture by niceness? Or calloused palm, erotic handshakes? "Yeah," he answered suspiciously.

"Good. I picked some wild blueberries yesterday and have muffins cooling inside."

He didn't immediately follow her but sat down on one of the chairs to take off his wet shoes and socks. Meanwhile, the delicious aroma of baked goods wafted out to him. The rat dog trotted over and eyed his shoes. Just as it was about to take a chomp out of the fabric, Caleb grabbed the shoe and set it and its mate up on the arm of the chair. When he turned, he saw the dog running off with one of his wet socks in its mouth.

"Boney!" Dr. Cassidy yelled out through the screen

door at the thief. There were four more cats of various sizes rubbing themselves against her ankles.

To his surprise, the dog stopped, looked back at its mistress dolefully, dropped the sock, and went off the porch and into the brush.

"You named your dog Boner?"

She made a clucking sound of disgust. "Not Boner. Boney. You know. Napoleon Bonaparte. Little dog. Napoleon Complex."

Well, at least she has a sense of humor. Okay, I see five cats so far and one semidog. What next?

What next, he soon learned, was Indian tom-tom music, along with some guttural chants, coming from a tape deck inside. "Ay-yi-yi-yi! Ay-yi-yi-yi-yi . . ." Two cages in one corner, one holding what looked like a porcupine with a splint on its leg and the other holding a bird with mangled feathers. *And* the good doctor taking off her T-shirt, whose sleeves were wet, leaving her with just a sports running bra kind of thing. Nothing scandalous. It was midway between a granny-type cotton undergarment and a hoochie-mama Victoria's Secret scrap of sexiness, but still . . . It was pink. And there was all that skin. Bare arms. Bare midriff. Bare collarbones. Plus, she was ripped, which would explain the exercise mat and hand weights. Not weight lifter ripped, but female athlete ripped. And worst of all—or best of all—she had breasts that could make a grown man weep.

Good thing I am not looking. Nope. I. Am. Not. Looking. And I am not getting turned on.

"It's hot in here, don't you think?" she asked, belatedly explaining her "strip tease," he supposed.

At least it felt like a strip tease to him.

She began to set a tray with supersized muffins, butter, mugs of coffee, sugar and cream, unaware of how tempting she looked. Forget muffins. He'd like a taste of—

To his surprise, she gave him a once-over, too. A once-over that gave special attention to his wet shorts. Then, with a bland expression, giving no clue to her assessment, she said, "It feels like today will be a scorcher."

Tell me about it! "It's probably your oven." *Shit! Could I sound any more dorky?*

She looked at him again, and this time she smiled.

While she continued to set the tray with small plates and napkins and other crap, he looked around her cabin. It was either that or ogle her body, which would not be smart. *Pink? What kind of serious archaeologist wears pink? Shiiit!*

The cabin was nice. Dried herbs hung from the low rafters of the kitchen, giving it a fragrant, cozy atmosphere. Colorful dream catchers at the windows caught and reflected the light like prisms. He assumed that a bedroom and bathroom were off to the left. To the right was the addition, which was completely open, making a combination kitchen/den/living room. A huge stone fireplace was flanked on one side by a half dozen baskets, some woven, others coiled, and on the other by a rustic, low, armless rocking chair that looked homemade. Two log walls of the addition held floor-to-ceiling bookcases with a built-in PC desk in the corner. The shelves overflowed with books, many of them related to the Lenni-Lenape tribe of the Delaware nation. Also, there were Indian relics: an impressive arrowhead collection, a peace pipe, several tomahawks, and framed photographs.

He walked over to check out one of the pictures.

Then wished he hadn't.

It was a side view of Dr. Cassidy facing some man of obvious Native American heritage. Her long auburn hair was in braids. His black hair was, too, and adorned with a single feather. They both wore Indian ceremonial outfits. His chest was bare. On top she appeared to be nude as well, except for the numerous bead and feathered necklaces she wore. On the bottom, he sported a loincloth-type outfit with leather flaps covering his belly and ass. She wore a low-riding, knee-length, fringed leather skirt and beaded moccasins. Her arms were raised, shaking some kind of rattles. He could care less about the man. But her—wow! Her side was bare from armpit to hip. From that view, Caleb got a perfect view of the side of one of her breasts.

Good Lord! Not the way I want to be picturing the archaeologist assigned to our project. She'll be talking Indian legends and I'll be thinking, "Wanna come over to my tepee and show me your beads?"

A thought suddenly occurred to him. "Are you married?"

"No. Why do you ask?"

He was walking back to the kitchen and waved over his shoulder at the photograph. "Geronimo back there."

She made a tsking sound at the political incorrectness of his remark. "That's Professor Henry Hawk from the University of Pennsylvania. He's a full-blooded Lenni-Lenape Indian. Geronimo was Apache."

Well, big whoop!

"I'm not topless in the photo, by the way." She

grinned, obviously reading his mind. "Lots of people think I am, but I'm wearing a flesh-colored leotard."

That's just great! Ruin a guy's fantasy, why don't you? "Don't you believe in historical accuracy?"

"Yeah, but I was young and naive then. I let the promoter talk me into it. Turned out that more people were watching my jiggling breasts as I danced, instead of learning about Indian rituals. That was the last time they tried that."

Oh, good Lord! Now I add jiggling to my fantasy.

Dr. Cassidy carried the tray out to the deck and motioned for him to move the laptop. While closing the lid, he noticed it contained notes on some Indian mating ritual. He wasn't dumb enough to ask if that's what she and Geronimo were doing in the photograph. *Not now. But I'll bet my Navy SEAL Budweiser pin that I hot damn will later.*

After three muffins and sipping his second cup of coffee, he leaned back. "That was great, Dr. Cassidy. Thanks."

"You're welcome. The wild berries are smaller, but I think they're sweeter. And, please, call me Claire."

He nodded. "So, what were you doing in the woods when you were *not camping?*" he asked, repeating her words back to her.

"I don't camp in the traditional sense, you know, tents and kerosene stoves. I build a wigwam up in the mountains like the Lenni-Lenape Indians did and cook over an open fire."

"Alone?" He was picturing her with some guy— okay, him—bending over the fire. Maybe dancing a little, making those beads and other things jiggle. Then, they'd go into the wigwam, and—

"Usually."

"Huh?"

"I usually go alone. I like the solitude. And I'm able to explore and dig for Indian artifacts at my leisure."

He could understand the solitude part—he was a loner himself—though he liked his fantasy better. "And you planned all along to be back here for the start of the project tomorrow?"

"Of course. I always honor my commitments."

And she couldn't have told me that. Not even one little phone call or e-mail. He decided to hold his tongue. "You're not going to make me fill out those forms, are you?"

She shook her head. "Not all of them. I'll help you, if you're willing."

He liked the fact that she was willing to bend the rules and decided reciprocation was in order. "I'll help you."

"You're staying at the Butterfly Bed & Breakfast?"

"Uh-huh. It's convenient, with the cavern right there on the property. Abbie is giving us a nice deal on rooms."

She cocked her head to the side, probably at his use of Abigail Franklin's first name.

"I met her grandson Mark in Afghanistan, and we've kept in touch occasionally."

"The Navy pilot?"

He nodded.

"How's he doing?"

"As well as a young man with one arm could be, I suppose. You should know, Jinx is here because Abbie contacted me."

"Abbie is a smart cookie. Don't underestimate her because of her age."

"You say that as if I should be wary."

"Let's face it, cave pearls don't have a huge value. They lack luster."

"There's some kind of chemical bath that's been invented recently. It supposedly gives them luster. Market value could be over five hundred thousand dollars, maybe a million."

She didn't look convinced.

"What?"

"Abbie's always been kind of secretive about her home, which is on the National Register of Historic Places, and the cavern. I wonder if there might be something else, and she's just using your firm on the pretext of the pearls."

In other words, we do the grunt work, and she skips off with the real bonanza. This was something Caleb would have to investigate further, but not with Ms. Indian Preservation on his tail. "All I can say is that Abbie has been very accommodating. Not just to me. The other members of my team will be staying at her B and B, too."

"And they are . . . ?"

"Adam Famosa, a professor at Rutgers, and John LeDeux, a police officer from Louisiana. This is a relatively simple job. No need for the usual six-man team."

"And you're the project manager?"

"Yep. You'll meet Veronica Jinkowsky, owner of Jinx, and her on-again, off-again husband Jake Jensen. Ronnie is a lawyer, and Jake is a professional poker player. They won't be staying, though. They're off to another treasure hunt in Mexico."

She nodded.

Caleb wouldn't be surprised if she had already researched every one of them, as well as the cavern to be explored and the targeted treasure.

"A college professor, a police officer, a poker player, a lawyer, an ex-Navy SEAL . . . What qualifies you guys to be treasure hunters?"

"Good question. Actually, each of our fortune-hunting expeditions is different and requires different skills. Could be anything from deep-sea treasure to buried gold to a lost heirloom. Once an elderly Southern belle hired us to dig up her backyard hoping to find her family's silver from the Civil War days. Some of us are climbers. Others have diving experience. Those of us on this project put in an additional fifty hours to get further certified in cave diving."

"Is cave diving so different?"

"Actually, yes. There are almost forty different swimming techniques just for negotiating underground water passes. We don't take on jobs we can't handle, or if we do agree to a project requiring special expertise, we hire someone to join the team. Mostly, though, we all share a love of adventure."

"Did you find the lady's silver?"

"Yeah. That and a couple of dead Yankee soldiers."

She appeared to be satisfied with his explanation.

"What is it *you* hope to find on this project, Claire?"

"Well, artifacts most likely. Arrowheads, tools, that kind of thing. Caves have long been used as dwelling places, burial sites, storage houses, places of worship. Add to that the fact that Pennsylvania has been homeland to the Lenape tribe for more than ten thousand years."

"Ten thousand years!"

She shrugged. "As you probably know, a cavern of any size is at least a million years old. We're talking ancient and near history here. Near history being the past few hundred years of which we have more concrete evidence. For example, the Lenape were among the first Indians to come in contact with Europeans in the 1600s."

"Uh-hum," he said. *Good God! She's giving me a lecture, like I'm one of her students.*

"It would be really great if there were pictographs as well. Cave paintings," she blathered on, pleased no doubt that she had a captive audience. "Oh, and aside from the usual artifacts, I would love to discover some new fetishes. I only have a few now."

He couldn't help himself. He had to grin. "Yeah? I've got a few myself. I'll tell you mine if you'll tell me yours."

She stared at him for a long moment, then laughed. "Oh, you! I meant Indian fetishes. Like small carvings in wood or stone. A turtle, for example. Things that hold some mystical spirit important to . . ." She let her words trail off as she realized he'd known what kind of fetish she'd meant all along.

"Yeah, well, back to what you hope to find. I've studied all the maps and history. I suspect the only things, other than pearls, that we're going to find there are bats and bugs and"—he shivered reflexively—"snakes. I do hate snakes."

Claire tilted her head to the side. "Didn't Abbie tell you about Sparky?" Then she smiled. Smirked, actually.

The fine hairs stood out on his body. "Okay. Who's Sparky?"

"A snake."

"A snake with a name?" *Uh-oh, this does not sound good.*

He must have turned a bit green because she grinned.

Oh, great! A sadist, on top of everything else.

"A big ol' snake."

"Define big."

"Twelve feet long and as wide around as your tattoo." She pointed to his left biceps where the thin chain tattoo peeked out from under the sleeve of his T-shirt. "Sparky's been living in Spruce Creek Cavern for at least ten years. Not that there aren't other snakes, but Sparky is the Big Daddy. Every so often, he sticks his head out, but then slithers back in before anyone can catch him."

Yeah, but has anyone ever shot him? With an AK-47?

"Are you pulling my leg?"

"I wouldn't think of touching your leg."

Okay, I recognize an insult when I hear one. He thought about taking her hand and placing it on his bare thigh, just to annoy her, but sanity persuaded him to restrain himself. "I. Hate. Snakes."

"Afraid of them?"

"Hell, no. Just don't like 'em." Probably stemmed from all those years as a kid when he'd helped handplow the fields and uncovered lots of the slimy buggers—usually black or garden variety, but even the occasional rattler. And he'd had to deal with plenty in SEAL survival training, too.

"Well, you had to know coming here that an underground cavern would have snakes."

"Sure, I knew that. I just didn't expect any anacondas."

She laughed, and her whole face lit up, even her eyes, which were a pale, pale green.

Nice. But he could see how some people might consider her eyes sort of woo-woo, fitting into the crazy category.

"Don't worry, he's not poisonous . . . though he has been known to bite."

"You're really enjoying yourself at my expense, aren't you?"

"Yep!" But then she switched subjects and floored him. Women had a talent for doing that to a guy, one minute talking about the latest hot chick movie and the next asking him something personal, something he absolutely does not want to discuss, like the size of his, oh, let's say, rifle, or why hasn't he ever married, or what's that huge chip on his shoulder with the word *family* chiseled on it.

What Claire zinged him with was: "Peachey . . . that's an Amish name, isn't it? An Amish Navy SEAL? That's an oxymoron, isn't it?"

I'm a moron, all right. Left myself wide open. Why don't I just paint a target on my chest that says, "Shoot Me."

Wendy Markham

"A fun, yet unique voice which we'll enjoy
for a long time."
—*Rendezvous*

SOCCER MOM CHRONICLES
0-446-61843-8

BRIDE NEEDS GROOM
0-446-61454-8

HELLO, IT'S ME
0-446-61453-X

ONCE UPON A BLIND DATE
0-446-61176-X

THE NINE MONTH PLAN
0-446-61175-1

More Warner Books romances . . .
From authors who'll make you laugh
and fall in love . . .

Lani Diane Rich

"Wacky characters, non-stop action,
riotous dialogue."
—*Publishers Weekly* on *MAYBE BABY*

THE COMEBACK KISS
0-446-61579-X

MAYBE BABY
0-446-61578-1

Lori Wilde

"A unique voice that will soar to publishing heights."
—*Rendezvous*

THERE GOES THE BRIDE
0-446-61845-4

YOU ONLY LOVE TWICE
0-446-61516-1

MISSION: IRRESISTIBLE
0-446-61515-3

LICENSE TO THRILL
0-446-61366-5

CHARMED AND DANGEROUS
0-446-61367-3

Kelley St. John

"Fast-paced, sexy, and witty."
—*Booklist* on *GOOD GIRLS DON'T*

REAL WOMEN DON'T WEAR
SIZE 2
0-446-61721-0

GOOD GIRLS DON'T
0-446-61720-2